W9-CUJ-421

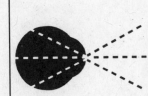

This Large Print Book carries the
Seal of Approval of N.A.V.H.

No Safe House

No Safe House

Linwood Barclay

THORNDIKE PRESS
A part of Gale, Cengage Learning

GALE
CENGAGE Learning®

Farmington Hills, Mich • San Francisco • New York • Waterville, Maine
Meriden, Conn • Mason, Ohio • Chicago

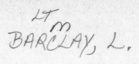

BARCLAY, L.

GALE
CENGAGE Learning®

LIBRARY OF CONGRESS CATALOGING-IN-PUBLICATION DATA

Barclay, Linwood.
  No safe house / by Linwood Barclay. — Large print edition.
    pages ; cm. — (Thorndike Press large print basic)
  ISBN 978-1-4104-6761-4 (hardcover) — ISBN 1-4104-6761-9 (hardcover)
  1. Older people—Crimes against—Fiction. 2. Murder—Investigation—Fiction. 3. Murderers—Fiction. 4. Large type books.
  I. Title.
  PR9199.3.B37135N6 2014b
  813'.54—dc23   2014025655

Published in 2014 by arrangement with NAL Signet, a member of Penguin Group (USA) LLC, a Penguin Random House Company

Printed in Mexico
1 2 3 4 5 6 7 18 17 16 15 14

For Neetha

PROLOGUE

Richard Bradley had never thought of himself as a violent man, but right now he was ready to kill someone.

"I can't take it anymore," he said, sitting on the side of the bed in his pajamas.

"You're not going out there," said his wife, Esther. "Not again. Just let it go."

Not only could they hear the music blaring from next door; they could feel it. The deep bass was pulsing through the walls of their house like a heartbeat.

"It's eleven o'clock, for Christ's sake," Richard said, turning on his bedside table lamp. "And it's Wednesday. Not Friday night or Saturday night, but Wednesday."

The Bradleys had lived in this modest Milford home, on this hundred-year-old street with its mature trees, for nearly thirty years. They'd seen neighbors come and go. The good, and the bad. But never had there been anything as bad as this, and it had been going on for a while. Two years back, the owner of the house next door started renting it to students attending

Housatonic Community College over in Bridgeport, and since then the neighborhood had gone, as Richard Bradley liked to proclaim on a daily basis, "to hell in a handcart."

Some of the students had been worse than others. This bunch, they took the cake. Loud music nearly every night. The smell of marijuana wafting in through the windows. Shattered beer bottles on the sidewalk.

This used to be a nice part of town. Young couples with their first homes, some starting families. There were some older teenagers on the street, to be sure, but if any of them acted up, threw a raucous party when they were left on their own, at least you could rat them out the next day to their parents and it wouldn't happen again. At least not for a while. There were older people on the street, too, many of them retired. Like the Bradleys, who'd taught in schools in and around Milford since the 1970s before packing it in.

"Is that what we worked so hard for our whole lives?" he asked Esther. "So we could live next door to a bunch of goddamn rabble-rousers?"

"I'm sure they'll stop soon," she said, sitting up in bed. "They usually do at some point. We were young, too, once." She grimaced. "A long time ago."

"It's like an earthquake that won't end," he said. "I don't even know what the hell kind of music that is. What is that?"

He stood up, grabbed his bathrobe, which was thrown over a chair, knotted the sash in front.

"You're going to give yourself a heart attack," Esther said. "You can't go over every time this happens."

"I'll be back in a couple of minutes."

"Oh, for God's sake," she said as he strode out of the bedroom. Esther Bradley threw back the covers, put on her own robe, slid her feet into the slippers on the floor by the bed, and went running down the stairs after her husband.

By the time she caught up with him, he was on the front porch. She noticed, for the first time, that he had nothing on his feet. She tried to grab his arm to stop him but he jerked it away, and she felt a twinge of pain in her shoulder. He went down the steps, walked down to the sidewalk, turned left, and kept marching until he reached the driveway next door. He could have taken a shortcut across the grass, but it was still wet from a shower earlier in the evening.

"Richard," she said pleadingly, a few steps behind him. She wasn't going to leave him alone. She figured there was less likelihood that these young men would do anything to him if they saw her standing there. Would they punch out an old man while his wife watched?

He was a man on a mission, mounting the steps to the front door of the three-story Victorian home. Most of the lights were on, many of the windows open, the music blaring out for all the neighbors to hear. But it wasn't loud enough to drown out the sounds of raised voices and laughter.

Richard banged on the door, his wife stationed at the bottom of the porch steps, watching anxiously.

"What are you going to say?" she asked.

He ignored her and banged on the door again. He was about to strike it with the heel of his fist a third time when the door swung open. A thin man, maybe twenty, just over six feet tall, dressed in jeans and a plain dark blue T-shirt and holding a can of Coors in his hand, stood there.

"Hey," he said. He blinked woozily a couple of times as he sized up his visitor. Bradley's few wisps of gray hair were sticking up at all angles, his bathrobe had started to part in front, and his eyes were bugging out.

"What the hell's wrong with you?" Bradley shouted.

"Excuse me?" the man said, bewildered.

"You're keeping up the whole damn neighborhood!"

The man's mouth formed an O, as if trying to take it in. He looked beyond the man and saw Esther Bradley, holding her hands together, almost in prayer.

She said, sounding almost apologetic, "The music is a bit loud."

"Oh yeah, shit," he said. "You're from next door, right?"

"Jesus," Richard said, shaking his head. "I was over here last week, and the week before that! You got any brain cells left?"

The young man blinked a couple more times, then turned and shouted back into the house, "Hey, turn it down. Carter! Hey, Carter! Turn it — yeah, turn it the fuck down, will ya!"

Three seconds later, the music stopped, the sudden silence jarring.

The young man shrugged apologetically, said, "Sorry." He extended his free hand. "My name's Brian. Or have I told you that before?"

Richard Bradley ignored the hand.

"You want to come in for a beer or something?" Brian asked, cheerily raising the bottle in his hand. "We've got some pizza, too."

"No," Richard said.

"Thank you for the offer," Esther said cheerily.

"You're, like, the people in that house, right?" Brian asked, pointing.

"Yes," Esther said.

"Okay. Well, sorry about the noise and everything. We all had this test today and we were kind of unwinding, you know? If we get out of hand again, just come over and bang on the door and we'll try to dial it down."

"That's what I've been doing," Richard said.

Brian shrugged, then slipped back into the house and closed the door.

Esther said, "He seems like a nice young man."

Richard grunted.

They returned to their house, the front door slightly ajar from when they'd run out of it in a hurry. It wasn't until they were both inside and had closed and bolted the door, that they noticed the two people sitting in the living room.

A man and woman. Late thirties, early forties. Both smartly dressed in jeans — was
that a crease in hers? — and lightweight
jackets.

Esther let out a short, startled scream
when she spotted them.

"Jesus!" Richard said. "How the hell did
you — ?"

"You shouldn't leave your door open like
that," said the woman, getting up from the
couch. She wasn't much more than five-
two, maybe five-three. Short black hair,
worn in a bob. "That's not smart," she said.
"Even in a nice neighborhood like this."

"Call the police," Richard Bradley said to
his wife.

It took a moment for the command to
register. But when it did, she started for the
kitchen. The moment she moved, the man
shot up off the couch. He was a good foot
taller than the woman, stocky, and swift. He
crossed the room in an instant and blocked
her path.

He grabbed her roughly by her bony
shoulders, spun her around, and tossed her,
hard, into a living room chair.

She yelped.

"You son of a bitch!" Richard Bradley said
and charged at the man while he was turned
away from him. He made a fist and pounded

13

it into the intruder's back, just below the neck. The man spun around and swatted Richard away as if he was a child. As he stumbled back, the man glanced down, saw Richard's bare foot, and drove the heel of his shoe down onto it.

Bradley shouted out in pain and collapsed toward the couch, catching the edge and falling onto the floor.

"Enough," the woman said. She said to her partner, "Sweetheart, you want to turn down some of these lights? It's awfully bright in here."

"Sure," he said, found the light switch, and flicked it down.

"My foot," Richard whimpered. "You broke my goddamn foot."

"Let me help him," Esther said. "Let me get him an ice pack."

"Stay put," the man said.

The woman perched her butt on the edge of the coffee table, where she could easily address Esther or look down to the floor to Richard.

She said this:

"I'm going to ask the two of you a question, and I'm only going to ask it once. So I want you to *listen* very carefully, and then I want you to *think* very carefully about how you answer. What I do not want you to do

14

is answer my question with a question. That would be very, very unproductive. Do you understand?"

The Bradleys glanced at each other, terrified, then looked back at the woman. Their heads bobbed up and down weakly in understanding.

"That's very good," the woman said. "So, pay attention. It's a very simple question."

The Bradleys waited.

The woman said, "Where is it?"

The words hung there for a moment, no one making a sound.

After several seconds, Richard said, "Where is wh— ?"

Then cut himself off when he saw the look in the woman's eyes.

She smiled and waved a finger at him. "Tut, tut, I warned you about that. You almost did it, didn't you?"

Richard swallowed. "But —"

"Can you answer the question? Again, you need to know that Eli says it's here."

Richard's lips trembled. He shook his head and stammered, "I — I don't — I don't —"

The woman raised a palm, silencing him, and turned her attention to Esther. "Would you like to answer the question?"

Esther was careful with her phrasing. "I

15

would appreciate it if you could be more specific. I — I have to tell you that name — Eli? I don't know anyone by that name. Whatever it is you want, if we have it, we'll give it to you."

The woman sighed and turned her head to her partner, who was standing a couple of feet away.

"I gave you your chance," the woman said. "I told you I'd only ask once." Just then, the house next door began to thump once again with loud music. The windows of the Bradley house began to vibrate. The woman smiled and said, "That's Drake. I like him." She glanced up at the man and said, "Shoot the husband."

"No! No!" Esther screamed.

"Jesus!" Richard shouted. "Just tell us what —"

Before the retired teacher could finish the sentence, the man had reached into his jacket for a gun, pointed it downward, and pulled the trigger.

Esther opened her mouth to scream again, but no sound came out. Little more than a high-pitched squeak, as though someone had stepped on a mouse.

The woman said to her, "I guess you really don't know." She nodded at her associate, and he fired a second shot.

Wearily, she said to him, "Doesn't mean it's not here. We've got a long night ahead of us, sweetheart, unless it's in the cookie jar."

"We should be so lucky," he said.

ONE

TERRY

I don't know where I got the idea that once you've come through a very dark time, after you've confronted the worst possible demons and defeated them, that everything's going to be just fine.

Doesn't work that way.

Not that life wasn't better for us, at least for a while. Seven years ago, things were pretty bad around here. Bad as they can get. People died. My wife and daughter and I came close to being among them. But when it was over, and we were whole, and still had each other, well, we did like the song says. We picked ourselves up, dusted ourselves off, and started all over again.

More or less.

But the scars remained. We went through our own version of post-traumatic stress. My wife, Cynthia, certainly did. She'd lost all the members of her family when she was fourteen — I really mean *lost;* her parents and her brother vanished into thin air one night — and Cynthia had to wait twenty-five years to learn their fate. When it was all over, there were no joyful reunions.

There was more. Cynthia's aunt paid the ultimate price in her bid to shine the light on a decades-old secret. And then there was Vince Fleming, a career criminal who was also just a kid when Cynthia's family vanished, who'd been with her that night. Twenty-five years later, against his own nature, he helped us find out what really happened. Like they say, no good deed goes unpunished. He got shot and nearly died for his trouble.

You might have heard about it. It was all over the news. They were even going to make a movie about it at one point, but that fell through, which, if you ask me, was for the best.

We thought we'd be able to close the book on that chapter of our lives. Questions were answered; mysteries were solved. The bad people died, or went to prison.

Case closed, as they say.

But it's like a horrible tsunami. You think it's over, but debris is washing ashore half a world away years later.

For Cynthia, the trauma never ended.

20

Every day, she feared history repeating itself with the family she had now. Me. And our daughter, Grace. The trouble was, the steps she took to make sure it wouldn't led us into that area known as the law of unintended consequence: the actions you take to achieve one thing often produce the exact opposite result.

Cynthia's efforts to keep our fourteen-year-old daughter, Grace, safe from the big, bad world were pushing the child to experience it as quickly as she could.

I kept hoping we'd eventually work our way through the darkness and come out the other side. But it didn't look as though it was going to happen anytime soon.

Grace and her mother had shouting matches on a pretty much daily basis.

They were all variations on a theme.

Grace ignored curfew. Grace didn't call when she got to where she was going. Grace said she was going to one friend's house but ended up going to another and didn't update her mother. Grace wanted to go to a concert in New York but wouldn't be able to get home until two in the morning. Mom said no.

I tried to be a peacemaker in these disputes, usually with little success. I'd tell

Cynthia privately that I understood her motives, that I didn't want anything bad to happen to Grace, either, but that if our daughter was never allowed any freedom, she'd never learn to cope in the world on her own.

These fights generally ended with someone storming out of a room. A door being slammed. Grace telling Cynthia she hated her, then knocking over a chair as she left the kitchen.

"God, she's just like me," Cynthia would often say. "I was a horror show at that age. I just don't want her making the same mistakes I made."

Cynthia, even now, thirty-two years later, carried a lot of guilt from the night her mother and father and older brother, Todd, disappeared. Part of her still believed that if she hadn't been out with a boy named Vince, without her parents' permission or knowledge, and if she hadn't gotten drunk and passed out once she'd fallen into her own bed, she might have known what was happening and, somehow, saved those closest to her.

Even though the facts didn't bear that out, Cynthia believed she'd been punished for her misbehavior.

She didn't want Grace ever having to

blame herself for something so tragic. That meant instilling in Grace the importance of resisting peer pressure, of never allowing yourself to be put into a difficult situation, of listening to that little voice in your head when it says, *This is wrong and I've got to get the hell out of here.*

Or as Grace might say, "Blah blah blah."

I wasn't much help when I told Cynthia almost every kid went through a period like this. Even if Grace did make mistakes, it didn't follow that the consequences would have to be as grave as what Cynthia had endured. Grace, God help us, was a teenager. In another six years, if Cyn and I hadn't killed ourselves by then, we'd see Grace mature into a sensible young woman.

But it was hard to believe that day would ever come.

Like that night when Grace was thirteen and hanging out at the Post Mall with her friends at the same time Cynthia happened to be there looking for shoes. Cynthia spotted our girl outside of Macy's sharing a cigarette. Cynthia confronted her in full view of her classmates and ordered her to the car. Cynthia was so rattled and busy tearing a strip off Grace that she ran a stop sign.

Nearly got broadsided by a dump truck.

"We could have been killed," Cynthia told me. "I was out of control, Terry. I totally lost it."

It was after that incident that she decided, for the first time, to take a break from us. Just a week. For our sake — or more specifically, for Grace's — as much as her own. A time-out, Cynthia called it. She bounced the idea off Naomi Kinzler, the therapist Cynthia had been seeing for years, and she saw the merit in it.

"Remove yourself from the conflict situation," Kinzler said. "You're not running away; you're not abandoning your responsibilities. But you're going to take some time to reflect, to regroup. You can give yourself permission to do that. This gives Grace time to think, too. She may not like what you're doing, but she might come to understand it. You suffered a terrible wound when you lost your family, and it's a wound that will never completely heal. Even if your daughter can't appreciate that now, I believe someday she will."

Cynthia got a place at the Hilton Garden Inn, over behind the mall. She was going to stay at the budget-minded Just Inn Time to save money, but I said no way. Not only was it a dump, but there'd been a white-slave operation running out of it a few years back.

24

She was only gone a week, but it felt like a year. What surprised me was how much Grace missed her mother.

"She doesn't love us anymore," Grace said one night over microwaved lasagna.

"That's not true," I said.

"Okay, she doesn't love *me* anymore."

"The reason your mother's taking a break is because she loves you so much. She knows she went too far, that she over-reacted, and she needs some time to get her head together."

"Tell her to speed it up."

When Cynthia returned, things were better for a month, maybe even six weeks. But the peace treaty started to crumble. Minor incursions at first, maybe a shot across the bow.

Then all-out warfare.

When they had one of their battles, feelings would be hurt and it'd take several days for our normal life — whatever that was — to resume. I'd attempt mediation, but these things had to run their course. Cynthia would communicate anything important she had to tell Grace through notes, signed *L. Mom*, just the way her own mother used to do when she was pissed with her daughter and couldn't bring herself to write *Love*.

But eventually the notes would be signed

25

Love, Mom, and a thaw in relations would begin. Grace would find some pretext to ask her mother for guidance. Does this top work with these pants? Can you help with this homework assignment? A tentative dialogue would be opened.

Things would be good.

And then they'd be bad.

The other day, they were really bad.

Grace wanted to go with two of her girl-friends to New Haven to a huge used-clothing bazaar that was running midweek. They could only go at night, because they had school through the day. Like that concert in New York, it would mean a late return home on the train. I offered to drive them up, kill some time, and then bring them back, but Grace would have none of it. She and her friends weren't five. They wanted to do this on their own.

"There's no way," Cynthia said, standing at the stove making dinner. Breaded pork cutlets and wild rice, as I remember. "Terry, tell me you're with me on this. There's no way she's doing that."

Before I could weigh in, Grace said, "Are you kidding? I'm not going to fucking Budapest. It's New Haven."

This was a relatively new wrinkle. The use of foul language. I don't suppose we had anyone to blame but ourselves. It was not uncommon for Cynthia or me to drop the f-bomb when we were angry or frustrated. If we had one of those swear jars where you drop in a quarter every time you used a bad word, we could have used the money to take a trip to Rome every year.

Just the same, I called Grace on it.

"Don't you ever speak to your mother that way," I said sternly.

Cynthia clearly felt a reprimand was inadequate. "You're grounded for two weeks," she said.

Grace, stunned, came back with: "How long are you going to take it out on *me* that *you* couldn't save your family? I wasn't even born, okay? It's not my fault."

A verbal knife to the heart with that one.

I could see, in Grace's face, instant regret, and something more than that. Fear. She'd crossed a line, and she knew it. Maybe, if she'd had a chance, she'd have withdrawn the comment, offered an apology, but Cynthia's hand came up so quickly, she never had a chance.

She slapped our daughter across the face. A smack loud enough I felt it in my own cheek.

"Cyn!" I shouted.

But as I yelled, Grace stumbled to the

27

side, put out her hand instinctively to brace her fall in case she lost her footing.

Her hand hit the side of the pot that was cooking the rice. Knocked it to one side. Grace's hand dropped, landed on the burner.

The scream. Jesus, the scream.

"Oh God!" Cynthia said. "Oh my God!"

She grabbed Grace's arm, spun her around to the sink, and turned on the cold tap, kept a constant stream of water running over her burned hand. The back of it had hit the hot pan and the side had connected with the burner. Maybe a millisecond of contact in each case, but enough to sear the flesh.

Tears were streaming down Grace's face. I wrapped my arms tightly around her while Cynthia kept running cold water on her hand.

We took her to Milford Hospital.

"You can tell them the truth," Cynthia told Grace. "You can tell them what I did. I deserve to be punished. If they call the police, they call the police. I'm not going to make you tell them something that isn't true."

Grace told the doctor she was boiling water to cook some macaroni, iPod buds in her ears, listening to Adele's "Rolling in the

Deep," dancing like an idiot, when she flung her arm out and hit the handle on the pot, knocking it off the stove.

We brought Grace home, her hand well bandaged.

The next day, Cynthia moved out for the second time.

She hasn't come back yet.

Two

"Reggie, Reggie, come in, come in."

"Hi, Unk."

"Did you find her?"

"Jeez, let me get my coat off."

"I'm sorry. I just —"

"I didn't. I didn't find . . . her. Not yet. No money, either."

"But I thought — You said you found the house and —"

"It didn't work out. It was a false lead. Eli lied to us, Unk. And it's not like we can go back and ask him again."

"Oh. But you said —"

"I know what I said. I'm telling you, we struck out."

"I'm sorry. I guess I got my hopes up. You seemed so sure last time I talked to you. I'm just disappointed is all. There's coffee there if you want it."

"Thanks."

"I still appreciate everything you're doing

30

for me."

"It's okay, Unk."

"I mean it. I know you get tired of my saying it, but I do. You're all I got. You're like the kid I never had, Reggie."

"Not a kid anymore."

"No, no — you're all grown. You grew up fast, and early."

"Didn't have much choice. Coffee's good."

"I'm just sorry I wasn't there for you sooner."

"I've never blamed you. You know that. We don't have to keep going over this. You see me obsessing about this? Huh? And *I'm* the one it all happened to. So if I can move on, you should be able to, too."

"It's hard for me."

"You live in the past. That's your problem, Unk. God, that's what all this latest shit has been about. You have a hard time getting over things."

"I . . . I was just hoping you'd found her."

"I'm not giving up."

"But I can see it in your face. You think this is all stupid. You think it doesn't matter."

"I didn't say that. Not the last part. Look, I get why this is important to you, why she matters so much. And you're important to

31

me. You're one of only two people I give a shit about, Unk."

"You know what I can't figure out about you?"

"What's that?"

"You understand people, you get how they think and how they feel, you've got a real insight into them, yet you've got no . . . what's the word?"

"Love?"

"No, that's not what I was going to say."

"Empathy?"

"Yeah, I guess that's it."

"Because I love you, Unk. Very much. But empathy? I suppose. I understand what makes people tick. I know what they're feeling. I need to know what they're feeling. I need to know when they're afraid. I very much need to feel that they *are* afraid, but I don't feel bad for them. Otherwise, I couldn't get things done."

"Yeah, well, I'd be better off if I was more like you. I guess it was empathy I felt for that damned Eli. He seemed like a lost kid — hell, he was no kid. He was twenty-one or -two. Something like that. I thought I was doing right by him, Reggie. I really did. And then the son of a bitch stabs me in the back."

"I believe he approached the other inter-

32

ested party."

"Shit, no."

"It's okay. Just an initial contact. He was holding back details until there was a face-to-face, which, of course, won't be happening now. I think he told us the truth about what was done with her, but lied about where. And the teachers' house was a nonstarter. Also, I'm starting to wonder about whether any of the people know. Whether they've given consent."

"I don't understand."

"That's okay. But what I was going to tell you is, I'm going to need more people, and it's going to take a lot more up-front money."

"Eli took all I'd set aside, Reggie."

"That's okay. I can put up money of my own. The tax refund thing's going well. I've got reserves. And when this is over, I'll not only get back my investment, and your money, but plenty of other money, too. There's a silver lining to all this, as it turns out."

"I still don't understand."

"That's okay. You don't have to. You just let me do what I do best."

"I just can't believe . . . after all these years, I finally win her back, and then I lose her again. Eli had no right, you know. He

33

had no right to take her from me."

"Trust me, Unk. We'll get her back."

THREE

TERRY

Just because Cynthia was no longer living with Grace and me didn't mean we were strangers to each other. We spoke daily, sometimes met for lunch. Her first week away, the three of us went out to Bistro Basque, over on River Street, for dinner. The girls both had the salmon and I went with the chicken stuffed with spinach and mushrooms. We were all on our best behavior. Not a word about our visit to the hospital, even though Cynthia couldn't keep her eyes off Grace's bandaged hand. The unreality of the meal was exceeded only by the end of the evening, when Grace and I dropped Cynthia off at her place and we drove on home alone.

She really lucked into the apartment. Cynthia had a friend at work who was leaving the last week of June for a trip to Brazil and not planning to return until August, or maybe even September. Cynthia remembered her saying she'd tried to sublet the place for the summer, get someone who could take over the rent while she was away. She'd found no takers. A day before her friend was to fly out, Cynthia said she'd take the apartment. The friend cleared it with the landlord, an old guy named Barney, and then it was a go.

I hadn't expected her to be gone until Labor Day, but as each day passed, and Cynthia showed no inclination to return, I was starting to wonder. At times I lay awake at night, half the bed empty next to me, wondering whether Cynthia would look for another place if this dragged on until early September when her friend returned.

About a week and a half after she'd left, I dropped by her place around five, figuring by then she'd be home from her job with the Milford Department of Public Health, where she was involved in everything from restaurant inspections to promoting good nutrition in the schools.

I was right. I saw her car first, parked between a sporty-looking Cadillac and an old blue pickup I recognized as Barney's. He was cutting the grass down the side of the house, limping with each step, almost as if one leg was shorter than the other. Cynthia was sitting on the front porch, feet propped up on the railing, nursing a beer, when I pulled up out front of the house.

It was, I had to admit, a pretty nice place, an old colonial house on North Street, just south of the Boston Post Road. It no doubt belonged to some prominent Milford family years ago before Barney bought it and converted it into four apartments. Two on the ground floor and two upstairs.

Before I could say hello to my wife, Barney spotted me and killed his mower.

"Hey, how ya doin'?" he called out. Barney viewed Cynthia and me as minor celebrities, although ours was not the kind of fame anyone would want, and he seemed to enjoy brushing up against us.

"I'm good," I said. "Don't let me keep you from your work there."

"I got two more houses to do after this one," he said, wiping his brow with the back of his hand. Barney owned at least a dozen homes that he'd turned into rental units between New Haven and Bridgeport, although, from what he'd told me in previous conversations, I'd learned this was one of the nicer ones and he spent more time on its upkeep. I wondered whether he was planning to put it on the market before long.

"Your missus is right up there on the

porch," he said.

"I see her," I said. "You look like you could use a cool drink."

"I'm good. Hope things are working out."

"Excuse me?" I said.

"Between you and the wife." He gave me a wink, then turned and went back to his mower.

Cynthia rested her beer on the railing and stood out of her chair as I came up the porch steps.

"Hey," she said. I was expecting her to offer me a cold one, and when she didn't I wondered whether I'd come at a bad time. Worry washed over her face. "Everything okay?"

"Everything's fine," I said.

"Grace is okay?" she asked.

"I told you, everything's fine."

Reassured, she sat back down and put her feet back up on the railing. I noticed that her phone was facedown on the arm of the wooden chair, holding down a health department flyer headlined, "Does Your Home Have Mold?"

"May I sit?"

She tipped her head toward the chair next to her.

I pointed to the flyer. "Problems with your new place? You show that to Barney and he'll flip out."

Cynthia glanced down at the flyer, shook her head. "It's a new awareness campaign we're doing. I've been talking about household mold so much lately I'm having nightmares where I'm being chased by fungus."

"Like that movie," I said. *The Blob.*

"Was that fungus?"

"Fungus from outer space."

She rested her head on the back of the chair, kept her feet perched on the railing. She sighed. "I never did this at home. Just decompressed at the end of the day."

"That's probably because we don't have a porch with a railing," I said. "I'll build you one if you want."

That prompted a chuckle. "You?"

Construction was not one of the manly arts at which I excelled. "Well, I could have someone build it. What I lack in hammering skills I make up for in writing checks."

"I just — at home, there's always something I have to do, right then. But here, when I get home from work, I sit here and watch the cars go by. That's it. It gives me time to think. You know?"

"I guess."

"I mean, you've got the summer to chill out." She had me there. As a teacher, I had July and August to recharge my batteries.

Cynthia had been working for the city only long enough to get a couple of weeks off every year. "So my holiday is an hour at the end of every day, where I sit here and do nothing."

"Good," I said. "If this is working for you, then I'm happy."

She turned and looked at me. "No, you're not."

"I just want what's good for you."

"I don't know anymore what's good for me. I sit here thinking I've removed myself from the source of my anxiety, all the fighting and nonsense at home with Grace, and then I realize I'm the source of my anxiety and I can't get away from myself."

"There's a Garrison Keillor story," I said, "about the old couple who can't get along, wondering whether to take a vacation, and the man says, 'Why pay good money to be miserable someplace else when I can be perfectly miserable at home.' "

She frowned. "You think we're an old couple?"

"That wasn't the point of the story."

"I won't stay here forever," Cynthia said, having to raise her voice some as Barney shifted his mowing activity to the front yard. The smell of freshly cut grass wafted our way. "I'm taking it a day at a time."

As much as I wanted her to come home, I wasn't going to beg her. She had to do it when she was good and ready.

"What have you told Teresa?" Cynthia asked. Teresa Moretti, the woman who came in to clean our place once a week. Four or five years ago, when Cynthia and I found ourselves so busy we couldn't seem to get to the most basic household chores, we'd asked around about a cleaning lady and found Teresa. Even though I was off for the summer and possessed the requisite skills to tidy a house, Cynthia thought it was unfair to Teresa to lay her off for July and August.

"She needs that money," Cynthia'd said at the time.

Normally, I wouldn't even see Teresa. I'd be at school. But six days ago I was there when she let herself in with the key we provided her. She didn't miss a trick. After noticing that Cynthia's makeup and other items were not in evidence, that her robe was not thrown over the chair in our bedroom, she'd asked if Cynthia was away.

Now on the porch with my wife, I said, "I told her you were enjoying a little time on your own. Thought that would do it, but then she wanted to know where you'd gone, whether I'd be joining you, was Grace going, how long would we be gone . . ."

41

"She's just worried we're going to cut her back to every other week or once a month."

I nodded. "She comes tomorrow. I'll put her mind at ease."

Cynthia tipped the bottle up to her lips. "Did you know those teachers?" she asked.

Those two retired schoolteachers who had been killed in their home a few days ago, not more than a mile from here.

From what I'd read and seen on the TV news, the cops were baffled. Rona Wedmore, the police detective we'd been involved with seven years ago, was the lead investigator and had as much as said they couldn't come up with a motive and there were no suspects. At least none the local police would talk about.

The idea that a couple of retired folks, with no known connections to any criminal activity whatsoever, could be slaughtered in their own home had led to a sense of unease in Milford. Some — particularly the news shows — were calling this the "Summer of Fear" in this community.

"We never crossed paths," I told Cynthia. "We didn't teach in the same schools."

"It's a horrible thing," she said. "Senseless."

"There's always a reason," I said. "Maybe not one that makes much sense, but a

42

reason nonetheless."

There were beads of sweat on Cynthia's beer bottle. "Hot one today," I said. "Wonder if it's going to be nice this weekend. Maybe we could all do something together."

I went to reach for her phone so I could open the weather app, check the forecast, the sort of thing I did at home all the time if my phone wasn't nearby. But before I could grab it, Cynthia moved the phone to the other arm of the chair, beyond my reach.

"I heard it's going to be nice," she said. "Why don't we talk on Saturday."

Barney went down the other side with the gas mower.

"He said he hopes we work things out," I said.

Cynthia closed her eyes for two seconds and sighed. "I swear, I really haven't said a thing. But he puts things together, sees you coming over but not staying. Likes to offer advice. Seize the day, that kind of thing."

"What's his story?"

"I don't know. Mid-sixties, never married, lives alone. Likes to tell everyone how his leg got busted up in a car accident back in the seventies, hasn't walked right since. He's kind of sad, actually. He's okay. I listen to him talk, try not to hurt his feelings. I might have a plugged toilet one night and need him to come over."

"Does he live here?"

Cynthia shook her head. "No. There's a young guy across the hall from me — there's a hell of a story there I'll tell you sometime. And on the first floor, there's Winnifred — swear to God, *Winnifred* — who works for the library, and across the hall from her another sad sack named Orland. Older than Barney, lives alone, hardly anyone ever comes to see him." She forced a grin. "It's the House of the Damned, I tell you. They're all here living alone. They've got no one."

"You do," I said.

Cynthia looked away. "I didn't mean it that —"

There was a sudden noise from the house. Someone coming down a flight of stairs, fast.

The door swung open and a man, late twenties to early thirties, slim, dark hair, stepped out. He spotted Cynthia before noticing me.

"Hey, good-lookin'," he said. "What's shakin'?"

"Hi, Nate," Cynthia said, an awkward smile on her face. "I'd like you to meet someone."

"Oh, hey," he said, his eyes landing on

44

me. "Another friend dropping by?"

"This is Terry. My husband. Terry, this is Nathaniel. My across-the-hall neighbor." Her eyebrows popped up briefly as she looked at me. This was the guy there was a hell of a story about.

His face quickly flushed, and it took him maybe a tenth of a second to decide to extend a hand. "Good to meet you. Heard a lot about you."

I glanced at Cynthia, but she wasn't looking at me.

"Where you off to?" Cynthia asked. "You don't walk dogs this late in the day, do you? Isn't everyone home by now?"

"Just going out for something to eat," Nathaniel said.

"You have dogs?" I asked.

He smiled sheepishly. "Not here, and they're not mine. That's what I do. I've got a dog-walking business. Go from house to house through the day, take my clients' mutts out for a stroll while their owners are at work." He shrugged. "I've had a small career change. But I'm sure Cyn— I'm sure your wife has told you all about that."

I looked at Cynthia again, expectantly this time.

"I haven't," Cynthia said. "Don't let us hold you up."

"Again, nice to meet you," he said to me, then trotted down the stairs, got behind the wheel of the Caddy, and took off on North Street.

"A dog walker with a Cadillac?" I said.

"Long story. Short version goes like this. Hit it big in the phone app business, market went south for a while, lost it all, had a nervous breakdown, now walks dogs for people every day while he gets his life back together."

I nodded. This house seemed to be a place where people came to regroup.

"Well," I said.

Neither of us spoke for the better part of a minute. Cynthia watched the street the entire time.

Finally, she said, "I'm ashamed."

"It was an accident," I said. "It was just a crazy accident. You never meant for that to happen."

"I do everything I can to protect her and I'm the one who ends up sending her to the hospital."

I didn't know what to say.

"You probably need to get home and make Grace dinner," Cynthia said. "Give her a hug for me." She paused. "Tell her I love her."

"She knows," I said, getting up. "But I'll do it."

She walked me to the car. The smell of freshly mown grass wafted up my nostrils.

"If there was anything going on, if Grace were in trouble, you'd let me know," Cynthia said. "Right?"

"Of course."

"You don't have to tiptoe around me. I can take it."

"Everything's fine." I grinned. "Mostly she watches me to keep me out of trouble. I try to throw any wild parties, she nips that right in the bud."

Cynthia rested her palm on my chest. "I'm coming back. I just need a little more time."

"I know."

"You just keep an eye on her. This thing, about those teachers being killed, it's got my mind going all kinds of places it shouldn't."

I forced a smile. "Maybe it's some former student, years later, getting even with teachers who gave him a hard time for not doing his homework. I better watch my back."

"Don't even joke."

I lost the smile. I realized I hadn't been funny. "I'm sorry. We're okay. We are. We'll be better when you come back, but we're

47

getting by. And I'm watching her like a hawk."

"You better."

I got in my Ford Escape, keyed the ignition. Driving home, I couldn't get out of my head two things Nathaniel had said.

Hey, good-lookin' was the first.

And the second was: *Another friend dropping by?*

FOUR

"Wanna have some *real* fun?" the boy asked.

That worried Grace. Maybe not a lot, but a little.

She had a pretty good idea what Stuart was getting at. They'd already been having some fun — just above-the-waist stuff — parked out back of the Walmart in his dad's old Buick. This car, it was an aircraft carrier. Massive hood and trunk, and inside, well, you hardly had to get into the backseat. The front — which went all the way across, no console or shifter in the middle — was the size of a park bench but way, way softer. The car was from the seventies, and when it went around corners, she felt as if she was in a huge boat way out past the sound, out in the Atlantic or something, getting carried away by the waves.

Grace was okay with what they'd done so far — she'd let him touch her in a couple of places — but she wasn't sure she wanted to take things any further. Not yet, anyway.

She was still just fourteen, after all. And even though she knew, with absolute certainty, that that meant she was *not* a kid anymore, she had to admit that Stuart, being sixteen, might know slightly more about the whole sex thing. It wasn't even so much that she was scared about doing it for the first time. What scared her was looking like a total amateur. Everyone knew, or thought they knew, that Stuart had already been with plenty of girls. What if she ended up doing it all wrong? Ended up looking like a total idiot?

So she decided to play things cautiously. "I don't know," she said, pulling away from him, leaning against the passenger door. "This has been, like, good, you know? But I'm not sure about taking things, like, to the next level."

Stuart laughed. "Shit, I'm not talking about that. Although, if you're thinking you're ready, I've come equipped." He started to reach down into the front pocket of his jeans.

Grace slapped his hand playfully. "Then what are you talking about?"

"It's something totally cool. I swear, you'll wet your pants."

Grace could guess. Maybe some pot, or

50

X. What the hell? She could give something like that a try. It was actually a little less scary than letting him get into her pants. "So what is it? I've tried a few things. Not just pot." A lie, but one had to keep up appearances.

"Nothing like that," Stuart said. "You ever driven a Porsche?"

That took her by surprise. "I've never driven anything, you idiot. I won't have a license for two more years."

"I mean, you ever *ridden* in a Porsche?"

"Like, is that the sports car?"

"Jesus, you don't know what a Porsche is?"

"Yeah, I know. Okay. Why you asking me if I ever had a ride in a Porsche?"

"Have you?"

"No," Grace said. "At least, I don't think I ever have. But I don't exactly pay a lot of attention to what kind of car I'm getting into. Maybe I was in one and didn't know it."

"I think," the boy said, "if you'd been in a Porsche, you'd kinda know. It's not like an average car. It's all low and swoopy and shit and fast as fuck."

"Okay, so no."

Stuart was kind of hot looking, and one of the cool kids, although not exactly in a good way. He had that don't-give-a-shit thing going on, which had some appeal to a girl who was sick to death of having to make safe choices. But after being out with him three times, she was starting to think there wasn't a whole lot going on inside that head of his.

Grace hadn't told her father she was seeing Stuart, because he knew exactly who the boy was. She could recall her dad bringing up his name more than once, back when Stuart was in her dad's English class two years earlier. He'd be marking papers in the evening at the kitchen table and say something about this Stuart kid being thick as a plank, which her dad didn't do very often because he said it wasn't professional. He said it wasn't right to comment on the work of students his daughter might know, but once in a while, if the kid was dumb enough, he slipped.

Grace remembered a joke her dad had made. For a long time, right up until this year, she'd thought she might like to be an astronaut, someone who went up to the International Space Station. Her dad had said maybe Stuart could be an astronaut, too, because all he did in class was take up space.

Tonight, Grace had to wonder whether maybe her father had this boy nailed.

One time, Stuart had asked her what she wanted to do when she finished school, and when she'd told him, he'd said, "Seriously? They only send guys up into space."

"Hello?" she'd shot back. "Sally Ride? Svetlana Savitskaya? Roberta Bondar?"

"You can't just make up names," he'd said.

Oh well. It wasn't like she had to marry him. She just wanted to have some . . . fun. She wanted to take a few . . . risks. And wasn't that just what he'd asked if she'd like to do?

"I have definitely never ridden in a Porsche."

Stuart grinned. "Want to?"

She shrugged. "Yeah, sure. Why not?"

A cell phone started buzzing.

"That's you," Stuart said.

Grace dug her phone out of her purse, glanced at the screen. "Oh, jeez."

"Who is it?"

"My dad. I'm kind of supposed to be home by now." It was nearing ten.

Adopting a deep baritone voice, Stuart said, "You get home right now, young lady, and do your homework."

"Stop it." Even if her dad was a huge pain in the ass at times, she didn't like other people mocking him. She hated it, at school, when she'd hear other kids running her dad down. It was no picnic, going to the same school where your dad taught. All these extra expectations to be a good kid, have above-average marks. After all, they'd say, she's a teacher's daughter. Talk about a cross to bear. Not that her marks were bad. She did pretty well, especially in science, although sometimes she'd write a couple of wrong answers just so she wouldn't get a hundred percent and have the boys call her Amy Farrah Fowler, the nerdy scientist girl on that TV show.

"You gonna talk to him or not?" Stuart asked as Grace's phone continued to buzz.

She stared at it, tried to will it to stop, which it finally did after a dozen rings.

But seconds later, a text. "Shit," she said. "He wants me to call home."

"He's got you on a tight leash. Your mom a control freak, too?"

If she were home, Grace thought. If she hadn't bailed on them two weeks ago, after the thing with the pot of boiling water. She'd gotten the bandage off only three days ago.

She ignored his question and turned things back to the topic at hand. "Okay, so did your dad buy you a Porsche?"

"God, no. You think he'd be driving around in a shitbox tank like this if he had?"

54

"Then what?"

"I know where I can find one and take it for a spin."

"What are you talking about?"

"I can get my hands on one in, like, ten minutes, one that we can borrow."

"What, like at a car dealership?" Grace asked. "Aren't they all going to be closed?" Who'd let you take a test drive this time of night?

Stuart shook his head. "No, at somebody's house."

"Who do you know who's got a Porsche?" She grinned. "And how dumb would they have to be to let you borrow it?"

"No, it's not like that. It's at a house that's empty this week. It was on the list."

"What list?"

"A list, okay? That my dad's got. They try to keep it up-to-date, when people are on vacation, that kind of thing. I check out places where people are away, see what kind of wheels they got. One time I took out a Mercedes, just for, like, twenty minutes, and no one ever knew. Not a scratch on it. Put it back in the garage just the way it was."

"Who keeps a list like that?" Grace asked. "What's your dad do? Does he do, like, security stuff, too?" The thing was, she had an inkling of what this boy's father did and

55

would have been surprised to learn it had anything to do with making people feel safer in their homes.

"Yeah," he said offhandedly. "That's what he is. Security."

Grace kept thinking about the call, and the text from her father. When she'd left the house, she'd told him she was going to a movie with another girl from her class. Her mom was going to drive. It was a seven o'clock show that was supposed to get out around nine, and she'd get a lift home after.

What would her dad do if he found out she'd lied? Because as lies went, this was a doozy. Grace wasn't with that girl, and they weren't at the movies. Stuart — not her friend's mother — was going to drop her off a block from home. Her father would never have let her go out with a boy who was old enough to drive.

And certainly not this boy, this onetime pain-in-the-ass know-nothing student in her father's class. With, as Grace suspected her father knew, a kind of questionable home background.

"What you're talking about sounds like stealing," she said.

Stuart shook his head. "No way. Stealing is when you take a car and keep it, or sell it to someone who packs it up in a big cargo container and ships it over to some guy in Arabia or something. But we're only going to *borrow* it. Won't even try to see what it can do, because the last thing you want when you're borrowing somebody's car is get a speeding ticket, you know?"

Grace waited a long time before she said, "I guess it would be fun."

He started up the land yacht and headed west.

FIVE

Detective Rona Wedmore was about to collapse into bed when she got the call that they'd found a body.

Lamont was already under the covers, and asleep, but began to stir when he sensed his wife was putting her clothes back on.

"Babe?" he said, turning over in bed.

She never got tired of hearing him talk, even a single word like that. Didn't matter what he said, not after she'd been through that period when he didn't speak a word. Traumatized after coming back from Iraq, the things he'd seen, he'd gone kind of catatonic on her. Not speaking for months, until that night three years ago when she got shot in the shoulder and he showed up at the emergency room and said to her, "You okay?"

It was nearly worth taking a bullet to hear those two words. No, actually, it *was* worth it.

"I gotta go out," she said. "Sorry I woke you."

" 'S'okay," he said, the side of his face still pressed into the pillow. He knew better than to ask how long she was going to be. She'd be gone as long as she had to be gone.

She locked up the house, got in her car, and, as she drove to the scene, thought this was just what Milford needed. Another murder. As if people here weren't already on edge. Wedmore hoped it was something simple, like some guy getting stabbed in a bar fight. People dying in bar fights did not spread fear through a community. One idiot kills another idiot at a bar and most people shrug and think, What do you expect when a couple of yahoos have too much to drink? Sitting in the safety of their homes, the good people of Milford didn't feel threatened by a crime like that.

But the Bradley double homicide, that was a horse of a different color, as Wedmore's late father liked to say. Two retired seniors shot in their living room? For no apparent reason?

That freaked people out.

Damned if Wedmore could get a handle on it. Neither Richard nor Esther Bradley had had any kind of criminal record. There wasn't so much as a single unpaid parking ticket registered against either of them. They had a married daughter in Cleveland, who checked out just as clean, too. There was no marijuana grow op in the basement, no meth lab in an old Airstream out back.

Yes, earlier in the evening Richard Bradley had stormed over to the house next door to tell some students to keep the noise down. At first, the kids were the only suspects Wedmore had. But the more she checked into them, the more convinced she became that they had nothing to do with killing the Bradleys.

So who the hell did it, then? And why?

The daughter had flown in from Cleveland, and when she wasn't going to pieces about losing her parents, she'd helped Wedmore go through the house in an attempt to determine whether anything was missing. As far as the daughter could tell, nothing had been stolen, and besides, her parents didn't have anything all that valuable anyway. And the killer, or killers, hadn't even bothered to take cash or credit cards out of Richard Bradley's wallet or Esther Bradley's purse.

Which tended to rule out drug addicts looking for a way to pay for their next fix.

So maybe it was a thrill kill.

But there was nothing ritualistic about the

murders. No writing of "Helter Skelter" in the victims' blood on the living room walls.

Rona wondered whether the fact that they had both been teachers was a factor. One possible scenario: Some kid one of them had flunked years earlier believed that Richard or Esther had ruined his life. He'd come back for revenge. It seemed a bit out there to Wedmore, but in the absence of any other theory, she found herself reaching. And overreaching. But revenge killings were not generally so tidy.

Richard and Esther Bradley had each been killed with a single bullet to the head. A cool and efficient double hit. No fingerprints left behind. People who killed for revenge tended to overdo it. Twenty stab wounds instead of three. Six bullets instead of one.

So, okay. If it was a professional hit, why? Who the hell would put out a contract on two retired teachers?

It was driving Detective Rona Wedmore crazy.

Maybe another murder, if not what Milford needed, was exactly what she needed. Something to clear her head of the Bradley case. Focus elsewhere. That sometimes worked for her. It might mean that when she went back to the double homicide, she'd notice something she hadn't seen before.

It wasn't, as it turned out, a bar that Wedmore had been summoned to, but Silver Sands State Park, forty-seven acres of sandy beaches, dunes, marshes, wetlands, and forest on the sound. She went south on Viscount, past the seniors apartment building on the right until the street ended, then turned left onto the roadway that paralleled the beach and the boardwalk. She took it right to the end, where three Milford police cars with rooftop lights twirling were parked.

A uniformed male officer spotted her unmarked car and approached.

"Detective Wedmore?" he asked as she got out of the car.

"Yeah. What's up, Charlie?"

"Same old. Wife and me just had a kid."

"Hey, no kidding? Congrats. Boy, girl? Something else?"

"A girl. Calling her Tabitha."

"So, what've we got here?"

"Dead male. White, early twenties. Looks like he took a couple in the back. Maybe he was running away."

"Witnesses?"

Officer Charlie shook his head. "Not even sure it happened here. Think he might have been dumped."

Wedmore was pulling on a pair of gloves.

"Lead the way."

She followed the cop down along the boardwalk. It had taken quite a beating during Hurricane Sandy, just like everything else along here, but had now been pretty much repaired.

"Over here." Charlie pointed into the tall grasses to the left of the boardwalk, away from the sound.

There were several other cops there already. Some lights had been set up on stands.

Wedmore made her way through the waist-high grass. She caught a whiff of decomposition, but there was a breeze coming in off the water, so she didn't feel the need to rub some Vicks beneath her nose.

"Who found him?" she asked of anyone who would answer while she got a penlight out of her jacket pocket.

A uniformed woman said, "Couple kids, making out, wandered this way. They ran out, called us, waited around on the boardwalk till we got here."

"You let them go?"

"We got names, all that. Their parents came and got them."

The body was facedown. The man was probably two hundred pounds, short blond hair, oversized blue T-shirt and khaki shorts with half a dozen pockets. White socks and running shoes. Wedmore knelt down, caught a glimpse of something in a lower pocket. She fished out a wallet, opened it up, shined her penlight on a driver's license visible behind clear plastic.

"Eli Richmond Goemann," she said. Wedmore studied the two bullet holes in the back of the blood-soaked shirt. "Roll him over."

A couple of officers did the dirty work.

"Hardly any blood," she said. "He didn't bleed out here. So yeah — where's Charlie? Anyway, what he said, that he was moved here, that seems likely. Joy been called?" The forensic examiner.

Someone said, "Yes."

Wedmore took a look through the wallet. Sixty-eight bucks in cash. Credit card receipts from bars, liquor stores. That'd give her a place to start.

She took another look at the Connecticut driver's license. The man was born in March 1992, so that made him twenty-two.

"Hello," she said.

"What?" said someone.

Wedmore kept staring at the license. At Eli Goemann's address.

"Son of a bitch," she said.

She knew the street. She'd been there

recently. Eli's former address was just two numbers off from the house where Richard and Esther Bradley had been murdered.

Wedmore was pretty sure that was the house where the students lived.

Six

"You look all freaked-out," Stuart said to Grace on their way to the house where they were going to find a Porsche. "But believe me, it's going to be fine. There's, like, no risk at all."

"How are you going to start it? Like on TV, you touch some wires together under the steering wheel?"

"Shit, no, that's totally unrealistic. Like, the guy, he gets under there, finds the wires, and in two seconds he's got the car going. Doesn't happen. And even if you could get it to start, how are you supposed to unlock the steering column, right? You need a key for that. In the movies, yeah, *maybe* you could get the car running, but you could only drive it in a straight line. I hate stupid stuff like that in movies."

"So you've got the key?"

"Not yet." He patted her thigh with his right hand. "Okay, it's just up the street here, but we'll walk up half a block."

She hadn't paid much attention to where they were going. But they were on a dead-end street now, in a nice part of town. Well-manicured lawns, mature trees, houses set back from the curb. Big driveways.

"Come on," Stuart said as she got out of the car slowly. They were a few steps away when the boy stopped suddenly. "Wait here a sec. Forgot something."

He went back to the Buick, opened the passenger door, put one knee on the seat, and leaned forward, as if rummaging around in the glove box for something. Whatever he found, he tucked it into the front waistband of his jeans and pulled his jacket over it.

"What did you get?" Grace asked when he rejoined her.

"Flashlight," he said.

He was reading house numbers. He stopped out front of a two-story Colonial. "This is it. Come on. We can't stand around staring at it. People notice."

Except there was no one around.

He grabbed her hand and pulled her up the drive. There was one light on over the front door, another at the side of the house, but he was pretty sure no one from any neighboring houses could see them.

"Whose place is this?" she asked.

"Somebody named Cummings or something. What a name. Someone says, Who are you?, you say, I'm Cumming. And they say, Oh, you that happy to see me?" He snorted. "Let's double-check the garage first, make sure it's there, that we haven't come here for nothing." He tightened his grip on her wrist.

A garage big enough for two cars was around back, attached to the house. Four rectangular windows ran horizontally along the door at eye level. "I just want to make sure," he said.

He reached into his jacket for his cell phone, used the app that turned it into a light, and put it up to a window.

"I thought you went back for a flashlight," Grace said.

"Jackpot," he said, staring into the garage. "Can you see that? Look in there."

She looked. "I see a car." Two, actually. A plain white four-door sedan and a low two-door sporty number in red.

"That's not a car," the boy said. "That's a 911. A goddamn Carrera. Now we just have to get inside and get the keys."

For the first time, Grace was starting to think this was a really, really bad idea. Her stomach started to float. "I don't think so. I don't like this."

"I told you, it's okay. They're away. We get in without tripping the alarm. Word is, they've got a dog — they've got it boarded or something for the week — but it means they won't have motion detectors inside. Stupid pets set them off all the time."

She wrenched her wrist from his grip. "No. No way."

He whirled around. "What are ya gonna do? Walk home? Do you even know where we are? You gonna sit on the curb till I get back? Come on. I wasn't able to get the key or find the pass code with my dad's stuff, but that's okay — we'll get in through a basement window."

Grace's phone dinged. Another text from her father.

"Your old man again?"

She nodded, then put the phone away as he turned away from her and knelt by a basement window.

"The sensor should be in the corner here," he said. He kicked in the glass. Grace jumped, put both hands to her mouth. "Just sounds loud because you're standing there. No one'll hear that. And there's carpet on the basement floor." Shards of glass lined the edge of the frame like sharks' teeth. "I could fit through here, but I'd bleed to death after."

He reached into the pocket of his jeans and came out with a credit card that had a couple of short pieces of duct tape stuck to it, and then something shiny about the size of a matchbook. He looked back at the girl, unfolded the shiny item, and grinned. "Tin foil. We just slip that over the contact and hold it in place . . ."

He had his hand inside the window, working on the upper right corner.

". . . and now, when we open the window, the alarm does . . . not . . . go . . . off." His arm still snaked into the house, he cranked open the window, creating a larger opening, without any shards to catch him on the way in. "I gotta be honest — that's the part that always scares me. I was ready to run if I had to."

He dropped his legs in first, supporting himself with his elbows, then dropped about a foot. "Piece of cake," he said. "Come on."

She felt chilled, even though the summer night air hadn't dipped below seventy. She tilted her head back, scanned the heavens. Despite the light pollution, she could make out stars. She remembered the telescope she used to have when she was a little girl. How she used to study the stars from her bedroom window, searching for asteroids, worried one of them would strike and wipe out her and her parents.

The whole planet, too. But once you'd lost your whole family, the rest of the world seemed incidental.

Lost families. Something of a theme in her household.

And now her family was less than whole, what with her mom living in an apartment in an old house on the other side of Milford. Grace thought she'd have moved back by now, but nope. Was she trying to make a point, staying away this long? Was all this talk that she needed some time to "get her head together" the truth, or just some bullshit story to cover up the fact that she just didn't love Grace and didn't want to be in the same house with her?

Not that things weren't a little more calm these days, with just her dad at home.

Her mom was so uptight, so worried some calamity would befall her daughter. Freaking out all the time. Wanting to know where she was every second of the day. Who she was seeing. Making her phone home every couple of hours. Wasn't that all supposed to be over? *Years* ago? After her mom had finally found out the truth about what had happened to her when *she* was a teenager?

Well, I'm fourteen now, Grace thought. How long was this going to go on? Would

71

her mom want her to wear one of those ankle bracelets when she went to college so she could monitor her every move?

Grace sometimes thought her mother had her so convinced something awful would happen to her that she just wanted to get it over with. Bring it on. The anticipation was always worse than the event.

Was that, Grace wondered, why she was with this boy now, about to do something very stupid? Because it would create some kind of crisis, force her mother to come home?

That's nuts. Like I want my mom to find out about this.

"Hey!" Stuart whispered, his head framed in the window. "You coming or what?"

She got on her knees, back to the window, and worked her legs through. The boy grabbed hold of her and eased her down gently.

"Don't turn on any lights," he said.

"Like that's the first thing I'm gonna do," she said.

They were in a basement rec room. Leather couch, two recliners, big flat-screen TV bolted to the wall. They crossed the carpet, glass crunching underfoot, and found their way to the stairs.

From what she could see, it was a nice

house. Modern furniture and decorations, plenty of leather and aluminum and glass. Not like her house. Her parents bought used, sometimes went to Ikea in New Haven.

"Aren't the people gonna know someone was here when they find the window broken?" Grace asked.

"So what? Won't matter then." He still had his phone in flashlight mode, guiding them through the house. "People usually keep their car keys somewhere near the front door, like in a drawer or a dish or something." They'd reached the front hall, where a long, narrow table with four drawers was pushed up against the wall.

"Yeah," he said. "This'll be the spot. I can guarantee it."

He pulled open the first one, held the illuminated phone over it. "Just gloves and shit here."

When he pulled on the handle of the second drawer, it stuck, and he bumped himself with his hand as it broke free.

Something heavy hit the marble floor.

"What was that?" Grace asked.

"I just dropped something."

"What the — is that a *gun*?"

"No, it's a tuna fish sandwich. The hell you think it is?"

"You keep a fucking gun in your car?"

"It's not my car, and it's not my gun. It's my dad's. Hold it for me while I do this."

"I'm not holding —"

"Just fucking do it!" Stuart said, shoving the gun at her. "You're starting to be a total pain in the ass — you know that?"

"What are you gonna do? Shoot somebody?"

"No, but if somebody tries to mess with us, they'll think twice when they see this."

She still resisted as he pushed the gun on her, but she could tell he was getting angry. Would he hurt her if she didn't hold it? Punch her in the face? How would she explain that when she got home? A bloody nose, a black eye?

"Okay," Grace said.

The gun was heavy and warm and foreign in her hand. She couldn't remember ever holding one before. It felt as if it weighed fifty pounds, pulling her arm toward the floor.

"Just don't put your finger on the trigger," he said. "You have to know what you're doing before you start shootin' one of those."

"Like you do," she said. "Like you're some sort of expert."

"Don't turn all bitchy on me, okay? Shit,

no keys in this drawer, either." He opened the third one and shook his head. "Damn, where do they keep those friggin' Porsche keys? It just makes sense for them to be —"

"Did you hear that?" Grace asked.

Stuart froze. "Hear what?"

"Shut up," she said. "Listen."

The two of them held their breath for a good ten seconds.

"I don't hear anything," he whispered. "What did you hear?"

"I thought I heard somebody moving around. Like a floor creaking or something." Without thinking about it, she tightened her grip on the gun, but kept it pointed at the floor.

"You're just imagin—"

He stopped. He'd heard something, too.

"Shit," he said, looking toward the kitchen.

Grace moved toward the front door. On the wall, just next to it, the security keypad, a small green light glowing.

Green? Doesn't that mean — ?

"No!" Stuart hissed. "Open that and the alarm'll go off!"

"But the light is —"

"The noise sounded like it was in here," he said quietly, moving on the balls of his feet toward the kitchen.

"No!" she whispered after him. "Let's go." She was thinking, even if they went out the front door, and the alarm was set to go off, and it did, they could still get to his car before the police or the security company showed up.

"It's probably nothing. I'm not runnin' out of here for no good reason. We're gonna find those keys."

He held his phone at arm's length, casting light on the floor head of him.

"Please," Grace said.

"Stay close to me," he said, inching forward, reaching out an encouraging hand to her.

"I'm scared."

He grinned. "You're the one with the gun, Grace. What's there to be worried about?"

SEVEN

TERRY

One phone message and a text. No response to either.

I struggled to remember the name of the girl Grace said she was going to the movies with. Sarah? Sandra? I was pretty sure it was Sandra Miller. Sandra's mother was going to be dropping Grace home on the way back from the theater. But I had no number for Sandra, or her mother, and how many Millers would there be listed in Milford? I didn't even have to look. These days, now that every kid on the planet had a cell phone, we were letting down our guard when it came to getting info on how to reach their friends.

Cynthia would've known. She'd have been able to tell me who Sandra Miller was, where she lived, her favorite pop star, how long she and Grace had been friends. She'd have probably talked to Sandra's mother at some point, too, and had the woman in her phone's contact list. Whenever Grace met someone new, Cynthia would manage to get all their particulars in case she might need them later.

Maybe, if I'd been through what Cynthia had, this kind of thoroughness would be second nature to me, too.

I liked to think I kept a close eye on Grace, but there was no doubt I didn't watch her the way her mother did. I cut her some slack. If she was ten minutes past curfew, I didn't launch into the Spanish Inquisition. I kept the waterboarding to a minimum. I wanted to be able to trust her. Or maybe it would be more accurate to say that I wanted to trust that she had some common sense. But no teenager is trustworthy. I wasn't at that age, and Cynthia was the first to admit she wasn't, either.

So much about being a parent is holding your breath and hoping everything will be okay.

So yeah, I gave Grace more freedom. I made deals with her. I told her I'd cut her more slack if she'd promise me that even while her mother was living elsewhere, that when we were all together as a family, she'd dial it down. Not everything had to be an argument.

Grace said okay.

But now she'd burned me.

I could sit here and wait for her to show up, or I could strike out looking for her. Trouble was, I had no idea where to begin. And the odds were, the moment I left, she'd show up here. I wanted a word with her the moment she came through that door.

I was standing in the kitchen when the phone rang. I had the receiver to my ear before the end of the first ring. But before I said a word, I saw from the caller ID that it was not Grace.

"Hi," I said.

"You must have been sitting on the phone," Cynthia said.

"Just in the kitchen, sneaking a cookie," I said. "What were you doing?"

"Nothing. Just . . . I felt bad about the beer."

"The what?"

"When you came by. I didn't offer you a beer."

"I didn't even notice."

"When you left, I realized what I'd done. Sat there and had one right in front of you. It was rude."

"Don't worry about it," I said.

She hesitated. "It was deliberate."

"Oh."

"I needed that time, just for me. I thought if I offered you a beer, you'd have — I feel sick about this."

"It's okay," I said.

"The thing is, the moment you left, I burst into tears and hated myself for not getting you one. Because I realized then I didn't want you to go. Jesus, Terry, I'm a mess. I really am."

"Have you seen Naomi this week?"

"Yeah. I look at her sometimes and think she must be so fucking tired of me. Listening to me still whining after all these years."

"I doubt that."

"It's just, I can't shake this post-trauma. That's what's making me hell to live with for Grace." A pause. "Is she back from the movies yet?"

"No," I said honestly.

Even though she wasn't here, in this house, Cynthia often needed to know that Grace was safely home before she could get to sleep at her place.

"When was she supposed to be back?"

"Cyn," I said.

"I know, I know. All I was thinking was, since she works tomorrow, I hate her to be out too late, to go to work tired. You can get hurt in a kitchen if you're not paying attention."

Grace had a summer job at the Milford Yacht Club, waiting tables in the dining room.

"Don't worry. She's only a few minutes late. I texted her a couple of minutes ago. Everything's fine."

Not quite a lie.

"Okay," Cynthia said.

"What'd you do tonight?"

"I had to go over and see Barney. I forgot this was the day I was supposed to pay the rent, and he likes cash, so I went to an ATM a couple of hours ago and drove over to his place to pay him."

"He offer you any marital advice?"

Cynthia laughed, but not hard. "He says to me, 'I've been alone my whole life, never had anyone. You don't know how lucky you are to have somebody, so don't throw that away.' That's what he said."

And she went silent.

"Cyn?"

Nothing.

"You okay?"

"Yeah. I'm fine," she said.

"You're not throwing anything away. I know that."

Unless I was wrong. Had I misread things? I'd believed Cynthia when she'd said she needed some space because of how she'd been dealing with Grace. Did her concerns extend beyond that issue? Was she having second thoughts about me?

Which led me to think about what Nathaniel had said. About *another* friend dropping by to visit her. I was about to ask who it was when the line beeped. It's was Grace's cell.

"Hang on a second. That's our girl on the other line."

"Sure."

I hit the button.

"Grace?" I said, an edge already in my voice. "You know what time it is?" I wasn't yelling, however. It was as if I somehow thought Cynthia could hear me on the other line.

"Dad? Dad? You have to come."

She was talking rapidly, her voice shaking.

I could tell, instantly, that something was not right, so I switched from Angry Dad to Concerned Dad.

"Honey, you okay? I thought what's-her-face's mom was bringing you home?"

"You have to come. You have to come *right now.*"

"Where are you? What's going on?"

"Something's happened, Dad. Something's happened."

EIGHT

TERRY

She told me I could find her in a small store attached to a gas station at the corner of Gulf Street and New Haven Avenue. I tried to get her to tell me what was going on, but all she'd say was that I should hurry.

And one last thing.

"Don't tell Mom."

"I'm on my way," I said, then clicked back to Cynthia. "Hey."

"I wondered when someone would say, 'Your call is important to us.' Is everything okay?"

"Yeah," I said. "There was a problem with her ride, so she's asked me to pick her up."

"If you want, I could pick her up, bring her home."

"No," I said, maybe a little too quickly. "That's okay."

I was thinking about those two words Grace had said. *Something's happened.* Just what a parent wants to hear. The mind races. If she were old enough to drive, I'd have guessed fender bender or a speeding ticket. But I could rule that out, given that she was only fourteen, unless she'd decided to get behind the wheel of one of her friend's cars illegally.

Jesus, don't let it be that.

Maybe she'd been stopped by the cops for drinking underage or having alcohol in her possession. Maybe she'd smuggled beer into the movie theater. I wasn't naive enough to think Grace was an angel in that regard. A year ago, when she was thirteen, her mother had discovered a liquor store receipt in the front pocket of her jeans while doing the laundry. We needed the intervention of a UN peacekeeping team after that one. We finally got her to confess she'd gotten a girlfriend's much older brother to buy her some Baileys Irish Cream — the girls felt very sophisticated adding it to their coffee — and he'd given her the receipt so she knew how much to pay him back.

Yeah, it could easily be something like that tonight.

And even though Cynthia had said she didn't need to be protected, that she could handle it if there was a problem with our daughter, she sounded fragile tonight and she didn't need this. If I took Cynthia up on her offer to pick up Grace, we might be into World War III within the hour.

"Are you sure?" Cynthia asked. "I don't mind."

I thought of inventing some excuse. Telling her we might be coming down with the flu and there was no sense exposing her. But if that were the case, why had I allowed Grace to go to the movies? Anything I could think of seemed incredibly lame, and I didn't want to start spinning a whole web of lies over something that, for all I knew, and hoped, wasn't that big a deal.

Besides, I needed to get going. I'd been off the phone only a few seconds with Grace but was feeling an urgency to get in the car and fetch her.

"No," I said firmly. "I got this. But thank you."

"Okay, then," Cynthia said, sounding slightly miffed.

"I'll talk to you tomorrow," I said.

"Sure, fine, whatever. Go get our girl."

She hung up.

I grabbed my keys out of the dish and bolted out the front door. I hit the remote to unlock the Escape, got behind the wheel, and backed onto Hickory. From there, it was a short distance to Pumpkin Delight

Road. I headed north on it to Bridgeport Avenue, then east, down through the Milford Green, and in only about five minutes was at New Haven and Gulf. The gas station was on the northeast corner.

As I wheeled into the lot, Grace came charging out of the convenience store. Head down, brown hair hanging down over her eyes. She ran to the car. She pulled on the door handle before I had a chance to unlock it. I hit the button, but she grabbed for the handle too quickly and a second time couldn't get into the car.

"Wait!" I shouted through the glass.

She dropped her arm, waited to hear the click, then swung open the door and got into the front passenger seat. She wouldn't look at me, but the brief glimpse I had of her face revealed damp cheeks.

"What the hell happened?" I asked.

"Just go."

"Where's your friend? How did you end up here? Why are you alone?"

"Just go," she said again. "Just drive. *Please.*"

I drove out between the pumps, got back onto New Haven, and headed west.

"Grace," I said, firmly but gently, "you can't expect me to drive out to some gas station in the middle of the night to pick you up without your offering up some kind of explanation."

"It's not the middle of the night," she said. "It's only after ten. Ten *fifteen*. You always exaggerate."

"Okay, it's ten. What's going on? You said something happened."

"I just want to get home. Then . . . maybe . . . I can tell you."

We rode in silence the rest of the way. I kept glancing over at her. Her head hung low, her hands were in her lap, and she appeared to be studying her fingers, which she laced together, took apart, laced together again. It looked to me like she was trying to keep them from shaking.

She was getting out of the car before I had it in park, then made a beeline for the front door. By the time I'd caught up to her, she was trying to unlock it with her own key, but her hand was shaking so much she couldn't slide it into the lock.

"Let me," I said, edging her out of the way and using mine.

Once the door was open, she ran up the stairs as fast as she could.

"Grace!" I shouted. If she thought she was going to hole up in her room and close the door and avoid an interrogation, she was very, very wrong. I chased her up the stairs, but she didn't run into her room. She was in the bathroom, on her knees in front of the toilet.

She attempted to pull back her hair as she retched once, then a second time. I had mixed feelings about whether to help her. When your kids experiment with drinking, maybe they need to endure the consequences without sympathy. Although if Grace had been drinking, surely I'd have smelled it on her breath when she got into the car. I hadn't noticed anything.

Grace gave it a third try, but hardly anything came up. I handed her a thick wad of tissues to blot her face, squatted down next to her, and reached over to the handle to flush the toilet. Grace slid back from the toilet and propped herself up against the wall.

It was my first real look at her, and she did not look good.

"You going to be okay?" I asked her.

No response.

"What did you drink? I didn't notice anything on your breath."

"Nothing," she whispered.

"Grace."

"Nothing! Okay?"

Maybe she really was coming down with the flu or something, and I was giving her hell for being sick.

"You sick? Did you eat something bad?"

"I'm not sick," she said, so quietly I could barely hear her.

I said nothing for the better part of a minute. I took the wadded tissues in her hand, tossed them in the basket, then ran a washcloth under a cold tap. "Here," I said. She wiped her mouth again, then put the cool cloth on her forehead.

"It's time," I said.

Grace fixed her wet eyes on me. I thought I saw fear in them.

"You weren't with Sarah," I said.

"Sandra."

"Okay. You weren't with Sandra, were you?"

Her head moved side to side half an inch.

"And you didn't go to the movies."

"No."

"Who were you with?" I asked. When she didn't respond, I added, "What's his name?"

Grace swallowed. "Stuart."

I nodded. "Stuart what?"

She mumbled something.

"I didn't catch that," I said.

"Koch."

I had to think a second. "Stuart Koch?"

A furtive glance my way, then she turned away. "Yeah."

"I taught a Stuart Koch a couple of years ago. Tell me it's not that Stuart Koch."

"It might be," she said. "I mean, yeah, it is. He went to Fairfield, but he dropped out this year."

That was the Stuart I knew. "Jesus, Grace, how did you hook up with him?" I was trying to get my head around it. Stuart Koch was the kind of kid who'd ask you how to spell DUI. A chronic underachiever if ever there was one. "Where'd you meet him?"

"Does it matter?"

"He's a lost kid. Hopeless. Going nowhere. Honestly."

She shot me a look. "So what are you saying? He wasn't worth saving because he's not a girl?"

Her aim was good with that one.

I knew that was a reference to a student I'd had seven years ago. Jane Scavullo, her name was. A troubled kid, always getting into fights. No one on staff had any use for her. But I'd thought there was something there. It came through in her writing assignments. She had a real gift, and I ended up going to bat for her. Of course, there were some extenuating circumstances, too, but those aside, Jane had struck me as a kid who could amount to more than she herself could have imagined. She ended up going

90

to college, and not that long ago, I'd run into her.

I'd talked about her from time to time with Grace, so she knew the story.

"It's not that," I said defensively. "Jane had . . . potential. If Stuart has any, it wasn't evident to me at the time." I hesitated. "If I've misjudged him, feel free to set me straight."

She had nothing to say to that, and I let it go — I sensed there was a more immediate problem involving this kid. Were they going together? If so, when had it started? How long had this been going on without my knowledge? Had they had some kind of fight this evening? A breakup?

"What were you doing at that gas station?"

"I walked there," she said, wiping a tear from her cheek. "I walked for, like, ten minutes or so, and when I got there I figured it would be an easy place for you to find to come get me."

"Was Stuart driving?" A nod. "But he left you to walk on your own at night, to that gas station? That sure as hell speaks well of him."

"It's not like that," she said. "You don't understand."

"I don't understand because you haven't told me anything. Did Stuart hurt you? Did he do something he shouldn't have?"

Her lips parted, as if she was about to say something, then closed.

"What?" I asked. "Grace, I know that maybe some things would be easier to talk about with your mother, but did he . . . did he try to make you do things that made you uncomfortable?"

A slow, torturous nod.

"Oh, honey," I said.

"It's not what you think," she said. "It wasn't . . . it wasn't that kind of stuff. He knew about this car."

"What car?"

"A Porsche. He knew where there was one that he wanted to take me for a ride in."

"But it wasn't his car?"

Grace shook her head.

"Did it belong to someone he knew?"

"No," she whispered. "He was kind of going to steal it. I mean, not forever, but just for a little while, and then he was going to take it back."

I put a hand to my forehead. "Good God, Grace, tell me you and this boy didn't take someone's car for a joyride." My mind made several leaps in a nanosecond. They'd stolen a car. They'd hit a pedestrian. They'd fled the scene and —

"We didn't steal it," she said. But she

didn't say it in a way that gave me any reason to feel relieved.

"You got caught? *He* got caught? Trying to take the car?"

"No," Grace said.

I folded the lid down on the toilet and took a seat. "You gotta help me here, Grace. I can't play twenty questions with you over and over until we get to what happened. Tell me that when Stuart went to take this car, that's when you walked away."

"Not totally," she said, and sniffed. I handed her more tissues and she blew her nose. Even if she wasn't sick, she looked terrible. Eyes red and bloodshot, skin pale, her hair in tangled strands. An image of her when she was five or six flashed before my eyes, when Cynthia and I took her to Virginia Beach and she was covered in sand from head to toe, building a castle at the water's edge, flashing a smile with three missing teeth.

Did that girl still exist? Was she still here? Buried deep inside this one curling in on herself in front of me?

I waited. I could sense her steeling herself. Getting ready to tell me, and then face the music after I knew what she'd done.

"I think . . ."

"You think what?"

"I think . . ."

"Jesus, Grace, you think *what?*"

"I think . . . I think I might have shot somebody."

NINE

Gordie Plunkett was starting to think everybody was going to be late for this meet tonight. Even the boss.

He spoke to the guy behind the desk in the motel office, rented the room, and not for the going rate, either, since they wouldn't be messing up the sheets. This was the kind of place many customers would take for an hour, and Gordie knew Vince wasn't going to need it for much more than that, unless their latest customers were late.

Even then, it wouldn't be an issue. If people you were meeting with didn't show up on time, you didn't wait around. Made you look weak. Vince had taught Gordie that. You didn't sit on your ass while someone disrespected you. You got up and you left. Besides, someone being late could mean something bad. Maybe the cops had picked them up. You didn't wait around to find out.

Gordie just hoped the boss, and Bert and Eldon, managed to get here before their latest clients.

Bert Gooding showed up first.

"Where's Eldon the Cock?" Bert asked, getting out of his car and walking over to Gordie, who was standing on the sidewalk outside of room twelve.

"Eldon? What about you? Where you been? And where's Vince?"

"I think maybe he had a doctor's appointment this afternoon and it took a lot out of him," Bert said.

"He looks like shit lately."

"Yeah. First his wife, and then he gets it. But he should be along any second. I don't know where Eldon is."

"Jeez," Gordie said. "Eldon's supposed to be covering the front door. You're supposed to be out back —"

"I know where I'm supposed to be."

"And I'm inside. That's the way Vince likes it."

"Yeah, well, Vince don't run as tight a ship as he used to," Bert observed.

Gordie's eyes narrowed. "What's that supposed to mean? You mean because he's been sick?"

"That's just part," Bert said. "He's not cracking the whip. Things are sliding. We should be out jacking cars, pulling over trucks, the kind of stuff we used to do."

"Vince hasn't got the energy for that anymore," Gordie said.

"He should do the chemo."

"He doesn't want to."

"He doesn't do the chemo, he's just hurting himself."

"Don't argue with me about it," Gordie said. "Where the fuck is Eldon?"

"All I'm sayin' is, I don't like the way things are going."

"Then maybe you should bring it up with the boss," Gordie said, using a tone almost daring Bert to do it, knowing he never would. Vince Fleming might not be the man he once was, but you didn't cross him. "Anyway, what's your excuse?"

"For what?"

"For being late."

Bert shrugged. "Jabba." As in Jabba the Hutt, his pet name, at least away from home, for his wife, Janine.

Gordie didn't have to ask for details. Janine had a face that would make a Pamplona bull turn around and go back, and a disposition to match. Gordie figured it was a testament to Bert's character that he hadn't killed her. God knows he had the wherewithal, and plenty of experience at

97

getting rid of bodies. He could take her up to the farm, feed the pigs for a couple of days. Unlike Bert, Gordie had never married. He'd always figured paying someone once a week was a simpler way to take care of one's needs. The irony was, Bert did the same.

"There's Vince," Bert said, pointing to the Dodge Ram pickup turning into the lot. He parked the truck, got out and walked over to the two men.

"Where's the Cock?" Vince asked. It was Eldon's bad luck to have a last name that, while spelled differently, looked as though it would be pronounced similarly to the male member.

"Don't know," Bert said.

Vince Fleming angled his head to one side. "And why don't you know?"

Slowly, he said, "Because I haven't called him."

"Why don't you do that, then?"

Bert got out his phone as Vince said to Gordie, "This the room?"

"Yeah. I did a Dunkin' run. There's some coffee and shit in there."

Vince grumbled something unintelligible as he went into the unit. Gordie sidled up to Bert, who was waiting for Eldon to pick up, and said, "I was sure you were going to ask the boss why he was late."

"Fuck off." Bert shook his head in frustration. "Eldon's not answering. It's going to voice — Hey, asshole, Bert here. You should already be here. If you're not here in the next two minutes, you better call with a good reason why." He ended the call, put the phone back into his pocket.

"I'm goin' 'round back," he said. It was their standard operating procedure. Watch the meeting place from all sides.

Gordie went into the motel room. It had all the charm one could expect for twenty bucks an hour. Vince was putting cream into one of the takeout coffees, helping himself to a strawberry-filled donut. Biting into it, he said, "They say these things'll kill ya."

Gordie didn't know whether he was supposed to laugh at that, so he played it safe and said nothing.

"What's up with Eldon?"

"Bert left a message."

Vince went to the window, used two sugar-dusted fingers to pry apart the chipped and grimy blinds. "I need someone out there before these assholes arrive."

"You want me to cover the front, have Bert come inside?"

Vince took another bite. "No, let's wait. Hang on — someone's coming."

A pair of headlights swept the lot as a car turned in off the street. It was an old, rusted VW Golf that sounded like a lawn mower, with Eldon behind the wheel. Bald as a cue ball, but a head more basketball-sized. Vince had been expecting to see Eldon in his massive old Buick.

"I'm going out," Vince said to Gordie, who was prying another coffee out of the cardboard takeout tray. Eldon was backing the Golf into a spot across from the unit so he'd have a good view of anything that went down. But what was going down now was Vince, and he looked pissed. He was walking toward him slowly but deliberately. Vince hadn't been able to run for some time, not since he'd been shot seven years earlier. The bullet damaged the muscles in his gut, among other things, and made it difficult for him to move quickly.

Eldon put down his window. Vince leaned in, his face in Eldon's.

"Where the fuck have you been?"

"Sorry," he said. "I got held up. Nothing's happened, has it?"

"They're not here yet."

"No harm, then," he said, forcing a smile and shrugging. "I'm here. We're good."

Vince pulled his head out of the car and walked back to the motel room. Gordie was exiting the bathroom as Vince came in, doing up his belt, checking his zipper.

"Fucking gang who couldn't shoot straight," Vince said. The cell in his hand buzzed.

"He here?" Bert asked.

"He's here," Vince said, and ended the call. He sat wearily on the edge of the bed.

Gordie said, "Did I hear right? Eldon's here?"

"Yeah. So we're good to go." Gordie noticed Vince was breathing heavily. "You okay?"

"I'm fine."

The cell phone in Vince's left hand buzzed yet again. "Yeah?"

"Our boys are here," Eldon said. "Just pulling up in a Lexus SUV."

"How many?"

"Unless they got someone hiding in the back, just the two, like you said. But . . . hang on. There's another car, a Beemer, holding back, down the street. Can't see who's in it."

"The Beemer's just sitting there?"

"Yeah."

"Cops?"

"I don't know," he said. "No, wait. It's driving off."

"You sure?" Vince asked.

"Yeah, it's gone. Okay, and the driver's getting out of the Lexus — now the other guy. The other guy has the bag. A black backpack. I'm getting out, will tell 'em which room."

Vince Fleming killed the connection, said to Gordie, "They're here."

He nodded. His duties were limited, at least on this occasion, to standing, watching, and guarding. A gun that he'd tucked into his belt he now took out and held. If things got out of hand, he wanted to be ready. Gordie had hurt a lot of people in his time working for Vince, but then again, so had Vince. But the boss didn't quite have the energy for it he once did.

Five quick raps on the door. Knuckles on metal.

Vince rose from the edge of the bed and opened the door. The men resembled each other. White, stocky, neither of them over five-six, both with black greasy hair, although one kept his shorter than the other. Couple of fireplugs. Looked like, if you wanted to push one of them over, you'd have to lean and put your back into it.

"Hey," Vince said, and closed the door once they were inside. "Which one of you is Logan?"

"I'm Logan," said the one with the shorter

hair, who also looked about five years older. He tipped his head toward the one who was holding the backpack. "This is Joseph."

"You two related?" Vince asked.

"He's my brother," said Logan.

Joseph went over, uninvited, and examined the pastries in the Dunkin' Donuts box. He selected a jam-filled one, bit into it, then frowned.

"Shit, cherry." He tossed the donut with the bite out of it back into the box and selected a chocolate. Bit into it, smiled. "This is better."

"The hell?" Gordie said.

Vince glared but said nothing.

After two bites, enough of the donut was gone that he was able to shove the rest into his mouth. Vince eyed the backpack he was holding and said, "So whaddya got for us?"

Joseph's mouth was too full to talk. His brother Logan said, "Couple things I need to get straight first. How do we know we can trust you?"

Vince looked at him with dead eyes. "You wouldn't be here if you hadn't checked me out."

Logan shrugged. "Yeah, okay, we did that."

"You want to do business, I'm ready. You not sure? Take your pig of a brother here and get the fuck out."

"Excuse me?" Joseph said, licking his fingers.

Vince kept his eyes on Logan. "Yes or no?"

Logan tried to meet the stare, but after five seconds looked away. "Yeah, I want to do business."

"You gonna let him talk to me that way?" Joseph asked his brother.

"Shut up," Logan said. "Give me the backpack."

Joseph handed it over.

"I got a lot in here for you to look after," Logan said.

"Just cash?" Vince asked.

Logan cocked his head. "I thought that was all you took."

"Whatever you can fit in that backpack, we'll take."

"Like a head?" Joseph asked.

Now Vince looked at him. "What?"

"A head. A head would fit in a bag like that. Let's say we had a guy's head and we needed to save it for something later, could you tuck it away for us?" Joseph grinned. "If we wrapped it up, like, so it didn't smell?"

Logan said, "We don't have a head."

Vince said, "Let's start counting." He pointed toward the cheap dresser, the laminate on the top and drawers heavily chipped. Sitting on it, next to an old, non-flat television that had to weigh three hundred pounds, was a currency-counting machine that looked, at a glance, like an oversized computer printer.

"Why do you need to know that?" Logan asked.

"When you go into your local Bank of America branch with a stack of cash, do you just tell them how much it is and they say okay?"

Logan grunted. He put the backpack on the bed, unzipped it, and reached in with both hands to bring out stacks of bills held together with rubber bands.

"Each stack is a thousand," Logan said. "There's seventy of them."

"Seventy grand," Vince said flatly. "I thought you said it was a lot."

He shook his head, grabbed three stacks at random. If they each came out to a thousand, Vince wouldn't bother counting the rest mechanically. He slipped off the rubber bands and set the stacks, one after the other, into the machine. Once he had the bills nicely tucked in, he hit the button and the bills fanned like tall grass in the wind.

After he'd checked the third stack, Vince

105

said, "Okay. Now we'll see that we have seventy of them stacks."

It didn't take Vince long to count them, making them into seven piles of ten. Gordie didn't help. As he'd been instructed, he was there to watch, and besides, it was hard to count bills with a gun in your hand.

"Now what?" Logan asked.

"I take my service charge," Vince said, pocketing five thousand-dollar stacks. "That covers you for six months."

"Motherfucker. That's high. What if I want it back before the six months is up?"

Vince shook his head. "Minimum charge."

"Fine," Logan muttered. "I'm outta options. The police may be watching us. Last week, they had a warrant to search our warehouse. Didn't find anything, the fucks. But they know what properties we own. And Swiss banks aren't what they used to be, either."

"No," Vince concurred. "I think we're done here."

Logan appeared uncertain. "Aren't we supposed to get something?"

Vince cocked his head. "A toaster?"

"A receipt?"

Vince shook his head. Vince had brought some brown paper Whole Foods shopping bags to put the money in, but Logan pointed

106

to the backpack and said, "You can keep that."

Joseph said to his brother, "Check it out." He was pointing at Vince's crotch. "Guy's pissed himself."

Vince bent his head down to examine himself, saw the dark, wet stain to the side of his zipper. "Son of a bitch," he said under his breath.

Gordie bit his lip. This happened occasionally, but it wasn't the sort of thing you wanted to point out to the boss. At least not in front of others.

Joseph took a step toward Vince. "Hey, I was out of line pointing that out. Sorry about that. Don't be embarrassed. My uncle, he's older than you now, but there's been times when he's had the same problem. Thing is, though, those times it happened, he was three years old."

He flashed that grin again. Vince turned his head away from Joseph and fixed his eyes on Logan.

"Your mother still alive?" he asked.

"Huh?" Logan said.

"Your mother. The one who pushed you and your brother out her cooz. She still alive?"

Logan blinked. "Yeah. She is."

"What are you gonna tell her?"

"What am I gonna tell her about what?"

"What are you gonna tell her when she asks why you didn't do more to save your brother? Why you didn't get him to control his mouth? Why you let him get himself killed by being an asshole?"

Logan's eyes shifted to the left, looking beyond his brother to Gordie, who had his arms raised and extended, a gun pointed at the back of Joseph's head.

Logan swallowed slowly, then said to his brother, "Apologize to the man."

Joseph turned around long enough to assess his situation, then looked at Vince and said, "I may have spoken out of turn. You have my sincerest apology."

"It's gonna cost you another five to leave your stash with me," Vince said.

Logan nodded, caught his brother's eye, and tipped his head toward the door. The two of them left the room.

When the door closed behind them, Gordie lowered his weapon and said, "All you had to do was give me the nod."

Vince glanced down again at his pants. "I got a change of clothes in the car."

"I'll go," Gordie offered. He was used to this.

Before he reached the door, Vince's phone buzzed again. He looked to see who it was and frowned. Not with disappointment, but curiosity. It wasn't one of his guys keeping watch outside.

He put the phone to his ear.

"Hey, sweetheart," he said. "What's up?"

His face grew dark as he listened. "Tell me again which house." He listened a few more seconds. "Okay. Thanks for letting me know. You done good."

Vince put the phone into his jacket and spoke to Gordie. "We need Bert. Tell Eldon to take care of the money. Then tell him to take the rest of the night off."

"Why? We're not going back to your place for a drink or —"

"Do it. Get rid of him."

"What's going on?"

Vince put a hand out to the dresser, steadying himself. "We may have been hit."

"Jesus," Gordie said.

"It's worse than that," Vince said.

TEN

TERRY

I was thinking I must have heard Grace wrong. There was no way she could have said what I thought I'd heard.

"You what?"

"I think — I don't exactly know for sure — but I think I might have shot somebody," she said.

So I'd heard right. But it didn't make any sense. I felt as though I'd just been pushed off the top of a tall building and there was no one down there with a net. The sidewalk was coming up very, very fast.

"Grace, I don't understand. How could you think you shot somebody?"

"He gave me the gun."

"Who gave you the gun?"

"Stuart."

This was going to be bad.

"He wanted me to hold on to it. But then we thought we heard something, and it was

dark, and I don't know what exactly happened. But there was this loud noise, like a
gun went off. Like, this huge bang. And I
didn't think it was me, that I was the one
who made the gun go, but I was the one
who was *holding* the gun, and Stuart didn't
have one, but I'm not sure because it was
all so dark and crazy and I've never touched
a gun before and I was so scared and then I
thought I heard a scream but I don't even
know now if it was somebody else or me. I
just ran. I was going to go out the front
door, even if it set off the alarm, although
the little light was green, but when I turned
the knob, it was locked and I couldn't figure
out how to open it, so I went back through
the basement and went out the window and
I didn't know what to do at first — I was
kind of paralyzed or in shock or something,
I don't know, and I got my phone out and
then I just ran and ran until I got to the gas
station and I wasn't sure what to do and
finally I decided the person I had to call
was you even though I knew you and Mom
would be really mad but I didn't know what
else to do and it wasn't my fault. I mean,
maybe it was my fault, but I don't know. I
don't know what happened."

And then she dissolved into tears. Not just
tears, but huge, racking sobs.

"Oh God, oh God, oh God," she said, wrapping her arms around herself and rocking against the wall. She raised her head, and even though her eyes were looking my way, it was as if she didn't even see me.

"My life's over," she said. "My life's completely fucking over."

I got down on the floor next to her, putting my arms around her and holding her as tight as I could.

"Okay, okay," I said. "We're going to sort this out. We're going to sort it all out."

Knowing, even as I said the words, how unlikely that was. This was no fender bender. This wasn't getting arrested for drinking underage. This wasn't something we'd be able to smooth over in a hurry.

"If somebody did get shot, are you saying it was Stuart?" I asked between her sobs. "Did you get the sense that there was somebody else there? Someone else who could have fired a gun? And is it possible Stuart had a second gun? That he gave one to you and held on to another one for himself?"

"He — I'm pretty sure — he had just the one. He went back to the car to get it. I . . . I called for Stuart and he didn't say anything. I think . . . I think I actually screamed for him. But then I thought I could still hear something moving around, and I put my hands over my eyes for a second, screamed again, I was totally freaking out, and I felt someone run by me, or I heard someone running . . . I don't know. It was dark in the house. He told me not to turn on any lights, so no one would know we were there. I think I got bumped. If Stuart was okay, wouldn't he have answered me? Maybe — maybe what I heard was a dog or something running through the house. He said the people there had pets, so they didn't have those, you know, those things in the house that can tell if you're there."

"Motion sensors."

"Yeah."

"Did you hear a dog? Was there any barking?"

"No, I didn't hear anything like that."

"Okay. Grace, where did this happen?"

"A house."

"Where's this house?"

"I don't know." She took several deep breaths. "I mean, I sort of know, but I don't exactly know. Not far from the gas station. I wasn't running that long."

Ten minutes, she said. Could be a radius of half a mile to a mile or so around that location.

"So it wasn't Stuart's house?"

She shook her head. "No. It was some house that he said was on the list."

"What list?"

"He didn't say. Just a list where they kept track of things. It might have been a list his dad had."

"What's his dad do?"

Grace sniffed and shook her head. "I don't know, just stuff. But Stuart knew the people who lived in the house were away and figured if he could get into the house, he could get the keys and take the car for a drive."

"Jesus," I said. I seemed to be saying that a lot.

"I'm so sorry," she said. "I'm sorry. I'm really, really sorry. It was really stupid. I'm so sorry. I know this is it for me. My life's finished. What's Mom going to say when she finds out? She'll probably kill herself. After she kills me."

"Grace, listen to me. Is it possible you didn't actually shoot him? Did you see him get shot? What did you see?"

"I don't know. I heard the shot, but I didn't really see anything."

"Were you pointing the gun? Were you holding it up, or was it down at your side?"

"I think — I don't think I was pointing it. Stuart told me not to put my finger on the trigger, but then when I started to follow him, I kind of moved it in my hand because it was heavy and I might have got my finger on it. Maybe it went off when it was pointed down, and the bullet bounced or something."

"Tell me again, where did this gun come from?"

"It was in the glove compartment."

"He keeps a gun in his car?"

"It's not his car. It belongs to his dad. It's really old."

"Is it possible his father's a cop or something?"

Grace shook her head. "He's definitely not a cop." I had the sense she knew more than she was saying about Stuart's father. "And it was just a dumpy old car, not a police car or anything. It was huge."

"Okay, so Stuart got the gun from the glove compartment. Why did he want to have a gun?"

"In case we ran into anyone. He said he wasn't going to use it to shoot anybody, just to scare them off if they gave him a hard time."

In my head, I was screaming.

"How did it end up in your hand?" I asked.

"He dropped it while he was looking for

the keys, so he asked me to hang on to it. I told him I didn't want to, I swear. I didn't want to touch it even. But he got really mad at me."

"When the shot happened, did your arm kick back hard?" I didn't know much about guns but was aware of the principle of recoil.

"I don't know. It's all kind of hard to remember."

"Grace," I said, trying to get her to look me in the eye. "Grace, look at me."

Slowly, she raised her head.

"If this boy has been shot, then we need to get him some help."

"What?"

"If he's in that house, if he's been wounded, then we have to help him. If you did shoot him, and we don't know if you did or not, but if you did, he might be alive. And if he is, we have to get him to a hospital. We have to call an ambulance."

Another sniff. "Yeah, I guess."

"Think. Do you know the address?"

"I told you. I don't even know where I was. Stuart drove, and then when I left, I didn't even pay attention to where I was exactly. He said the name of the people who lived there, but . . ." She struggled to remember. "I don't . . . I can't think what it was."

"Then we're going to have to find that house," I told her.

"Huh?"

"We're going to have to go back. You're going to have to help me find it. If we drive around that area, maybe you'll recognize it."

She started to shake.

"I can't do that. I can't go back."

"Look," I said. "Call him. Try calling Stuart on your cell. Maybe he's fine. Maybe's he's okay."

"I tried," she said. "After I ran away. I made — I made some calls before I called you, most of them to Stuart. He didn't answer."

"Try one more time. If you get him and find out he's okay, then we'll sort out what we have to do. But if you can't get him, we're going to have to find that house. Right now, if I called an ambulance, I'd have no idea where to send them."

Grace swallowed again. "Okay." She pointed to her purse, which she'd dropped by the bathroom door. "Can you reach that for me?"

I crawled over, got the bag, and set it by her knee. She dug into it, pulled out the phone. She went into her recent calls, tapped the screen, put the phone to her ear.

Waited.

Looked at me.

Waited a little longer.

A large tear formed at the corner of her right eye and left a damp trail down her cheek.

"It went to message," she whispered.

I stood. "I guess we better go."

ELEVEN

"Hello?"

"I almost gave up there. That was ten rings, Unk. I wake you?"

"I guess I'd nodded off. What time is . . . It's almost eleven. I was watching TV and fell asleep. I think I was dreaming about your father. About when the two of us were growing up together. He liked to light firecrackers under turtles. Mom always said he wasn't wired right in the head. Something happen?"

"Just thought I'd bring you up to speed."

"Yes?"

"First of all, they took the bait. Again."

"That's good, right, Reggie?"

"Yes and no. What we're finding is, there's not just one hiding place. She could be anywhere. It's a risk-reduction strategy. Multiple spots. I get the wisdom of it. And like I said before, there's a chance for a real payoff here. Something I wasn't expecting at the outset."

"I want you to come out okay. You deserve it."

"It just means I may have to come up with another strategy. I can't hit a dozen locations at once. I've got help — I've had to bring in a couple of extra guys — but it's not like I've got an army. Instead of us finding a way to get it, maybe we're going to have to find a way to get them to bring it — and her — to us."

"You think she's okay?"

"I've got no reason to think otherwise. But we need to move quickly because we're not the only one looking for her."

"He can't have her back. I won't allow it."

"I know."

"You know, I nod off watching TV, but when I actually go to bed, I can't sleep. I can't stop thinking about her. About how we met."

"It was at a funeral, wasn't it?"

"We both went to Milford High — this was before they closed it and turned it into offices — but she was a year ahead of me. Couple of years after I graduated, and there was this kid name of Brewster. Clive Brewster. Not that bright, drunk half the time. One night he's goofing around and — You know that little bridge downtown, past the green, with those turrets at one end and those big stones with people's names on them?"

"Yeah."

"He decides to jump in. Water's not that deep there, but it hardly matters because he does this little spin and whacks his head on one of those stones. That was the end of him. So lots of kids came to the church, and I end up sitting next to her, and she nudges me, whispers that the minister's got this funny little strand of hair that's sticking out the side of his head, and every time he moves this hair goes waving along with him, like it's an antenna. And she starts to get the giggles."

"Wow."

"It was kind of like — you remember that *Mary Tyler Moore* episode where Chuckles the Clown died? He was in a peanut costume at a parade and got crushed by an elephant?"

"Before my time, Unk."

"She can't keep it together. Her body's starting to shake, so I put my arm round her, like I'm consoling her, like she's crying instead of laughing, and whisper, 'Follow my lead. Act really upset.' We're right at the end of the pew, so I stand and take her with me, my arm still around her, and she's making these noises that sound like sobs but she's actually laughing. I get her out of the church, and the door closes, and she explodes with laughter. But I'm worried the people in the church can still hear, so I pull her in close to me, practically smother her, and I can feel her heaving in my arms, and when she slows down and has herself under control, she looks up at me, and I don't know what happened, but right then, I looked at her and thought she was the most beautiful girl I'd ever seen, and I kissed her. I kissed her, Reggie, right on the mouth."

"What a story."

"Yeah. And the second I did it, I thought, Shit, this is wrong, I'm going to get my face slapped, but she threw her arms around my neck and kissed me back. Know what we did then?"

"Tell me."

"Drove to Mystic, got a motel and stayed there till the next day."

"You dog, you."

"I was never happier."

"I know, Unk."

"Get her back. Do whatever you have to do."

TWELVE

TERRY

I grabbed a bottle of water from the fridge for Grace as we headed out of the house. I opened the car door for her, assisting her as though she'd suffered some physical injury. She was on autopilot, going through the motions in a daze. I uncapped the bottle and told her to drink, which she did. I got her buckled in, and by the time I'd gone around the car and settled myself in behind the wheel, she'd drunk a third of the bottle.

"I need to know how you're feeling," I said.

She turned her head. "Seriously?"

"Yeah, this is a serious question. Your breathing seems okay. Are you still feeling sick to your stomach?"

"I guess not."

"You dizzy?"

"I just feel . . . I feel like I'm in a dream."

"Chest pain?"

"Am I going to have a heart attack?" she asked, alarmed.

"I need to know whether you're going into shock," I told her.

Grace blinked a couple of times. "I . . . I don't even know what I'd be feeling if I was in shock. Mostly I'm just really scared. And numb. It's like I'm not feeling anything, like I'm watching all this happen to someone else. It can't be me."

I wished. I reached out, touched her knee. "You can do this. Where should we start?"

"I guess the gas station," she said. "Maybe I can figure it out from there."

So back we went.

"Mom can't know about this," she said. "She can't be home when they come to arrest me and charge me with murder, like in *Law and Order.*"

"We'll find out first what we're dealing with," I said. "But whatever happened tonight, it's probably not going to be the kind of thing we can keep from your mother. Unless this whole thing turns out to be some huge practical joke."

I didn't believe we'd get lucky that way.

"I guess, if I end up in jail, she'll start wondering what happened to me, so she'll have to know. Or she'll see me on TV, when they walk the killer past the cameras and·

put them into the backseat of a police car."

"Don't talk that way."

"That's what'll happen. They'll send me off to one of those juvie places, with other kids who've killed people. I'll probably get stabbed in a shower. I'll never come out."

"Grace," I said, trying to keep my voice level, "let's get some facts before we go off the deep end. Okay? I need you thinking clearly. You get that?"

"I guess."

"No, not a guess. Tell me again. What happened just before there was a shot?"

She closed her eyes briefly, trying to put herself back into that house. I had a feeling she'd be having to tell this story many times before this mess was over. To me, to Cynthia.

To the police.

To lawyers.

I had to prod her. "Tell me about when Stuart gave you the gun."

"Okay, like I said, he dropped it, when he was looking for the keys, and then he told me to hang on to it and I said no."

"But eventually you took it."

She nodded. "He was getting really mad at me. So I took it, and tried to keep my finger off the trigger like he said, so I just held on to it by the handle part."

"The butt."

"Yeah, I guess. And then I thought I heard something, and then Stuart thought he heard it, too, in the kitchen. I mean, I guess it was the kitchen. It was dark and I'd never been in there before. Stuart wanted to check it out, but I wanted to leave, but he told me to follow him."

"The gun's still in your hand."

"Yeah. I think . . . I might have moved it to my other hand, and then back again. I'm not sure. It's all mixed up in my head."

Up ahead were the lights of the gas station.

"Okay," I said. "Then what?"

She cocked her head slightly to one side, as if she was remembering details she hadn't thought about before.

"Someone said, 'You.' I remember that."

" 'You'?"

"Yeah."

"Who said it? Was it Stuart?"

"I'm not sure. It could have been. And then —" She covered her mouth with her right hand. "And then there was the shot. And then it sounded like somebody falling down."

"The shot," I repeated. "Where did it sound like it came from?"

"It sounded like it was everywhere. And

then I tried to get out the door, and couldn't, and next thing I knew I was outside. I'd gone back out through the basement window."

My mind had already imagined the worst-case scenario. That Grace's fears would be realized, that she had actually fired that gun.

And that the bullet had hit Stuart Koch.

And that Stuart Koch was dead. In that house.

If there was nothing I could do to save him, I had to do everything in my power to save Grace. To help her get through this as best she could. I wasn't thinking about the morality of this. I wasn't thinking that justice should run its course, that Grace should get what was coming to her.

I was thinking like her father. I wanted to save her from this. Even if she was guilty of something horrible, I wanted her to get off. The bigger picture wasn't my concern. Justice didn't enter into it. I didn't want my little girl going to prison, and was already thinking about what I could do to ensure that didn't happen.

The gun.

It would have her fingerprints on it. The police would be able to match it up against the bullet they'd take out of Stuart Koch. If, in fact, he was shot. And if, in fact, Grace had shot him.

If I could find the gun, if I could get my hands on it before anyone else did, I could take a drive west on Bridgeport Avenue, stop on the bridge that crossed the Housatonic, and pitch it over the railing.

And I'd fucking well do it. There wasn't a doubt in my mind.

"Grace," I said gently. "About the gun."

She turned and faced me. "What about it?"

"Where is it? Where's the gun now?"

Her face went blank. "I don't know. I have no idea."

THIRTEEN

Detective Wedmore didn't have to worry about waking anyone up this time of night. Her only concern was whether anyone would hear her banging over the blast of the music.

She made a fist and pounded on the front door of the house, prepared to walk in on her own if someone didn't answer soon. She was reaching for the doorknob when it swung open and she was looking into the slightly bloodshot eyes of a man in his early twenties.

She figured they would remember her. After the Bradleys were murdered next door, Wedmore had talked to the three young men who were living here while attending some college in Bridgeport. She had conducted thorough interviews with all three of them, separately, and had come to the conclusion they not only had nothing to do with the double homicide, but didn't know anything useful. She wasn't actually sure they knew anything useful about anything.

Now she was here for a completely different reason. But in the back of her mind, she couldn't stop wondering whether there was a connection.

Rona Wedmore didn't like coincidences.

When the young man saw her standing there, he blinked a couple of times, then said, "Hey, hi, I remember you. Did someone call the cops about the music?"

He shouted back into the house, "Turn it off!"

Seconds later, the music died.

"That okay?" he asked Wedmore.

"They don't send me out on noise calls," she said. "You're Brian, right?" Brian Sinise, if she remembered correctly, and it wasn't very often she remembered incorrectly. She knew the other two who lived here were Carter Hinkley and Kyle Dirk.

"Yeah, right."

"Carter and Kyle here?"

He nodded. "You're good," he said. "Guys! The black cop lady wants to talk to us! Not about the noise!" He smiled and led her into the living room of the house, which was littered with empty beer bottles, overflowing ashtrays, and empty pizza boxes.

"We just had dinner," he said. "You want a beer?"

Wedmore shook her head. "No, thanks."

Two sets of footsteps could be heard coming down the stairs. Carter and Kyle were both around the same age as Brian. Of the three, Carter was on the heavy side.

"Hey, man," Carter said to Brian. "You don't shout out 'black cop lady.' What's wrong with you?"

Brian winced and looked apologetically at Wedmore. "Sorry."

She said, "Can we all sit down?"

Kyle rushed over to clear a pizza box off a chair so Wedmore could sit. She had a good look at it first, brushed away a few crumbs. Kyle said, "So, have you figured out who killed those old folks?"

"We haven't made an arrest in that yet," Wedmore said. "I guess you've all been feeling pretty on edge ever since."

They glanced at one another, evidently assessing one another's level of anxiety, and finally all three shrugged. "I guess so," Kyle said. "It's pretty fucked-up, but we're all kind of busy."

The other two nodded. Wedmore thought, *Dumb as shoes.*

"So you've got more questions about that?" Carter asked.

"I wanted to ask you about someone else, someone who I think may have lived here at some point."

"Oh," Brian said. "Shoot."

"Nice choice of words, douchehead," Kyle said.

"I can't say anything right," Brian said. "It's the beer. I think I might have a problem." His friends chuckled.

"Did someone named Eli Goemann live here?"

"Oh yeah, Eli," Kyle said. "He was here for, like, a couple years. I moved in when it was his last year, same time as Brian moved in. And then, when Eli left, that was when Carter moved in."

"So I never met the guy," Carter said. "I just heard the stories."

"But you two know him," Wedmore said to Brian and Kyle. They nodded.

"What's up with Eli?" Brian asked. "Because he, like, left without paying his share of the rent for the last month he was here."

"Was he attending school while he lived here?" Wedmore asked.

"Yeah. Same place as us."

"Why'd he move out?"

Brian shrugged. "He was kind of an ass. I didn't want him around. Neither did Kyle."

"Why?"

Kyle said, "He didn't pull his weight. We try to keep the house running smoothly, you know? Make sure there's beer in the fridge, keep the place looking good."

Wedmore's eyes roamed the room.

"But Eli never pitched in. It was like housework and chores were beneath him."

"Yeah," Brian said. "And if we ordered pizza and had to split it three ways, he'd always say, Shit, like, I didn't get to the ATM — can I pay you back tomorrow? And then when you asked him the next day he'd say, Well, I didn't even have that much pizza, only a slice — you guys had most of it."

"So we said, Why don't you find somewhere else to live?" Kyle said. "We started freezing him out. Finally, he got the message and left."

"When was this again?" Wedmore asked.

"A year ago," Brian told her.

"But his driver's license gives this as his address."

"Yeah, well —" Brian shrugged. "Mine's still got the address from two moves ago."

Wedmore gave him a reproachful look. "You're supposed to notify them of a change of address."

He nodded sagely. "I will certainly get on that."

"Where did Eli go after he left here?"

133

He and Kyle glanced at each other. "Beats me," said Kyle. "He got the odd bit of mail coming here after he left, but he didn't tell us where he was going, so we just threw that shit out."

Brian said, "You didn't say why you're asking."

"So you haven't talked to him since he moved out. Neither of you?"

"I haven't," Brian said.

"Me, neither," Kyle said.

"And I wouldn't know the asshole if I saw him," Carter piped up.

"You ever know him to get into any kind of trouble? Outside of the house here? With other people, or the police?"

Heads shaking.

"You know anything about his family? Where his parents are? They in Milford?"

Brian said, "I think they're in Nebraska or Kansas or someplace like that."

"You don't know which it was? Kansas or Nebraska?"

Brian shook his head. "I always think of them as kind of interchangeable."

That didn't worry Wedmore too much. Goemann wasn't that common a name, and a Web search for phone numbers in those two states wasn't likely to produce too daunting a list.

"But it is kind of weird," Brian said.

"What's weird?" the detective asked.

"That this would be, like, the second time in a week or so when someone has come around looking for him."

Wedmore leaned forward in her chair. "Someone else was here? Who?"

Brian shrugged. "I don't know. I thought at first maybe he was a cop, you know, like you. But he didn't show me a badge or anything."

"He give you a name?"

Brian shook his head.

"Why'd you think he was a cop?"

"He just had that cop thing going on. A suit, big guy, short hair. And I don't know if I'm allowed to say this" — he shot a glance at Kyle — "but he was black. Looked like a detective out of *The Wire* or something like that."

"And what did he want?"

"Said he was trying to find Eli, that he had some business with him, that he'd been in touch, but they hadn't gotten back to him. Thought he might live here. I told the guy he hadn't lived here for, like, a year."

Wedmore had a thought. If this guy had been a cop, he would have shown a badge. But if he came across like one, he might be a former police officer who'd gone private.

"This guy who came around asking," she said. "How tall?"

Brian said, "Like, six feet? Six-two? Looked like he could have played football when he was younger."

"How old would you say he was?"

"Pretty old. Mid-forties."

Wedmore let that one go.

"And he had sort of a gap between his teeth, right here." Brian touched his finger to his upper teeth.

Wedmore raised an eyebrow. "You sure about that?"

Brian nodded.

"How about his nose?" she asked. "Did it look like it was kind of pushed over to one side, like maybe it got broken a long time ago?"

Another nod from Brian. "Yeah, I think. I even asked him about it."

"You would," Kyle said.

"He said it happened when he played ball."

That nailed it for Detective Wedmore. That sounded very much like Heywood Duggan.

Of course, back when he worked for the state police, and he and Wedmore were sleeping together, she'd always called him Woody. For more reasons than one.

FOURTEEN

TERRY

"I kind of blanked out, you know?" Grace told me, sitting in the car next to me as we tried to find the home she and Stuart had broken into. "Next thing I knew, I was out of the house. I guess I dropped the gun somewhere. Or maybe back in the house. Probably in the house, because it would have been hard to hold on to when I was crawling out of the basement, you know?" She was thinking. "Unless I put it on the ground outside before I got out. Maybe I picked it up and then threw it in the bushes on my way to the gas station."

"Think, Grace. It's important."

She turned away, dropped her head, studied her hands. "I don't know. The house. I'm pretty sure. I remember when I tried to open the front door, I think I was using both hands."

"Okay," I said. "That's good."

137

But then she added, "I think."

I slowed the car when we got to the intersection of New Haven and Gulf. "Which way did you come from?"

She pointed right, onto Gulf. "Down that way. That much I know."

I put on my blinker and lowered my speed to allow Grace a chance to refamiliarize herself with the neighborhood. The first cross street we came to was George.

"Was it down here?" I asked, pointing left. Then, glancing in the other direction, "Or that way?"

"I don't know. I don't think so. Everything looks the same."

That was true. At night, with only a few streetlights to distinguish one house from another, I could understand her difficulty.

"Maybe when I see his car," she said, "then I'll know if we have the right street."

"What kind of car?"

"I don't know, but it was old and really big. And sort of brown. I think I'd know it if I saw it. He didn't park it right out front of the house. It was a few houses away."

I drove past George. I passed Anchorage on the left, and shortly after, Bedford on the right.

"Wait," Grace said. "I remember that." She was pointing at a yellow fire hydrant. "I remember running by that."

"So you must have come up Bedford," I said, making a right.

"Yeah, I think I came along here."

I barely had my foot on the gas. "Recognize any of these houses?"

She shook her head but said nothing. "Where's his car?"

"This might not be the right street, hon." We'd reached another street that came up from the south to join Bedford. Glen Street.

"Here!" she said. "I remember that sign. It was Glen. I'm sure it was Glen."

I turned the wheel hard to the left. Glen took a gentle bend to the right a short distance ahead.

There were no big old cars parked along the street. There were no cars parked on the street at all. The homes along here all had driveways large enough to accommodate more than one car, so there wasn't much need for people to leave vehicles on the street.

In a few seconds, I realized we had no place else to go. Glen dead-ended.

"If it's on this street, then we must have passed it," I said.

"I keep looking for the car. There's no car."

"Maybe Stuart's okay and he went home,"

I said, desperate for any positive development.

"Maybe," she said.

I did a three-point turn at the end of Glen. "Okay, so study the houses on the way back, see if any of them look like the place."

I was also trying to take some comfort from the fact that the street was not overrun with police cars, their lights flashing. If something had happened along here, it sure looked as though no one had any inkling of it yet. And a gun going off — someone would have heard that, right? Called the cops?

Maybe. Maybe not. A lot of times, people hear one shot, wait for a second, and when another one doesn't come, they go back to sleep.

"Tell me about the house," I said.

"It had two floors, and you couldn't see the garage from the street because it was tucked around the back. It could be that one, or it could be that one, too, or — Cummings!"

"What?"

"That was the name. That was the name of the people who live there. Stuart said it was Cummings."

I stopped the car, got out my cell, and opened the app that allowed me to find ad-

140

dresses and phone numbers. I entered "Cummings" and "Milford."

I looked up from the phone, and then at the first house Grace had pointed to. "It's that one."

I killed the lights and the engine. "Let's have a look-see."

I grabbed a flashlight I kept under the seat. Grace was out of the car by the time I got around to her side. Tentatively, the two of us walked up the driveway.

"I never wanted to do this," Grace whispered, taking hold of my arm, clinging to me. "You have to believe me."

I said nothing. There was a part of me that wanted to go ballistic. To ask her what the hell she'd been thinking. To scream at her until I went hoarse. But not now. It was important that we both make as little noise as possible. Lectures would come later, but I feared a stern talking-to was going to be the least of Grace's worries.

"Where did you go in?"

"Around back," Grace said. "Stuart knew this trick, this thing he did, so the alarm wouldn't come on. He was pretty good at it." She turned to see whether I was looking at her, and I was. "Maybe he's done stuff like this before."

I still resisted the urge to scold, but my

look conveyed the message. Her head slunk down lower on her shoulders.

Once we were around the back and the double garage was visible, I clicked on the flashlight. First I shone it through the garage windows, saw a red Porsche and another car in there. I'd wondered whether, after Grace had fled, Stuart had continued with his plan to take the car.

Assuming he was okay.

The fact that the car was there was not a good sign. But then again, was it a bad sign?

I turned the flashlight on the house and saw the open basement window. The first thing I looked for was a gun on the ground.

No sign of one.

"That's where we got in," Grace said.

I got close to the window, shone the light down into the basement, saw some shards of glass down there on the carpet.

"Let's see if we can look inside without going in," I said. I wanted to look through the kitchen windows. Most houses had the kitchen at the back of the house. The first-floor windows sat up some, the sills hitting me around the base of the neck. Low enough to get a peek.

There was flagstone right up to the wall's edge, so I didn't have to step into any gardens to put my face up close to the glass.

A set of blinds covered the entire window, but they were turned to let the sun in, so I was able, at least in theory, to peer between the slats. I held the flashlight over my shoulder and angled it to shine light through them and into the house.

It worked. I was looking at the kitchen. There was a large granite-topped island, a fridge on the far wall.

"Can you see anything?" Grace asked.

Problem was, from my angle I couldn't see below the level of the countertops. If someone was on the floor, I wasn't going to be able to tell from out here.

"Not really," I said.

There was one obvious solution, of course: call the Milford Police. They'd be able to get into this house without going through a basement window. They'd know how to contact the security firm that monitored the house. They'd know how to handle things properly.

They'd also have questions for Grace. About her and her boyfriend's plan to steal a Porsche. About breaking into this house.

On the off chance that things were not as bad as they seemed, I wanted to keep the police out of this mess as long as possible. Preferably forever. I had a feeling Grace would accept whatever punishment her mother and I dished out if it meant she wasn't spending time behind bars.

Stop going there.

I lowered the flashlight and backed away from the house a couple of steps. "I really can't see anything," I said. "And that's just the kitchen. Maybe whatever you heard happened someplace else."

I had to make a decision. Call the police, or —

"I'm gonna have to go in," I said, glancing over at the open basement window.

"I can't," Grace said, eyes wide with fear. "I can't go in there."

"I'm not asking you to. You stay by the window. Better yet, call me on your cell. We'll be connected the whole time I'm in there."

We both got out our phones. I instructed her to mute the ring, and I did the same. Grace dialed mine, it buzzed in my hand, and I accepted the call.

"Okay. If there's a problem out here, you just give me a shout."

She nodded as I slipped the phone into my shirt pocket. Close enough that if she called out to me, I'd hear her.

I got down on my hands and knees and worked my way back through the open basement window.

FIFTEEN

Cynthia Archer was pissed.

Why wouldn't Terry let her pick up Grace? Why did he insist on doing it? He had to know it was important to her. He had to know that she wanted her daughter to know that even though she was taking a break away, she still loved Grace and wanted to be there for her.

Even for something as simple as a lift home.

Was Terry angry with her? Was this about the beer? About her being rude? Did it have anything to do with Nathaniel? Did Terry pick up some kind of vibe from him, even in the few seconds they'd spoken? Maybe Terry wasn't upset about anything that had happened today, but just generally fed up about the whole time-out.

Or maybe it was something else.

Maybe it was something to do with Grace. Maybe Terry didn't want Cynthia picking up Grace because the girl was in some kind of trouble. Not necessarily something big, just big enough that it might set Cynthia off.

Was that how they saw her? she wondered. Like she was dynamite? Handled incorrectly and she'd explode?

It depressed her.

Terry and Grace were always trying to protect Cynthia, shield her from anything that might raise her anxiety level. Well, really, it was just Terry trying to protect her. Grace was probably more interested in protecting herself whenever she kept something from her mother.

The problem was, the more they tried to keep her from worrying, the more she worried. When she suspected this was what they were up to, Cynthia couldn't stop thinking about what it was they were hiding. Was Grace having trouble at school? Was she skipping classes? Failing to turn in her assignments? Staying out too late? Getting into trouble with boys? Smoking? Drinking? Drugs?

Sex?

There was no end of things to make yourself crazy about when it came to teenage girls.

Cynthia knew better than anyone. She was

146

willing to concede she was a terror at that age. But she also knew, despite the headache she must have been to her parents — at least while she was still in their lives — that she was a pretty good kid. True, she made some stupid choices, like all teenagers. She shouldn't have been out that night with Vince Fleming, who was seventeen and had what they called back then a "reputation." It wasn't just that he liked to raise a little hell, drove too fast, drank too much. His father was a known criminal, and, to recollect a phrase both her mother and her aunt Tess used to say, "the apple doesn't fall far from the tree."

Even though she was half in the bag at the time, she could recall every detail of that night back in May 1983. At least the parts before she got home and passed out. She remembered her father tracking her down, finding her in that Mustang with Vince, how he dragged her out, drove her home. The ugly scene that followed.

And the horrible, horrible events that happened after that. Waking up the next morning to an empty house, and not knowing for another two and a half decades what had happened to her mother and father and brother. And then struggling to come to terms with knowing her family — that family, the one she grew up with — was now forever gone.

But none of it was her fault.

After all these years, it was one of the few things she'd finally accepted, thank you very much, Dr. Naomi Kinzler. The irony was, her bad behavior that night when she was fourteen, her excessive drinking, undoubtedly saved Cynthia's life. She'd passed out, missed the whole thing.

Stop dwelling on the past . . .

But that was the whole problem, wasn't it? She couldn't stop. When you suffer a trauma in your teens, it never really leaves you. She knew these deep-rooted anxieties fed her worries about Grace, and Terry, too. It wouldn't matter how perfect their lives were — she'd always be steeling herself for what was around the next corner.

There were medications she could take, of course. But she didn't like how they made her feel, and really, wasn't it a good thing to always be on guard? To be ready for whatever bad thing that might come along? You couldn't allow yourself to be lulled into a false sense of security, right?

Except it was no way to live.

And she didn't want to live here, in this apartment, nice as it was. A combined living room and kitchen, plus bedroom and bath. Nathaniel across the hall. Downstairs, Winnifred the librarian and Orland, the lonely old guy. Not exactly a place where you had to be worried about loud parties.

The only one she'd really gotten to know was Nathaniel Braithwaite. A very distinguished name for a man who made his living taking people's pets for a stroll while their owners were at work.

Cynthia chided herself for mocking him in her thoughts. Nathaniel was a nice man. Thirty-three, jet-black hair, slim. From the looks of him, walking dogs got you in as good a shape as if you went to the gym. He told her he covered probably ten miles a day. Plus, all that bending over to clean up after them — well, it was the next best thing to calisthenics. Lots of stretching.

He'd had his own software company in Bridgeport, designing apps for that cell phone company that went bankrupt a couple of years back. He'd had the fancy car, a condo overlooking the sound, a place in Florida. But when his major client went under and failed to pay Nathaniel's company the millions he was owed, his company got dragged down with it.

Nathaniel didn't just lose the company and the condo and just about every dime he had in the bank.

He lost his wife, too. She'd met Nathaniel as he was riding the wave and had grown accustomed to a certain lifestyle. When it ended, so did the marriage.

And then, as he'd told Cynthia during the chats they'd had in the hall or when they met on the stairs, he lost his mind.

He called it a nervous breakdown. A mental collapse, with a dollop of depression thrown in for good measure. Lasted the better part of a year, even spent a week in the hospital when he went through a suicidal period. When he finally emerged from the darkness, he opted for a simpler, less ambitious, much less stressful existence.

He might not get back into the proverbial fast lane for six months, or a year. Or maybe never. He got his small apartment, then began considering ways to keep food on the table and beer in the fridge.

Nathaniel liked dogs.

He'd always had them as a kid. He wasn't about to go back to school for several years to become a veterinarian, but he was pretty sure he didn't need a degree to walk them. He acquired several clients whose dogs needed to be liberated from the house to do their business every day.

Cynthia liked Nathaniel. She tried hard not to feel sorry for him. He claimed to be happy, that he wasn't looking for pity, but he always seemed to be on the edge. She couldn't help but feel a tenderness, an almost motherly feeling toward him. He was, after all, thirteen years younger.

A handsome man.

But right now, at this moment, she wasn't thinking about Nathaniel. She was thinking about why Terry didn't want her to give Grace a ride home.

Something was going on.

She could feel it.

The question was whether she should do anything about it, and if the answer was yes, then what? At the very least, she could call back in half an hour and make sure Grace had gotten home safely. She paced the apartment wondering what she should do.

Make a cup of tea and go to bed. That's what you should do.

As if that would happen. She had tossed the pamphlets warning about household mold on her small dining table — just the sort of thing she wanted to read while eating dinner — and now picked one up to reread the copy. She'd written it, and now that she was looking at it again, she realized she could have used simpler, less technical language — and that was when she heard a noise in the hall.

Maybe Terry had decided to drop by with Grace. Was there a chance of that? That they might decide to surprise her with a late-night visit?

But then she heard raised voices. Two. Both men, although neither sounded like Terry.

Cynthia swung open her door to see Orland from downstairs trying to open the door to Nathaniel's apartment. He kept twisting the knob, but the locked door wouldn't yield.

Cynthia guessed Orland was in his seventies. He was sapling thin and had probably been over six feet tall at one time, but now, round shouldered, he was no more than five-nine. His thinned, wispy hair was all over place, as if he'd just taken off a hat, but there was none in evidence. His eyebrows were bushy and there was hair sticking out of his ears. His silver-framed glasses were askew.

Nathaniel was ten feet away at the end of the hall by the top of the stairs.

"Orland?" he said. "Can I help you?"

Orland's head craned around. "Huh? Yeah, you can help me. You can help me get this damned door open."

He made a fist, banged on the door. "Honey? Open the damn door!" He turned and looked at Nathaniel again. "My wife's locked me out. Goddamn bitch."

Cynthia stepped out into the hall and gently placed her hand on the man's shoulder. His head moved around and he eyed her over the top of his glasses. "You're not my wife."

"It's me, Cynthia. Your upstairs neighbor. I think you're on the wrong floor."

"Huh?"

"Orland," said Nathaniel, "why don't you let us take you downstairs, to your place."

"My wife's moved?"

Nathaniel and Cynthia guided him toward the stairs. Nathaniel led and Cynthia followed. The door to Orland's apartment was unlocked. They settled him into his La-Z-Boy chair in front of the television, which was already on.

"I was watching TV," Orland said.

There was no one else in the apartment, and Orland took no notice of that. The hunt for his spouse was over, for now.

"You going to be okay?" Nathaniel asked.

"Sure, I'm fine. What are you doing here?"

"Good night, Orland," Cynthia said as she and her upstairs neighbor slipped out of the apartment and closed the door.

"I've never seen him like that," she said.

"Me, neither," Nathaniel said. "Good

thing I got home when I did. He might have got into my place and I'd have found him in my bed."

When they'd returned to the second-floor hallway, she said, "I wonder if I should let Barney know. I mean, if Orland's starting to lose it, he could set the place on fire or something."

"Jesus, I hadn't thought of that."

They'd reached the door to his apartment. "Listen, you want a coffee or something? I feel a little, I don't know, wound up."

"It's late," Cynthia said.

"I was going to make decaf, if you're worried about not being able to get to sleep." He smiled, flashed his perfect teeth, and opened the door. "Take two seconds."

She knew she should go back into her apartment and close the door. But it would be nice to talk to someone, anyone, about just about anything. She hadn't realized, when she decided to stay here, just how lonely she'd feel at times. How even turmoil was a form of company.

Talking to Nathaniel might ease the anxiety she was feeling about what Terry and Grace might be keeping from her.

And the things that she was keeping from them.

"Sure," Cynthia said. "A cup of decaf sounds great."

Sixteen

TERRY

I pushed my legs into the house, let them dangle a second, then dropped in. It was barely a one-foot drop to the basement floor. I surveyed the room with the flashlight. All the things you might expect. Big couches. TV. Dartboard on the wall. Bookshelves jammed with as many DVDs and old VHS tapes as actual books. I shone the light around my feet looking for glass, not wanting to step in it even with shoes on. Shards could get caught in the treads.

But it was impossible to avoid, and broken glass crunched beneath my shoes.

"What is it, Dad?" Grace asked, appearing to me only from feet to knees, her shoes just beyond the window.

"Nothing," I said. "Just glass." I got the phone back out of my pocket and put it to my ear as I hunted for the stairs up to the first floor. "You hear me?" I said.

"I hear you," Grace whispered, still close enough that there was a slight echoing effect in my ear. "It's making a weird noise, like your voice is repeating. It did that before tonight, when I got out of the house. My phone might be wonky."

"It should go away once we get farther apart," I said.

Phone in one hand, flashlight in the other, I found the stairs and ascended to the first floor. The stairs brought me off to the side of the front hallway. One of the drawers on a shallow table pushed up against the wall was half open. I raised the flashlight, cast the beam ahead into what looked to be the kitchen.

It would have been nice to turn on all the lights, but I knew that wasn't an option. Couldn't afford to have any of the neighbors spotting me wandering around in there.

"What do you see, Dad?"

"Nothing yet." The echoing had stopped.

Three hours earlier, I'd been sitting in front of the TV watching *Jeopardy!* Now I was exploring, illegally, the house of someone I did not know with a flashlight, in the dead of night, hoping not to come across a body.

At that moment I thought of those two retired people slain in their home. What it must have been like for them to find a stranger — assuming it was a stranger who killed them — in their house.

That's what I was now. *I* was the stranger. And while I knew I didn't pose any threat, if I confronted someone in this house, they wouldn't know that.

I hoped to encounter no one here — dead or alive.

I stood at the entryway to the kitchen, which was combined with a family room. To the right, a large central island, bar stools, all the usual appliances, and then opposite that a high-ceilinged room with skylights decorated with easy chairs, a couch, a fireplace, and a TV angled in one corner.

The kitchen floor was smooth. Some kind of tile, crisscrossed with what looked like a million tiny scratches. I bent down for a closer look.

"Dog," I said to myself.

"What?" Grace said. "There's a dog there?"

"No. I was just noticing all the scratches on the floor. Probably from a dog's toenails. From its claws."

"Oh."

The countertops were cluttered with a toaster, Cuisinart, regular coffeemaker, Nespresso coffeemaker, waffle iron, bread maker, pretty much every gadget Williams-Sonoma carried. I lowered the beam, slowly scanned the floor again, saw more scratches. I figured that if Stuart, or anyone else, had been shot, they wouldn't have ended up on the countertop. There'd be evidence — blood — on the floor. As I rounded the island, getting closer to the window, I held my breath. I had a very bad feeling that there was something around the corner, and I steeled myself for the discovery.

But there was nothing.

I came around the fourth side of the island, the space between it and the stove, and still nothing caught my eye.

"I've been through the kitchen," I said. "I don't see anything." No response. "Grace?"

"I'm here. I heard you." A pause. "Dad."

"Yeah?"

"There's a police car going by."

Son of a bitch.

I killed the flashlight and held my breath. "Grace?"

"I'm just hiding behind the corner of the house. It just drove by real slow. I think it's going down to the dead end."

My car was parked out front. Was that what had attracted some officer's attention? Had he wondered what it was doing there, the only car on that whole stretch that wasn't pulled into a driveway? Would he take note of the license plate? Would he stop and do a check of the house?

"You want me to see where he — ?"

"No! Grace, just stay where you are."

"Okay."

We both waited. I was tempted to run to the living room at the front of the house, peek through the drapes, but with the flashlight off I'd probably end up tripping over something.

"I see headlights coming back," Grace whispered. "He must have turned around."

Shit shit shit shit.

"He must be going real slow so — there he is!"

Drive on by. Just drive on by.

"He's stopping, Dad."

"Where?"

"He's . . . he's stopped next to your car."

"Is he getting out? What's he doing?"

"I can just sort of — It's not a guy cop. It's a woman. She's got the light on inside her car."

"What's she doing?"

"I don't know. Don't they have, like, computers in their cars?"

"Yeah," I said. "Maybe she's running my plate."

"She's starting to — I think she's getting out of the car. Dad, you have to get out of the house."

And go where? To the car? The cop was sitting on it. Suppose I could escape out the basement window, grab Grace, and cut through the property that backed onto this house? Once the police found the broken window, found out who belonged to the car out front —

We'd be toast. Grace and me both.

"Just sit tight, hon," I said, trying my best to tamp down the panic I was feeling. Droplets of sweat were forming on my forehead. Even if Grace managed to hide, if that cop walked around the back of the house, saw the open window —

"Wait," Grace said. "She's getting back in the car. I think she's on the radio or something."

"Is she leaving? Is she — ?"

"She's driving away! Dad, she's going! She's going!"

I clicked the flashlight back on, kept it pointed to the floor, and found my way to a living room window. Through some sheers, I saw the Milford police car drive up the street, round the bend, and disappear.

"That was a little too close," I said.

"Can we go now? Can we get out of here?"

The second time in as many hours that she wanted to get the hell away from this house.

"I've only checked the kitchen," I said. "Before I leave, I've got to take a quick look through the whole house."

SEVENTEEN

The car, an oversized GM SUV, rolled to a stop, the engine continuing to rumble. Vince was in the passenger seat, Gordie behind the wheel. The backseats were folded down, an extension ladder stowed there. Behind them, in the old Buick, was Bert. He'd come to a stop barely a car length behind them.

"Bert'll help you when he's done, but you get started," Vince Fleming told Gordie. "Every location. See if anything looks out of the ordinary. If no one's there, go in tonight. If the place looks occupied, we do it tomorrow through the day. Everything — fucking everything — has to be moved by tomorrow."

"What if the people are home? What if — ?"

"Figure it out!" Vince said. He reached for the door handle, fumbling a couple of times. His hand was shaking.

"What about Eldon?" Gordie asked.

163

"What about him?" Vince snapped.

Gordie tried to hide how taken aback he was by the question. "When are you going to tell him?"

"I want to know a hell of a lot more before I talk to him. Take a run by his place, too. See if he's there. I want to know if he's home. You may end up running into him at one of the other houses."

Gordie looked uncomfortable. "What are you saying? You saying Eldon's in on it? That he did this? That doesn't make any sense. He's hardly going to —"

"Maybe not," Vince said. "But maybe he's got his kid and others helping him. Maybe things went wrong at one house. Who knows what the fuck is going on at the others? This is a nuclear meltdown, that's what this is."

He had the door open. "Just get moving." Vince got out, slammed the door, slapped the sheet metal with his palm, hard, as if the SUV was a horse he wanted to bolt. Gordie hit the gas, squealing the tires as he took off.

Vince took the few steps to the Buick, leaned over, and rested his arms on the window-down passenger door.

Bert said nothing, waited for orders.

"Soon as you take care of this, work with Gordie."

"Got it," Bert said.

"Not a word to Eldon," Vince said. "Not yet. There's only so many ways this can shake down."

"It's not him, boss," Bert said. "No way."

Vince pressed his lips together, shook his head very slowly back and forth. "It was his kid in there. Maybe he put him up to it. Or maybe the kid came up with the idea on his own. Either way, Eldon's on the hook for this."

"Yeah, but there had to be somebody else in on it, too. I already told you who I'm putting my money on."

Vince nodded. "I'll check him out, but I don't think he's got the balls for it."

"He coulda told somebody."

"But the son of a bitch doesn't even know. The cleaning ladies don't know. The nannies don't know. Even if they did, they wouldn't know where to look. But yeah, maybe." The man sighed. "Clusterfuck City."

Bert didn't know what to say. What words could make things better? He just wanted to get moving. He had an unpleasant task awaiting him, and he wanted it behind him. Then he could help Gordie.

"I should get going," Bert said.

165

Vince retreated from the open window. "Go."

Before Bert hit the gas, Vince took a step and stood next to the trunk. He went to touch the broad metal surface with his palm, the way one might lay one's hand on a casket at a funeral service.

Then thought better of it. Bert would wipe down the car, but might not think of the trunk lid.

The Buick pulled away and Vince watched it head up East Broadway, hang a left, and then disappear.

Wearily, he mounted the wooden steps that took him up to the main floor of the beach house. Back in the day, he took these two at a time. Back before he'd been shot. And back before the diagnosis. He was getting too old for this. It was one of the reasons why he'd pulled back on the kinds of jobs they used to do. Warehouse robberies, truck hijackings. Stuff that required a lot of heavy lifting. Sometimes, running.

So he started a sideline, one that didn't take such a physical toll. A service for people who didn't feel comfortable with financial institutions.

Seemed like a pretty good plan.

Until tonight.

Now it looked like the whole thing was

going to blow up in his face. He hoped to know more, soon, once he'd had a chance to talk to an old friend.

EIGHTEEN

TERRY

Given Grace's confusion about what had happened in the house, it occurred to me that what she thought she'd heard in the kitchen might easily have taken place someplace else. I couldn't see limiting my search of the house to the first floor.

In for a penny, in for a pound.

Standing in the living room, I couldn't see that anything was amiss, unless someone was jammed in between the sofa and the wall — and I was not going to start moving around furniture. Nor did there appear to be anything out of the ordinary in the adjoining dining room. When what you're looking for is a body, it doesn't take long to cross a room off your list. This wasn't looking for a needle in a haystack.

As I was headed for the stairs that would take me to the second floor, I glanced in the direction of the front door and the security system keypad mounted on the wall next to it. The light was red, indicating the system was engaged. If I opened that door without entering the code, alarms would go off, police would be dispatched.

I remembered Grace saying the light had been green when she was in the house.

That was a puzzle I couldn't solve right now. I was looking for Stuart.

Heading up the stairs, I nearly touched the railing out of habit. I had the phone in that hand and wouldn't have been able to do more than use the railing to steady myself, but even if I couldn't grip it, it was best not to touch it at all.

Don't touch a damn thing.

Off the upstairs hallway, which ran about twenty feet, were three bedrooms and a bathroom, all with doors slightly ajar, so I was able to ease them open with my elbow. I went into each one, shined the light around the beds, and peeked behind the shower curtain in the bathroom.

So far, so good.

I had a brief debate with myself about closets. Should I go back into each bedroom and inspect them or not? I knew it wasn't something I wanted to do. I was freaking myself out enough already, just being in this house, moving stealthily from room to room.

For Stuart, or anyone else for that matter, to be stuffed in a closet suggested there would have been at least a third person in the house to put him there. Maybe even a couple of people. Grace had said she felt someone brushing past her.

Sometimes you had to do things you didn't want to do. But I was going to need something on my hand before I started turning doorknobs.

I tucked my cell back into my shirt pocket without breaking the connection with Grace and grabbed a fistful of tissues from a Kleenex box in the bathroom. Then I went into the first bedroom, which gave every indication of being a girl's room, with stuffed animals by the pillows and posters of horses on the walls, and stood in front of the closet.

"Here goes," I said under my breath. With a tissue-wrapped hand I opened the door and shined the light in.

Nothing special there. Skirts and blouses and shoes and other items of clothing, all small. Barbie boxes. More stuffed animals. A girl maybe seven or eight years old, I guessed. These looked like the kinds of things Grace surrounded herself with at that age. I closed the door and went down the hall to the next bedroom.

Another girl, but older, probably mid-teens. A poster of what looked like the latest hot boy band on one wall, and while there was the odd stuffed animal, everything was a little less "itsy." An iPod dock on the table next to the bed, a hodgepodge of earrings and other jewelry on the top of the dresser. Bottles of nail polish remover, hairspray, body lotion.

I stood before the closet, took a breath, and turned the knob.

"Shit!"

I managed, even startled as I was, to keep my outburst to a whisper, but it was loud enough for Grace to hear.

"What?" said her voice, coming from my shirt pocket. "Dad? What's happened?"

I took out the phone. "You know how sometimes, when we ask you to clean up your room, you just dump everything in your closet and keep stuffing it in until you can get the door closed?"

"Yeah?"

"You're not the only one."

I put the phone back into my pocket. A stack of clothes had tumbled out and was covering the toes of my shoes. I set down the flashlight, shoveled the mess back into the closet — hoping fingerprints wouldn't show up on a pile of jeans and tops and underwear, since I couldn't do this with a wad of tissues in my hand — and managed to get the door shut once more.

I didn't run into Fibber McGee's closet in the master bedroom. And even at that moment, I thought, Where the hell did that reference come from? I wasn't old enough to have ever seen, or heard, the old *Fibber McGee and Molly* movies or radio shows, but it was a phrase my grandparents always used to describe a closet that was jam-packed. Whenever Fibber opened the hall closet, a hundred things cascaded out onto his head. Hilarity, evidently, ensued.

I could use a laugh right about now.

The master had a walk-in closet, so nothing rained down on me as I opened the door. It was tidier than either of the children's closets, with nothing on the carpeted floor. Shoes, and there were dozens of pairs of them, about ninety percent of them a woman's, were all neatly stacked on shelving. I noticed eight small rectangular impressions in the carpet, clustered in groups of two and each about the size of a domino, which, if you were to draw a line between them, would have made a square roughly two feet by two feet. Given that I was looking for a body, I didn't spend much time thinking about them.

I left the closet and did another inspection of the en suite bathroom. Glanced into the tub to see whether anyone had been dumped there.

I reached into my pocket for the phone.

"I'm almost done," I told Grace. "I'll take a quick look through the basement before I come back out. Everything okay out there?"

"Yeah. So you haven't seen Stuart?"

"Haven't seen him or anybody else, sweetheart."

"Thank God."

I thought it was premature to be offering up those kinds of thanks yet, but I hoped she had reason to be optimistic.

On my way to the basement I aimed the flashlight back into the kitchen for a final sweep, then went down the last flight of stairs. In addition to the rec room, where I'd come through the window, there was a furnace room, a laundry room, and a small workshop. Tools of every description hung on one wall, a table saw, a drill press, a small lathe bolted to the workbench. An aluminum ladder leaned up against the wall. And while there was a faint scent of sawdust in the air, there wasn't a trace of it on the painted concrete floor.

There, on the far wall, a chest freezer.

Waist high, about six feet long. A small amber light on the side to indicate that it was running.

"Oh no," I said under my breath. If I didn't open it, I might end up kicking myself later. And I was not — ever — coming into this house again.

I approached the freezer, held the light in my left hand, raised above my shoulder, angled down, and lifted the top with my right.

Lots of frozen food.

As I came back out of the workshop, I felt somewhat encouraged. The home looked to me to be corpse free. Not the sort of thing generally mentioned in a real estate listing, but a good thing nonetheless.

Stuart Koch — dead or alive — was not here. But if he was okay, why wasn't he answering his phone?

I could think of any number of reasons, but the first that came to mind was that he was a chickenshit little weasel and didn't want to take a call from the girl he'd dragged into a terrifying situation. He didn't have the guts to apologize. He didn't have the guts to admit he'd done a pretty goddamn stupid thing.

I didn't want to have to come up with

another reason. That one suited me just fine.

The trouble was, it didn't explain what had happened in this house an hour and a half or so earlier.

Something was nagging at me.

It wasn't the business of trying to figure out what had gone down here. I'd seen something, and it was only now registering.

When I'd waved the light past the kitchen on my way down, something had caught my eye. I hadn't really thought about it until I'd gotten to the basement.

Something not quite right. Something shimmery.

Something on the kitchen island. Not on it, exactly, but on the *side* of it.

"Are you done, Daddy?" Grace asked.

"Just another minute," I told her.

I went back up to the first floor, stood at the entrance to the kitchen, aimed the light at the base of the island. The sides were done in paneled wood. Light in color, probably a bleached oak.

About a foot up from the floor, the finish was marred. Droplets of something that had hit the vertical plane and then trickled down.

Something, in the glow of the flashlight, that could have been, say, spaghetti sauce.

I knelt down and brought the light up

close. The drops were fresh to the touch, and when I put the tip of my finger to within an inch of my nose, I detected no whiff of tomato or spices.

My heart sank. Something had definitely happened here. But — if this was any consolation — there was so little blood my guess was that whoever suffered an injury had managed to leave the scene.

The hospital. That was where we should go next. Milford Hospital.

I wiped the blood off my finger, wadded up the tissue, and stuck it into the front pocket of my jeans. Then I took the cell from my pocket.

"Hey, sweetheart. I'm comin' out. I think we've got another stop to make on the way home."

In fact, I was thinking, maybe two. The hospital would be our first, and if we didn't find Stuart sitting in the ER, we'd go past his house on our way home.

We needed to find this kid. We needed to find him, and find out what, if anything, had happened to him.

I was waiting for Grace to respond.

"Grace? You there? I'm thinking we check the hospital on the way home. I found what looks like just a little — and I mean just a little — blood here in the kitchen."

Grace still had nothing to say.

"Grace?" I said. "Grace, are you there?"

Nothing.

I looked at the display on my phone. The connection had been broken. I moved quickly to the kitchen window to see whether she was still standing out back of the house.

She was not.

I brought up her number and was about to call her back when I stopped myself. If Grace had run into the bushes to hide — maybe that Milford cop had returned and was snooping around the house — and if she'd forgotten to mute her phone, the last thing she'd need would be me calling her. Even if I texted her, it would make that brief jingle and alert anyone around her.

I thought about running downstairs and scrambling out the basement window, but then reconsidered. If there was a cop wandering around, this wouldn't be the best time to make an appearance. But then again, if someone spotted that broken window and decided to come into the house, I was trapped here.

I was not then, and never have been, adept at what you'd call grace under pressure. I couldn't decide what to do next. I was paralyzed, terrified that whatever choice I made would be wrong.

I took a few deep breaths and attempted to focus. I needed to know what was going on, and I wasn't going to learn a damn thing standing here in the kitchen trying to keep myself from wetting my pants.

I killed the flashlight and gingerly made my way through the living room to the front window so I could get a look at the street. No cop car, which was a blessing. Of course, my car was still sitting there, like a big blazing advertisement that read: "SOMEONE'S HERE! CHECK IT OUT!"

I detected some movement out of the corner of my eye.

Near the end of the driveway, sheltered by a tall hedge that separated this property from the next, I could make out two dark shapes.

Two people, facing each other. Talking.

I was pretty sure one of those people was Grace.

While it was too dark to read facial expressions, there was nothing about her posture that indicated this was a confrontation. The other person, who was about the same height, wasn't waving his arms or pointing a finger.

And it didn't look like a he, either.

178

Grace was talking to another girl. Or woman.

That cop she'd spotted was a woman, but this woman didn't appear to be wearing a uniform or a heavy belt loaded down with assorted cop accessories. Plus, there was no cruiser on the street, at least not on the part of the street that I could see.

Time to find out what the hell was going on.

I returned to the basement, hoisted myself up through the open window, and got back on my feet outside the house. As I came around the corner, I could hear the hushed conversation of two people whispering.

Grace glanced my way. "Dad!"

She ran toward me. The other woman didn't move.

She put her arms around me, her head on my chest. "I thought you'd never get out of there."

"Your phone," I said, not taking my eyes off the woman.

"Oh," she said, glancing at it, still in her hand. "I must have hit the button or something."

"Who's that?" I asked.

"It's okay," Grace said. "You know I told you I made another call before I called you, soon as I got out of the house. I mean, I kept trying Stuart, but I called someone else, too."

I eased myself out of Grace's embrace and walked in the direction of this mystery woman. I kept the flashlight off and down at my side, hoping that once I'd closed the distance, I'd be able to get a look at this person.

I stopped when I was within two feet of her.

"Hey, Teach," she said.

"Jane," I said.

Jane Scavullo.

NINETEEN

Cynthia Archer had been in Nathaniel's apartment only five seconds when she realized she didn't have her cell phone. Cynthia was not necessarily expecting Terry to call her about Grace, or anything else for that matter, but she wanted the phone with her just in case. So she ran back across the hall for the phone, then reentered Nathaniel's place.

She'd told herself she had a good, and perfectly innocent, reason for accepting his invitation for coffee. She needed the distraction. Chatting with Nathaniel would keep her mind occupied with something other than Terry and Grace, and what might be going on that they didn't want her knowing about.

It had nothing to do with the fact that he was an attractive young man. Let's face it, a *damaged* attractive young man. He had more baggage than the lost and found at

LaGuardia. And that short episode with Orland — the poor man — had been unsettling.

Nathaniel, reaching into the cupboard for two coffee cups, said, "It was nice to meet your husband, um —"

"Terry," Cynthia said.

"Yeah, Terry. I hope I didn't interrupt something when you guys were talking on the porch there. I didn't realize — I mean, I never notice things like rings on fingers, so I didn't even realize you were married. And you know, considering that you're living here by yourself — but that's none of my business anyway, so — Jesus, I'm rambling."

Cynthia smiled. "That's okay. Don't worry about it."

"He seems like a nice guy."

"He is."

"Grab a seat," Nathaniel said, pointing to the small island in the kitchen nook. There were two stools tucked under the counter overhang. Cynthia pulled one out and perched her butt on the edge, one foot resting on the rung. At the island sink Nathaniel filled a glass carafe with cold water, turned around, and poured it into the top of an electric coffeemaker on the opposite counter, then slid the empty carafe into the base.

"I drink it, but the whole idea of decaf just seems wrong," he said. "Like wine without alcohol. Cake without icing. Sex without orgasm." He glanced at her. "Too far?"

"Yeah, the cake thing was a bit much," Cynthia said.

"Thing is, decaf is all I can drink this late. It's hard enough for me to sleep, and the last thing I need is to be more jittery."

"What's given you the jitters, aside from Orland?"

He forced a laugh. "Nothing really. Just — I was heading back, and I kind of let it rip on the turnpike, cruising around ninety, and I glanced in the mirror and thought I had a cop behind me. 'Bout had a heart attack. It was a Charger — the cops use them a lot for their unmarked cars. But it turned out just to be some guy."

"Where were you driving back from?"

"Nowhere. A lot of nights, I just drive. Think about things. What used to be, and like that."

"You know, I really think I should give Barney a call," Cynthia said. She'd already put his number into her phone. She brought up her contact list, tapped the screen, and put the phone to her ear.

After three rings, "Hello?"

"Barney? It's Cynthia? Over on —"

"I know."

"Sorry to call so late, but there's something I thought I should let you in on." She told him the story.

"Oh no," Barney said. "Orland's been okay for a while, but he must be taking a turn for the worse. The other day, I went to call on him, heard him talking to somebody, but when he opened the door, there was no one else there and he hadn't been on the phone, either."

"He was looking for his wife," Cynthia said.

"She's been dead thirty years, at least. He could hurt himself if he's starting to lose it."

"That's why I called. I was thinking, he leaves something on the stove . . ."

"Okay, I'll check in on him. Thanks for this."

Cynthia set her phone down on the counter and watched Nathaniel spoon in some ground coffee from a tin into the coffee machine, spilling some of it.

"Shit," he said, using his hand as a broom to clear the spilled coffee into his other hand. He slapped his hands over the sink, then rinsed his hands to get all the granules off. "I always do that." He forced another laugh. "Maybe I've caught something from the dogs. Distemper or something."

Cynthia smiled. "Might be fleas. You need one of those collars."

He nodded. "That might stop me from trying to scratch my neck with my foot."

"That'd be something to see," she said.

"Oh, I'm flexible," he said, then, maybe thinking the comment had some sexual connotation, quickly added, "It's all that stooping and scooping. It's better than yoga. You ever tried yoga?"

"No."

"I gave it a shot, didn't like it. Took all kinds of things. Yoga, spinning — you know, the stationary bikes. A step class, but that was really a chick thing. Karate, but only until I got to the purple belt level, which is not all that impressive. I can still remember a couple of things, but those katas? You know, the movements you have to go through? I could never get those right. Tried jogging, too, and I still sort of do that, with the dogs. Instead of just walking them, we'll run flat out for a half mile or so."

The coffeemaker gurgled as the pot began to fill.

"So how many people's dogs do you walk every day?" Cynthia asked.

"I've got ten. I zip from house to house,

do four in the morning, six in the afternoon, walk each one for about forty-five minutes. I can jam a couple extra in after lunch because some of my clients live on the same street and I can walk two at a time."

"They get along? The dogs, I mean, not your clients. Although if you have some gossip on them, I'm all ears."

"Yeah, the dogs get used to each other, like to play, although sometimes I don't cover as much territory with them. They spend more time sniffing each other than walking."

Cynthia shook her head. "You really have to love dogs to spend your day doing what you do."

"We always had them when I was a kid. Never more than one at a time, but when one died of old age or got hit by a car or whatever, we always got another."

She winced. "Your dog got hit by a car?"

He made a V with his fingers. "Two. We lost O'Reilly when I was three years old, and Skip when I was ten. We were on a country road, up near Torrington — I've still got a lot of family up there. My brother lived up that way. I got nieces and nephews there still. Anyway, my parents never kept the dogs tied up. Wanted them to run free. My dad said if that meant one of them got run over, well, so be it. Better a dog have five great years running its ass off than fifteen years chained to a tree."

"Gee, I don't know," Cynthia said.

"Anyway, after I left home and was working all the time, I never had a dog, and my ex, may she get crabs, was allergic, so there was no dog in my life for several years. Then, when the shit hit the fan and I needed something to do, well . . ." He threw up his hands.

"But you're getting by okay."

"Oh yeah. Twenty-five bucks a dog, ten dogs, that's two-fifty a day, twelve-fifty a week, and it's all cash, so it's almost like making eighteen hundred a week or so if you had to pay Uncle Sam." He eyed her suspiciously. "This isn't where you tell me you actually work for the IRS and not the health department."

"You're so busted," she said.

"And you know, there's the odd other bit of cash coming in. The one thing I wanted to hang on to after my company went south was my ATS."

"Your what?"

"My car. The Cadillac."

"Oh."

"Anyway, it's not exactly a hybrid where gas is concerned, and the insurance ain't

187

cheap, but damn it, I just wanted to hang on to my wheels." He laughed. "You should see people's faces, I show up to walk dogs in a Caddy."

Cynthia asked, "So these dogs don't go crazy when you come into the house when their owners are away?"

"You have to get to know them first, yeah, or they might go nuts on you. And I got one Doberman and a German shepherd — I don't walk those two together — which are not the kind of mutts you want going squirrelly when you come through the front door."

"So people give you their keys?" Cynthia said.

He pointed to a ring by the toaster with what looked like a dozen keys on it. "Some places I need the security code, too. But if they don't mind giving that stuff out to their babysitter, they don't mind giving it to me." He sighed. "I must seem like the world's biggest loser to you. Guy my age, and this is what I do. You know, I used to be worth hundreds of thousands? What I make in a week walking goddamn dogs I made in ten minutes. I could buy anything I wanted. I'd walk into a store, see a pair of shoes that cost three hundred bucks — I wouldn't even think about it. I'd say, Yeah, I'll take those.

And I'd get them home, wear them once, find out they hurt my feet, and I wouldn't even try to return them. Didn't give a shit."

Cynthia shook her head. "I don't think you're a loser. What do they say? Life's a journey, and when you think about it, yours is more interesting than most people's. Like you said when I first met you, you're taking a breather. You won't be doing this forever. At some point you'll think, Okay, it's time to move on."

And that was when it hit her.

It was time to move on.

She was going to give up this apartment.

She was going to go home.

You didn't solve your problems at home by moving out. You solved your problems by staying home and solving the goddamn problems.

I'm not going to run away. I'm going to go home.

"Cynthia?"

"Hmm?"

"You there?"

"Yes, I'm listening."

"I said maybe you're right. Everything just takes time, right?"

She nodded slowly, then said, "I'm going to move out this week."

"And go where?"

"Home?"

"You've only been here a few weeks," he said.

"It's been a few weeks too long. This was . . . this was a mistake."

"No," Nathaniel said. "Maybe you had to move here to find out that moving here was a mistake. As goofy as that sounds. I figured you were here kind of clearing your head, figuring yourself out. Maybe living here has made you appreciate whatever it is you left. Your husband and — you've got a kid, right?"

"Grace," she said wistfully. "I abandoned my family because I thought I was sick, but they're the only thing that can make me better."

"What do you take?"

"I've tried a couple of things, like Xanax, but I don't feel right being on them. For me, I have to solve my problems on my own, without any artificial interference."

"I meant in your coffee."

"Oh!" Cynthia laughed.

"Cream, sugar?"

"Just black, thanks."

Nathaniel removed the carafe and filled two mugs. He set one in front of Cynthia, then banged his forehead with the heel of his hand. "What the hell am I making coffee for? Tonight's a special night for you. If you're moving out, going home, that calls for a celebration."

He took the mug back before Cynthia could touch it and emptied it into the sink. He swung open the door to the refrigerator and brought out a bottle of white wine.

"No, that's okay," she said.

"Nonsense."

"Really, it's —"

"Hey, look, it's a screw-top pinot gris, and it's already been opened. This isn't as grand a gesture as it looks. Unless — you do drink, don't you?"

She sighed. "I do."

"Well, fine, then." He found two peanut butter glasses in the cupboard, twisted the cap off the bottle. He glanced at the label. "A very nice vintage. March, I believe."

Cynthia smiled uncomfortably. Having a coffee with this boy across the hall — and really, compared with her, he was a *boy* — was one thing, but sharing a bottle of wine, that was another, wasn't it?

Stop it. He's just trying to be nice.

He filled the two glasses, handed her one. "Cheers," he said, raising his, clinking it lightly against Cynthia's. "To fresh starts."

"To fresh starts."

"Mine's just going to come a little later,"

he said. "I used to belong to a wine club. Very, very snooty. My wife and I, we'd get invited to tastings, fancy cheeses and chocolate. They'd send me the latest chardonnay or merlot or whatever in these fancy wood boxes. Cost a fortune. This bottle here, this ran me seven bucks. And you know, it gets me drunk just as efficiently as the expensive stuff. Which, by the way, I do quite frequently, and often by myself."

He tipped the glass to his mouth, emptied it in one go, refilled it.

"I was something," he said. "And now I'm not."

"I'm sorry, Nathaniel," she said. "You got a raw deal."

"Have I never told you to call me Nate?"

"I —"

He smiled, patted her hand. "Call me Nate."

"Okay, Nate."

"In some ways, it was a blessing. I was so stressed out all the time. Every minute was about work. I think, even if I hadn't lost everything, I'd have found myself heading for a nervous breakdown. But I did lose everything. Ev. Ry. Thing. Worst of all, I lost Charlotte."

"She's your . . ."

"My wife, yeah. Once the flow stopped,

192

man, she started looking for the exit. Ended up with this asshole — someone I thought was a friend of mine — who's still got his platinum card. Runs a computer game company. Made that guy rich, and now —" He shook his head.

Cynthia didn't know what to say.

"You ever lost everything?" he asked her.

She hesitated. "I know a bit about that."

He grew curious. "Really? You had a fortune and then it was gone? Big house, fancy car? All that shit?"

"No. It wasn't a financial loss." She put the glass to her lips and sipped.

Nathaniel's eyes softened. "Oh, sorry. Shit. But you don't mean your husband and your kid. You've still got them."

She moved the wine around her tongue, as if it cost more than seven dollars a bottle, then swallowed it slowly. "It was a long time ago. My family. I lost my family."

"What do you mean? Like, your parents died?"

Cynthia had neither the energy nor the desire to tell the story. "More or less," she said. "And my brother, too. I was the only one left. After that, I went to live with my aunt."

"Jesus," he said. "What happened?"

She shook her head.

"Sorry, sorry. It's not even any of my business. God, I'm such an ass. I'm all 'pity me' and you've been through something probably a thousand times worse." He grabbed his glass and the bottle and came around the island, parked himself on the stool next to her so their shoulders were just touching. Cynthia felt a kind of charge come off his body. "Really, I'm sorry."

She shook her head. "Don't feel bad. What happened to you, what happened to me, they're both life-changing. They're both traumatic in their own ways."

"Yeah, but still. Let me top you up there."

Cynthia had had only half a glass but let him refill it. He'd nearly finished his second glassful and helped himself to more, which emptied the bottle.

"Do you ever think," he said slowly, "when you've been through something really horrendous that . . . I don't know how to put this. You ever think, I'm sick of playing by the rules? Like, the hell with it. I just don't give a fuck. Like you want to get even. Not just with some person, but the whole world."

Cynthia took another sip. "I went through that, when I was in my later teens. You think you're entitled to do whatever you want because you got the short end of the stick. But I got over it. I didn't want to be a huge pain in the ass to my aunt. I mean, she was good enough to take me in. If she'd kicked me out, I'd have had no place to go. Just because something shitty happens to you doesn't mean you get to make life harder for those around you."

"Well, yeah, sure. Your aunt, she still around?"

Cynthia felt a constriction in her throat, a moistening in her eyes. "No."

They sat there, shoulders touching, for a while, neither one saying anything.

Cynthia finally said, "Look, I should go."

"I've got another partial bottle in the fridge. Seems stupid not to kill it off." She felt the pressure from his shoulder grow ever so slightly.

"Nate," she said.

"I feel like I've wasted these last few weeks. Having someone like you across the hall, and now you're getting ready to leave."

"Nate."

"I'm just saying, I like you. You're nice to talk to. *Easy* to talk to. Maybe, because of what happened to you, maybe you have more empathy than most people."

"I don't know about that."

He opened his mouth to say something, stopped, tried again. "I think I may have done something I shouldn't have," he said.

195

He shifted on the stool so that he was facing her more directly, his face only inches from hers.

"Nate, it's okay. Whatever it is, don't worry."

"Your husband, he's lucky you're coming home. If you were my wife, I'd have never let you go in the first place."

"I should really —"

"No, I mean it. You're a very —"

"I'm old enough to be your mother," Cynthia said.

"Bullshit, unless you got knocked up when you were ten," he said quietly.

"And you're wrong — you haven't done anything you shouldn't have, and neither have I. We're just having a drink. And now I'm going home."

"No, wait — that's not what I meant," Nathaniel said. "The reason I asked you over here — I mean, I did ask you over here because I like you, you know? But there was something I wanted to ask you about."

Hesitantly, she said, "Okay."

"It's about your friend."

"My friend?"

"The one who dropped by here a couple of weeks ago."

Cynthia recalled the encounter he was talking about. "What about him, Nate?"

"Remember he asked what I did, and I told him. About the dog walking."

"Yeah."

"So you must have told him a bit more about me that after, right?"

She tried to recall. "If I did, I didn't have a lot to say, Nate, honestly."

"The thing is, he got in touch with me later."

Cynthia felt a shiver. "Oh."

"Yeah. He must have Googled me or something because he kind of knew what I'd been through, read up on my financial problems, that what I was doing now was just a *bit* of a comedown from selling apps and making hundreds of thousands of dollars, right? He even looked into my personal life, knew my wife had left me, found out she was seeing some new guy."

"Nate, what on earth — ?"

"Anyway, he said he could help me out, if I could help him out."

"Help him out how?"

He hesitated. "I don't want to get into that part."

"Well, what did you say?"

"I thought about it, and said sure," Nathaniel said. "Because he said, and he was really firm about this, that nothing bad

197

would happen. That no one would ever know."

"Nate, I have no idea what you're talking about. Tell me, what did you agree to do?"

He put his palm over his mouth, dragged it down over his chin. "I think it's probably better if I don't tell you everything."

That suited her fine. Cynthia wasn't sure she wanted to know.

"But what I was wondering was, since he's a friend of yours, I wonder if you could talk to him. The thing is, I want to end our arrangement. I want to break things off. I'm even willing to give back every dime he's paid me so far. Well, most of it anyway. I spent some of it. But he doesn't strike me as the kind of guy who'd be inclined to let someone out of a business arrangement, even though we don't exactly have what you'd call a signed contract."

"You want me to talk to him?" Cynthia said.

Nate nodded. "Yeah, I'd really appreciate it. I mean, Vince is your friend, right? He said he'd known you from way back, all the way to high school, that you'd kept in touch."

TWENTY

TERRY

It had been six months since I'd last seen Jane Scavullo.

I was in Whole Foods getting a small container of egg salad, English muffins, and some fresh pasta — enough to set me back twenty bucks — when I noticed her going through the checkout ahead of me.

I debated whether to get her attention. This was a different girl from the one I'd taught seven years earlier, when she was seventeen and a student in my creative writing class. The one who got suspended for fights with other girls, who'd rather spend her days smoking in the girls' restroom than show up for class, who had a perpetual chip on her shoulder, who didn't take shit from anybody, but also didn't seem to give much of a shit about anything, either.

And she could write.

Whenever I had a stack of assignments

from that class to mark, I'd always save her submission for last, assuming that she'd actually handed one in on this occasion. I still remembered this part from one of them:

"*. . . you're a kid, and you think things are pretty fucking OK, and then one day this guy who's supposed to be your dad says so long, have a nice life. And you think, what the fuck is this? So years later, your mom ends up living with another guy, and he seems OK, but you think, when's it coming? That's what life is. Life is always asking yourself, when's it coming? Because if it hasn't come for a long, long time, then you know you're fucking due.*"

She wrote that assignment after her mother had moved in with a man named Vince Fleming, an individual who was, as they say, known to police, and not just here in Milford. I spent one long, harrowing night in his company seven years ago, the night he played a role in helping us find out what happened to Cynthia's family.

He nearly died in the process.

But Vince's good deeds that night didn't make him a citizen in good standing.

He as much as admitted, that night, that he was responsible for one murder when he was a young man, and I suspected there were more. He made me uneasy, but he never struck me as a psychopath. Whatever acts of violence he committed were, in his world, just part of doing business. But as I'd reminded myself at the time, just because a scorpion doesn't sting you out of spite doesn't make it a good idea to hang out with a scorpion.

One thing he'd made clear to me in the short time we spent together: even though Jane Scavullo was not his daughter, she meant a great deal to him and he wanted the best for her. When Vince was in his early twenties, he'd become a father. A young woman he'd gotten pregnant had a baby girl, but it wasn't long before mother and daughter were killed in a tragic accident.

I think Vince often saw, in Jane, the girl his own daughter might have grown up to be.

Seven years back, he made me promise to do what I could to help her. Although I transferred out of Old Fairfield High School for a few years before returning, I continued to encourage Jane with her writing. But it wasn't as simple as that. It wasn't enough to tell her she was good at stringing words together. I had to persuade her that hers was a life worth writing about. That you didn't have to be some big-name, lame-brained celebrity to be interesting. That there was value in, and lessons to be learned from, the lives of each and every one of us. That her experience, as much as she tried to diminish it, was worthy of examination.

"What do you care?" Jane asked me, more than once.

"If I tell you I'm doing it because I care about you, you'll think I'm full of it," I told her. "You won't believe me. So I'll give you a more selfish reason. I'm doing it for myself. If I can get you to give more of a rat's ass about your future, I'll feel better about who I am and what I've accomplished as a teacher."

"So it's a huge ego thing," she said.

"Yeah. It's all about me. It's got absolutely nothing to do with you."

Jane remained stone-faced. "So if I just pretend to give a shit, you get to be all Mr. Holland's Opus."

I smiled. "Yeah. Just fake it. Don't do well because in your heart you want to be better. Do it to see if you can pull one over on us."

"Okay," Jane said. "I'm like your Eliza Donothing."

"That's a good one," I said.

"You think I don't read. I know shit."

"See? You're getting into the spirit of this already."

Other teachers at the school who I kept in

touch with reported that Jane Scavullo was starting to make an effort. Not exactly Yale material yet, but she might actually get out of the building with a diploma.

"That act is going very well," I told her.

"I'm going for an Oscar," she said.

By the time she was in her last year, she'd stopped skipping so many classes. She completed assignments. Her grades improved.

"I don't think you're acting anymore," I told her one day. "I promise not to tell anyone, but I think you're starting to give a damn."

"I'm not doing it for you," she said.

"You're doing it for yourself," I said.

"God, you think you're so smart, but you're really not, you know," she said. "I'm doing it for him."

For Vince.

I should have figured that out much earlier. She was trying to make things up to him by making something of herself. What I was slow to realize was that Jane was carrying around a lot of guilt where Vince was concerned. It had been Jane who'd persuaded Vince to help me that night when he nearly died.

I assisted Jane with her college applications, wrote letters on her behalf. Her teachers were right: she wasn't Yale material. But she was accepted at the University of Bridgeport, where she took advertising. "It's perfect for me," she said. "I've spent my whole life trying to make people believe shit that isn't true." Advertising allowed her to apply her gift with words and her powers of persuasion.

She e-mailed me once in a while, mostly during her first year. I wondered whether I'd rate an invitation to her graduation, but was quietly relieved when I didn't. There was a good chance she might not have bothered attending anyway. Jane didn't put a high value on ceremony. But if she did go, and if I'd attended, there would have been a good chance I'd have run into Vince, and that wasn't something I'd have wanted.

For a long time, I felt my neck where Vince was concerned.

Cynthia and I visited him twice when he was recovering in Milford Hospital from his gunshot wound. Our times with him weren't long enough to really qualify as visits. He wasn't particularly happy to see us.

"Fucking stupidest thing I ever did was get mixed up with you two," he said the first time we walked into his hospital room.

It was hard to argue. It was Cynthia who'd insisted we go back a second time to see how he was doing.

"His disposition may have improved if he's feeling better," she said. "We owe him a lot."

So we tried.

Looking at Cynthia, Vince said this: "If I could find myself a fucking time machine, I'd get in it, set the dial back to 1983, and instead of going out that night with you, I'd have looked for — shit — the *ugliest* girl in Milford. I'd have even gone out with a fag and done whatever the hell he wanted to do if it meant I'd never have gotten dragged into your mess and ended up here getting shot in the fucking gut all these years later. So you can keep your get-well cards and your fucking flowers and get the fuck out of here."

We opted against a third visit, and hadn't seen him since.

I didn't tell Jane about the encounter, but kept my promise to Vince to help her out.

"What's going on between you two?" she asked me once. "I asked him if you guys talk and he just grumbles."

"We've kind of gone our separate ways," I said.

"You think you're too good for him, don't you?" Jane said. "He's the guy from the wrong side of the tracks. You don't want to be seen with him."

That touched a nerve.

Even if Vince had been willing to associate with me, wanted to meet for a beer now and then, I'd probably have resisted, but not because I'd have thought I was too good for him. Vince was not the kind of person I had the nerve to pal around with. He was a tough guy, and so were the people he hung out with. Vince made a living breaking all the rules.

I was a high school teacher who paid his parking tickets.

Vince killed people.

I really couldn't see the two of us as pals.

So when I saw Jane at Whole Foods, I was ambivalent. It would have been nice to see her, to catch up. But the conversation would inevitably turn to Vince, and I didn't want to talk about him.

I was getting into my car when a voice behind me said, "You spotted me but didn't say anything. I know it."

I turned around, saw her standing there in front of me, brown recyclable bag in her hand.

"Don't try to deny it," Jane said.

"I won't," I said. "You look good."

She did, too. No ripped jeans, no nose stud, no streaks of pink in her hair. She looked . . . polished. Tailored clothes, smart jacket, nails polished, hair shorter than I remembered it, nicely trimmed.

"You kinda look like shit," she said, and then smiled. "Sorry. I guess that's the old me talking. Let me try again. How are you?"

"I'm okay," I said. I guessed there was a heaviness in my voice that she'd picked up on. Things at home were sapping my strength.

"I didn't mean to get all first-degree on you there. If you didn't want to talk to me, that's cool."

I smiled. "I'm sorry. I did see you. But you looked like you were in a hurry and I didn't want to slow you down. How are you?"

"I'm good. You know, okay. Just heading back to work."

"Which is where?"

"After I finished school, I got a job with Anders and Phelps." She waited a half second to see whether I recognized the name. When she saw that I did not, she said, "They're a small advertising firm here in Milford. It's not like we've got the Coke account or anything. It's just local stuff, but it's fun. I'm putting together a radio spot for a furnace repair guy."

"That's fantastic," I said, and meant it.

She shrugged. "It's not exactly *Mad Men*, but you gotta start someplace. So, when I said you looked like shit, I didn't mean that, but you look kinda, you know, tired."

"Some," I said. "But hey, who doesn't have something going on at one time or another, right? This is just one of those times."

"God, after all that shit that went down, what, six years ago?"

"Seven."

"Everything wasn't okay after that?"

"We're doing our best."

"How's your kid? Grace? How old's she now?"

"Fourteen. Although it feels more like nineteen."

"Hell on skates?"

"She has her moments." I hesitated. "How's Vince?"

Another shrug. "Okay, I guess. He and my mom made it legal five years ago, got married."

"Great."

She shook her head. "Yeah, but then, a month ago, she died. Breast cancer."

My face fell. "I'm so sorry."

She shook her head. "Hey, like you said, who doesn't have something going on at some time, right? So I was officially a stepdaughter until four weeks ago, and then maybe not." A pause, during which she appeared to be composing herself. "I moved out a while ago anyway."

"How's Vince holding up?"

"You know Vince. You don't know whether to pity him or just write him off as a total dick. Anyway, I'm better off on my own. I got an apartment on the water. It's pretty kick-ass. And there's more."

"Tell me," I said.

She grinned. "There's this guy. Bryce. We've been going out for a long time, and when I moved out, he and I moved in together."

"That's terrific. I'm glad things have worked out for you on that score."

Jane Scavullo paused, seemed to be sizing me up. "You were pretty stand-up, Teach. You believed in me when nobody else did."

"It wasn't hard."

"That," she said, "is total bullshit." An awkward silence ensued. "Look, I should let you go. Nice seein' ya."

"Sure thing."

She gave me a hug and went over to her car. A blue Mini. She gave me a wave as she drove off.

And now, here we were, running into each other again. In the most unlikely of places, and circumstances. In the driveway of a home where my daughter was afraid she might have shot someone. A home I had searched illegally.

Where I hadn't found Stuart. But I'd found blood.

"What are you doing here, Jane?" I asked her.

"It's Vince," Jane said. "He wants to have a word with you."

TWENTY-ONE

TERRY

Vince Fleming wanted to talk to me? Now? At this time of night? What the hell sense did that make? I hadn't spoken to the man in seven years, not since that second visit to the hospital. Why would he want anything to do with me now?

Unless.

Had I just been prowling around Vince Fleming's house? So far as I knew, he still lived on East Broadway, his place on the beach.

"Tell me this isn't Vince's house," I said to Jane. The idea that I might have burgled that man's home made my insides flip.

She shook her head. "No."

"Well, thank Christ for that. If this isn't his house, then I don't know what he wants with me. Grace and I have to go."

I wanted to get my daughter into the car and head straight to Milford Hospital to see whether Stuart Koch had been admitted. And depending on what we learned there, I might very well be looking for a lawyer for my daughter before the sun came up. Someone had lost some blood in that house, and the sooner we found whose it was, and how it had been spilled, the better chance we had of coming to grips with this mess. It was hard to get someone out of trouble when you didn't know just how bad the trouble was.

"How the hell did you even know we're here?" I asked my former student.

Jane's eyes shifted to Grace.

"I called her," Grace said. "A while ago. Before I called you to come pick me up."

Grace had called Jane? Since when did Grace have Jane's contact information? Since when did Grace even know Jane?

"What?" I asked my daughter. "Why would you call her?"

Grace said something so quietly I couldn't make it out.

"What?" I said.

"Because she's a friend," Grace said. "Because I thought she could help me."

Jane said, "I told her the person to call was you, not me."

"What did you find?" Grace asked me. "In the house. Did you find anything?"

212

"Excuse me," I said to Jane, then led Grace a few feet away so I could speak to her privately.

"I found some blood," I told her.

"Oh God."

"A small amount, in the kitchen. I searched everywhere else and didn't find anything or anyone. But something happened in there. We'll go by the hospital, see if Stuart went to the emergency room, and if that doesn't pan out, we'll —"

"Mr. Archer." It was Jane. She'd never called me by my first name. It was always Mr. Archer or Teach.

"We're talking," I said.

"Vince really hates to be kept waiting," she said. "Whatever you're talking about, trust me, it's more important that you talk to Vince."

"I'm not getting this, Jane. What's this got to do with him?"

She shook her head, raised her right shoulder half an inch like she was too weary for a full shrug. I remembered the gesture from when she sat in my class.

"You know I don't get involved in his business. He does his thing and I do mine. The less I know about it, the better. It's not like he calls on me to help him, but he figured, in this case, it might be better if I approached you. And he's kind of got a lot on his plate at the moment."

I looked back at the house. "This — this house — has something to do with Vince."

Jane gave no indication either way. "Like I said, you're going to have to find out from him." She hesitated. "He's gonna want to talk to Grace, too."

"Not a chance," I said.

"I told him you'd say that. So I made him a deal, which I'll make with you. Grace can hang with me while he talks to you. That okay?"

I couldn't stand there and debate this all night with her. If I refused, Vince would send some of his goons after me the way he had once before, long ago.

"Fine," I said.

The three of us walked down the driveway to the street. Half a block up, I saw Jane's Mini parked under a streetlight.

"Come on," Jane said to Grace.

"Hang on," I said. "The house on the beach?"

"Yeah," Jane said. "Where you first had the pleasure. Remember?"

Would have been hard to forget.

It took less than ten minutes to get there. I'd driven along here many times in the last seven years, and not because I wanted to remind myself of my encounter with Vince Fleming. East Broadway was simply a Milford street I often used to get from one part of town to the other. It was also one of my favorite areas, this strip along the beach that looked out onto Long Island Sound and Charles Island, which was officially part of the Silver Sands park. Rumor had it that Captain Kidd had buried a treasure there hundreds of years ago, and I was betting if anyone had found it, it was Vince.

This wasn't quite the idyllic part of town it was two years earlier, before Hurricane Sandy swept through, laying waste to many of these beach houses, dropping trees, devastating countless home owners and their families, dumping tons of sand hundreds of feet inland.

We'd gotten off relatively easy at our house. We had a tree come down in the yard, one window blew in, and some shingles were ripped off the roof, but it was nothing to complain about compared with the destruction so many of our neighbors endured.

East Broadway was coming back. The street had been lined with contractors' trucks for more than twenty months. Not all homes could be repaired. The storm leveled many, knocked others off their foundations. Some houses that looked relatively unscathed still had to be torn down because they were structurally unsound.

Vince's place fell into the repairable category. I walked down here several times in the days after Sandy came through — cars weren't allowed as crews worked to clear the streets of sand and debris. Part of the roof was missing from Vince's two-story residence, windows had shattered, some of the siding had been ripped off. But compared with the houses on either side of him, he'd been lucky. Those two places looked as though they'd been dynamited.

Jane drove ahead of me, thinking maybe I couldn't find the place without help. Her brake lights flashed and I could see her pointing to the house, Grace barely visible in the passenger seat. She brought the Mini to a stop and I parked behind her.

As I walked up to the passenger side, Grace put down her window. "If you have any kind of problem or you hear anything about Stuart," I said to her, "you call me, okay?"

She nodded.

The lower level of Vince's place was mostly garage. A place for two cars, or boat storage. A set of stairs went up the left side of the house to a small landing. Looking up, I could see lights on. I mounted the stairs. Not too slow, but not too fast, either. I figured Vince would be listening for me, and I didn't want to go charging up there like I was some dog who came whenever you whistled for it. You try to preserve your pride in whatever small ways that are available to you.

I reached the landing and rapped on the screen door.

" 'S'open," he said.

It had been a long time since I'd heard that voice. Still recognizable, but more gravelly. Maybe even less forceful. But I knew better than to estimate this man based on his vocal abilities.

I pulled open the door and stepped in. The living area was on the beach side, the kitchen at the back. I glanced out at the sound, but there wasn't much you could see this time of night beyond a few stars and the faint lights of some boats out on the water.

The room hadn't changed any since I'd been brought here by Vince's henchmen seven years ago. Kidnapped, really. I'd been asking around town for him, thinking he might be able to help me find Cynthia, who, along with Grace, was missing at the time, and when he got wind that someone was snooping around looking for him, he had his employees scoop me up and deliver me to him.

At least, this time I'd come under my own power.

He was sitting at the kitchen table, putting down a cell phone, making no effort to get up and greet me. He'd lost some weight and his hair was peppered with more gray. The word that came to mind was "gaunt." I wondered whether he was sick.

He pointed to the chair opposite him.

"Siddown, Terry."

I walked over, pulled out the chair, and sat. I kept my hands in my lap, off the tabletop. Didn't want Vince to play any knife games with me this time.

"Vince," I said, nodding.

"Long time," he said.

"Yeah."

"You don't call, you don't write."

"Last time I saw you, you didn't exactly encourage it."

He waved a hand in the air. "I was feeling kind of cranky. Getting shot will do that to you."

"I suppose," I said. "We tried to tell you then, and I mean it when I tell you now, Cynthia and I remain grateful to you for your help and we regret the price you had to pay in offering it."

Vince stared at me. "That's nice. That's lovely. The truth is, I think about you most every day."

I swallowed. "Really."

"That's right. Every time I empty my bag."

I blinked. "I'm sorry. What?"

Vince placed his meaty palms on the table and pushed himself back in his chair. He came around the end of the table, stood about two feet from me. I started to get up, but he raised a hand. "No no, just sit. You'll get a better view from there."

He undid his belt, lowered his zipper, pushed his pants down about six inches, and lifted up his shirt to reveal a plastic bag attached to his abdomen. The lower half contained dark yellow liquid.

"You know what that is?" he asked.

"Yes," I said.

"That's good. I'm impressed. Before I got shot, I'd never even heard about these ostomy bag things. But the bullet fucked up my interior plumbing so I can't piss out my dick anymore. Had to get used to wearing one of these twenty-four/seven. So now, every time I go into the can to drain this bag, I think of you."

"I'm sorry," I said. "I didn't know."

"It's not the sort of thing you put on Facebook."

I hadn't given up trying to be nice. "And I'm sorry about your wife, too. I ran into Jane a while back and she told me."

Vince tucked his shirt back in, did up his zipper, and buckled his belt. He sat back down across from me.

"You didn't ask Jane to get me here so you could update me on your health," I said.

"No," he said. "It's about your kid."

I felt a shiver run down the length of my spine.

"What about my kid?" I asked slowly.

"She's stepped in the shit, that's what."

TWENTY-TWO

Bert Gooding was running the Buick's headlights off the battery. He wasn't too worried about anyone noticing the lights out here in the country on a farm, but thought leaving the engine running might attract some attention. It was a big V-8, sounded like a tractor, and pumped out exhaust like a coal plant.

But he needed to see what he was doing. So he positioned the car just right.

He'd brought an ax along, given the kind of job it was, and a change of clothes. It was hard to do something like this and not make a mess of yourself. When he was a kid, his dad used to take him twice a year to a cabin up in Maine, where they had a woodstove, and Bert always volunteered to split the already cut firewood into smaller pieces. He loved the feeling that came from making a perfect swing, blade meeting wood, forcing its way through cleanly without getting stuck. That satisfying sound of cracking wood. Using sufficient force so that you didn't have to hold the wood down with your boot to pry the blade free. It was all physics.

Not quite the same as what he was doing now. But the principle remained the same. You wanted to take a good, strong swing, connect in just the right place, make as clean a cut as possible. But there wasn't much chance of getting your blade stuck, and the sound wasn't nearly as satisfying.

Sickening was more like it.

Didn't feel good about this. Didn't feel good about this at all. But sometimes you just had to do what you had to do, at least so long as you were still working for Vince Fleming.

He raised the ax over his head, swung down hard in a perfect arc.

Smoosh.

Moved over about a foot, swung again.

Smoosh.

It wasn't quiet out here, not even with the car turned off. He was right up against the pen where the pigs were kept, and all the commotion had awakened them. They were grunting and snorting and bumping up against one another against the fence. They knew a treat was coming.

222

Bert tossed some morsels into the pen.

"Eat that, you fat fucks," he said.

He had the ax up over his head, was getting ready to put some momentum into it, when his phone rang.

"Shit," he said. Threw him off. He brought the ax down to his side, leaned the handle up against the front bumper of the Buick. He fetched the phone from his pocket, getting some blood on the screen, but not enough that he couldn't see where the call was coming from: HOME.

Jabba.

He put the phone to his ear. "Yes, Janine?"

"Where are you?"

"Work."

"Do you know what time it is?" she asked.

"I've got a pretty good idea."

"You said you were going to be back by ten. You had a short thing with Vince and you'd be back."

"Something came up," Bert said.

"You've forgotten, haven't you?" she snapped.

"Forgotten what?"

"The meeting? At ten? At the home?"

How could he forget? She'd been reminding him about it all week. They'd moved Janine's eighty-year-old mother, Brenda, out of her apartment and into a seniors home

223

in Orange a month before, but it wasn't working out. Brenda was making everyone's life hell. Hated the food, dumped it on the dining room floor in protest. Accused staff of stealing from her even though she couldn't tell them what was missing. Cheated at cards with the other "inmates," as she called them. Pushed people in wheelchairs out of her way so she could get on the elevator first.

The managers of the home had compiled a list of grievances about her, and now they wanted her out.

Janine said there was no way her mother could return to her apartment, so she'd just have to move in with Bert and her.

Bert had objected. But Janine wasn't hearing any of it.

"I won't be able to make the meeting," Bert said.

"You have to be there. We're probably going to have to move her out right then and there," Janine said.

"I told you, something's come up, and it's going to take all night to sort it out."

"I'm not happy, Bert."

"You've never been happy," he said. "Jesus could return to earth and paint a smiley face on your puss and you'd still be miserable."

"Don't you —"

He ended the call, muted the phone. She'd call back. She always did.

Bert returned to the task at hand, imagining that it was Janine he was cutting up into pieces and feeding to the pigs.

He wondered whether the beasts had any kind of standards. If he brought his wife here, tossed her into the pen in bite-sized bits, would they turn their snouts up at her? Give her a pass? Bert guessed she'd be too distasteful even for them.

TWENTY-THREE

TERRY

"It's obvious you know about tonight," I said to Vince Fleming, "but I don't understand how."

"This is going to go better with me asking the questions and you answering them," he said.

"Bullshit," I said. "My daughter's scared out of her wits. She got mixed up with some dumbass kid, got dragged into something she had no business being involved in, and now she's not even sure what the hell happened. *You* want answers? *I* want answers."

"Don't be so sure," he said. "What'd your kid tell you?"

"Grace," I said.

"Hmm?"

"Her name is Grace."

A long hesitation. "Okay. What did *Grace* tell you?"

I brought up my hands, folded my arms

in front of me, and leaned back in the chair. "No."

"Excuse me?"

"No," I repeated. "You want to know what she told me, then you tell me why you care."

"You got a lot of balls for an English teacher," Vince said.

"Clearly you've never taught in the high school system."

"Don't push me, Terry."

"Look, I'm not an idiot. I know what you do and what you're capable of. Your band of merry men could haul me out of here and I'd never be seen again. So, okay, you're an intimidating son of a bitch, but I'm not the same guy you met seven years ago. You and I have a history, Vince, and I'm saying that warrants some mutual respect. Yeah, you helped Cynthia and me, and you got shot and now you wear that bag. I'm sorry. You want pity? I can't imagine that. It's beneath you. We're all scarred, one way or another."

I took a breath.

"I think you know what happened in that house tonight. Not all of it, obviously, or I wouldn't be sitting here. You want me to answer your questions? Then you answer mine. Tell me what the hell is going on."

Vince glowered at me for several seconds,

then pushed back his chair, took four steps over to the kitchen counter, grabbed two shot glasses from the cupboard and a bottle of scotch, put them on the table in front of me, and sat back down. He splashed some brown liquid into each glass and shoved one toward me. He knocked his back before I'd touched mine.

I hate scotch.

But this seemed to be a peace offering, so I put it to my lips and downed half, doing my best not to make the face I made when I was four and my parents made me eat a brussels sprout.

Vince sighed. "Let's say I have an interest in that house where . . . Grace was tonight."

"What kind of interest?" I asked.

"You might already know. That's why I needed to talk to you."

I waited.

"And if you don't already know, it'd be better to keep it that way. Believe me when I tell you, that's for your sake, and your daughter's."

"But it's not your house," I said. "You don't own it."

"I do not."

"It's about the boy," I said.

Vince nodded.

"Stuart Koch," I said. "You know this kid?"

"I do."

"How?" I asked.

Vince weighed whether to answer, then probably figured that if I didn't already know, it wouldn't be a difficult thing to find out. "He's one of my guys' kids. Eldon. You might remember him. Bald guy, gave you a lift when you came to visit me here before."

I remembered. I hadn't known his name, but I remembered the bald guy as one of the ones who'd tossed me into a car to bring me to my first meeting with Vince. So I had taught the son of one of Vince's thugs.

Small world.

"Eldon's been raising Stuart on his own for several years now, ever since his wife left him for a Hells Angel and moved to California, and doing a lousy job of it. Lets the kid get away with all kinds of shit and doesn't know where he is most of the time."

"Where's Stuart now?"

"He's being taken care of."

"So he's okay?"

Vince hesitated. "Like I said."

I didn't know how to interpret that. I wanted to believe it meant Stuart was alive, and that if he had been shot in that house, he was on the mend. Somewhere.

"Grace would like to talk to him. So she knows he's okay," I said.

"Great," Vince said. "Let's get her up here. Then I can ask her some questions, face-to-face, at the same time."

I did not want Grace talking to this man.

"I'll talk to him myself," I said. "Pass on a message to Grace."

"Would you recognize his voice? Would you really know it was him?"

I wasn't sure, after all this time, whether I'd know Stuart's voice on the phone. But I could ask him questions about when he was in my class. Then I'd know.

"I'd give it a shot," I said.

"I'm trying to be nice, Terry. I'm showing you a courtesy. If I want to talk to your kid, there's not a damn thing you'll be able to do to stop me. But I talked to Jane, and she thought it'd be better to talk to her for me. And I went along with that. You want to keep it that way?"

"Yes," I said.

"Then help me out. What'd she tell you?"

I decided to tell him what I could.

"This Koch boy wanted to take the Porsche that was in the garage at that house for a spin. His plan was to break in, find a key, take the joyride, then return the car."

"And that was the only reason?"

"Yes."

"Grace didn't mention anything else?"

I blinked. "What other reason would there be?" The only thing I could think of was sex. But there were a million places a couple of horny teenagers could make out. They'd hardly need to take the risks that came with breaking into a house. To my mind, the Porsche was the prize.

"You tell me," Vince said.

"That's what Grace told me. It was about taking the car. So you tell me. Why else would Stuart want to break in there?"

"Where'd they go in the house?"

I replayed Grace's story in my head at fast-forward. "They were in the basement. They came up to the first floor. They were standing around the entrance to the kitchen when they thought they heard something. Stuart went to check it out, a shot went off, and Grace got the hell out of there."

"A shot went off," Vince repeated.

"Yeah."

"And who fired this shot?"

"Grace isn't sure," I said.

"What's that mean?" Vince asked.

"Like I said."

Vince gave me a look.

"Did Stuart bring a gun?" Vince asked.

"Grace said he got one out of the car. His

father's car. So that'd be your Eldon. I guess he kept a gun in the glove box."

"So this shot that was fired, it could have been Stuart that fired it?"

I didn't like where this was headed. "I don't think so," I said slowly.

Vince raised the bottle of scotch. "Another?"

I held my palm over the glass. "I'm good."

He refilled his. "Terry, I understand there's shit you don't want to tell me, that you're trying to protect your kid. I get that. I'm not out to get Grace. But I need to know what happened, and you being all dodgy with your answers, that's not helping. That's not good for you, or your kid."

When I said nothing, he continued. "There's stuff I already know you probably think I don't. Grace has already talked to Jane. I'm not talking about now. I'm talking about earlier. Your kid called Jane soon as she got out of the house, told her she was scared shitless she might have shot Stuart. Jane's known Stuart for eight, nine years, ever since her mom and I hooked up, and Jane got to know the people who work for me and the members of their families. Grace said Stuart gave her the gun to hold on to. That sound about right to you?"

"Yes," I said.

232

"What else did she say?"

I swallowed. My mouth was dry, but I still didn't want the scotch. "I think she blanked out. She doesn't know what happened in that house. She'd never even held a gun before and when she heard the shot wondered if somehow she'd made the gun go off. I asked her if it had kicked back, you know, recoiled, and she couldn't remember one way or another. And one more thing."

Vince waited.

"She doesn't have the gun. She doesn't know what she did with it. She thinks she dropped it in the house, but I didn't see it."

His eyebrows went up. "You were in the house."

I nodded.

"You went in through the broken window?"

I nodded.

"What *did* you see?"

"Some blood. A trace. In the kitchen."

"Shit," he said. "We'll have to do a more thorough cleanup. It's amazing we got done as much as we did in the time we had. We'll do it when we go back to fix the window. The people who live there won't be returning until next week. There's time."

I wondered how much blood was there before they'd started their tidying efforts.

"Did Grace see anyone else in the house?" he asked.

"She said she thought someone ran past her."

"She get a look at him?"

I shook my head. "No." Something Grace had said came back to me. "The security system wasn't engaged."

"Huh?"

"They went to all the trouble to break in through a basement window, but Grace said the light on the security keypad by the door was green."

Vince looked like he had a bad taste in his mouth. While he was trying to make sense of that, I was trying to figure out what must have happened after Grace phoned Jane.

I said, "Jane had to have called you right after she heard from Grace. Stuart being Eldon's son, she knew you had to be her first call. So you and your boys rushed in to cover things up, clean up the scene, make like none of this ever happened."

Vince said nothing.

"But there's more going on than just some stupid teenage shenanigans, isn't there? More than an aborted joyride."

Still nothing.

"Vince, level with me."

"We're done," he said. He poured the

234

remaining contents of his shot glass down his throat and pushed back his chair.

"No," I said. "We're not. I don't know if we should be going to the hospital to look for Stuart, or to the police, or try to track down this gun, or —"

"Fuck!" Vince said, kicking over his chair as he stood. "You think you've gotten tough but you're the same pussy you were when I first met you. Listen to me and listen good. You will do none of those things. You will not go looking for Stuart. Not at the hospital and not anyplace else. You will not go to the police. You will not call some fucking lawyer. You will not go to that fucking woman from that *Deadline* TV show and tell your life story again. You will go home and you will forget any of this ever happened."

He'd come around the table and was jabbing a short, stubby index finger to within an inch of my nose.

"You will get up tomorrow morning and go about your day like it was any other day, and if you're smart, you and Grace won't even talk about any of this ever again. She won't say a word to her friends. She won't try to get in touch with Stuart. Far as she's concerned, she never even met the kid. You know why? *Because it didn't happen.* None of this happened. And you won't be keeping your mouth shut just for me. You'll be keeping your mouth shut for your kid."

When I didn't say anything, he asked, "Am I getting through?"

"I hear ya," I said.

"Hearin's not enough. I gotta know you're on board. I have enough on my plate right now without having to be concerned about what you might do."

"I need to know if the kid is okay," I said. "I need to know what happened to Stuart."

"No, you don't," Vince said. "You don't have to worry about him. Because — and you worry me, Terry, because you seem to have some kind of comprehension problem — Grace doesn't even know him. Remember that part? She's never even heard of him."

"What if the police come around, asking about what happened at the house?"

"That's not going to happen."

"But it might," I insisted.

"I told you, you're not saying anything, because you want to do everything you can to protect your little girl."

"Don't threaten my daughter, Vince."

"I'm putting myself in your place. You want to do what's best for her. And you seem to be forgetting something, Terry."

"What?"

"The gun."

That got my attention. "What about the gun?"

"Maybe the reason you didn't find it is because it's already been found."

I waited.

"We know for sure your daughter's fingerprints are on it. But did that gun go off? Did it hit somebody? Let's say the answer's yes, on both counts. Just for the sake of argument. Then that becomes a very special gun. That's what you call a *smoking* gun in every sense of the word. A gun the police would like to get their hands on. Well, right now, I can make sure that never happens. But that doesn't mean I'm gonna get rid of it. It means I'm going to keep it for insurance. You don't know whether that gun's bad news for your kid or not, but you're a lot better off if it never surfaces, now, aren't you?"

I said nothing.

"You take your girl home and you read her a nice story and tuck her in and give her a little kiss good night from me."

TWENTY-FOUR

"Its gonna be okay, Grace," Jane said, sitting behind the wheel of the Mini. "Vince'll know what to do."

Grace, teary eyed, was unconvinced. "I know I'm going to go to jail. I'm going to go to jail and I won't get out until I'm, like, fifty or something."

Jane took Grace's hand and squeezed it. "No way. That's not going to happen. I know it's, like, impossible to tell you to stop worrying, but everything'll work out. You wait. Vince wouldn't have lasted as long as he has if he didn't know how to get out of these situations."

Grace sniffed. "Doesn't it bug you?"

"What?"

"That he's, you know, like, the Mafia or something."

Jane shook her head. "He's not Mafia."

"But he's a criminal, right? And he has a gang? And Stuart's dad is one of the people

238

in his gang?"

Jane sighed. "Look, I'm not proud of any of this, okay? But calling Vince and Eldon and Bert and Gordie a gang, it makes them sound like a bunch of teenagers on motorcycles going around terrorizing the neighborhood. What they are is a business. That's all. A different kind of business, but that's what it is."

"But he's a criminal."

Jane shrugged. "What do you want me to say?"

"So, like, how do you deal with that? I mean, there are days I'm totally ashamed of my dad, and he's just a teacher."

"Just because he does bad things doesn't mean he's a totally bad person. Look, this is who he is, and this is what his father did. He's got good in him, even if, lately, he and I are kind of . . ."

"Kind of what?"

"I don't know. Since my mom died, it hasn't been the same with him, and that's okay, you know? I'm not a kid anymore, and I don't need a father figure in my life every day. But right now, the guy's in a bind, and he needs your dad's help, and your help, too."

"Help to find out what happened, or help to cover everything up?"

Jane looked at her straight on. "Both."

"If I did something wrong, I have to pay the price for it," Grace said. "I have to do the right thing."

"Sometimes doing the right thing is complicated."

"A few weeks ago," Grace said slowly, "my mom and I had a fight." She wiped her eyes. "I didn't tell you about this."

"What kind of fight?"

"You remember you asked about this mark on my hand?" Grace showed her.

"Yeah. You said you accidentally burned it."

"My mom pushed me and my hand hit a pot on the stove. It was kind of both our faults, but if she hadn't pushed me, it wouldn't have happened. I had to go to the hospital and my mom told me to tell them the truth, that it was her fault, and if that meant they had to call the police, then that's the way it would have to be."

Jane took Grace's hand and gently squeezed it. "Wow. So what did you do?"

"I told them I was just goofing around, that I was dancing, and my arm hit the pot."

"You covered for her."

Grace nodded. "Yeah, but she was willing to pay for her mistake. She was willing to do the right thing."

"But you didn't let her, because you love her too much to let that happen. That's kind of what's happening now. I care about you, and Vince, well, he cares about the people he's got around him, and we'd all rather go with a story that's not exactly what happened if it means you're going to be okay in the long run."

"I don't know," Grace said.

Jane took a breath. "Okay, the first thing we have to do is figure out what really went down. You need to remember everything you can about what happened in the house. You heard a shot. Maybe it was you. Maybe it was somebody else. But you need to remember. Did you see anybody, other than Stuart?"

"No. I mean, I think someone ran past me. But I didn't see anybody."

"You're sure?"

Grace nodded.

"Okay, but even if you didn't see anyone, maybe you heard something or, I don't know, *smelled* something. Maybe there's something you noticed without even realizing it. Close your eyes."

"What?"

"Just close them," Jane said. "Put yourself back in that house, after the shot."

"I don't want to do that. I don't want to

241

think about it."

"Grace, here's the thing. You're going to be thinking about this and thinking about this for a long time, whether you want to or not, so you might as well do it now and try to learn something. Okay?"

"I guess." Grace closed her eyes.

"After the shot, what do you hear?"

"I'm screaming."

"What are you saying?"

"I'm going, 'Stuart! Stuart!' Like that."

"And what does he say?"

"He's not saying anything."

"But you hear something?"

Grace tried to close her eyes more tightly. "I hear steps."

"Okay, that's good. Fast steps, slow steps?"

"Kind of — running? It's not hard steps, like if someone was wearing dress shoes. It's kind of soft and squeaky. Like maybe running shoes."

Jane smiled encouragingly, even though Grace couldn't see her. "That's good. So someone was running, getting away. You think it was Stuart? You think he ran off and just decided to leave you there? Maybe you accidentally pulled the trigger, or there was someone else there with a gun, and he got scared and ran?"

"He wouldn't do that," Grace said, opening her eyes. "Would he?"

Jane gave her a pitying look. "Gracie, honey, please. I know these characters. Vince is solid, but the rest, and their kids — I mean, I thought I was just an idiot in school when I was there, but I was a Rhodes scholar by comparison."

"A what?"

"Never mind. Close your eyes again."

Grace complied.

"So you heard steps. Running. Are you saying it couldn't have been Stuart?"

"I don't know. I'm, like, trying to hear them again."

Jane thought a moment. "After the shot went off, that must have been really loud. Did you kinda lose your hearing for a second?"

"Maybe."

"So if you were able to hear footsteps, even if the person was wearing running shoes, the person would have to be pretty heavy, you think?"

Grace slowly said, "I guess so."

"And did you say someone bumped you running by in the dark?"

"Yeah."

"Hard?"

Grace concentrated. "I think I kind of lost my balance. I think maybe I got hit by a bag, like, something the person was carrying."

"What I'm thinking is, if you heard these steps even after you might have gone partially deaf, and you got bumped hard, it could have been a pretty big guy."

Grace opened her eyes and looked at Jane. "Maybe. But that's not exactly very much to go on, is it?"

"Well, it's something," Jane said. "But you're right, it doesn't really narrow down the field of suspects."

Grace twigged to that. "Suspect in what?"

"You know. Like, whoever else might have been there."

Grace felt tears trickling down her cheeks and wiped them away. "Stuart's dead, isn't he, Jane?"

"I got a pretty good idea what Vince is telling your dad right now. He's telling him to take you home and forget any of this ever happened. And that's real good advice. Vince has got this. And he's going to be real grateful when I tell him how you helped me."

Grace heard footsteps on gravel. She turned and saw her father standing by her door. Grace fumbled around, looking for the handle, and opened it.

"See ya," Jane said as Grace was led back to her father's car.

TWENTY-FIVE

"This is an unexpected pleasure," Heywood Duggan said, slipping into the all-night coffee shop booth across from Detective Rona Wedmore. He had to squeeze himself in. He wasn't a fat man, but he was big, and there wasn't any room between his stomach and the edge of the table.

"Sorry to call you so late," Wedmore said. "And to be so mysterious."

Heywood grinned, flashing his pearly white teeth. He still had that gap between the two top ones. Back when they were seeing each other, he'd talked about getting that fixed, but Rona had told him it gave him character.

"It's good to see you," he said, placing his meaty palms flat down on the table. "I don't get called out to midnight meetings with beautiful women all that often."

"Oh, shut up," Wedmore said, slipping her own hands down to her lap, not wanting to give him the opportunity to reach out and hold hers, which she figured he might do at some point. Not that there wasn't some part of her that didn't long for his touch after all this time. "It's good to see you, Heywood."

He grinned. "You always used to call me Woody."

She smiled. "I did." She cocked her head. "And I wasn't the only one."

He flicked his hand, as if shooing away a fly, dismissing the comment. "You're looking good."

"I've put on a few since you saw me last," she said.

"More to love," he said.

She brought up her left hand not only to wave a finger at him, but to let him see her ring. "I'm spoken for," she said.

"That was not a pass, just an observation." He smiled warmly. "How are things with Lamont? I heard he had a rough go of it in Iraq."

Rona nodded. "He's good. It was hard for him over there. He saw things no one should have to see."

"I heard he didn't say a word for months."

"Well, he's talking now," Wedmore said with a forced laugh. "And he's got a job, with Costco. They're good to him there."

"I'm glad to hear that — I really am."

Heywood Duggan's face fell. "I wondered, when you called, if, you know, maybe something had happened. Maybe the two of you were going through a rough patch. That maybe you needed someone to talk to."

Wedmore's eyes narrowed. "Or fall into the sack with."

He raised his palms. "I did not say that." Heywood shook his head. "You hurt me, Rona."

"Oh, bullshit," she said.

A waitress came by and they both ordered coffee.

He grinned. "You and I, we had a good run there, you have to admit."

She tried to hide her smile. "When'd you quit being a trooper?"

"Eight, nine years ago," he said.

"Why?"

He turned a simple shrug into a ten-second shoulder exercise. "You know. Different opportunities. Didn't want to be with state police forever."

"That's not what I heard."

"And what'd you hear?"

"I heard some evidence — cash — went missing after a drug bust and not long after that you decided to take an early retirement rather than face an internal affairs investigation."

Another wave of the hand. "You can't believe everything you hear."

"Is that when you started to go freelance?"

"I've done a bunch of things, private security — you know the drill. So why the hell did you ask me to meet you tonight? I'm starting to think this isn't as personal as I was hoping it might be."

"Eli Goemann," Rona said.

"Eli what?"

"I hope, for your sake, that your hearing is the only thing you've lost since I saw you last."

"I just didn't catch the name."

"Eli Goemann. Don't be cute."

"Eli Goemann, Eli Goemann." He shook his head. "I'm sorry. I don't know the name."

"Then why did you go ask his former roommates where you could find him?" Wedmore asked.

He pushed himself back against the seat. The space was so tight, he suddenly looked trapped to Rona. The waitress put two mugs of coffee on the table in front of them and walked away.

"What do you want from me?" he asked.

"I want you to tell me why you've been looking for Eli Goemann. I'm guessing someone hired you. Who wants you to find

Eli and why?"

"Rona, come on, you know how this works. Clients expect confidentiality, and I can't be bought for a cup of coffee." He smiled slyly. "If you were offering something more substantial . . ."

"Stop acting like you're twelve," Rona said. "So you admit you're looking for him."

"Okay, yeah, I am. But it's a private matter."

"Not when there's a homicide."

His eyebrows went up. "Say again?"

"Goemann's dead. His body was found at Silver Sands."

Duggan grimaced. "Son of a bitch."

"Help me out here."

He put a hand over his mouth, rubbed his chin. "Shit."

"I'd like to know who killed him, Heywood. And you've been asking around about him. Right now, you're my best lead to finding out what happened."

"They figure out how long he's been dead?"

"So now you want me to answer *your* questions?" Wedmore said.

"Okay, look, I'll have to talk to my client, clear it with him before I talk to you."

"It's not his call," Wedmore said.

"Here's what I can tell you. Goemann

called my client, said he had something he believed my client would like to have returned to him."

"Goemann stole something from him and was trying to get your client to buy it back?"

"Half right. He didn't *steal* this item — at least that's what he told my client — but had come into *possession* of it. And yes, he was willing to sell it back."

"What's the item?"

Heywood Duggan moved his head left and right half an inch. "Why don't you tell me if he was found with anything of interest. If what you found is what he was flogging, I'll tell you."

"He wasn't found with anything. And we haven't figured out where he was residing."

"Then all I can tell you is, it was a personal item. Not the sort of thing you'd assign a commercial value to. Well, only partly."

"But it's worth a lot to your client. How much was Eli asking?"

"He threw out a crazy number. A hundred thousand. I told him that wasn't possible. My client is not a rich man."

"Rich enough to hire you."

He shrugged. "I come for a lot less than a hundred g's."

"So this Goemann character approaches your client, asks for a hundred grand to get this *thing* back, and then what happens?"

"Nothing."

"What do you mean, nothing?"

"My client doesn't hear from him again. He didn't even know who it was who called him. He hires me, I get the number off his phone, find out it belongs to Goemann, then trace him through DMV to that house where he once lived with the other students, but he hasn't lived there in a year or so. Sounds like he was bouncing around, sleeping on couches, working odd jobs the last twelve months or so, no fixed address. When he never called back with a counteroffer, to try and set something up, started to wonder whether he ever had anything to sell."

"You still working it?"

Another shrug. "Client's only got so much to spend. And I said to him, Look, this may have been a bluff. Maybe there's nothing to this."

Wedmore took a sip of her coffee. "Woody," she said, and he smiled, "this is me you're talking to. Off the record. What the hell was Goemann selling? What was your client trying to get back?"

"Basically, he was trying to get back what you were to me."

"What the hell are you talking about?"

"He was trying to get back the love of his life."

TWENTY-SIX

Cynthia had sent Vince a sympathy card when she'd seen the item in the paper's death notices that his wife had died.

She didn't mention it to Terry. After those two disastrous visits to Milford Hospital to see Vince during his recovery, Terry had been adamant that they were done. We've made an effort, he'd said. We tried to show our appreciation, and he doesn't want any of it. There's nothing else for us to do.

Cynthia agreed, to a point, but she still felt she owed Vince something for helping them seven years before. If Vince hadn't helped Terry put together some of the pieces in the puzzle of what had happened to her parents and her brother, Todd, Terry would never have found her and Grace in time.

They nearly died.

The way Cynthia saw it, she owed Vince. For her life, and the life of her daughter. The least she could do was send a card. So she picked one up at the mall, as unsentimental a one as she could find, but wrote inside:

I was very sorry to learn about the passing of your wife, Audrey. You, and Jane, are in my thoughts at this time. But I also wanted to tell you that I've been thinking of you. You made a tremendous sacrifice on our behalf, and I remain immensely grateful. I understand you may not have been in the mood to hear that message when we last saw you, but it remains as true today as it was then. With every good wish in this difficult time, Cynthia.

She could have signed it from herself and Terry, but decided not to. The note, really, was from her. Even though she hadn't told Terry about it, if it ever came up, she wouldn't deny it.

Cynthia hadn't heared anything back from him. And that was fine.

But a few days after she'd settled herself into the apartment, she noticed an old Dodge Ram pickup roll up to the curb as she pulled into the driveway. She'd gotten out of her car and saw Vince Fleming open the door and slide off the seat.

"Hey," he'd said.

He was thinner and grayer — not just his hair, but even his pallor — and when he walked toward her, she noticed a deliberateness in his gait that suggested low-level pain.

"Vince," she said.

"I was at a cross street back there, saw you drive by, was pretty sure it was you. Thought I'd say, you know, hello. But this — this isn't your house."

"No," Cynthia said. "When I finish work, I like to sit on the porch with a beer. Join me?"

He hesitated. "No reason not to, I guess."

She went up to her room, dropped her purse, kicked off her heels, grabbed two Sam Adams, and came back down in her bare feet. Vince was in one of the porch chairs staring out at the street.

She handed him a bottle, beads of sweat already forming on it in the humid air.

"Thanks," he said.

Cynthia sat down, tucked her legs up under her butt, and put the bottle to her lips. "You doing some work around here?" she asked, like he was a friendly neighborhood contractor or something. If Vince was doing work around here, it was probably best to alert Neighborhood Watch.

"No," he said, not looking at her. "Listen, thanks for the card."

"You're welcome," Cynthia said. "I'd seen the notice in the paper."

"Yeah," he said.

"Had she been sick for a while?" Cynthia asked.

"About a year." He swallowed some beer. "Hot today."

Cynthia fanned herself with her left hand. "Yeah."

"So, you guys downsize? Renting a room? Doesn't seem big enough for you two and the kid."

"Just me."

"Oh. So you guys split up."

"No. I just needed some time."

"Time to what?"

"Just some time."

He grunted. "I get that. Sometimes it's nice living alone. Lot less drama."

"Jane still with you?"

He shook his head. "Nope. She's living with some half-wit."

"A what?"

Vince shrugged. "Half-wit, dipshit, fucktwat, whatever. A musician. Plays in a band. I don't like it, her living with him. Maybe I'm old-fashioned, but that doesn't sit right with me."

Cynthia asked, "Were you and Audrey married when you first started living to-

257

gether?"

"That's different," he said. "We'd been around. She'd been married before. Nobody's business what we do at that age."

"Maybe that's what Jane thinks. That it's nobody's business what she does."

He gave her a look. "Did I come here for you to bust my balls?"

"I don't know. Did you?"

Vince glowered at her. "No." Long pause. "I came by to apologize."

"For what?"

"When you came to the hospital to see me. I was a horse's ass. This might seem kinda late coming, but I take my time when it comes to admitting I was wrong."

"Forget it," Cynthia said. "All is forgiven."

"Well, shit, that was easier than I thought it'd be." He drew on the bottle. "So, I opened up to you. Now tell me what happened between you and Terry."

"You call that opening up?"

"I said I was sorry. So what are you doing here?"

She settled back in the chair, watched a car go by. "I lost it. With Grace. I was . . . out of control. So I'm on a self-imposed time-out."

"You smack her around some?"

She shot him a look. "I did not smack her

around. Jesus. But I've been trying to control her every move. We're fighting all the time."

Vince looked unimpressed. "That's what parents do. How else kids going to learn?"

"It's beyond that. I'm fucked-up, Vince. You find that surprising?"

"What, you mean about that shit with your family?" Vince shook his head. "That was years ago."

She eyed him incredulously. "Really? So I should, what, just walk it off?"

He looked at her. "Things got sorted out. Move on."

Cynthia studied him with a small sense of wonder. "You should have your own show. Dr. Phil's got nothing on you."

"There you go." Vince stretched out his legs. He seemed to be struggling to get comfortable in the chair. "I'm not trying to be an insensitive asshole."

"It just comes natural."

"But you have to move forward. No sense looking back."

"How about you, then? You moved on? You nearly died."

He twisted uncomfortably in the chair, lightly touched his abdomen with his free hand. "I've been better."

He drank some more beer.

A Cadillac came charging up the street, turned into the driveway, and parked. Nathaniel Braithwaite got out, slammed the door, spent about half a minute brushing dog hair off his clothes, and approached the house. As he mounted the steps to the porch, he slowed when he saw Cynthia and her guest.

"Oh, hey," he said. He glanced at Vince, nodded.

"Hi," Cynthia said. "Nathaniel, this is my friend Vince. From high school. Vince, Nathaniel."

"Nice wheels," Vince said.

Nathaniel smiled. "Thanks."

"Always liked Caddies. But not so much now. They're trying to turn them into Kraut cars. I liked them when they were big and long and had huge fins on them. Like the '59. Bit before my time, but that was a car. Thing spanned two zip codes."

Vince craned his neck, took another look at the car, then cast his eye back at the house. Cynthia could guess what he was thinking. Nathaniel had a pretty nice car for someone renting a room in an old house like this.

"What line of work you in?" Vince asked.

"Used to be in computer software," Nathaniel said.

"Not anymore?"

"I'm taking a break from all that."

Vince, motioning to Nathaniel's pants, said, "If you're having an affair with a collie, you're gonna have to do a better job hiding the evidence."

Nathaniel looked down at himself. "Occupational hazard."

Vince cocked his head, waiting for an answer. Cynthia didn't feel it was her place to explain what Nathaniel did for a living now.

"I walk dogs," he said.

"For what?" Vince asked. "Like, for a hobby?"

He shook his head, forced out his chin defiantly, struggling for dignity. "It's what I do. I go to people's houses through the day and take their dogs out for a walk."

Vince moved his tongue around in his mouth.

"That's your job?" he asked. Not in a patronizing way. Just interested. "Must pay good to be driving a car like that."

Nathaniel dug his upper teeth into his lower lip and said, "Hung on to it from my software days. Look, nice to meet you." He offered Cynthia an awkward smile. "Catch you later."

He went into the house. They both listened to his feet stomping up the stairs to the second floor.

Looking at the street, taking another draw on the bottle, Vince said, "I'm guessing there's a story there."

Cynthia thought back to that day in the moments after she returned to her apartment after having a glass of wine with Nathaniel. Thought about Nate asking her to help him get out of an arrangement he had with her high school friend.

What the hell had Vince gotten Nathaniel into? Cynthia had no intention of talking to Vince on his behalf. Nate was on his own. There was a part of Vince that Cynthia still liked, but she had no illusions about the man.

Helping Nate extricate himself from an arrangement with Vince would be like one fly letting itself getting snared in a spider's web to save another.

She thought about that, and other matters, as she rested her back against the large oak tree, her arms folded across her chest, half a block down from the house she intended to return to soon. Cynthia had parked her car around the corner so it would not be spotted.

She wondered where Terry's car was and

why it was taking him so long to pick up Grace and bring her home.

This was Cynthia's favorite spot. She could stand here by this tree, and if a car showed up in the distance coming from either direction, she could scurry around to the other side and not be seen.

How many nights had she done this? Pretty much every night since she'd moved out.

Cynthia needed to know everyone was home safe.

She wanted to phone Terry, ask what was keeping him, whether Grace had run into a problem, but how did she do that without giving away the fact that she was spying on them?

So instead, she waited, took out her cell to check the time. How long had it been since she'd been on the phone with Terry? Nearly an hour and a half? Where the hell could — ?

Wait.

A car was approaching. It looked like Terry's Escape.

She moved around to the other side of the tree, waited for the car to pass her. It was Terry's car.

He was behind the wheel. And there was Grace beside him.

She watched the car turn into their driveway. Cynthia wondered what sort of trouble Grace had gotten herself into. Drinking maybe? But when she got out of the car, she seemed to be walking okay. But she didn't look well. Her head was hanging low. Her clothes were a mess, as if she'd been rolling around on the ground in them.

Something was wrong.

But at least she was home.

Cynthia watched until they were in the house, then walked back to her car and returned to her apartment. But she had a difficult time getting to sleep.

She kept wondering what Grace had done.

Twenty-Seven

TERRY

"What happened?" Grace asked as we walked back to my car out back of Vince's beach house. "What's going on?"

"Get in," I said.

I let Grace handle her own door this time. I was keying the engine as she got into the passenger seat.

"What are we going to do now?" she asked. "Did Vince know what's happened to Stuart? Was Stuart with him? Are we going to the hospital? Are we going to Stuart's house? What about — ?"

I slammed the heel of my hand against the steering wheel. "Enough. No more questions."

"But —"

"Enough!" I put the car in drive and did a U-turn on East Broadway. "We'll talk at home."

Grace turned away and pressed herself up

against the passenger door. I glanced over, noticed her shoulders trembling slightly.

We were back at the house in five minutes. We got out of the car like two people coming home from a funeral service. Moving slowly, not talking, wrapped up in our own thoughts. She stood next to me while I fumbled with the key to let us in.

"Kitchen," I said.

She walked ahead of me like a condemned prisoner. I pointed to a chair and she sat down compliantly. I pulled out a chair and sat down across from her.

"There's no point in looking for Stuart," I said.

Her eyes filled with tears. "Oh my God."

"It looks like Vince, or his crew, or both, were in the house between the time you left and when we got back there. They cleaned the place up. They're going to go back, finish up, fix the window."

"But what — ?"

"Whatever happened to Stuart, Vince has taken care of it."

Grace's face was flushed. "What does that mean?"

"I don't know," I said.

"What do you *think* it means?"

You want to protect your kids from bad things, but sometimes there's no way.

Especially when they're the ones who got themselves into the mess in the first place.

"I think it means he's dead," I said.

She put her hands to her face, covering all of it save for her frightened eyes. "I shot him," she said, the words coming out muffled. "I killed him."

"That part's less clear," I said. "I don't have all the information when I say this, but I don't think so."

She brought her hands down. "Why?"

"A few things. One, from what you've said, it's pretty clear someone else was in the house. Two, if you'd fired that gun, I think you'd have known it. The kickback, when you pulled the trigger — it would've knocked you on your ass. I think you may have been — maybe you still are now — suffering from a mild form of shock when things started getting scary in that house. So your perception of things is skewed. You don't really know what went down."

She swallowed. "What else?"

"Vince says you're to forget any of this ever happened."

"Yeah, like that's going to happen."

I grabbed both her wrists and squeezed. "You listen to me and you listen good."

She gulped.

"Vince isn't kidding around. You won't

forget what happened tonight, but you're going to have to pretend you have. He wants you to forget you ever even met Stuart Koch. He doesn't want you, or me, talking to anybody about this. He doesn't want us looking for Stuart — he doesn't want us checking the hospital, going to his house, nothing. And he sure doesn't want us going to the police about it."

Even without Vince leaning on us, I'd have had pretty mixed feelings about calling the Milford cops. What the hell would I have told them? That my daughter broke into a house with her boyfriend, who may or may not have been shot? Point the cops in the direction of Vince Fleming for the full story? Who had as much as told me he had, in his possession, the gun Grace had been holding?

That gun was a wild card. Even if Grace hadn't fired it, what if, after she'd dropped it, someone else had? What if Grace's prints were still on it?

"But isn't that wrong?" Grace asked.

The question snapped me out of my thoughts. "What?"

"Isn't it wrong? If something has happened to Stuart, whether I did it or somebody else did, isn't it wrong not to go to the police? Don't we have to tell them what happened?"

I felt like this was a test. Of whether I was a good father. Of whether I was a good man. It struck me at that moment that being one did not necessarily mean you were both.

I squeezed her wrists harder and looked down at the table briefly, then met her eyes with mine.

"Grace, you and that boy broke into a house. You were going to steal a car. You're vulnerable. Very vulnerable. If there's a way to keep you out of this, I'm going to do it and I don't give a good goddamn whether it's the right thing or not."

"You're hurting me," she whispered.

I let go of her wrists. "The only thing that matters to me right now is you. Making sure that you're safe, that nothing bad happens to you. There's a lot we don't know right now, and without knowing everything, it's hard to figure out what the best thing to do is. And as much as I don't like having to follow orders from a thug like Vince Fleming, right now I don't see a lot of other options."

"This feels wrong."

"Grace . . . I don't have all the answers right now."

She searched my eyes for some sort of comfort. I shifted my chair around the corner of the table and hugged her. She buried her face into my shoulder and wept.

"I'm so scared," she said.

"Me, too."

"I don't know what to do."

"We have to ride this out. Maybe, soon, we'll have an idea what we're dealing with. But until then — and I hate this, believe me, I hate this — I'm not sure we have much choice but to go along with what Vince wants."

She pulled away and asked, "What if my friends start asking?"

"Start asking what?"

"What's happened to Stuart? What am I supposed to say?"

I felt a constriction in my neck. We were on borrowed time. I could keep Grace out of trouble maybe for a while, but at what point would all this catch up to us? When would the unraveling begin?

"How many know you were seeing Stuart?"

"A couple of my friends. And Stuart might have told somebody. I mean, we weren't, like, going out, but we'd hung out together a few times, is all. I might have mentioned him on Facebook."

Jesus. Once it was online, it was out there forever.

"If there are any mentions of him, delete them," I said. "Delete anything you can. No, wait. Later, if they find you were deleting everything about him the same night he disappeared — Shit. I don't know. If your friends ask what's going on with him, you haven't seen him lately. You drifted apart, something like that. Did anyone know you and Stuart were going to be together tonight?"

Grace thought a moment. "I don't think so. I didn't tell anyone."

"What about Sandra?"

"Sandra?"

"Sandra Miller. The girl you were supposedly going to the movies with tonight."

Grace winced.

"Yeah," I said. "Did you tell her she was your cover story, so if I called her or her mother she'd know what was going on?"

Grace shook her head. Kids think they're so smart sometimes, but the perfect crime is beyond them.

"You told me Sandra's mother was going to drive you home? How were you going to make that work?"

"I was going to get Stuart to drop me just down the street, so you wouldn't have seen any car pull into the driveway," she said.

I pushed my chair back. It was difficult, in

the midst of trying to comfort my daughter, not to be furious with her, too.

"Tell me about Jane," I said.

"What about her?"

"When did you two connect?"

Picking up the accusing tone, she pulled back. "I found her online and became her friend."

"Being a friend online and being someone you call in the middle of the night when you think you've shot somebody, those are two very different levels of friendship," I said. "Why did you call her? When did you get so chummy?"

"I got to know her over the last few months. I wanted to know."

"You wanted to know what?"

"I wanted to know about Mom, and you, and what happened back then." She sniffed. "You guys never really talk about it. I mean, you talk about how Mom's still all freaked-out about what happened to her, that it was this big trauma and all, but you never get into the details so I could really try to understand, you know?"

I listened.

"But I knew that Vince Fleming helped you guys back then, and that he was with Mom the night her family disappeared back in, like, 1983. And I knew you used to be

Jane's teacher and that Vince was kind of her stepfather. I wasn't going to ask Vince about things. He was way too scary, and too old to talk to. But I thought if I asked Jane, she'd answer some of my questions."

"You could have just asked us," I said.

"Oh yeah, right," Grace said. "You guys have been, like, superprotective forever about this. When I was seven, and Mom and I nearly got killed, it's like you guys put me in this bubble. It's the thing you always say we'll talk about one day, but we never do. And it's like Mom's the only one who gets to be a basket case about it. What about me? You think because it happened a long time ago I'm not still freaked-out, too? I haven't forgotten being in that car at the top of that cliff. I can close my eyes and it's like I'm right back there. I remember. And I want to know. I want to know everything about it, not just discuss my stupid *feelings* about it, like that time you sent me to that shrink Mom sees. And even if Jane wasn't right there when it all happened, she knows a lot about what went down and she doesn't mind talking about it with me. She's *helping* me, okay? Is that okay with you and Mom? That I talk to someone who can *really* help me?"

My neck was getting too tired to hold my

head up. I let it fall again while I considered her words. "So you got together," I said.

"Yeah. We met a bunch of times. For coffee and like that. And we didn't just talk about all the shit that happened a long time ago, either. We just talked about stuff. I like her — I like her a lot — and when I was in trouble, I called her."

"Because you thought she could help you more than I could?" I asked. It was hard not to feel slightly wounded.

"Not . . . exactly," she said. "It was because of Stuart. And her connection."

"Because she knew him," I said. "Because Stuart's dad works with Vince."

"Yeah. I'd seen Stuart around school and all, but it was Jane who actually introduced us."

"When was this?"

"Like, a few weeks ago? We were in the food court, and she saw him and called him over, and we all got talking. And after that, Stuart texted me and we hung out."

"Did you know that Stuart was connected to Vince Fleming? That his father is Eldon Koch? That he works for Vince?"

"Yeah, I knew that."

"You knew that, and you went out with him? This kid whose father is some kind of fucking gangster? You know he kidnapped me off the street back when all that stuff happened?"

I shook my head in disbelief.

"But he also helped you, right? If it hadn't been for him helping you figure out what happened, I'd be dead, right? And Mom, too? Not bad for a fucking gangster."

I had no comeback for that.

"That's the stuff I found out from Jane. Maybe if you guys would tell me something once in a while, I'd have known."

"You should never —"

I stopped myself. I was letting things get out of hand. Now I was the one losing control. Of the situation, and myself.

"You're always about not prejudging people," Grace said.

"What?"

"Just because someone's dad is bad doesn't have to mean the kid's bad."

I looked at her, dumbfounded. "Stuart broke into a house so he could steal a car. Who's prejudging? The kid already proved himself to be bad news. Just like his father."

Grace got up, ran upstairs to her room, and slammed the door hard enough the house shook.

Hard enough that it shook something free that I'd been thinking about without actually realizing I'd been thinking about it.

For all he knows, she saw him.

This person who ran past, who may have shot and killed Stuart.

Did he know Grace failed to get a good look at him?

If he believed Grace had seen him, that she could identify him . . .

We might have more to worry about than the police finding out Grace was in that house.

TWENTY-EIGHT

"Hey," Vince said as Jane Scavullo let herself in. He'd heard her coming up the stairs and was expecting her.

"Hi," she said tiredly. She stood by the door.

"Come in," he said.

"I'm fine here."

"Oh, for Christ's sake, come in and sit down."

Jane advanced into the room and sat in the chair Terry had been in moments earlier.

"So what'd she say? She see anything?" Vince asked. "No, wait. Hold that thought. I gotta empty this thing before I blow up." He went into the bathroom, closed the door.

Jane closed her eyes for a moment, laid her hands down on the table to rest them. Her father emerged a couple of minutes later, wiping his hands on his shirt to dry them, and took a seat opposite the young woman.

"So?"

"She wasn't much help."

"Shit. She must have noticed something."

Jane recounted her conversation with Grace as close to word for word as she could.

"So we know nothing about this guy," Vince said. "Not one goddamn thing." Jane said nothing. "That's just great. Did she say whether they were there for anything other than the car?"

Jane shook her head. "Like what?"

"Did she or didn't she?"

"She didn't. Stuart broke in to get the Porsche keys. If he was there for anything else, Grace doesn't seem to know about it."

"So they didn't go upstairs?"

"I *told* you what she said."

"Whoever else was in there didn't have to bust in," Vince said.

"You asking me?"

"I'm thinking out loud. Stuart broke a window, the dumb shit. But the alarm system was already off. So it could have been someone who had a key, who knew how to disarm the security system."

"Maybe the owners have someone who checks the house for them. So they have a key, know the code." She said it as if it was obvious.

Vince thought about that. "But if it was someone there with their blessing, why was he creeping around with the lights off?"

Jane shrugged. "I don't know, Vince. It's late." She cocked her head to one side, eyeing him critically. "You're so worried about them getting into that house and how somebody else got into the house and what they were looking for, blah blah blah, but are you even this much concerned about Stuart?" She held her thumb and index finger a fraction of an inch apart.

"Of course I am."

"Does Eldon even know yet?"

"No."

"When you going to tell him?"

Vince strummed his fingers on the table. "When the time is right. I got a few questions for him first."

"You're kidding me," Jane said. "Before you tell him about his kid, you're going to grill him?"

"Yeah. Like how'd Stuart know to pick that house? Eldon must have got sloppy and let him see the list."

"What list? Why are you so freaked-out about that house anyway?"

"Never mind. The fact Stuart was there goes right back to Eldon. He fucked up. Something about this is just not right."

"I don't know what you're talking about."

"Maybe Eldon was there. In the house. He was late for our meet tonight."

Jane put her fingertips to her forehead, looked downward. "Vince, really, are you saying Eldon shot his own kid?"

"No. I mean, I don't know what happened. Maybe Eldon was there, and didn't tell his kid, and they surprised each other."

"This is crazy talk," Jane said.

"Maybe Eldon was ripping me off," Vince said, more to himself than to Jane.

"How the hell could Eldon have been ripping you off? He wasn't in *your* house. He was in somebody *else's* house. So Eldon could shoot his own kid, then show up for this meet you had? That's what you're saying? Does Eldon strike you as someone who could pull that off?"

"I'm gonna find out. I guarantee it."

Jane pushed back her chair and stood. "Well, good luck with that." She turned and headed for the door.

"Wait," Vince said to her back. She stopped without turning around. "I just want to . . . I want to thank you for the heads-up. Grace calling you and then you letting me know, I want you to know, you did the right thing."

"What else was I going to do?" she said,

facing him now.

"I know, but still. I get that you're pissed, being dragged into this. I don't like you getting mixed up in my business, but this was different. I figured Grace'd tell you more than she'd tell me."

"You don't want me involved in your business?" Jane countered. "Since when? You think somehow I haven't always been involved? Come on. You were living with my mother. Then you guys got married. I was living under your roof. So maybe you didn't have me ripping off a shipment of iPads, but you think I wasn't involved? Every time my mom got a phone call, her heart was in her mouth, worried you were dead or in jail. Someone came knockin' at the door, I figured maybe it was the cops, or someone standing there with a gun, looking to blow your brains out. So don't be all sorry about my having to take Grace's call, because that was nothing compared to the kind of stuff I lived with for years."

Vince went to say something, but no words came out.

"I gotta go. It's late."

Vince took a step toward her. "Jane."

An exasperated sigh. "What?"

"This is . . . this isn't an easy time for me. You gotta know that."

"Whatever you say," she said.

"I know I've been kind of busy lately, that you and I, we haven't spent as much time together, but hey, you know, you've got your life, and there's all this other shit, with the doctor and —"

"Which doctor? What's the latest?"

"Nothing. Forget about that. The point is, I've been changing my whole operation this last couple of years, trying to be more creative."

"I thought you'd always been pretty creative," she said. "Hijacking trucks, stealing SUVs, shipping them overseas. That's pretty creative."

Vince didn't try to deny it. "But it's all labor intensive. I'm not as young as I used to be. And I've had . . . cash flow problems. But I'm turning things around."

"You think any of that has anything to do with why I'm pissed at you?" she snapped.

He said nothing. He just waited.

"Why didn't you go visit her?"

"I did," he said defensively.

"Oh, like twice?"

"That's not true, Jane, and you know it. I was into the hospital to see your mother regularly."

"But not that night. Where were you then?"

"I was on my way," he said. "I was going to come over. I was."

"Really? Something come up? You got delayed? I know where you were. Mike's." A Milford bar where Vince spent a lot of time. "If you'd tried to drive to the hospital in your condition, you'd have plowed right into the emergency ward."

"So I was at Mike's. Big deal."

"And what were you doing there?"

"Having a few drinks," he admitted. "I didn't know it was gonna happen that night."

"No, you didn't, because you hadn't gotten your ass in there for days to see how she was. If you had, you'd have seen how bad she was getting. You'd have known it was coming. I tried to tell you but you had your head up your ass and didn't hear me."

Vince mumbled something.

"What's that?"

"I couldn't."

"Couldn't what?"

"I couldn't see her like that. I just . . ." He stopped, took a breath as though he were winded. "I loved your mother very much. She was everything to me. Watching her suffer, watching her get worse every day, that was hard."

"Hard for her, too," Jane said.

"Why do you think I was at Mike's drinking myself into a stupor? Because I couldn't stand to lose her, that's why."

Jane's eyes were piercing. "Feeling sorry for yourself. You know what I never would have guessed all these years? That you were a pussy."

Vince glared at her. His cheeks flushed.

"Yeah, I said it. You didn't have the guts to be there. I mean, it's not like you haven't been around death all your life, is it? You don't mind causing it. You just don't want to see what it looks like."

"No one else talks that way to me and gets away with it, Jane."

She opened her arms, a "bring it on" gesture. "Take your best shot."

"Jesus, Jane," he said, and shifted closer to the table, put out a hand to steady himself. "I don't want to do this." He dropped his head, shook it slowly. "I know I've disappointed you. I don't blame you. I'm not the man you thought I was. I probably never was. I've lost your mother, and it looks like I've lost you now, too. I won't disappoint you much longer."

Jane started to respond, but something made her hang back.

"Besides," he said flippantly, "it's not like I'm really your father. You're not my real daughter. So what's the big deal, right?"

He tried to force a laugh, but it sent him into a coughing fit.

Jane hesitated. She was only a foot from the door, but it was hard to walk out on someone when he was in the middle of trying to catch his breath.

"You okay?" she asked.

"Yeah," he said. His cell phone started ringing. "I gotta get that."

"Sure."

He got out the phone, put it to his ear. "Yeah, Gordie . . . good . . . yeah . . . Hang on."

Vince said to Jane, "I got stuff I gotta take care of."

"Sure," she said. She turned, went out the screen door, and let it swing shut with a loud clap behind her.

Vince spoke into the phone. "Off the top of my head, I'm thinking it could be the dog walker. Braithwaite. The security pad was green. Someone used a key, knew the code. Keep doing the other checks, but I'm liking him for this. If other places got broken into, then it's not him. But if it's just the Cummings place, that's different. We'll pay him a visit tomorrow. He's living across the hall from Archer's wife. I'll give

285

you the address — you got something to
write it down?"

TWENTY-NINE

TERRY

I could have gone up to Grace's room, knocked on the door, and tried to calm the waters, but I had nothing left. If she wanted to stew about this for a while on her own, that was fine by me.

So I kept my ass in the kitchen chair.

Said to myself, *Shit shit goddamn motherfucking shit.*

Because that's what we were in. Right up to our goddamn necks.

Was I a fool to do what Vince had ordered me to do?

Probably.

Did I have a better idea about how to deal with this mess?

Not exactly.

Did Vince honestly believe he could keep the lid on this? Did he think he could make these problems disappear? Even if he could make Grace and me forget Stuart ever existed, did he think he could erase all evidence that the boy ever existed?

Had Stuart ceased to exist? And if he had, what the hell had actually happened to him? If he was dead, what had Vince done with him? What about the boy's father, Eldon? What was his reaction going to be? Maybe, just maybe, Grace and I could be counted on to keep our mouths shut, but Stuart's father? If his kid was dead, was he going to do whatever Vince wanted?

What was it about that house? Why was Vince going on about whether Stuart and Grace had plans to do anything besides stealing the Porsche? Why did he want to know if they'd been anywhere else but the basement and the main floor?

The man was rattled. If he didn't have a handle on what was going on, if he couldn't contain things, what would be the fallout for Grace later when everything came out? What price would she pay for not coming forward in the beginning?

And if whoever else was in that house believed Grace was a witness, and knew who she was and how to find her, was Grace safer going to the police and putting all her cards on the table?

Man oh man oh man, what a mess.

In the morning, I'd see a lawyer. Someone

288

I could tell all this to, with complete confidentiality. Lay it all out for him. See what our options were.

I couldn't imagine any of them were good.

As if all this were not enough, there was another matter.

Cynthia.

What the hell would all this do to her? Unless Vince really could bury this mess deeper than Captain Kidd's treasure, I was going to have to tell her everything. She deserved to know.

More than that, I *needed* her to know. Cynthia might be more high-strung and stressed-out than the next person, but she was still my rock, and I wasn't going to be able to get through this without her. And as much as Grace might want to keep her mom in the dark, she wasn't going to be able to get through this without her, either.

The question was when to bring her into the loop.

Not tonight. Definitely not tonight.

I went upstairs, stood in front of the bathroom sink, looked at myself in the mirror for a good minute before I remembered what I'd gone in there to do. I brushed my teeth, stripped down to my boxers, and crawled into the queen-sized bed that had felt far too empty the last few weeks.

I lay there staring at the ceiling for several minutes when I decided enough time had gone by that it was okay to check in on Grace. I got out of bed, threw on a bathrobe, and went down the hall to her room.

The door was ajar an inch and I pushed it open. Her light was off, but there was enough illumination coming through the window to see that she was in bed.

"I'm awake," she said.

"I figured," I said, perching myself on the edge of her bed.

"I don't think I can go to work tomorrow."

"I'll phone you in sick in the morning."

"Okay."

She brought an arm out from under the covers and held my arm.

"What about Mom?" Grace asked.

"I was just thinking about her."

"If it all comes out, and I have to, you know, go to jail or something, we'll have to tell her."

"I think we might have to bring her up to speed sooner than that," I said, smiled, and rubbed her arm.

"You think that's what'll happen? That I'll go to jail?"

"No," I said. "We won't let that happen. Let me ask you something."

Grace waited.

"What's your gut tell you?" I asked.

"About what?"

"About Stuart. Did you shoot him or not?"

She took a second to think about the question. "I didn't."

"What makes you say that?"

"I've been lying here thinking about it and thinking about it and thinking about it, you know?"

"Sure."

"It's the order of things."

I gave her arm a slight squeeze. "Go on."

"I did hear a shot. And all this time I've been wondering if I'm the one who did it. And when it happened, I screamed. But the shot came first. If I'd gotten scared and screamed, I might have done something dumb like pull the trigger when I was all freaked out about something. But I didn't freak out *until* I'd heard a shot."

"You remember anything else?"

Her head bounced back and forth on the pillow. "I don't think so."

"You going to be okay here or do you want to come into my room?"

"I'll give it a few minutes. If I can't sleep, I'll come in."

"Okay," I said. I was going to tell her my

thoughts on getting a lawyer, then decided against it. I leaned in and kissed her forehead. "We'll get through this." I hesitated. "We need a couple of new rules."

"Yeah, I know. I'm grounded forever. I figured that."

"I'm not talking about that exactly. I mean, you need to be, you know, careful. Paying attention. About answering the door, who you talk to online, like if somebody new wants to meet you or —"

"What are you talking about?"

I didn't want to upset her. God knows she was going to have a hard enough time sleeping as things were now.

I searched for words that didn't sound too alarmist. "He — whoever bumped into you — might think you saw him."

"But I didn't."

"But what I'm saying is, he might not know that."

Her eyes sharpened as she grasped my meaning. "Shit."

"Yeah."

"If Stuart's dead, and if this guy in the house did it —"

"Yeah," I said again.

"But how would he even know who I am?" Grace asked.

"He might not. But he might figure it out."

She sat up in bed and put her arms around me. "I'm scared, Daddy."

I held her tight. "Me, too. But you're safe here, right now, with me. I'm not going to let anything happen to you."

Grace buried her face against my chest, her words coming out muffled. "I didn't see him. I didn't see anything. I didn't."

"I know. We're going to get through this."

I held her like that for a good five minutes before she let go and put her head back down on the pillow.

"You come get me if you need me," I said, easing off the bed.

"I will. I'm okay."

I slipped out of her room, leaving the door slightly ajar so I could hear her if she called.

As I expected, I didn't sleep. At least not until around five in the morning, when I finally dozed off. But I was awake again before seven, and couldn't see the point in staying in bed. I got up, showered, dressed, and on my way down to the kitchen peeked into Grace's room to see whether she was asleep.

She was not in her bed.

Her bathroom was directly across the hall, but the door was open. She wasn't in there.

"Grace?" I called out.

"Down here," she said.

She was sitting at the kitchen table. Just sitting there. Not eating breakfast, not doing anything. Just sitting there in the over-sized T-shirt she liked to sleep in. She was bleary eyed, and it looked as though she'd done her hair in a wind tunnel. Not that I looked any better.

"You gave me a start," I said. "How long you been sitting there?"

She glanced up at the clock on the wall. "Since around five."

She must have come down after I'd finally fallen asleep. Otherwise I would have heard her moving about.

"I've got something to say," Grace said.

I looked at her. "Okay."

"I don't care what Vince says. I don't care what he said to you. And I don't care what happens to me." She paused, took a breath. "I have to know."

And with that she got up, sidled past me, and went back upstairs to her room.

THIRTY

Eldon Koch was asleep when he heard banging on the door.

He and his boy, Stuart, lived in an apartment above an appliance repair shop on Naugatuck Avenue. The entrance was up a flight of stairs that ran up the side of the building.

He opened his eyes, looked at the digital clock, saw that it was nearly seven a.m. He figured it was Stuart, that somehow he'd lost his keys and needed him to open the door. It wasn't unusual for Stuart to be gone all night, or even for a day or two. If he'd lost his keys, that meant Eldon's second car, the old Buick, was out there somewhere. So Eldon would have to find his spare set and the two of them would have to head back out there, pick it up, and bring it back.

Unless Stuart was drunk. There was every

reason to think he'd come home pissed, or stoned.

Eldon believed he'd done the best he could with the kid, but Jesus Christ on a hubcap, you could spend your whole life trying to teach a fish to operate a backhoe but at some point you had to face the fact that some goals were unachievable. Maybe, when Stuart got older, he'd develop some common sense. Eldon could only hope. Raising a kid on your own was no picnic. Maybe his wife was the smart one, running off when Stuart was only five. She ended up getting killed six years after that in a motorcycle accident, riding on the back of a Harley somewhere north of San Francisco, but at least she had those six years of no responsibility. He kind of envied her for that, even if she did end up leaving an imprint of herself on a bridge abutment.

"Hold on!" he shouted. "You lose your damn keys again?"

He threw back the covers, stood up in his boxers, took a second to get over the dizziness he felt when he got up quickly, then slid his feet into a pair of threadbare red-and-black-plaid slippers. He shuffled out of the bedroom and crossed the combined living room/kitchen. There was a man silhouetted in the window of the door, the morning sun rising behind him.

Didn't look like Stuart, but Eldon wasn't sure. The man continued banging.

"I said hold on!"

He got to the door, turned back the dead bolt, and swung it open.

"Oh," he said, squinting, blinded by the sunlight. "Hey, Vince."

"Eldon," Vince Fleming said. He was wearing a puffy Windbreaker zipped up halfway and holding a takeout tray in his left hand with two coffees in it. "Got something to help wake you up. Four sugars, right?"

"Yeah. What's going on?"

"You gonna invite me in?"

"Shit, yeah, sure." He opened the door wide and Vince, one hand in his jacket pocket, stepped in. "What's going on? Everything okay?"

"We've got a situation, Eldon. Hopin' you can help me with it."

Eldon blinked a few more times, his eyes adjusting to daylight as Vince stepped into the kitchen area. He put down the tray and handed Eldon his coffee. The nearly naked man took it awkwardly in two hands.

"A situation?" He looked back out the door, but he couldn't see down to the parking lot from up here, not without going out

297

onto the landing. "Gordie and Bert with you?"

"No. They've been busy all night. Still going at it. Everything work out with you last night?"

"Huh? Yeah. I took care of the money. Came home after that. If something was going on, you shoulda called me."

"That's okay."

"So what's this situation?" He was still holding the coffee, hadn't taken a sip. Vince had removed the lid from his, was blowing on it.

"Damage control," Vince said.

"What?"

"Yeah. They're checking on all our locations. We got hit last night, Eldon."

The man's jaw dropped. "Fuck, no. You gotta be kidding."

"I wish."

"That's bad. That's really bad."

"No shit. Sit down, Eldon."

Eldon set the coffee down on the small table in front of the couch. Vince had left his in the takeout container back on the counter. "Why don't I get dressed first. I can be ready in a couple of secs." The man looked vulnerable, standing there in his boxers and ratty slippers.

"No, have a seat."

298

Eldon took the couch while Vince struggled to lower himself into a low, swoopy Ikea chair.

"You're not curious about where we got hit?" Vince asked.

"Of course. I was just about to ask."

"The Cummings house."

"Whoa," Eldon said. "You're talking two hundred thou in there, plus incidentals. Fuck, Vince, that's not a hit. That's a catastrophe."

"Yeah, it is."

"Whose money is that? That the bank manager from Stamford? Took him three years to embezzle it? He's thinking about heading off to the Caymans, but he might be wanting that money soon. He's not gonna be happy."

Vince shook his head. "No. Whose money it is doesn't matter. The fact that it's gone is what matters."

"Was it just the one place?"

"Like I said, we're checking."

"We shouldn't be sitting here," Eldon said. "We need to get out there."

Vince shook his head, raised a palm to get Eldon to stay put. "What's interesting about last night is, it looks like the Cummings place got hit twice."

"Huh?"

"Yeah. Twice in one night. Looks like one party was already there when the second one arrived."

Eldon Koch looked baffled. "I don't get that. Like, did they know each other? Were they working together?"

"Not sure. Looks like someone got in the regular way. With a key and a code. Then someone else came along and broke in through a basement window, didn't know they could have walked through the front door and not set off the alarm."

Eldon continued to look mystified. Suddenly, he snapped his fingers and pointed a finger at his boss. "The dog walker could have got in the regular way."

"Maybe," Vince said. "That was my first thought."

"He's got a key. He knows the code. That's one of his houses."

"Maybe," Vince said again.

"What?" Eldon asked. "What you thinking?"

"You were late getting to the meet last night."

"Huh?"

"At the motel. You were late."

"I told you, I'm sorry," Eldon said. "I let Stuart take the Buick, and that left me the Golf. Thing wouldn't start for me. Had to

300

fiddle around with it to get it running. If I'd had a brain, I'd have given Stuart the Golf, let him deal with it, but I think Stuart was seeing some girl, and the Buick, well, it's got more space in it, you know?" He grinned amiably. "More make-out room, right? Shit, I was young once. I know what that's like, so I let him take it. The Buick, it's a tank — thing won't die. I really am sorry. I meant to be there on time."

"Once you got the Golf started, you make any stops on the way to the motel?"

"No, I floored it. Shit, you have to floor it just to make it go. I went straight to the meet. What's going on, Vince? Why you asking me questions like this? You got a beef with me? Okay, I was late. I'm sorry. It won't happen again. But what's that got to do with us getting hit?"

"Where do you keep the list?"

"Huh?"

"Stop saying that, Eldon. It's annoying."

"You want to know about the list? Where I keep it?"

Vince sighed. "Yes. That's what I'd like to know."

"I never put it on the computer, like you said. I keep things up-to-date in my notebook. You tell me stuff, and I write it down in there."

"Where's the notebook?"

"Right this second, it's in my pants," he said.

"Get it."

Eldon got off the couch, his slippers making swishing noises as he walked into his bedroom. Vince heard pocket change jangling as Eldon picked his jeans off the floor. He returned in a few seconds, notebook in hand, and sat back down on the couch.

"See?" he said, handing it over to Vince.

Vince opened it, flipped through the pages.

"You always have this thing on you?"

Eldon shrugged. " 'Cept maybe when I'm writing in it. I might set it down or something at the shop."

The auto body shop that served not only as Vince's headquarters, but as a business front to funnel through some of his funds.

"So you might leave it around where someone could pick it up and look at it. What about here, in the apartment? You ever leave it sitting out?"

"Jesus, Vince, where is this — ?"

"Just answer the question, Eldon."

There was fear in Eldon's eyes for the first time. "Um, maybe. But it wouldn't matter. Only one ever here is Stuart. You could ask him, but I don't think he's come home yet."

Eldon glanced at the closed door to his son's bedroom. "I could check."

"Don't bother," Vince said. "You tell your kid how you keep track of things?"

Eldon scratched his head. "I . . . He asked me one time about the addresses. I told him I take one off each number, how 264 Main Street would be 153, and like that. It was just father-son stuff, you know?"

"And the dates?"

Eldon swallowed. "I told him it was the same thing. Like, say, March tenth to twentieth would be February ninth to nineteenth. Like we worked out. But Jesus, Vince, are you thinking Stuart would try to rip us off? There's no way. Even if he looked at my book, he wouldn't have a key."

"Where are your keys right now?" Vince asked.

"They're right in the bedroom where —" He stopped. He sprung to his feet, went back in there. "I always leave 'em . . . Okay, I usually leave them on the table right here next to the bed." He emerged from the bedroom with a single key. "I got the one for the house I had to get into last night."

"Where are the rest?"

Slowly, he said, "I guess they're at the shop."

Vince smiled. "Not really an issue anyway.

303

That's not how Stuart got in. He busted a basement window."

"Oh, goddamn!" Eldon made a fist and brought it down on his knee, hard. "Are you kidding me? That stupid little shit! I'll beat his fuckin' head in." His face, angry, suddenly shifted to concern. He jumped up again, strode into his bedroom, came back with a cell phone. He stood behind the couch and entered a number, put the phone to his ear.

"I'll get him here," he told Vince. "You wait. I'll get the little bastard here right now and we'll sort this out. I can't believe it. The stupid bastard."

Vince waited while Eldon listened to Stuart's phone ring.

"Pick up, you little pisser. Shit! Voice mail. Hey, where the fuck are you? You get your ass home right now! Now!"

He ended the call, shook his head in frustration.

Waited.

"I can't believe he'd — Wait. Shit, how do you know this? How do you know he actually did this?" Alarm washed over his face. "Cops? Shit, did the cops pick him up?"

"No."

"Then what? How? Maybe you've got it wrong. There's no way he'd do this. He

304

respects you, Vince. He may be dumber than a bag of hammers, but he respects you — he does."

"I don't think he was there for the money," Vince said calmly. "He knew about the Porsche in the garage. He broke in to find the keys, go for a joyride."

Eldon almost looked relieved. "That's all?"

"No. Not by a long shot. Even if all he wanted was car keys, he must have known, from reading your notebook when it wasn't safely stored away in your fucking pants, when the Cummings would be away. So he thought it'd be a safe time to break in, get the keys, have some fun."

"Okay, the kid's an idiot. I don't know what to say. I'll talk to him. We'll make this right. What'd he do? Confess? Was he there when somebody else ripped us off? He try to stop them, and figured he had to tell you what went down? Vince, come on, I need to know."

"If Stuart could get a look at the book, who else might have seen it?" Vince asked. "Who might he have told? About which houses were on the list? About when people were away? About which houses had security systems and which ones didn't? About where the stuff was stashed in the house?"

Eldon furiously shook his head. "Nobody.

305

Look, do you know where he is? You've got him, right? Is he with Gordie? Bert?"

"Sit back down, Eldon."

The man came around the front of the couch, sat, leaned forward, elbows on knees.

"What aren't you telling me, Vince?"

Vince paused. "I want you to listen carefully. I'm going to tell you how we're going to do this."

The color started to drain from Eldon's face. "What are you talking about?"

"You're going to tell people — anyone who happens to ask — that he's gone away for a while."

"What are you talking about?"

"Does Stuart go back to school in September? Or'd he drop out when he turned sixteen?"

"He says he's not going back, but I've been telling him he has to stay in school. He wants to make anything of himself, he has to stay."

"So if he doesn't return, that's not going to surprise anyone."

Eldon appeared to be suffering from some kind of tremor, his head moving back and forth by tiny degrees, almost too fast to see. "No, no."

"There'll be cell records. You'll get calls from his phone, from across the country, while he sees the good old U.S. of A. Anyone asks, you can tell them about the places he's been. How this was something he talked about doing for a long time, hitching across this great country. We'll arrange cash withdrawals from ATMs to match. Here and there."

"Stop, Vince. Please stop."

"So there'll be a record. You understand the importance of that. And then, one day, you'll stop hearing from him. Maybe the last call will be from California, or Oregon. Someplace like that. So that's where the police will start looking for him. By then, the trail will be so cold, it won't ever lead back here, to the business we run."

"No."

"Is that a no, you won't go along with that?" Vince asked. "Or is it just difficult for the realization to sink in?" His tone softened, and he extended a hand, close to Eldon's knee, but he could not bring himself to touch him. "He put all of us in a very difficult spot."

"You didn't do it. Tell me you didn't do it."

"I didn't. Someone else. And we're gonna find out who. Bert and Gordie and me, we're going to do that, for you. We're gonna find who killed your boy and make them pay — you can count on that."

Eldon's chin quivered.

"But where Stuart was when this went down, that creates a significant problem for us. We couldn't have the Cummings return home to find a body in their kitchen. Nor could we move him someplace and let him be found. There'd be questions. Things that'd be hard to explain to the cops. Stuart had his faults, but I know you loved him. I understand that. I know what it is to lose a child. I got an idea what you're going through. But I also see what has to be done. This son of a bitch who killed your boy, that's also the son of a bitch who took our money. Money that was entrusted to us. Left in our care. That all complicates things, Eldon. That's why I need to know I can count on you. I need to know that you're going to —"

"Where is he?" Eldon asked, the words coming out in a whisper.

"Eldon, we've looked after it."

Eldon stood, took a step toward Vince, pointed a trembling finger at him. "You son of a bitch. You're telling me my son is dead, and you don't have the decency to let me have one last look at him?"

"Things have been moving very quickly."

"I want to see him! I want to see my son!

You fuck! Where is Stuart?"

Vince wanted to get out of the chair, not have this man towering over him, but the chair, the way it sloped back, it was going to be an effort and a half to get the hell out of it.

"I told you, we've looked after him."

Eldon stared incredulously at him. His voice went low. "Tell me you didn't take him to the farm."

"Eldon."

"Tell me you didn't feed him to the pigs. Tell me you did not feed my boy to the pigs."

"I gotta get out of this fucking chair." Vince gripped the wooden arms, tried to pull himself forward, gain some leverage. But suddenly Eldon placed the flat of his hand on Vince's chest and shoved. Vince fell back, the front of the chair springing up for a second, the whole thing nearly toppling over.

"Eldon, you need to calm the fuck down."

"You miserable sack of shit. Do you feel *anything*? How could you do that?" He kept jabbing a finger in the air in front of his boss's face. "I bet it was you. All this talk about someone else being in that house. I bet it was you."

"No."

"This whole thing of yours, this plan to safeguard other people's money. It's all a scam, isn't it? The whole thing. You sucker these dumb, scared bastards into leaving their stash with you, and you've just been waiting until you've got enough. Then you're going to help yourself to all of it. One day, Gordie and Bert and me come to work and you're fucking gone, and then when these assholes drop by to get their money back, we're left with nothing but our dicks in our hands. Is that what Stuart figured out? Did he catch you in the act? Is that why you killed him?"

Spit was flying out of his mouth as he ranted. Vince glared at a drop on the sleeve of his Windbreaker.

"Is that how it went down?" Eldon continued. "Stuart broke in to steal a car and find you there? All these questions, asking me where I was, why I was late — that's all bullshit, isn't it? An act. You fuck."

"You shouldn't say things like that," Vince said. "Any other time, you talking to me like that, that'd be something I couldn't forgive. But I'm going to make some allowances. You've suffered a loss. You're in shock."

Eldon wasn't done. "You've been running on empty for too long. You're an old man.

You're sick and you're dying and you don't know what the hell you're doing anymore. But I've stuck by you, because you know why? Because loyalty means something, that's why. But it only goes so far. You feed a man's son to the pigs, you can't expect him to have your back any longer."

Eldon turned, started walking toward the bedroom, giving Vince time to gather up enough momentum to pitch himself forward out of the chair.

"What are you doing?" Vince asked. He rested his hand on the back of the couch, gripped the cushion in his fingers.

"Getting dressed," Eldon shot back.

"What are you going to do?"

The man was pulling on his jeans, doing up his belt. "I guess you'll find out soon enough."

"I'm sorry about your boy," Vince said. He pulled a cushion off the back of the couch with his left hand, reached into his jacket with his right.

Eldon was reaching across the bed for his shirt, his back turned, when Vince came into the bedroom.

"You're not sorry about anything, you asshole. You're not capable of it."

When he was less than two feet away, Vince raised the cushion, pushed the barrel

311

of the gun into it, and fired. It still made a noise, no question. All Vince cared about was that it not be heard outside the apartment, and on that score he thought he was reasonably safe.

The bullet caught Eldon below the right shoulder blade. He fell forward onto the bed.

"Shit!" he yelled.

Vince moved quickly. He forced himself on top of the man, held the pillow over his head, and fired a second time. Eldon thrashed briefly, then stopped.

"You're wrong," Vince whispered. "I am sorry. More than you could know."

Vince crawled off, breathing heavily as he did so. He put the gun back into his jacket. His joints felt stiff and his gut was sore. There was something warm and damp on his leg. He worried, for half a second, that somehow he'd shot himself. There was a dark spot on his upper thigh, just below his crotch.

All the sudden physical activity had caused his bag to leak. The tape that held it in place had come loose.

"Goddamn it," he said under his breath.

He went into the bathroom to tend to himself as best he could. When he was done, he washed his hands and looked wearily at his reflection over the sink. He hadn't shaved since the day before, hadn't slept all night.

Had to do it, he told himself.

He was tucking his shirt back into his pants and zipping up when he heard someone rapping sharply on the apartment door.

"Hello?"

A man's voice, muffled, coming through the glass.

Vince froze, worried any move he made might be heard.

"Hello! Is Stuart home? I'm looking for Stuart Koch!"

Carefully, Vince moved his head around the corner of the door far enough to get one eye on the entrance to the apartment. The blinds weren't closed, and the man had put his face tight to the glass, cupped his hands around his eyes to see into the apartment.

Vince was able to make out who it was.

Some people just don't listen.

Vince was confident the man at the door would not be able to see into Eldon's bedroom from that vantage point. But then the man did something that could change all that. He was trying the door to see whether it was locked.

Which it was not.

Vince watched the doorknob slowly turn, and reached into his jacket again for his gun.

THIRTY-ONE

TERRY

Fuck Vince Fleming.

It wasn't a point of view I'd come to right away. It grew on me. After Grace stated, quite clearly, that she had to know what happened, I had to make a decision about whose interests were more important.

I chose Grace.

I chose Grace because I loved her, of course, but also because, at that moment, I realized how brave she was. She wasn't going to crawl into bed and pull the covers up over her head. She was willing to face the consequences, and in the few short hours since this mess had begun, I'd started to feel it was the only way we were going to get through this.

It might also be the only way to save her. If Grace was perceived by someone out there to be a witness, getting to the bottom of this mess might expose who that person was.

But still.

Vince was formidable, and going against him was not going to be easy. I'd have to watch my back, try to find out as much as I could without his knowing it. And I didn't exactly have a plan for dealing with whatever it was I might learn.

"You going to be okay here if I go out and ask a few questions?" I asked Grace. She was in the bathroom, door open, brushing her teeth.

"Yeah," she said. "I'll phone work and book off sick. You don't have to do it. I'll do my best sick voice. I know I'll do something really stupid in the kitchen if I go in. Set someone on fire, drop a pot of lobsters, something, because I won't be able to concentrate."

"And I may need to talk to you," I said. "Best that you're here." I hit my forehead with the heel of my hand, remembering that this was the day the cleaning lady came. "Shit, Teresa."

"When does she usually show up?" Grace asked.

"In the mornings. Usually no one's home and she just lets herself in. If you want, I can call and cancel her."

She shook her head. "No, it's okay."

I asked Grace if she had continued to try reaching Stuart on his cell phone.

"Yeah, and I texted him, too. Nothing."

I decided I'd start with Milford Hospital. It was going to be the first place we would have checked last night after leaving the Cummings house, so it seemed like the logical place to begin this morning.

I gave Grace a kiss good-bye and headed out, but not before going over the new rules. She didn't answer the door for anyone she didn't know. She left the alarm on. She'd stay off all her social sites. No chatting with anyone.

"Got it," she said, and saluted.

The hospital is right downtown and getting to it took less time than finding a place to park there. I went in the main entrance and approached reception, where a woman was tapping away on a keyboard.

"Can I help you?" she asked.

"I'm looking for someone who might have been admitted last night," I said. "I wanted to see how he was doing."

"Name?"

"Stuart Koch." I spelled the last name for her.

She entered the name and studied the monitor. She asked me for the spelling of

Stuart, which I knew because he had once been my student. If I'd had to guess, I'd have spelled it with an "ew" in the middle.

She frowned. "I don't see anything. When would this have been?"

"Last night around ten. Maybe closer to eleven."

"And what was he brought in for?"

I hesitated. I almost said he'd been shot. But if it turned out Stuart wasn't here, a comment like that was going to open a can of worms, maybe prompt this woman to call the police.

So I said, "I think it was some kind of head injury. Tripped or something."

She reached for her phone, waited a few seconds, then said, "D'you guys treat a patient named Koch last night? Would have come in after ten, possible head injury? Yeah, well, just double-check. Okay, then."

She hung up the phone and gave me an apologetic look. "I'm sorry, but we've got no one by that name. Are you sure he was brought here?"

"I thought so," I said.

"I'd tell you to check with the walk-in clinic, but they close up at seven thirty. If your friend got hurt later than that, I don't know where else he would have gone but here."

"Thanks for your time," I said.

On the way back to the car I phoned Grace.

"No luck at the hospital. You heard anything?"

"Nope."

"Okay. You know where Stuart lives?"

"I've never been there, but I can look it up. Can you hang on?"

I said I could. I could hear her typing away, looking up an address.

"I found it," she said. She gave me an address. "Let me just check it on Whirl360." The Web site that gave you an actual image of any location. Some more clicking. "Okay, he told me he lived on top of some kind of repair shop or something and I'm looking at it right now. It's called Dietrich's Appliance Repair. There's stairs on the side of the building. I think they go up to his apartment."

I was pretty sure I knew the place. I'd driven past it many times. "Can you see Stuart's car there, on the computer?" I asked.

"Dad," Grace said wearily, "it's not a *live* shot. Duh."

"Right, okay. I'll get back to you."

I got back into the Escape and headed for Naugatuck Avenue. It didn't take long to find Dietrich's. I parked across the street, got out, and surveyed the surroundings. It was a stretch of residences and businesses. There was a parking lot next to Dietrich's that served a short stretch of stores on the other side. The lot was nearly empty. An old VW Golf, a pickup truck, but no huge Buick from decades past.

It was, after all, still very early. The odd car that drove past held someone going to work or school. A lot of people probably weren't even up yet. I hated to bang on someone's door at this hour, but this was one of those times when not all niceties could be observed.

I crossed the street and mounted the open-backed stairs that ran up the side of the building, not unlike the steps up to the second floor of Vince's beach house on East Broadway. When I got to the top, I rapped on the door.

"Hello?"

I waited a few seconds, then tried again.

"Hello! Is Stuart home? I'm looking for Stuart Koch!"

Blinds hung over the window, but they weren't turned shut. I put my face to the glass and shielded my eyes with my hands to keep out the sun.

The kitchen and living area made up the

room that I could see. Two doors on the far wall that were probably bedrooms or a bathroom. No sign of anyone, but Stuart or his father could still be here asleep.

Maybe they couldn't hear me shouting through the door.

I decided it wouldn't exactly be breaking and entering if all I did was open the door and stick my head in.

If the door was unlocked.

I tried the knob, and it turned. So I opened it about a foot and leaned my head into the apartment.

"Hello?" I called out. "Anyone home?"

No response.

"Stuart?"

I knew, from experience, that it could take a lot of noise to wake a sleeping teenager. Someone had to be here. People didn't head off for the day without locking the door.

So I opened the door wider, and stepped inside.

THIRTY-TWO

"What'd you end up doing last night?" Bryce Withers asked as he walked naked from the bed into the bathroom.

Jane Scavullo mumbled something into her pillow.

"What's that?" he said.

She forced herself to roll over, taking a tangle of covers with her, so he could hear her. "Just stuff."

"Stuff?"

"Yeah. Nothin' much. How'd it go last night?"

"This is working into a good gig," Bryce said. "So many bars these days, they don't even want to pay the band. But they're giving us five hundred a night, so that's a hundred bucks apiece. And all the drinks we want." He chuckled. "The other guys, I think they'd still do it just for the drinks, but we deserve to get paid. I told you about that other place? They got in touch, invited us to play on Friday and Saturday nights, and I said how much and they said two hundred. And I said, man, we can't afford to play a gig for two hundred bucks, have to split that five ways, and the guy says no, no, he was going to charge *us* two hundred to play there. Said it would be good exposure for us, we'd end up getting other gigs through him. If he'd been standing in front of me, I'd've kicked his fucking teeth in, I swear to God. The whole world's turning fucking upside down, thinks the talent should always work for nothing."

"Hmm," Jane said without enthusiasm.

"I got in around two and you were, like, totally comatose. So you did nothing? You weren't here all night, were you?"

"No," she said.

"What'd you do?"

"Saw Vince." Soon as she said it, she regretted it.

"That son of a bitch?" Bryce said. "I thought you weren't talking to him."

"I don't want to go over this again. And don't talk about him like that. It's okay for me to do it but not you."

"I'm just saying. He wasn't there for your mother when she was, you know, when all that shit was going down with her. And then you got screwed over on the house you thought she was leaving to you. He's an asshole — that's all I'm trying to say."

He came back into the bedroom and sat on the edge of the bed on Jane's side. He put a hand on her head, stroked her hair.

"I just want you to know I'm looking out for you. If he's not going to give a shit, I am."

"Don't worry about me," Jane said.

"So why'd you go and see him anyway?"

"He had a problem he wanted me to help him with."

Bryce twitched. "What kind of problem?"

"Just . . . something to do with his work. And this girl, a friend of mine. She ran into some trouble and it's sort of connected to Vince. So I ended up at his place."

Bryce twitched again and said, "What girl?"

"It's a long story, Bryce. I just need some sleep."

"I'm just curious. Was it Melanie? That one who got in touch with you?"

"No, not Melanie. Her name was Grace. Grace Archer. Her dad used to be my teacher, long time ago."

"Oh yeah," Bryce said. "You've mentioned him. The one who was nice to you. Isn't he the one whose wife had all that weird shit happen to her back when she was a kid or something?"

"Please stop talking." Jane tried to fold the edges of the pillow over her ears.

"Why'd this Grace chick want to talk to you? What was her problem and what did it have to do with Vince?"

Jane opened her eyes wide, threw her arms down on the bed, and said, "How come you're Mr. Twenty Questions this morning? Jesus."

He pulled his hand away from stroking her hair. "You don't have to bite my fucking head off. I'm just trying to be interested."

"Since when?" Jane asked. "You hardly ever ask me anything, except when it has to do with Vince and how you think he's fucked me over. Well, that's my problem and not yours, so you can stop worrying about it."

"I know he doesn't like me," Bryce said. "He got something against musicians? Is that it?"

"The whole world doesn't revolve around you, you know," she said.

He stood. "Fine. Let me know when you're not all PMSing and maybe we can have a normal conversation."

"Oh, good one," she said. "Every time I get pissed with you it's because of that and not because you're being a total asshole."

325

He went back into the bathroom and closed the door. Seconds later, she heard water running in the shower.

It was going so well for a while there, she thought. But ever since they'd moved in together, Bryce had started evolving into a total douche.

Always asking her about Vince. What he did, how he made his money, whether he'd ever actually killed anybody. Did what Vince did freak him out, or at some level did he think it was kind of cool?

She looked at the clock. Nearly eight. She was supposed to be at her job at nine thirty.

God. A lot to accomplish in the next hour and a half.

Maybe, if she lay here for just another five minutes, she wouldn't feel so terrible. She hadn't had much sleep. The events of the previous evening had left her unnerved.

Her thoughts were interrupted by the sound of a low-level buzz. She'd muted her phone, but it was still on vibrate, and sitting on her bedside table, it still made enough noise to be heard.

A text or an e-mail. Probably from work.

She reached over for the phone, looked at the screen.

Nothing.

She rolled over in bed, saw that Bryce had

left his phone on the table on his side of the bed.

She wasn't feeling particularly kindly toward him at this moment. Not kindly enough to let him know he had a message.

But then again, it might be something important, so she worked her way across to the other side of the king bed and reached for the phone.

It was a text message.

It had been sent by Bryce's friend Hartley, one of the other members of the band, which was called Energy Drink.

If there was a worse name for a band, Jane couldn't think what it might be. She worked in advertising now and had a feel for this kind of thing. But would Bryce listen?

She read the text.

It said: GIG WENT GOOD. SORRY U HAD TO BAIL. HOPE YOUR FEELING BETTER. LET US KNOW ASAP IF YOU CANT MAKE IT TONITE.

THIRTY-THREE

"I think it'll all come together before the day's over, Unk."

"You're the best, Reggie. You're the only one I should ever have talked to about this. You're the only one I can admit to what a fool I've been. Trusting that boy. Eli. I gave him work, helped him out. His roommates, they threw him out, you know. But I saw something of myself in that boy."

"He was no boy, Unk. He was a man."

"I suppose, but . . . I don't know. He was a kid who'd gotten the short end of the stick all his life. Parents never gave a shit about him. He'd had to fend for himself for a long time."

"A little too well, you ask me."

"You're right. I know that. But I never thought, giving him some work, helping him out, that he would turn against me. Me and Eli, we'd sit and talk in the evening. I ended up telling him all about her. All these stories

I've told you. Too damn much. One night, I guess I had a little too much to drink, and I told him what I'd done. Stupid, I was just stupid."

"He paid for his betrayal, Unk. He got what he deserved."

"Other than him, the only person I've ever confided in, is you. You know my secrets."

"And you know mine, Unk."

"You should have told me sooner. Just how much of a monster my brother was. At first I thought, after your mom died, raising you on his own would make him a better man, a good father."

"A good father doesn't expect his daughter to fulfill all the responsibilities of a wife. You've been the father I was meant to have, ever since you took me in when I was fourteen."

"I've never told a soul, you know."

"There's nothing to tell. There was a fire in the barn. The man died. End of story."

"About Eli, do you think he told Quayle it was me? When he tried to make the deal with him?"

"He told us no. If Eli had told Quayle everything, you'd have heard from him by now. I guarantee it."

"I hate that man. There are no words. I hate him with every fiber of my being."

"I know, Unk. He did a terrible thing to you when he took her away. But you got the last laugh."

"I suppose."

"Sit tight. This is the day we're all going to get what's coming to us."

THIRTY-FOUR

TERRY

I took three steps into the Koch apartment, leaving the door open behind me, stopped, and took the place in. I guess I was expecting a dump. After all, this was a father and son living over an appliance repair shop with no woman on the scene. I remembered, from when Stuart was my student, that his mother was absent. I never knew whether she'd walked out on them, had passed away, or what. Any efforts I'd made to get Eldon in for a parent-teacher night failed. Back then, I wrote him off as a father who didn't give a shit, and I might still have been right about that. But after my most recent chat with Vince, I now knew who Stuart's father was. It was possible he didn't want to come in and discuss his son's progress with someone he'd once grabbed off the street and tossed into the back of an SUV. Maybe he thought it was just possible I might hold a grudge against a student whose father had kidnapped me.

The apartment, though, was tidy. No dishes in the sink, no mess on the counter, aside from a cardboard takeout tray with one coffee in it. There were no clothes tossed about here and there. An Xbox and games were tucked neatly on a shelf below the television. There were some framed pictures on the wall, one in particular that caught my eye, a Sears-style portrait of Eldon, Stuart at about three years of age, and a woman I presumed was his mother. They all wore the pasted-on smiles we adopt for those kinds of shots.

Maybe being here wasn't such a good idea.

It wasn't quite as risky as what I'd done the night before. Crawling through a busted basement window, wandering through a house of people I didn't know, opening closet doors, snooping through every room. That was a new experience for me.

Stepping into an unlocked apartment without an invitation wasn't quite as serious a transgression, particularly when you considered I was looking for someone who lived here. But if someone came up those stairs behind me right now, I'd have a tricky time explaining myself. I could tell them the door was open, that I wasn't here to rob the place, but would they believe me?

Would Eldon take kindly to finding me here? It was a safe bet Vince wouldn't.

I decided to call out one last time, loud enough, I hoped, to wake the dead.

"Stuart! It's Terry Archer! Grace's dad! I just came by to see if you were okay."

Nothing.

I stood there another few seconds. Something made me reach over to the coffee in the takeout tray.

It was still warm.

There was a second cup on the table in front of the couch. I stepped over, wrapped my hand around it long enough to determine that it was as warm as the cup on the counter.

So someone had gone out for coffees, or arrived with them, but then not hung around long enough to drink them. Did that make any sense at all? It meant there'd been two people in this apartment in the last few minutes, and that something had prompted them to leave so quickly they hadn't bothered to take their drinks with them.

Or lock the apartment door.

Did this mean Stuart was alive? He'd shown up with two coffees — a peace offering for his father, maybe — but then they'd both immediately left? Maybe Stuart told his father what had happened, and they were on their way to the house he'd broken into last night?

God, I had no idea.

And I wasn't going to learn anything just standing here. So I backed out of the apartment, stood on the landing at the top of the stairs, and closed the door.

Maybe they'd come back. I decided to wait a few more minutes, but not up here at the top of the stairs. I walked back down, crossed the street, and got into my car. It was starting to get warm, so I turned the key far enough to let me get the windows down.

Sat there.

Pondered my next move.

If no one showed up here, I didn't really have one. If Stuart's fate couldn't be determined, I didn't know what else to do but proceed with the lawyer route. We needed to know where we stood, to be ready for anything that might happen.

I turned on the radio, listened to the news, traffic reports.

Wasted nearly ten minutes.

I was about to turn the key when my cell phone rang. I glanced at it, saw that it was HOME calling, and answered.

"Grace?"

"Hi, Dad. Did you find Stuart?"

"No, sweetheart. If I had, I'd've called you."

"I thought, maybe, if you'd found him, but he was, you know . . . you'd wait till you got home to tell me."

"I haven't found him, one way or another. I dropped by his place, but there's no one here. Not him, or his dad."

"Okay." She paused. "This is probably nothing."

I felt a small chill run the length of my spine. "What, honey?"

"There's this guy parked across the street, kind of down a bit."

A chill instantly ran down my spine.

"Okay," I said slowly, trying to keep the anxiety out of my voice. "What about him?"

"I was in my bedroom, looking out the window, but just through the crack in the drapes, you know?"

"Yeah."

"So I don't think he saw me."

"What are you saying? Is he looking at the house?"

"That's the thing. I'm not sure. But he's kind of looking this way."

I turned on the car. "Hang on," I said. "The Bluetooth thing is kicking in. Okay, you're on speaker."

"Can you hear me?" Grace said.

"Yeah," I said, setting the cell phone down on the seat next to me and pulling the seat belt across my body. I put the car in drive and hit the gas.

"You there?" Grace asked.

"I'm on my way," I said. "Five minutes tops."

"Like I said, it might be nothing. I'm just kind of on edge, you know? Especially after what you said. About my being a witness and all."

"I didn't mean to freak you out, sweetheart."

"I know, but you were right. I might have seen something I don't even realize I saw? You know? Or heard something?"

"Describe the car."

"It's just a car," she said. "Dark blue."

"What about the driver? Is there anyone else in the car?"

"Just the one guy. He's just a regular guy."

God. What was wrong with kids' observational skills?

"White guy? Black?"

"White," she said.

"Does he look older or younger than me?"

"About the same? It's kind of hard to tell because he's so far — Hang on."

"What?"

336

"He's getting out of the car, Dad."

"What's he doing?"

"He's kind of looking around. Looking both ways on the street."

I felt my heart starting to pick up speed along with the car. "Now that you can see him, how tall? My height?"

"Taller. And he's got kind of browny gray hair, and he's wearing sunglasses and he's wearing jeans and a white shirt and a jacket. Like, a sport jacket. It's kind of black."

"Okay, that's good," I said. "You recognize him? You ever seen him before?"

"No, I've never — He's crossing the street."

"Where are you, Grace?"

"I'm in my room. I'm watching him from up here."

"Is the front door locked?"

"Yeah. I locked it when you left. Like you said. And I turned the alarm on, too, so if he kicks the door in, it's going to go *whoop-whoop.*"

I didn't want that image in my head.

"Okay," I said. "That's good, that's good. It's probably nothing, okay? Probably nothing at all. I'm probably only four minutes away."

I was coming up to a stop sign. I slowed, glanced both ways, and blew through it.

Coming the other way, a school bus. And standing in a cluster on the sidewalk, on my side, a bunch of schoolkids.

"Shit shit shit," I said, easing my foot down on the gas a little harder.

"What is it?" Grace said.

"Nothing," I said. "Don't worry about me. What's he doing now?"

"He's standing in front of our house. He's looking at the house!"

"Okay, okay, just calm down. You're going to be okay. The house is locked. I want you to double-check that you turned on the alarm."

"Dad, I know —"

"Do it!"

I could hear her thumping down the stairs as she took the phone with her.

"The red light is on!" she said.

"Okay, that's — Shit!"

I slammed on the brakes. The school bus had stopped, engaged its flashing red lights, and half a dozen kids were crossing the street in front of me. The car came to a screeching halt.

"Dad! Dad?"

"I'm okay, honey," I said, although my heart was pounding like it was trying to break free. I glanced up at the school bus driver, a woman, who was giving me a dirty,

338

reproachful look. The last of the students passed by the front of my car and boarded the bus. A second later, the red lights stopped flashing and I tromped down on the accelerator once again.

"Grace?"

"Yeah?"

"Where are you now?"

"I'm near the front door."

"Can you see him?"

"No, I'm going to peek out the living room window . . . No, he's not standing across the street anymore. He must have —"

In the background, I heard our doorbell.

"Dad!" she whispered.

"Grace?"

"He's ringing the doorbell. He's at the door!"

"It's okay, honey. Don't answer it. Just stay away from the door. When no one comes, he'll go away. When he does, maybe you can get a closer look at the car. Maybe even get a license plate —"

"He's knocking now," she whispered. "He tried the doorbell and now he's knocking."

I raced through another stop sign, leaving honking horns in my wake.

"It's okay, sweetheart. I'm three minutes away. What's happening now?"

"He stopped knocking," she said, her voice sounding slightly less hysterical. "He's not ringing the doorbell or knocking or anything."

"That's good, that's good. He's given up. So run back up to your room and see if you —"

"Hang on," Grace said. "I'm hearing something."

"What? What are you hearing?"

"It sounds like . . . Dad, it sounds like he's putting a key in the door."

"That's not possible, honey. There's no way —"

"It's turning," she said.

"What's turning?" I asked, holding my breath as I pulled into oncoming traffic to pass a slow-moving van.

"The dead bolt thingy," Grace said. "It's turning."

THIRTY-FIVE

Vince Fleming held back in the bathroom of Eldon Koch's apartment for a full minute after Terry Archer had left and closed the door. He didn't want to take a chance that asshole would change his mind and come charging back in.

Maybe he should have shot him, too.

Damn you, Eldon.

Vince told himself it was Eldon who'd forced the play. He'd made it damn clear he wasn't going along with Vince's plan. And if Eldon wasn't going to help cover up what had happened to Stuart, well, it was like they said. If you're not part of the solution, you're part of the problem.

And covering up the circumstances of Stuart's death, steering the police away from anything to do with Vince and his operation, was a big problem.

If Eldon wouldn't play his role in a story that would place Stuart all over the country for several weeks, if not months, into the future, then what, exactly, was he planning to do? Go to the police? Work some kind of deal in return for testifying against his boss? He just might have, especially since he seemed to believe Vince was responsible for Stuart's death.

Where'd he get a crazy idea like that?

Eldon was spouting some pretty insane shit there, right before the end. Suggesting Vince not only killed his son, but was ripping off his clients. Taking their money, scamming them into thinking he'd safeguard it, when in fact he was waiting until he had enough squirreled away, at which point he'd round it all up and take off.

Vince didn't like it that Eldon had ideas like that in his head. He wondered whether Gordie and Bert had ever thought the same thing.

Vince emerged from the tiny bathroom and walked tentatively to the door. Looked to see whether Terry Archer was still out there, maybe standing on the steps. He saw a car parked across the street, Archer behind the wheel, just sitting there.

What the hell?

He was waiting. Waiting for Stuart or Eldon to come home. Vince touched the warm coffee on the counter.

"Shit," he said to himself. Archer was probably thinking someone would come back for the coffees. But sooner or later, he'd have to leave.

Vince was stuck here until then.

He went back to the bedroom, looked at Eldon's body sprawled across the bed, blood soaking into the sheets. "You dumb bastard," Vince said under his breath. "You think I wanted to do that?"

How were Gordie and Bert going to react? The three of them had worked together a long time. They were friends. Vince believed he could persuade them that he'd done the only thing he could. Eldon lost it, he'd tell them. Was spouting crazy talk. His grief had made him irrational, a liability. No telling what he might say, or who he might say it to. If he'd talked to the cops, it wouldn't have been just Vince who'd take the fall. Gordie and Bert would go down with him.

They'd see that. They'd understand.

They needed to know Eldon had screwed up. Big time. He'd been sloppy with the details of their operation, allowed his son to know what was going on. When you thought about it, Eldon was as much to blame for what had happened to his son as the person who'd pulled the trigger on him.

Gordie and Bert would see that.

Still, it wouldn't be easy for them, having to come back here, tonight, when it was dark, to clean up this mess. To get rid of the body of a man they'd come to know. Vince was sure they'd grieve, but they'd know it had to be done.

Jesus. First Stuart, now Eldon.

Vince had had a plan worked out to explain Stuart's disappearance. Let the cops think he died by misadventure while exploring America. Coming up with an explanation for Eldon's disappearance might take more work. He'd have to give it some thought. If there was one silver lining, the one person who'd have noticed he was missing was no longer around.

Vince propped himself against the door-jamb. "Weary" didn't begin to describe how he felt. Beaten. Defeated.

He could almost feel his insides being eaten away. The doctor wasn't able to say with any certainty how much longer he had. Six months? A year at the outside? He might be able to buy himself more time with aggressive treatment, but Vince wanted no part of that.

Better to just keep going, as best he could, for as long as he could.

Or maybe not.

Vince got out his phone, entered a number.

"Yeah?" said Gordie.

"Where are you?"

"I'm heading back to the shop. Done all I can do for the moment. Cleared out a few places where I could, but I still got some to go."

"Bert with you?"

"No. He's still doing the rounds. I've got, like, four hundred grand, some coke, some hardware in the car. What do you want us to do with it?"

Vince wondered whether he himself was going to have to open a safe-deposit box. The fucking irony of it.

"Leave that with me," Vince said. "I've got some new fires to put out."

"Great. We really need more of those."

"Archer's still snooping around."

"I thought you talked to him."

"I did, but he didn't get the message. I got an idea how we might solve that, at least temporarily."

He told Gordie his idea. "I can do that," Gordie said. "And what else?"

"I'll tell you when I see you."

"Okay. Look, the good news, if there is any, is so far it looks like our problems are limited to the Cummings house. Kinda puts the dog walker in the crosshairs."

Vince said, "See ya in a bit."

He took another look at Eldon, caught a whiff of the coppery blood smell.

He rolled the body up in the bedsheets, grunting and struggling with the effort. There was a roll of plastic sheeting in the truck, and some duct tape. He'd try to get Eldon wrapped up now. Save them some work when they came back here tonight. He'd turn up the AC unit tucked in the window full blast. Anything to help in this heat. He hoped Eldon wasn't too ripe by the time they returned.

"I'm sorry," Vince said. "I should have given you a chance to say good-bye to your boy."

THIRTY-SIX

Heywood Duggan made an early-morning call from home to his client Martin Quayle.

"Hello?"

"Mr. Quayle? Heywood Duggan here."

"Duggan! I wasn't expecting to hear from you. I thought you'd given up on this. Given up on me."

"There's a reason why you haven't heard back from Eli Goemann. Someone killed him."

Quayle gasped. "Good God. Who did it? What the hell was the man into? You thinking I wasn't the only person he was trying to scam? Because that's what I'm starting to think it was. I'm thinking he never had what he said he had. That he just saw the story on the news."

"I don't have the details. A police detective came to see me. A woman. She found out I'd been asking around about him. They haven't made an arrest."

347

"Did he have it?"

"Looks like he didn't. This detective, Wedmore's her name, didn't say anything to suggest he was found with anything on him."

"Then someone else may have it," Quayle said.

"If Eli even had it to begin with," Duggan said. "Like you say, he could have been running a game on you."

"I just . . . I just can't imagine why anyone would do such a thing. Whether it was Eli who did it in the first place, or somebody else. What would possess someone to do that?"

"I don't know, Mr. Quayle. My guess is someone thought the item itself, and not what was inside, was of value. But listen, I did come across some names yesterday I wanted to bounce off you. People Goemann crashed with over the last few months after his roommates booted him out. I've been doing some checking."

"Crashed?"

"Stayed with."

"Oh. Okay."

"There were a couple of girls. Selina Michaels was one, in Bridgeport. And a Juanita Cole here in Milford. I don't know if they were actual girlfriends, but he talked them into letting him sleep under their roof for a while. There was an older guy named Croft he may have done some work for, and someone I think he went to school with by the name of Waterman. But whether they had anything —"

"Did you say Croft?"

"Yeah."

Quayle was silent on the other end of the line.

"You there?" Duggan asked.

"A long time ago, there was a man named Croft. He . . . he'd been a friend of mine. We fought together. In Vietnam. We were both from around here. I lived in Stratford. He was in New Haven. We stayed in touch when we got back."

"Okay. You have any reason to believe he'd have anything to do with this?"

Again, nothing but silence from Quayle.

"Sir?"

"I stole her from him."

"You what?"

"We both loved the same woman. There was . . . an opportunity, and I stole her away from him."

"This was your wife? You're talking about Charlotte?"

"Yes." A pause. "It's him."

"Croft?"

"I know it. It's him. He's always wanted her back, and he finally did it. That son of a bitch. Now that I think of it, I was pretty sure I saw him. Two years ago. In the church. So he would have known."

"You might be right," Duggan said. "I can stick with this a little longer, see what I can find out."

"That bastard. I'm going to confront him."

"I wouldn't recommend that, Mr. Quayle."

"I'll put the fear of God into him. That's what I'll do."

"Mr. Quayle, listen to me. I think the best thing would be —"

"What if I tell him — here's an idea — I tell him we've got her back. If he laughs, calls my bluff, I'll know he's got her. But if he doesn't, if he sounds worried, we'll know she's still out there somewhere. Maybe he'll think we got her from Eli, that the deal was made. I know! I'll tell him —"

"Stop," Duggan said. "This is not the way you want to go about this."

"— tell him that we're checking for finger-prints! That if we find his prints, he's finished. I'll get my lawyer involved, the police, and —"

"Mr. Quayle," Duggan said, keeping his

voice level, but firm. "Don't do this."

"I'm gonna get the son of a bitch. That's what I'm gonna do."

Quayle ended the call.

Fuck it, Heywood Duggan thought. If that was what the man wanted to do, then let him. He'd be just as happy to forget this case, move on to something else.

This file was closed.

THIRTY-SEVEN

Cynthia Archer did not sleep well.

She lay awake, wondering what it was her husband and daughter might be keeping from her. Why had it taken so long for Terry to go pick Grace up and come home? They hadn't pulled into the driveway until after midnight, a couple of hours after he'd taken the call from Grace to come get her.

Something was wrong. She could sense it.

But she couldn't call Terry and ask why they had been out so late. Not without admitting she'd been spying on them from behind a tree, like some ridiculous character in a *Scooby-Doo* cartoon. If Terry found out she'd been watching the house, he'd jump to the conclusion that she'd been doing this other nights. Maybe every night since she'd moved out of the house.

And he'd be right.

By the time Cynthia's digital clock read 5:30, she didn't see the point in lying in bed any longer. She got up, showered, did her makeup, put on the clothes she'd selected for herself the night before.

She put a slice of bread into the toaster, peeled a banana, made some coffee, turned on the radio. But she couldn't have told anyone a thing she heard. Her mind was elsewhere.

Those buggers.

Thought they could pull something over on her, did they? She could understand why they'd do it. They were protecting her. They were doing what they could to keep her anxiety level down.

It was insulting. As if she couldn't handle things. As if she was some kind of baby.

Well, Cynthia Archer was not a baby.

She was going to find out what was going on. She was not going to go directly to work this morning. She was going to stop by their house. After all, it was still hers, too, and she could drop by anytime she wanted. She didn't need an invitation. She didn't need a reason.

She was going to go up to the door and let herself in and damned if she was going to knock.

Hey, thought I'd join you for breakfast. Coffee on?

So at six-fifty she stepped out of her apart-

353

ment and headed for the stairs. But there was a man there, about four steps down, blocking her path. She nearly screamed.

"Good morning, Cynthia."

It was Barney. He had a screwdriver in his hand, and an open red metal toolbox was perched one step down from the top. The wooden hand railing, which was normally secured to the wall with metal brackets, was half off.

"You scared me half to death," she said.

"Sorry about that. I decided to come over this morning, check in on Orland. I popped my head in — he's fast asleep, but I'm going to hang around until he wakes up. Figured I'd get some work done in the meantime. I've been meaning to fix this railing for a while. It's pretty loose, not safe. Let me get out of your way here."

"Thank you. I hope everything's okay with Orland."

"It might be he was just having a bad day. I've known him a long time. Went to high school together. Where you off to so early? Wait — let me guess. You're doing a restaurant inspection. See if somebody's serving bugs with the home fries."

"Just have a lot to do," she said. She started to squeeze past him when there was the sound of a door opening in the first-floor hallway. Then, Orland shouting, "What's all the racket?"

His face appeared at the bottom of the stairs, looking up through smudged glasses, hair all over the place. He was dressed in nothing but a tattered blue bathrobe and socks. "Barney!" he said. "What the hell you doin'?"

"Fixing this railing, Orland. Maybe you'd like to give me a hand?"

"I look like I'm dressed for work?"

"So get dressed. How you feeling today?"

"I feel fine," he said, then coughed. He looked quizzically at Barney and said, "Where's Charlotte?"

Barney sighed tiredly. "Charlotte's passed away, Orland. Years ago. You know that."

"Oh. I'm sorry to hear that. How long were you two married?"

"You're confused, Orland. Charlotte was never *my* wife."

Orland scratched his head. "Oh, that's right." He chuckled. "What the hell was I thinking?"

Cynthia gave Barney a weak, sympathetic smile. "I have to go," she whispered.

"Sure thing," Barney said.

"Have a nice day, Orland," Cynthia said as she scooted past the man and headed out the front door. Seconds later, she was in her car.

As she turned off Pumpkin Delight Road onto Hickory, she saw Terry's Ford Escape backing out of the driveway. She hit the brakes and eased the car over to the curb and watched as he headed off in the other direction, toward Maplewood.

Where the hell was he going this early? It wasn't as if he had a job to go to in July. She was pretty sure there was only one person in the car, which meant Grace was still at home.

Why would he head out so early? What kind of errand could he be running? A donut and coffee run? Was he fetching Grace an Egg McMuffin? That didn't sound like Terry.

Could he be sick? Was he off to the drug-store for some medicine? Could it be Grace? Was she sick? The CVS pharmacy out on the Boston Post Road would be open this early, she thought. It was a twenty-four-hour location.

She might as well follow him and find out.

Cynthia gave her husband a good head start, then took her foot off the brake.

He wasn't heading for the CVS. He was heading across town, ending up on Naug-atuck. Parked across the street from some place that fixed busted appliances. But it wasn't even open, and Terry had said nothing about a broken washer or dryer or —

He wasn't going to the repair shop. He was going up a flight of stairs on the side of the building. To what looked like an apartment.

What the hell was he doing there?

Terry happened to glance in her direction, just for a second, and suddenly Cynthia felt vulnerable. What if he spotted her? She was pretty sure he hadn't just now, but what if he did the next time he looked her way? It was one thing to be caught spying on them at home, but how would she explain following him all over Milford?

She turned the car around and started heading back. To the house. She'd play dumb. Let herself in, find Grace, ask her where her father was.

As she rounded the corner, she noticed there was a car parked on the street, just down from their place, that had not been there when she'd gone by minutes earlier. A man was crossing the street, right out front of their house.

Cynthia slowed, steered over to the side of the road.

The man walked up their driveway, approached the front door.

Rang the bell.

"Who the hell is that, this bloody early?" Cynthia said to herself. "Don't answer it, Grace. Do not answer that door."

She reached into her bag for her cell phone. She'd call Grace, tell her not to go to the door. But before she could place the call, she saw the man knocking. Hard enough that she could almost hear it through the windshield.

"Just go away," Cynthia said. "Go now. Get."

What she saw next — well, she almost couldn't believe her eyes. The man reached into his pocket and took out . . . It was a key.

Before he inserted it, he looked over his shoulder to check whether anyone was watching him. He failed to spot Cynthia sitting in her car, so he turned back to the door, slid the key into the lock.

Cynthia hit the gas.

The car leapt forward, the tires squealing. She didn't even wait until she reached the driveway before turning hard right. The car bounced up over the curb and charged right across the yard, the spinning tires digging up sod and dirt as Cynthia aimed the car for the front door, her hand pressing so hard on the horn it felt like it would go through the steering column.

The man whirled around, saw the car heading straight for him, and dived out of the way. Cynthia hit the brakes, the bumper coming to a stop about six feet from the door.

The man was running flat out now, heading for that blue car. Cynthia threw open her door and shouted, "Hey! Hey you!"

She debated running after him, but then she heard the familiar *whoop* of a house alarm. Cynthia spun around to see Grace, dressed in one of her oversized sleeping shirts, standing in the open doorway of the house.

Grace screamed, "Mom! Mom!"

Grace shot forward, arms outstretched. She fell into her mother's arms, weeping, and Cynthia clutched her tight, holding her like she'd never ever let her go.

THIRTY-EIGHT

TERRY

I wasn't expecting to see what I saw when I got to the house.

Tire tracks across the lawn, Cynthia's car, door wide-open, nosed up to the house, Grace and her mother locked in an embrace on the front step.

Grace sobbing. The security alarm *whooping*.

I slammed on the brakes, left the car in the street, and ran to them. Grace saw me through watery eyes. "Dad!"

"Grace! Grace! Are you okay?" I asked her once, then at least five more times.

Cynthia used my arrival to pry herself free of Grace — not, I suspected, because she didn't want to comfort her, but because she wanted to see where the man who'd been trying to get into the house had gone.

She ran halfway down the driveway, looking up the street into the distance.

"Shit," she said.

"He didn't hurt you, did he?" I said to Grace, hugging her, trying to be heard above the alarm.

"He didn't get in," she said. "Mom came. Almost ran him down."

A woman who lived across the street, still in her housecoat, had stepped out of her house with a mug of coffee in her hand. She called over, "You okay?"

I shouted back, "We're okay, thanks."

"Should I call the police?"

Cynthia started to shout yes, but I stopped her with a firm shake of the head. "No, it's okay!" I yelled. "We've got this."

Cynthia shot me a look. "Are you kidding?" she said. She started walking toward me at full tilt. "Someone tries to break in and attack our daughter and you don't want to call the police?"

"Let's get inside," I said. First thing I had to do was enter the code to stop the alarm from screeching. I didn't know whether the alarm had been activated by the man getting the door open or Grace opening it herself when she saw her mother.

"What the hell is going on?" Cynthia asked.

She went to her car — the engine was still running — and reached in to shut it off and grab her purse. She had her cell phone in her hand.

"If you're not calling the police, I will."

"No, Mom, wait," Grace said.

That got Cynthia's attention. "What?"

"Please," I said. "Let's go inside. You may be right — we may have to call the police. But first I want to make sure Grace is okay."

Her sobs had turned to sniffs. "I'm okay. I am. I told you."

Cynthia took that as permission to make the call, but again I stopped her. "*Please,* not yet."

We went into the house and closed the door, at which point the alarm, only annoying up to this point, became deafening. I went to the security panel, entered our four-digit code to cancel it. Once it was silenced, we could hear the phone was ringing. That'd be the security monitoring service. I ran to the extension in the living room and snatched the receiver off the cradle.

"Hello!" I said. "Alarm, right?"

"Is this Mr. Archer?" A man enunciating very carefully.

"It is."

"Are you having an emergency?"

"Everything's okay."

"We need your password, Mr. Archer.

362

Otherwise we will be dispatching the police."

I was so flustered it took me a second to remember it. "Telescope," I said. "Our password is telescope."

"Okay," he said. "Can you tell me what happened?"

"We — we forgot the alarm was on and opened the door," I said. "We're very sorry."

"Not to worry, Mr. Archer. The good news, your system's working. You have a great day now."

I put down the receiver and saw that Cynthia was back to holding Grace. My wife was looking at me fiercely.

"Why weren't you here?" she asked.

"I was out for a few minutes," I said.

"Doing what?"

I shrugged. "An errand."

"To an appliance repair place?" she asked. "At seven in the morning?"

I looked at Grace. "Did you tell your mother where I was going?"

She shook her head.

I looked back at Cynthia. "Were you following me?"

She broke away from Grace and took a step toward me and pointed a finger. "You said you'd look after her. But something's going on and I want to know what it is."

"How about answering my question? Were you following me? Have you been spying on us?"

When Cynthia hesitated, Grace said, "Jeez, is that true, Mom? You've, like, got us under surveillance?"

Cynthia must have decided a good defense was a good offense. She bristled and said, "Good thing, too! If I hadn't been, that man — he'd have gotten into the house!" Back to me. "And who was he? If you don't want me calling the police, does that mean you know who he was?"

"I don't," I said. "Grace, you sure you've never seen him before?"

She shook her head.

"Could he have been the man in the house?" I asked.

"There was a man in our house?" Cynthia asked.

"Not our house," I said.

"He might have been the guy," Grace said, "but I don't know. Even if it was him, how could he have a key, Dad?" she asked.

"Maybe he didn't," I said. "Maybe he had one of those, whaddya call 'em, lock-picking sets."

"But it didn't take him anytime at all. I heard a key go straight in and the lock started turning."

"I saw him use a key," Cynthia said. She looked at me. "Who did you give a key to?"

"No one," I said. "Did *you* give a key to anyone?"

"Of course not."

I looked at Grace. "Are you kidding?" she said. "You think I'm an idiot?" I gave her a look that suggested her last twelve hours made that a risky question.

I said, "Okay, the only people who have a key to this house are each of us, and Teresa."

"Well, that sure wasn't Teresa trying to break in," Grace said.

"Why would someone have a key and want to get in here?" I asked. I was looking at Grace.

"Like you said. I'm a witness."

Cynthia looked dumbstruck, trying to get her head around what we were talking about.

"Yeah," I said. "But what are the odds the person who was in that house would have a key to ours?"

She shook her head. "I don't know. I just — I don't know, Dad."

"What on earth are you talking about?" Cynthia asked. "What the hell is going on?"

I took a second to compose myself, let the proverbial dust settle around us. I said, "We've got some trouble."

■ ■ ■ ■

Sitting at the kitchen table, Grace and I told her everything, from the beginning. We didn't leave anything out. When Grace neglected a detail, I filled in a gap, and vice versa.

Cynthia, to her credit, mostly listened, asking only the occasional question, letting the story unfold. If it had been me hearing all this, I'd have been interrupting every ten seconds.

I finished by telling her where I'd just been, how I had hoped maybe I'd find Stuart Koch at home.

"So you still don't know what happened to him," Cynthia said.

We both shook our heads.

Grace said, "I know you probably want to chew me out and all that stuff, but Dad's sort of done some of it, and right now I really have to go to the bathroom, so can it wait until I get back?"

Cynthia nodded.

As Grace got up from the table, her mother grabbed her arm and pulled her in to give her another hug. Grace wrapped her arms around her mother's head and said, "I'm glad you're home. Even if it's just for a visit. And everything's going to shit."

Cynthia looked like she wanted to say something, but held back. All she said was, "Go."

When Grace was gone, Cynthia looked at me.

"You could chew me out now instead," I said.

She reached out and gripped my hand. "What a mess."

"What'd Tommy Lee Jones say in that movie? 'If it ain't, it'll do till the real mess gets here.' Yeah, this is bad."

"I think you're right about getting her a lawyer. Pronto. We don't know what's coming."

I nodded.

"But we've been through tough times before," Cynthia said. "Thanks to me. My troubles nearly got us all killed."

"It's nice that we can take turns," I said.

"You think that man at the door — that he was here to get Grace? That he was in that house and thinks she saw him?"

"Maybe," I said.

"Let's say you're right," Cynthia said. "How could that person have a key to the house?"

Good question.

Cynthia speculated. "Maybe Grace — or

you, or I — maybe we left our keys out somewhere, allowing someone to make a copy. You know, like when you leave your car keys with the dealership service department, or you give them to a valet and they're hanging there at some restaurant where anyone could sneak off with them for a while."

Except I was a schoolteacher and Cynthia worked for the health department. Okay, we had a cleaning lady, but we didn't exactly throw our money around that way. "When was the last time you used the valet service at a hotel or restaurant?" I asked.

"Never."

"Same here."

"Maybe one of Grace's friends? Got into her purse, took her key and copied it?"

"From the way Grace described the guy, it wasn't a kid. It was someone my age."

"But even if he got into the house," Cynthia said, "he'd have had to contend with the alarm system. Soon as that went off, he'd have had to run."

"He didn't know we had one," I surmised. "If he knew we had one, he'd have had to know the code to disable it."

We were both quiet for a moment.

"Stealing a key and copying it is one thing," Cynthia said. "But none of us would

368

be dumb enough to give out the code."

"Only people who know the code are you, me, Grace, and Teresa."

"Second time her name has come up," Cynthia said.

And again, we were both quiet.

"No," I said. "I mean, even if it was Teresa, that she gave someone a key and told him the code, what would be the point? What have we got? We don't have a security system to protect our valuables. We have it to protect ourselves, after what happened years ago. And that guy, when he was trying to get in, he figured no one was home. He rang the bell, he knocked, and Grace didn't answer. So maybe he wasn't coming in to attack her. He was coming in for some other reason. What would he steal? Your priceless jewelry?"

For the first time, Cynthia chuckled softly, despite everything.

"My rare coin collection?" I continued. "The thousands in cash that we keep stuffed under the mattress?"

"It doesn't make sense," she said, and her face grew dark. "I'm going to talk to Vince."

"Oh yeah, that's a plan. He loves us. When I saw him last night, he wasn't any more friendly than when you and I visited him in the hospital years ago."

"I've seen him," she said.

"What? You mean, recently?"

Cynthia nodded. "Yeah. He visited me at the apartment."

"Wait a minute," I said, breaking my hand free of hers. "You've been seeing Vince?"

"I haven't been *seeing* Vince," she said, leaning back in her chair away from me. "But I've talked to him. I wrote to him after his wife died, sent a card. He spotted me driving around, followed me to the apartment, thanked me. And he apologized for how he treated us way back then."

"I didn't get my apology," I said.

"I guess the card you sent got held up in the mail."

I had no comeback for that.

"Anyway," Cynthia said, "I want to talk to him. I think he'll be more forthcoming with me than you."

"I'll go with you," I said.

"No. I'll do it alone. Besides, someone needs to be with Grace. All the time."

I didn't disagree.

I pressed my back against the chair and folded my arms across my chest. "So how long have you been keeping an eye on us?"

She bit her lip. "Since I left."

"Wait a minute. You couldn't be watching us all the time."

"No. But most nights. I'd park around the corner. There's a tree — you know the one, out front of the Walmsleys' house?"

I nodded.

"It's wide enough to hide behind. I can't get to sleep unless I know you're both home safe. Especially Grace. I could see her window, and sometimes I'd wait until she turned off her light, and then I'd go home."

She swallowed. "What I wanted to do was just come in. I wanted to go up to her room and kiss her good night and turn off the light for her. But I guess, when you're fourteen, you're too old for your mother to do that."

"I think she'd have been okay with it."

"And then, after I'd done that, all I'd have wanted would be to slip into bed next to you." She sniffed. "But then I'd drive back to the apartment. Until the next night, and I'd do it all over again."

I should have known. I should have suspected from the very beginning that this was what she would do.

"Can you forgive me?" she asked. I uncrossed my arms, leaned forward, and took her hand.

I nodded. "For loving us? Yeah, I think so."

I was about to give her a hug when we

heard a scream from upstairs.

Grace.

Actually, not a scream. A shout. A single word: "Yes!"

Cynthia and I ran up the stairs and found her in her room, sitting on the bed, phone in hand, a smile on her face unlike any I had seen in some time.

"What is it?" I said, coming through the door first, Cynthia right behind me.

Grace looked up, and she was smiling.

"He's okay!" she said.

"What?" her mother said. "Stuart?"

"He just texted me! He's okay!"

She handed the phone to me and I held it so Cynthia could see the screen, too. We read:

GRACE: just let me know your ok

GRACE: im going out of my mind if something happened 2 u let me no

GRACE: if you cant talk get someone else to get in touch with me

GRACE: did i hit you? just let me know that much

Those messages had all been written this morning. Grace had sent a dozen others last night.

And then, just now, there was this:

STUART: *hey*

GRACE: *omg r u ok?*

STUART: *yeah. sorry if i freaked u out*

GRACE: *freaked out? im going out of my fuckin mind*

STUART: *had to run sorry i left u there. lotta shit going down, my dad mad*

GRACE: *but your ok?*

STUART: *yup.*

GRACE: *where r u*

STUART: *hidin out for while. dad mad boss too*

GRACE: *did i do it? shoot u?*

STUART: *fuck no! more l8r. see ya.*

Cynthia and I exchanged glances, then looked at Grace, who was beaming.

"This is, like, the best news ever," she said.

THIRTY-NINE

"Hello?"

"Reggie."

"I'm kind of busy right now, Unk. Let me call you back in a few —"

"He called me."

"What? Who called you? What are you talking about?"

"He knows."

"Who? Who knows what?"

"Quayle."

"Jesus. Just hang on a second. I'm coming out of the coffee shop. Let me get into the car. Hang on. Okay, I'm in. Start over."

"Quayle phoned me. Just now. He knows it's me."

"There's no way. Eli never told him. I'm sure of that. He — Shit!"

"What?"

"I just spilled some hot coffee in my lap. Unk, I don't get it. How would Quayle make the connection?"

"Quayle hired a detective. Eli must have called him once to sound him out about a deal, but when he never called back, Quayle wanted to find him. So he got a private detective to look for him."

"What did Quayle say? Exactly. What did he say, exactly, Unk?"

"He said he knew it was me. Said he should have known all along. Reggie, he must have done a deal with Eli after all."

"What?"

"He hasn't got her in his actual possession, but the detective does. Quayle said they're checking for fingerprints. That they're going to look for my fingerprints."

"That sounds like bullshit, Unk. It's a trick. He's trying to set you up."

"What if he isn't? If they find my fingerprints, they'll go to the police. I'll be arrested. And then they'll find out about Eli, about what happened to him."

"Let me think, let me think. If we knew who the detective was —"

"He told me."

"What?"

"He told me the detective's name. Duggan. Heywood Duggan. I looked him up in the book. He's a real private detective."

"Well, hell, you got an address, Unk?"

FORTY

At the body shop, Vince had closeted himself in his office. Gordie was outside the door asking Vince, through the frosted glass, whether he was okay.

"I need a minute," he said, dropping into the padded chair behind his desk. "Where's Bert?"

"He's coming in."

"When'd he get back from the farm?" Vince opened a drawer, took out a small glass and a bottle of Jack Daniel's. Poured himself a snootful, knocked it back, poured himself another.

"Around four in the morning. He joined up with me to do a couple more houses, then went off on his own."

"What'd he do with Eldon's Buick?"

"Left it at his place. He was in his own car when he caught up with me. Listen, I think things are more or less okay," Gordie said, "but he ran into a problem at one of the houses a little while ago."

Jesus, it never ends.

Vince asked, "Which house?"

Gordie told him. "He said he rang the bell, knocked, was sure no one was home, but the kid was there, and then the wife showed up. Nearly ran him over."

Cynthia.

"Shit," Vince said.

"Have you talked to Eldon yet?" Gordie asked. "I mean, is he going to show up here any minute and not know? 'Cause I don't want to be the one who tells him. I think it should come from you. I'm trying to weasel out of it, but you're the boss and all."

"Eldon won't be coming in."

"Why's that?"

"When Bert gets here, I'll fill you both in. You do that other thing I asked you?"

"The texts? Yeah, that's done. But I wanted to ask you if —"

"I told you. I need a minute."

Gordie's shadow moved away from the frosted glass.

Vince stared straight ahead, dazed. Poured himself a third shot, downed it, then placed his hands flat on the desktop. Concentrated on his breathing. Inhaled slowly. Exhaled slowly. He was feeling light-headed, and it had nothing to do with the booze. He felt a knot of anxiety in the center of his chest. He wondered, for a moment, whether he was going to be sick to his stomach.

Was this what they called a panic attack?

Get a grip. You got a lotta shit to deal with.

A shadow darkened the frosted glass again. "Bert's pulling in," Gordie said.

"I'll be out when I'm out."

The shadow slipped away again.

Vince was thinking about a show he'd seen on disasters. Probably on the Discovery Channel. How, when a plane came down or two trains ended up heading toward each other on the same track, there was usually more than one cause, unless it was a bomb. Events conspiring. Pilot error meets faulty switch. Engineer looking at a video on his cell phone as trackside signals malfunction.

Vince believed events had very much conspired against him. Stuart breaking into that house at the very same time as someone else was ripping it off.

Things were going to shit all around him. He could feel his empire — such as it was — slipping away. And it had been getting chipped away at before the events of the last twenty-four — God, it hadn't even been that long. More like twelve hours.

Audrey.

Maybe Jane was right. He had been a

pussy. But he couldn't bear to see his wife in that hospital bed those last few weeks. It tore him apart, filled him with despair and rage at the same time. He knew this wasn't supposed to be about him — it was about her, about being there for her. But it was too risky, going to see her. Vince had to be the rock. Always the rock. He was the guy who didn't let things touch him.

Most of the time, he could pull that off.

But not when he was in that room with Audrey, watching her die. It was bad enough, when she had her eyes open, seeing him become emotionally compromised. Seeing that tremble in his chin. The moistness in his eyes. But what if someone entered the room — a nurse, her doctor, Jane, Eldon or Gordie or Bert — and saw him that way? He'd never recover from the embarrassment. It would be a humiliation.

Now, though, he wondered.

He'd been so worried about how he'd be perceived during the time he was losing Audrey that now he was at risk of losing Jane.

Aw, fuck it. It's not like she's my real daughter or —

Maybe not. But damn it, he loved her. From the moment Audrey came into his life, dragging Jane along with her, there was something about the kid. Tough, but vulnerable at the same time. She'd been hurt so often by other men who'd come into her mother's orbit, starting with her own dad, who'd never been there for her. She'd stopped looking for any sort of father figure. As far as she was concerned, all the men her mother had taken up with over the years were assholes.

Vince was willing to concede that maybe he wasn't much different, but at least he cared about Jane in ways the others hadn't.

He'd had a daughter once.

Briefly.

It had always haunted him. He'd often thought about the girl that never was. Who would that baby have grown up to be? What would she have been like at five years of age? Ten? Fifteen. When he and Audrey began living together and Jane was around all the time, he could easily imagine her as the embodiment of what his own daughter might have been.

Headstrong. Stubborn. Not afraid of a fight. Goddamn intimidating at times. Sneaky, too, when it served her purposes.

And a pain in the ass, let's not forget that. But if his daughter had turned out like Jane, he would have been proud. This is a kid who can take care of herself. A kid who doesn't take any shit.

He didn't try to be her friend. From the beginning, he just tried to treat her with respect. Didn't bullshit her. When she asked him once — this was more than seven years earlier, before he got shot — whether he was going to marry her mother, he could have said something like, "Well, we'll see, your mother and I care about each other a great deal, and we don't know at this point where it will lead blah blah blah."

But instead he said, "I got no idea. If I had to make up my mind today, I'd say there's no way. I got enough people nagging me as it is. But I like her. And you're okay, too."

Another time, she asked him flat out whether he was a criminal.

"That's how you make your living, right? I mean, this body shop thing, that's just bullshit. A legit business to cover up all the other stuff that you and Bert and Gordie and Eldon are up to. Am I right or am I right?"

He took a second. "You're right."

Jane nodded appreciatively. "That was a test."

"Huh?"

"I just wanted to see if you'd lie to my face. I don't like what you do, but at least you're honest about it."

A pistol. That's what she was.

Maybe he was a fool to believe this, but he thought his directness had, over time, won her respect. And once he had that — and it sure as hell didn't happen overnight — he believed she came to feel something stronger. Was he kidding himself, or did she love him back?

Vince thought she did.

He knew he didn't come across as an educated guy. He'd barely finished high school, and never attended any institution of so-called higher learning. But he liked to read, and the shelves of his beach house were lined with books. History and biography, mostly. Vince liked to read about how important people made decisions, and took comfort in the fact that even smart people, as often as not, made the wrong choices.

Whenever it was his birthday or Christmas, Jane bought Vince a book. Everybody else tended to buy him scotch. He'd said to her once, "You know I'm a thinker, not just a drinker."

But what had really touched him was that last year, when her mother was still alive, before things got bad, Jane had bought him a book for Father's Day. The huge Keith Richards memoir *Life.* She'd written inside: *For a guy who rocks, a book about another guy who rocks. Love, Jane.*

She'd never bought him anything for Father's Day before.

This year, Father's Day had come in the weeks preceding Audrey's death. Jane's opinion of him had clearly taken a hit. There was no gift this time.

She hates me.

She hated him because he'd let his mother down. Let Jane down, too. Plus, there was the business of the house. A nice two-story up in Orange, on Riverdale Road, just off Ridge, not far from the shopping center. Audrey had owned it when she met Vince, and after moving in with him kept the place and rented it out.

When she died, Jane assumed the house would go to her, but her mother had willed it to Vince. Jane figured he'd do the right thing and give it to her, and in the normal course of events he would have, except for one thing.

Bryce. Bryce Withers.

There was something about that kid Vince didn't like. It wasn't just that he was a musician. No, that was giving him too much credit. He played in a band. Calling him a musician, that suggested schooling and training. Talent. Vince didn't believe Bryce needed any of those things to play in a band.

Turned out Vince was right. One night he'd wandered into a bar where they were playing. Energy Drink, they called themselves. What the hell kind of lame-ass name was that? Vince never told Jane he'd seen them play. He wanted to get a handle on this guy who was sleeping with his stepdaughter. What he heard convinced him Bryce was more of a noisemaker than a musician. You could put a guitar in a monkey's hands and it'd produce the same kind of music.

No, that was unfair to the monkey.

Jane was making something of herself. She'd landed a good job with a local advertising agency. Not making a fortune, not yet, but doing better than her boyfriend, who Vince had pegged as a first-class mooch. Someone willing to live off his girlfriend's earnings. And, by extension, any money or property she happened to come into.

Like her mother's house.

If she married this clown and they moved into that house, and then split up and had to sell the place, this dickhead would end up getting half of what had been left to Vince in the first place.

Vince was okay with everything going to Jane. But not Bryce.

So he hung on to it and endured Jane's disdain. Soon as she broke up with Bryce — and sooner or later she'd have to see the light — he'd sit her down, tell her the house was hers.

It had been weighing on him.

But now there were new problems. Chief among them was the money missing from the attic of the Cummings house.

"Vince?" More rapping on the frosted glass.

"What?"

"Bert here."

Vince put the glass and bottle away, slid the drawer shut, took another couple of deep breaths. He was okay. He was a rock again. He could see this through. Start what you finish, his father used to tell him.

He came around the desk and opened the door. "Gordie told me you had some trouble."

"Yeah. I thought nobody was home."

"Cops?"

"I don't know what happened after I left."

Vince needed to know.

"What's happening with Eldon?" Bert asked. Gordie was standing right behind, looking anxious.

"Eldon's dead," Vince said.

Stunned silence for two seconds, then

"Fuck me" from Gordie.

"What happened?" Bert asked.

"He took the news badly," Vince said. "He started acting crazy. Making threats. Blaming me for what happened. Accusing me. I think he was getting ready to call the cops." He took a breath. "I did what I had to do."

Bert looked disbelievingly at his boss. "Wait. Are you saying . . . you fucking killed Eldon?"

"We'll have to deal with him later," Vince said. "Right now, we got other priorities. You two need to pay the dog walker a visit. He's the only one I can think of who's got a key and knows the security code for that house. See if he got a little too ambitious. And I'm gonna have to call an old girlfriend and try to talk her out of calling the cops if it's not already too late."

FORTY-ONE

Heywood Duggan parked his car on the street behind a row of downtown Milford storefronts. His office was tucked in back of a shop that sold wedding dresses, with a ground-floor entrance a few steps from a Dumpster. It wasn't much more than a ten-foot-square room, with a bathroom he had to share with the women who ran the dress shop. He had a desk, a computer, two chairs, and a filing cabinet, and never met prospective clients here. But it was a good place to get paperwork and research done.

As he got out of the car and headed for his office entrance, his cell phone rang. He glanced at the screen, saw who it was, and answered.

"Mr. Quayle," Heywood said, phone in one hand, keys in the other.

"I did it," Quayle said. "I called the son of a bitch."

Was there any point in telling him he

shouldn't have done that? Not now. "What'd he say?" Heywood asked.

"He was spooked. I rattled his cage, no doubt about it."

Heywood fiddled with his keys, singled out the one for his office. "Rattled because he didn't know what the hell you were talking about, or rattled because you'd found him out?"

"Definitely the latter. Once I told him about the vase being dusted for fingerprints."

"You didn't really tell him that."

"I did. I told him you were doing that right now."

Heywood sighed as he slipped the key into the lock. It didn't turn the way it usually did. Had he forgotten to lock up the night before?

"Mr. Quayle, that was a foolish thing to do. Listen, I just got to my office. I'll call you back in an hour or so."

He slipped the phone back into his jacket and pushed open his office door.

There was a woman sitting in the chair behind his desk. She looked at him and smiled.

"How the hell did you get in here?" Heywood asked.

That was when he felt something cold and

hard, but no broader than a dime, press up against the back of his head. When Heywood went to turn around, the man holding the gun said, "I wouldn't." And then he closed the door.

The woman said, "I'm going to ask you a question, and I'm only going to ask it once. So I want you to listen very carefully to it, and then I want you to think very carefully about how you answer. What I do not want you to do is answer my question with a question. That would be very, very unproductive. Do you understand?"

Heywood said, "Yes."

The woman said, "Where is it?"

FORTY-TWO

TERRY

Grace was ecstatic about the text messages from Stuart Koch. Cynthia, only recently up to speed on our troubles, was eager to put a good spin on them, too.

"So she didn't do it," Cynthia said, unable to conceal her enthusiasm. "Grace didn't shoot that boy. And no one else did, either. He's okay."

We'd left Grace in her bedroom and gone into our own, closing the door almost all the way. "So it seems," I said.

"And you said Vince told you that he was going to see that the broken window at that house got fixed. So it'll be like it never happened. No one ever has to know what a stupid thing our girl did. And she's going to learn from this — I truly believe that. She'll never do anything like this again."

Cynthia shook her head in exasperation. "And there'll have to be some new rules around here. Strict curfews. When she goes out someplace — *when* we let her go out someplace — we're going to know *where* she's going, *who* she's going to be with, how long she's going to be there, *when* —"

"Sure," I said. "We'll have her fitted with one of those ankle bracelets. We can sit on the computer all night and watch where she goes."

"You're mocking me."

"I'm sorry."

"This happened on your watch," she reminded me.

"I'm aware of that," I said.

"I'm not saying it's your fault," she added quickly. "It's as much mine, because I haven't been here." She took a seat on the edge of the bed. "I'm just glad we're past this part. At least now we don't have to spend the day getting Grace a lawyer."

"Yeah," I said slowly.

"What's wrong?" she said. "You don't see this as good news?"

"Sure, yes, of course it is. I don't want to be the one who bursts the bubble. But it was just a text."

"What are you saying?" Her face started to fall.

"It's not like Grace actually talked to him."

"Yeah, but it came from Stuart's phone," Cynthia said.

"I know."

"Grace seemed to think it was him. These kids, they probably have their own kind of 'voice' when it comes to texting. You can tell who it is by the short forms they use and everything."

"You're probably right," I said. "Let's say Stuart's okay. He's hiding somewhere until things blow over. What's that got to do with someone trying to break into the house?"

Cynthia looked off to the side, as though the answer were written down on a pad on the bedside table.

"Maybe the two things aren't connected," she said. "This mess happened with Grace, and someone tried to break into our house." She paused. "A coincidence."

"Which would mean we *should* call the police," I said. "Because the reason Grace and I wanted you to hold off is because we thought it had something to do with her, and we didn't want police involved until things had sorted themselves out or we had Grace a lawyer. You want to call the cops now?"

I could see her struggling with it. She rubbed her mouth, then briefly put both hands on the top of her head, as if she had the world's worst headache and was trying to keep her brain from exploding.

"God, I have no idea. If that man really has nothing to do with what happened to Grace, then we *should* call the police. He could return, or break into someone else's house, or — hell, I don't know."

"But . . ."

She stood, went into the bathroom, ran some water into her hand and scooped some into her mouth. I followed, stood in the doorway.

"Here's what I don't get," I said. "If Stuart's alive, why didn't Vince just tell me? He could have said the kid's okay, but instead ordered me to let the matter drop. If he'd just told me Stuart was fine, I probably would have dropped it. I wouldn't have gone looking for him this morning, at the hospital and his apartment."

I paused, thinking it through. "Maybe that's why we got the text. Vince found out — don't ask me how — I was nosing around, and came up with that idea."

"So it was Vince texting Grace, on Stuart's phone."

"Vince, or one of his bunch."

"Oh shit," she said, bracing herself on the countertop with her hands, looking at me in the mirror.

"We still have to know," I said. "With certainty."

The phone in the bedroom rang, startling both of us. I got to it first. The ID declared the caller to be unknown.

I picked up. "Hello?"

"Is your wife there?"

I knew the voice.

"What do you want?"

"Just put her on," Vince said.

Cynthia was standing in the bathroom doorway, mouthing, "Who is it?"

I held out the receiver. "Vince," I told her.

Her eyes went wide. She reached out, put the receiver to her ear. "Vince," she said.

She let me put my head up next to hers so I could hear both sides of the conversation.

"Cynthia," he said. "I need to know whether you've brought in the police. Are they there now?"

"Why would I have called the police, Vince?"

"Because there was an incident. At your home. Not your apartment. About an hour ago."

"That's right," she said. "There was. How would you know about that?" She gave me a quick look.

"You haven't answered my question."

"No," Cynthia said. "The police are not involved." She paused. "Yet."

Another pause, at Vince's end. Was that a sigh of relief?

"That's good," he said. "I owe you an apology."

Cynthia's face started to flush. "An apology? That was you? That was one of your goons?"

"Like I said, I owe you an —"

"No!" she said. "You owe me a fuck of a lot more than an apology! You owe me — *us!* — some answers, that's what you owe us, you son of a bitch!"

"Cynthia, I —"

"No more bullshit! Why the hell was someone, working for you, trying to get into our house? How did you get a key? What's going on? And what about Stuart? Was it you? Did you send those texts?"

"What texts would those be?" he said.

"To Grace. She received text messages from Stuart, just a few minutes ago."

"I didn't send Grace any texts," he said.

Those sounded like weasel words to me. He didn't say he didn't know about it. But Cynthia was going in another direction.

"Our *house,* Vince. You sent someone to break into our house. What was the plan? Was it to get Grace? To keep her from talking? My God, is that what the plan was?"

"No," he said. "He thought the house was empty."

"He?"

"Bert. It was Bert."

I took the phone. "Why, Vince? Why would Bert be trying to break into our house?"

Another moment of silence at the other end of the line.

Finally, Vince spoke.

"Because that's where the money is."

FORTY-THREE

It was nearly ten thirty when Jane Scavullo arrived at the offices of the Anders and Phelps advertising agency with her purse over one shoulder, the strap of an oversized gym bag, the handle of a tennis racket sticking out one end, over the other.

"Hey, Jane," Hector, the young guy on the front desk, said as she walked through the lobby. "Lookin' a little wasted there."

"Fuck off, Hector," she said.

"Late, too," he said with pleasure.

She had to admit she'd looked better. Not nearly enough sleep last night. All that drama with the Cummings house and Grace and Vince. Then, this morning, finding out that Bryce had lied to her. Finally, making a stop on the way to work to deal with another matter.

She dumped the gym bag in the well under her desk and kicked it forward, then saw the light on her phone was flashing. She wasn't ready yet to face her messages, so she got up and went around the corner to the lunchroom to see whether anyone had put on a pot of coffee yet.

Yes.

She grabbed a mug and filled it. Jane drank her coffee black, the way Vince drank his. If you're going to have coffee, he'd told her, have *coffee.* Don't pussy it up with milk or cream and sugar.

She blew on it, then had a sip, caught her reflection in the glass of a framed newspaper ad: "Riverside Honda! We've Re-built and NOW We're Having a Fire Sale!"

Not one of her ads. That was before her stint here began, although she remembered when the car dealership burned down a few years ago. She hadn't worked at Anders and Phelps — A&P, everyone around here called it — long enough to earn a framed piece of work on the wall, not even here in the lunchroom. And these days, an effective ad was unlikely to be something you could frame. Who advertised in newspapers anymore? Who *looked* at newspapers anymore? Jane couldn't remember the last time she'd picked one up, not even the *New York Times.* When Jane wanted to know what was going on in the world — which was not that often, if you wanted to know the truth — she went online. That's where she liked to see her clients' ads placed. You just had to find the right Web site so you were going after the right demographic. Or figured out peoples' surfing habits and made the ad pop up wherever they went. There was radio, too, which seemed like the oldest medium on the planet next to newspapers. But it was still a good choice. People driving around in their cars all day, radio turned on for background noise. That could work.

Like she gave a shit about any of this.

Was this what she really wanted to do? Mr. Archer, he'd figured her out. She wanted to write, and not stupid jingles for gas stations and furnace repair companies. She wanted to write novels. She wanted to write about what it was like to be a young woman growing up today. Wondering what the hell you were going to do with your life. Having to fight for everything you got. Nobody wanting to give you a permanent job. All short-term contracts. No benefits. The whole 22-22-22 thing. If you were twenty-two, companies worked you twenty-two hours a day for twenty-two thousand dollars a year. And if you didn't like that, well, tough shit.

Kind of like Anders and Phelps.

She went back to her desk, set the coffee

down, and retrieved her messages. She'd made cold calls the day before to a couple of dozen random Milford-area businesses. She got three callbacks, all saying thanks but no thanks, they didn't have the budget to advertise at this time.

Dumbasses. If things were slow, you had to get your name out there. If there wasn't a lot of business, you had to make sure what business there was went to you. Jane tried to tell them, but some people were dumb as turnips.

Fucking Bryce.

Talking about his gig, how the evening had gone, but he hadn't even been there. Jane hadn't let on that she'd seen his text. She'd left his phone facedown on his bedside table. When he'd come out of the bathroom, she'd said his phone had buzzed. Bryce checked it, turned his back to her.

"What is it?" she'd asked.

"Nothing," he'd said. "Just Hartley, saying he thinks we should work on some new things."

She'd seen him fiddling about with his thumb, no doubt deleting the exchange in case she got curious.

If Jane was guessing, it was Melanie. Her supposed *friend* Melanie. She'd seen something going on between the two of them.

Nothing overt. It wasn't as if Melanie had leaned across the table the last time they were all out for drinks together and shoved her tongue down Bryce's throat. It was more the way she laughed at everything he said, and let's face it, Bryce was not exactly Jerry Seinfeld. And Jane was pretty sure she'd caught him looking at her out of the corner of his eye more than once.

Jane got out her phone, brought up her contacts, and tapped on Melanie. Considered how to go about this. What message could she send her friend that might trip her up?

She typed: Hey maybe a drink after work? Did you catch band last night? I couldn't make it.

Sent the message.

Jane set the phone down, took a file folder out of her desk. She had to write some copy for a law firm's radio spot and think up some way to make a protective mattress pad sound like something you just had to buy, without using the word "stain."

Her phone buzzed.

Melanie had texted: Yes to drink. Duh. Went by bar, Bryce not there. Sick?

That was interesting. Jane had to think about that response. Melanie wasn't covering for him. If she and Bryce had been out together, wouldn't she have lied? Wouldn't she have said yes, she saw the band, Bryce was great? Something like that?

She texted back: Shit just had ton of stuff dropt on me cant do tonite. Bryce seemed ok 2 me this morn.

So if he hadn't been out with Melanie, what was he doing? Who was he with?

The hell with it. She dialed Bryce's cell.

Seconds later, he said, "Hey, babe. Sorry about this morning. We just seemed to get off on the wrong foot or —"

"Don't lie to me, okay? Don't lie to me when I ask you this question."

"What are you talking about?"

"Where were you last night? I know it wasn't with the band."

Silence on the other end.

"You there, Bryce? This is not a good time to pretend you lost my signal."

"Look, uh, I couldn't make it to the gig. I was feeling off."

"So if you didn't do the gig, where did you go? Spend the night in the ER waiting for them to treat you for sniffles?"

"Jane, I can't — I can't do this right now."

"I can."

"It's just, things between us lately, they've

been kind of rocky, you know? And you've been totally on edge. Sometimes, when I'm talking to you, it's like you're on another planet. You don't hear a thing I'm —"

"Just tell me her name," Jane said. Hector had appeared and was standing in front of her desk.

A long sigh from Bryce. "I went for a drink with Steph. That's all it was. A drink."

"You were out with Staphylococcus?"

Hector had his arms crossed and was strumming his fingers on his elbow.

"Jane, don't call her that. She's just a friend, but she's a good listener and —"

Jane snapped at Hector. "I am on the phone."

"Sounds like a personal call."

"Wow. You're super perceptive."

"You shouldn't talk to me like that," he said.

"Like what?"

"When you came in and told me to fuck off."

"Oh, Hector, fuck off."

"That's what I mean, right there. It's contrary to the office code of conduct."

Jane spoke back into the phone. "Goodbye, Bryce."

"Yeah, we'll talk later, after you get —"

"No, good-bye, for good." She ended the

call and turned her glare back onto Hector. "The office code of conduct, and you can kiss my skinny, white ass. Was there something else you wanted?"

"There's a woman in the lobby who wants to talk to you," he said.

"About what? I hit her car or something?"

"She wants to hire you, bitch," Hector said. "You know, for an ad campaign? The thing we do here?"

"Show her to the conference room. I'll join her in a minute."

"You know," Hector said, leaning over the desk and whispering, "I'd complain to Mr. Anders about you, but my guess is, you're blowing him."

Jane batted her eyes twice and said, "Yeah, but he tells me I'm nowhere near as good as you."

Hector scurried off. Jane gathered together a notepad and a fine-point pen, plus an iPad in its handsome black leather case. If this potential client wanted to see or hear any of the work Jane had done for others, she could show it to her on the tablet. She allowed a minute to make sure the client was already in the room. That way Jane could make an entrance. Always looked better than being the one sitting and waiting, like you had nothing else to do. Make the client think you're doing her a favor, finding a spot in your busy day to talk to her.

The woman was there, sitting. Nice looking, black hair, small string of pearls around her neck. Big smile, good teeth.

"Hi," she said, standing.

"Don't get up," Jane said, extending a hand. "A pleasure to meet you. I just had to finish up a call there." All businesslike now, no more f-bombs.

Calm down, she told herself. *Put the Bryce thing away. Lock it up in the box. You've always been good at this.*

"No problem," the woman said.

"I'm Jane Scavullo." She presented the woman with a business card.

"I'm so glad to meet you. I've heard good things."

Jane almost said, "Really?" Had to catch herself. Don't act stunned when getting a compliment. What she did say was, "And you are?"

"I'm the best life coach in all of southern Connecticut," she said.

"A who?"

"Life coach. I've been trying to raise my profile and I thought, maybe I need to advertise more, you know? I mean, I have the Web site, but people have to *find* the

406

Web site, right? They have to know it's out there."

Jane was thinking, *Steph? Bryce was out with Stephanie?* That girl had nothing going on.

"What do you think?" the woman asked.

"I'm sorry?" Jane said.

"Do you think you could get my name out there, get me more clients?"

"Well, I guess the first place to start would be for you to tell me what your name is?"

"Oh!" The woman laughed and extended a hand. "My name's Regina. But call me Reggie. Everybody does."

FORTY-FOUR

Gordie and Bert took the panel van they kept parked out back of the shop. Bert got behind the wheel and Gordie jumped in next to him.

"I still can't believe it," Bert said, driving away from the body shop.

"Which part?" Gordie asked.

"You kidding me? Eldon. I can't believe he punched Eldon's ticket."

"If he did it," Gordie said, "he did it for a reason. Like he said, Eldon was gonna blow the whistle on us. I mean, yeah, it's pretty sad about what happened to his kid, and he'd have been upset and all, but if he can't handle it in a way that keeps us all safe, what's Vince supposed to do?"

Bert looked ill. "Don't talk to me about the kid. You weren't the one who had to go to the farm."

"Sorry, man. That couldn't have been easy."

"I can't fucking do this."

"Don't talk that way. Don't ever be talking that way," Gordie said. "Sometimes shit happens. You'll feel better in a day or two."

"Come on," Bert said. "You see things clearly. Tell me things aren't going south."

Gordie glanced over. "What are you talking about?"

"All I'm saying is, the boss is not the man he used to be."

"His wife died. He's been sick. He's got to ride this through. How do you think you'd be if your wife died?"

Bert looked at him and laughed. "Seriously?"

"Okay, maybe that's a bad example."

"That'd be the best thing that could ever happen to me. Janine wanted me at a meeting — be going on right about now — at the home where her mother's at? They're kicking the old bat out because she's a miserable bitch. And guess what Janine's plan is? Guess?"

"Just tell me."

"She's going to move her in with us."

"Oh man. No, you can't let that happen."

Bert waved a hand in the air in frustration. "What am I gonna do? You can't talk to Janine. The two of them there, ganging up on me, telling me everything I'm doin' wrong." He went quiet. "There are times, I just think, I'd rather hit the road and not come back. Life's shit at home, and it ain't much better at work."

Gordie watched him quietly.

Bert said, "Vince, the guy, I tell ya, he's running on empty. Things are falling apart. And now we've been hit. What happens when the guy that money belongs to comes back for it? And we ain't got it? What's gonna happen then?"

Gordie was silent.

"Huh? What would you do, you parked that kind of money with someone for safe-keeping and they lost it? Would you say, Okay, shit happens, and leave it at that? Or would you blow their fucking brains out? I sure know what I'd do."

"All the more reason," Gordie said evenly, "to find out what happened to the money."

"Yeah, but what I'm saying is, what if we don't? And we've still got our wagon hitched to Vince? That guy's on borrowed time, and as long as we're attached to him, so are we. This thing with Eldon, that's the last straw for me."

Gordie had gone quiet again.

"What? You got nothin' to say?"

"You shouldn't be talkin' this way, man.

Vince, he wouldn't like it."

"You gonna tell him?"

" 'Course not. But you're taking a chance even thinking this way. He took out Eldon. You think now he wouldn't take out either of us if we looked at him the wrong way?"

"Exactly what I'm saying. You want to live with that every day? Wondering if the boss is going to come up behind you and shoot you in the head or slit your throat?"

"I hear what you're saying but . . ."

"But? But what? I've been watching him. There's times it's like he's not quite there. You see him breathing heavy, like he's having a heart attack or something. That cancer's eatin' him up inside. He's holding on to things so he don't fall down. You seen him walk? He kind of limps along. I was with him the other day; he was saying it hurts like hell when he drives, all bunched up with that bag in his lap."

Gordie was looking straight ahead through the windshield.

"Okay, forget it." Bert hit the steering wheel with the heel of his hand. "Bury your head in the sand."

"Let's just see what happens. Maybe —"

"Do you know where we're going?"

"Down this way."

Bert hung a left, the van lurching. There

was almost nothing inside, but it still rattled with every bump and pavement seam.

"I don't have my head in the sand," Gordie said. "I've seen the things you've seen. But what're you gonna do? Hand in your notice? Tell Vince you got a better offer?"

Bert snorted.

"I got an idea," Gordie said. "Tell him you've been headhunted by the Mafia."

"That's just it," Bert said. "He's *not* the Mafia. They never let you quit. Once you're in, you're in forever. But Vince is one guy. If you quit, you quit."

"No, you're wrong. You — try making a right at the next light; we might find him down there — quit on Vince and he'll hunt you down. I'm tellin' ya, you don't want to fuck with the guy. You can quit when he's dead." He paused.

"Maybe I won't have to wait that long," Bert said, cranking the wheel.

"I'm tellin' ya, don't talk like that."

"I'm not saying I'd do it. What I'm saying is, the way he's going, he may not have that much longer. And I don't want to be there when —"

"There! Up ahead, other side of the street. Isn't that him?"

Bert pulled the van over to the curb so he

could take a good look without having to watch the road. On the other side, on the sidewalk, a man walking two dogs. A golden lab and a poodle, both straining at their leashes.

"Yeah, that's Braithwaite," Bert said. "I got a feeling about this guy. I think he did it. I'd bet on it."

"Gonna be tricky with the dogs."

"Labs are nice, and a fucking poodle?" Bert said. "He might as well be walking a couple of cats."

He checked his mirror, cranked the wheel hard, and did a U-turn, stopping the van at the side of the road several car lengths ahead of Nathaniel Braithwaite.

Gordie got out the passenger side and positioned himself in the center of the sidewalk.

Braithwaite stopped, the dogs still straining to go forward.

"Nathaniel, right?"

"Yes," he said hesitantly.

Gordie smiled. "We're associates of Mr. Vince Fleming, and we'd like to have a word with you."

"Oh, okay," he said. "I was actually going to call him. I, uh, I wanted to talk to him about, you know, the arrangement."

"Well, whaddya know? But you're gonna

have to lose the dogs."

Bert was out of the truck now, too, taking a spot up alongside Gordie. Sunglasses on, arms folded, playing the role.

"I'll finish walking them and then I guess I could meet him somewhere," Braithwaite said.

Gordie shook his head. "No. It has to be now. And we're not taking the dogs with us."

Nathaniel Braithwaite forced a nervous laugh. "I can't just let the dogs go."

"Sure you can. Just unsnap the leashes. Give 'em their freedom."

"You don't understand. I'm responsible for them. Their owners trust me to look after them."

"Their owners trust you, huh?" Bert said. "That's a good one."

Bert pulled back his jacket far enough for Nathaniel to see the gun tucked into his waistband.

"Please," Braithwaite said. "Just let me take them back to their homes."

"And give you time to run?" Gordie said. "I don't think so."

"Run? Why would I run?"

Gordie, talking out of the side of his mouth, said to Bert, loud enough for Braithwaite to hear, "Shoot the dogs."

Bert put his right hand on the butt.

"Okay, okay!" Braithwaite said. He knelt down, unfastened the leash first from the poodle, then the lab. The dogs bolted into a nearby yard, sniffing the grass, the trees, each other. Braithwaite watched, his face washing over with anxiety, as they got farther and farther from him.

Bert had slid back the van's side door.

"All aboard," he said.

Forty-Five

Terry

"What the hell are you talking about?" I asked Vince over the phone, Cynthia huddled close to me to hear what he was saying. "What money? There's money in this house?"

"You were always one of my first choices," Vince said. "There's no one squeakier clean than a teacher and a wife who works for the health department. Couple of responsible, decent civic employees. Police would never search your place. Not in a million years."

"You've hidden something here? In our house?"

"I don't want to talk about it on the phone. I'll be over in a while. I'll take it off your hands."

"You son of a bitch. If you've hidden something here, you've put us all at risk, you've —"

"I told you, I'll take care of it."

The line went dead.

"You heard that?" I said to Cynthia.

She nodded, but then she started shaking her head in disbelief. I could see the fear in her eyes.

"It doesn't make any sense. I don't get it."

"You heard what he said. Because we're squeaky clean. Because we're the kind of people no one would suspect of hiding something illegal. Like stolen goods. Stolen money."

I tried to get my head around it. Was that what Vince had been getting at when he asked me whether Stuart and Grace had gone anywhere in the Cummings house? Whether they'd been looking for something other than keys to the Porsche?

"Son of a bitch," I said under my breath.

"What?"

"That's what he's doing. He's hiding his money in other people's houses, in case the cops ever raid his place."

"That's insane," Cynthia said.

"Maybe. But if there's money hidden in this house, and we haven't got a clue about it, maybe it's not as crazy as it sounds."

We both looked at each other, dumbfounded. Finally, I said, "The basement. If that bastard hid something here, it's probably in the basement."

I walked hurriedly out of our bedroom, Cynthia close on my heels. Seconds after we passed Grace's room, she poked her head out and said, "What's going on?"

Neither of us answered. I was in the basement in less than ten seconds, heading for the furnace room. It was on the north side of the house, tucked into a corner of the rec room where we watched movies. A room four by eight feet, large enough for the furnace and the water heater and a few boxes.

"It could be in here," I said.

"I don't even know what we're looking for," Cynthia said. "A box of money? You gotta be kidding me. A shoe box? A wine box? What?"

"I don't know."

I grabbed the first two boxes I saw, both with Magic Marker scribbling on them. One read *Family Photos,* the other *2007 Receipts.*

I dragged them out onto the rec room floor. Once I was on my knees, I opened the flaps of both boxes and dug my hands into them, pushing aside bits of paper and photo shop envelopes of old vacation shots that we'd never bothered to put into an album.

"Grab some more boxes," I said.

"This is nuts," Cynthia said, but she

grabbed the boxes.

There were about a dozen of them. More receipts. More photos. Two boxes of movies on VHS that we'd somehow decided to save even though we hadn't owned a VCR in nearly ten years. Boxes jammed with CDs we no longer listened to. Essays I'd written back when I was a student at UConn. We'd scattered the contents of the boxes all over the floor, making one hell of a mess.

There was no money.

Grace was standing at the bottom of the stairs looking at us. "Have you guys lost your mind?"

"What do you want, Grace?" I asked.

"What should I do about Teresa?" she asked.

Cynthia and I looked at each other. "What?" Cynthia said.

"She's here. She's upstairs. Should I tell her this is kind of a bad day? Or is everything sort of good now, except for the part where that guy broke in to probably kill me or something?"

Neither of us said anything. We were still looking at each other, and I suspected we were thinking the same thing.

Cynthia said, "Tell her we'll be right up."

Grace said, "Okay." She disappeared back up the stairs.

"Vince's guy needed a key to get in here," I said.

"And the code," Cynthia said. "Like you said before, there's a bunch of ways he might have got a key, but the code? Only four people should know that code."

We went upstairs together, found Teresa standing just inside the front door. She was in her late forties, early fifties. So far as we knew, she'd been cleaning houses since she came here from Italy thirty or so years ago. Teresa still had an accent, but her English was flawless, and I knew she devoured books like crazy. We gave her all our used paperbacks when we'd read them.

"Are you okay?" she asked, her voice high-pitched. "The car! What happened with the car? Something wrong with the brakes? You almost hit the house!"

"The steering," Cynthia said gently. "I'm going to have to get them to look at the steering. There I was, driving down the street, and the next thing I knew, I was driving right across the lawn."

"Oh!" she said, putting her hands to her cheeks. "You could have been killed!"

"No kidding," Cynthia said, then smiled reassuringly. "It's been quite a day."

"I will make some tea," Teresa offered. "It will calm you."

"That's not necessary."

"I'm surprised to find everyone home. Him," she said, pointing at me, "I figured would be here, you teachers getting the summer off and everything, but I didn't expect to find you and Grace, too. And a car in the yard! Are you moving back in? Please say yes! I know it's none of my business, but it pains me that you two are apart. It's not right. What do you want me to do? I can work, or I can come back another day if there is something going on."

"Stay," Cynthia said. "I'm hoping you can help us with something."

"Oh yes?" she said, her face full of expectation.

"I want to tell you what happened this morning. Why I drove across the yard."

"It was not a steering problem?"

"No. I was driving past the house, and I saw a man."

"A man? What man? A man where?"

"There was a man trying to get into the house. I drove right across the lawn to scare him off."

Teresa's jaw dropped. "A burglar? Breaking in?"

"Well, he wasn't breaking anything. He had a key."

There it was. A small facial tic. A small

tug at the corner of her mouth. "A key? A man with a key?" she asked.

"That's right." Cynthia was keeping her voice soft, unthreatening. "You see, Grace was here, and she heard him ring the bell, and then knock, but she didn't want to answer the door to a strange man, so she did nothing. But then she heard him slipping a key into the lock."

"My God, that is awful," Teresa said. She saw Grace standing by the door to the kitchen. "You must have been terrified."

"Yeah, kinda," she said.

Cynthia continued. "It doesn't seem like this man was worried about the alarm going off. You know, there's that little sticker on the door that says the house has an alarm system, so he had to know the moment he opened the door he'd have to disarm it. So he had to know the code. He knew he'd be able to turn off the alarm."

Cynthia paused, getting ready to go in for the kill.

"What we were wondering was, how could this man have a key and know the code? He'd have had to get one of our keys to make a copy, and someone would have had to tell him the code."

Teresa swallowed. She glanced left and right, starting to look like a cowering, cornered animal. "Grace," she whispered, not to her, but to us. "Teenagers, they like to get into houses when people are away, have parties and have sex."

"Excuse me?" Grace said. "I heard that."

"I am just telling you what I know about kids," Teresa said apologetically, as if it wasn't her fault.

"So you're guessing that's what the man told me?" Cynthia said.

Oh, interesting. Cynthia was going to go out on a limb here.

Teresa, incredulous, said, "You talked to this man? I thought you said you scared him off. When you drove at him."

"Oh, I scared him," Cynthia said. "Scared him good. He was even more scared when he tripped jumping over some bushes, twisted his ankle. Terry jumped on top of him."

I was pleased to discover I had a role in this.

"That gave us a chance to ask him a few questions," Cynthia said. "Before the cops came and took him away. Can you guess what he told us?"

Teresa still looked like that cornered animal, but no longer cowering. She was going to come out fighting.

"He told you lies," she said, nearly spitting out the words. "Lies and bullshit."

"Really?" Cynthia said. "You don't even know what he said. What do you think he said? That you let him copy our key? That you told him the code?"

"The police . . . did he tell the police?"

"I don't think so," Cynthia said. "Maybe I could keep that from happening if you fill in the details."

Teresa weighed whether to come clean, as it were. Cynthia gave her a few seconds to think about it. The woman's eyes softened.

Finally, she said, "He said he would never do anything bad. He said he would never steal anything, break anything. He said no one would ever even know when he was here. He just needed to get into the house."

"Did he tell you why?" I asked.

"I don't know," Teresa said. "And I didn't ask him. All I asked was, was he a pervert, was he going to be putting in cameras to watch your daughter have a shower or something like that."

Grace made a creeped-out face.

Teresa added, "He was a scary man, hard to say no to."

"Describe him," Cynthia said. She'd seen the man who'd tried to break in, but whoever approached Teresa and the man at our door might not be one and the same.

Teresa gave a short description that could easily have been Vince. "And he had this funny bump under his shirt and his pants," she said.

Bingo.

"He came by here one day, almost three years ago. He had been watching the house, saw me letting myself in. Talked to me when I finished and was getting my car, found out I clean your house. He said maybe I could help him. I thought he meant clean for him, but he said no, something different. He'd already checked me out, knew my boy is in prison, said he could make it hard for him or easy for him because he knew people."

Cynthia and I exchanged a quick look. Teresa had a son in jail? Who knew?

"Said if I helped him, he'd put in a word for my Francis, and he would give me some money, too."

"So you sold us out," Cynthia said.

Teresa bristled. "You think you matter more than my son?"

"We didn't know anything about that," Cynthia said.

"Of course you didn't," Teresa said. "You never ask me anything about my life. I am just the person who comes into your house and cleans your mess and shit and picks up

425

after you."

If that made Cynthia feel guilty, it was hard to judge by what she said next.

"You're fired."

FORTY-SIX

"So, a life coach?" Jane said. "That must be interesting." *As if.*

The woman everyone called Reggie said, "If you're having trouble with your job or your boyfriend and are looking for someone to talk to, someone who'll listen and offer you some life choices, I'm your gal. Like you — I'm guessing you have a boyfriend. Are things good? Are you feeling fulfilled in the relationship? If not, why not? That's the sort of thing you might talk about with your friends, but what qualifications do they have to advise you?"

"But you have qualifications?"

Reggie nodded. "I have a life-coaching certificate. Look, I'm not trying to pass myself off as a psychiatrist or psychologist or anything like that. Those are people with real medical training, and if you've got a serious disorder, like, you know, you're bipolar or schizophrenic or clinically depressed, I'm not the one you should be talking to. But let's say it's a bit simpler than that. You can't seem to get your act together. You feel you're in a rut. You wake up each morning and don't think you can face one more day doing the same thing over and over again. But what you don't know is how to change your situation. You need someone to talk to, and a lot of people, they just don't have that. I mean, sure, they might have their mom or dad or someone like that, but often there's already a lot of prejudging going on in a situation like that."

"Uh-huh," said Jane.

"When someone comes to me, there are no preconceptions. I don't judge. I don't start off telling them, Well, you've never succeeded at anything, so what makes you think you can turn things around now? No, I don't do that. I'm all about positive energy. I'm about building up, not tearing down. I want you to know that you can make that change, that you can turn your life around, to achieve your goals, and what I do is facilitate that through dialogue and encouragement and, well, coaching. That's what it's all about. Being a coach."

"Wow," Jane said. She hadn't written one word on her notepad.

"And there are so many people out there

428

who could use that coaching. Men and women — well, mostly women, I have to admit, because I don't think men are comfortable going to someone and admitting they need advice. God knows they won't even ask for directions when they've been driving around for an hour without a clue as to where they are."

"Oh yeah," Jane said.

Reggie leaned back in her chair, studied Jane, and said, "You're skeptical. I can tell."

Jane held up her hands. "Hey, I'm not judging. You offer a service, you need to get your name out there. I totally get that."

"But you think it's bullshit."

"I never said that."

"You're in a relationship right now, and it's troubled. Isn't that right?"

"Excuse me?" Jane said.

"Your mascara's ever so slightly smeared. You've been crying."

Jane reached a hand toward her eye, blinked. She needed a mirror but there was none handy.

"Things are a bit rocky right now," she conceded.

"Another woman?"

"I . . . I don't know. I know he lied to me. About where he was last night."

"Do you think he's lied to you before?"

Reggie asked.

"I don't know. This is the first time I've really been sure."

"You have to ask yourself a very basic question. What's his name?"

"Bryce."

"You have to ask yourself, Do I trust Bryce? If the answer is no, you have to ask yourself a second question. Do you see yourself moving forward in life with a man you do not trust?"

Jane, rattled, gave her head a shake. "I don't want to . . . I think we should move on. What were you thinking? Radio spots? A greater Web presence? I'm thinking TV is out, because the cost is kind of prohibitive, but then again, I don't know what you charge. I guess if you're Tom Cruise's life coach, you can charge whatever you want."

Reggie offered a sympathetic smile. "Of course, let's get to the business. I —"

A small *ding* emanated from her purse. A text.

"Oh, better just see what that is . . ." Reggie said, and rooted around in her bag until she had found her phone. "Oh, one of my clients, just confirming that I'm coming to see her this morning. I swear, once people connect with me, they don't want to make a move without hearing what I have to say."

Regina, still looking at her phone, frowned. "I totally forgot I'm supposed to meet this woman for coffee in twenty minutes. You would not believe the kind of day I've had already today. I wonder, maybe —"

"Would you like to meet later, maybe this afternoon?" Jane asked, losing the tone she'd had earlier.

"No, that's okay. You know what? I brought along a whole bunch of promotional material I wanted you to look at — brochures, and a couple of articles that made the Milford paper and the *New Haven Register* — but it looks like I must have left it all in the car. I'd go down and get it but" — she looked at the time on her phone again — "I don't know that I'll have time to run it back up here."

Jane said, "Tell you what. Why don't I walk you to your car. We can talk a little more on the way, you can give me those materials, and then make your appointment. Then I can have a look at everything and make some recommendations. How does that sound?"

Reggie beamed. "That sounds perfect."

They both stood. Jane grabbed her cell phone.

"So, Reggie, how did you hear about me?" Jane asked as they headed for the elevator.

"Your name came up . . . I'm trying to remember where," Reggie said. "I think it was a meeting with some real estate people. Have you done any work with them?"

"I did a radio spot for Belinda Morton," Jane said. "Could it have been her? She's a Realtor here in Milford."

"I think it might have been," Reggie said as Jane pressed for the elevator. "She had very nice things to say about you."

Jane Scavullo smiled. "I'll have to thank her next time I see her."

The elevator doors parted and they boarded. Jane hit "G."

"Are you from Milford?" Jane asked.

"I didn't grow up around here, if that's what you're asking. I'm actually from Duluth."

"Oh," Jane said. "I've never been up that way. Must be cold in the winter."

"That's for sure. But I can't believe how much snow we've been getting around here the last couple of years. All this crazy weather. Hurricane Sandy! Were you here for that?"

Jane nodded. "That was unbelievable. My stepfather's place is right on the beach, on East Broadway. Lot of damage there. At least his house could be fixed. A lot of them, they just had to tear them down."

"What does he do?" Reggie asked. "Would I know him?"

"Well," Jane said, cracking a smile as the elevator doors opened, "I think I'm pretty safe in saying he hasn't engaged your services, or any other life coach's for that matter."

"It's like I said. Men don't want to appear weak."

"No kidding." They emerged from the building into the sunlight and the heat. "Where you parked?"

"Over this way," she said, pointing. "The lot was full when I pulled in, so I found a spot down an alley up here. I'm so sorry to drag you out of the office like this."

"No problem. Reggie, did you have any kind of advertising budget in mind for this?"

"Well, it's all so new to me. All I've done is the Web site, and I got this kid I know who's real good with computers to set it up so it hardly cost me anything except to get the whaddyacallit domain name registered. But I was wondering what I could do with a thousand dollars or so."

They turned into the alley.

Jane shook her head. "I have to be honest. A thousand really isn't going to buy you very much. That might pay for my time to come up with a couple of quick concepts, but let's say you want to buy some radio spots. That's gonna be a chunk of change."

"Here's my car," she said, getting out her key.

"Nice Beemer," Jane said. The car was parked next to a white Lexus SUV. "Looks like the life coach game pays better than I might have thought."

Reggie had the back door open and was leaning in to reach a briefcase. "Oh, I didn't get this from being a life coach. My husband, Wyatt, bought me this."

"Oh," Jane said. "What does your husband do?"

Reggie glanced back over her shoulder to answer Jane, but seemed to be looking beyond her. "Together, he and I commit tax fraud, and just a little while ago, he helped me kill a man who we'd been led to believe had something we wanted, but he didn't."

Jane stopped dead. "What?"

"Oh," she said, coming back out of the car. "And, I guess you could add, kidnapper."

That was when someone behind Jane swiftly pulled the canvas bag down over her head, and everything went very dark.

FORTY-SEVEN

"Is this going to be long?" Nathaniel Braithwaite asked. "Because I really have to find King and Emily."

"What and who?" Gordie asked from the front passenger seat of the van. Bert was behind the wheel, and they were on the move. Braithwaite was struggling to maintain his balance, given that the van had only the two front seats. He had his legs positioned wide apart on the metal floor, a hand gripping the top of each of the front seats.

"The dogs. Those are their names. King and Emily. I'm responsible for them. If I don't find them, their owners are going to be apoplectic."

"Appawhat?"

"They're going to be very upset. How would you feel if you'd entrusted your dog to someone and they lost him?"

"I would be peeved," Gordie said. "Yes,

that's what I would be. What about you, Bert?"

"I'd be peeved, too," he said.

"Come on," Braithwaite said. "What do you want? Does Mr. Fleming want to see me? Like I said, I've been wanting to talk to him. I want to end our arrangement. It's making me uncomfortable."

"Really?" said Gordie.

"That's right. And I'm willing to pay him back the money he'd already paid me. As a sign of good faith. But I'm not comfortable with it."

"You're going to pay him back, you say?" Gordie asked.

"That's right. In full. He's given me three thousand dollars. I can pay that all back."

"With what?"

"I'm sorry?"

"With what?"

"With . . . the money he gave me. I haven't spent it."

Gordie shifted around in his seat. "You sure you haven't come into any other money lately?"

"What are you talking about?"

The van lurched around a corner, and Braithwaite nearly fell over.

"When's the last time you were in the Cummings house?"

"It's been a few days. They're away on vacation. I sent you a note. Well, to Mr. Fleming. I let him know that they were going to be away for a week."

"And so you haven't been over there in the meantime?"

"No. They boarded their dog. There was no reason."

"But you could've if you wanted to."

Braithwaite said nothing.

"Hello? What do you say to that, *Nate*?"

"I don't know what you're getting at. Of course I could get into their house if I wanted to. You know that. I have a key. I know the code. I can get in anytime I want, but there's no point going there if Mandy's not there."

"That's the dog's name?" Bert asked. "Like in the Barry Manilow song?" Bert had always liked Manilow, although he never liked him as much as the Carpenters.

"Yeah," Nathaniel said.

"Are you sure you weren't in that house last night, Nate?" Gordie asked.

"What? No. I wasn't. Why would I have been there?"

"Maybe to solve your cash flow problems? I hear you haven't always been in the dog-walking game. I don't even think there's a community college course for that. What I

437

hear is there was a time when you were in a slightly higher income bracket. That right?"

"Yes."

"That you had some kind of computer company?"

"Apps."

"Hmm?"

"We designed apps for phones and tablets. That's what we did."

Gordie nodded. "So you were making gazillions doing that, and now you clean up after dogs doing a dump on the sidewalk. That is what I would call a downfall of fucking epic proportions."

Braithwaite struggled to maintain balance. "Yeah," he said. "Pretty much."

"So it strikes me that if you saw an opportunity to get back a little of what you once had, you'd take it."

"I have no idea what you're talking about."

"Why d'you think our boss wanted to get into that house in the first place?"

"I don't know and I didn't ask. He just gave me his word that he'd never take a thing, he wasn't going to steal anything, that the owners would never know anyone had ever been in the house. I figured — I don't know . . . I thought maybe he was using the house to watch some people across the street, or maybe he was putting in bugs, you

438

know, to listen in on the Cummings."

"And you were okay with that?"

"Your boss is hard to say no to." Braith-waite shook his head. "He said he did me a favor. I couldn't believe this. Some guy who's been seeing my ex, he had him beat up. Broke his jaw."

"Yeah," Gordie said. "I nearly busted my hand. Fucker never saw it coming."

"Jesus, you did that?" Braithwaite said.

Gordie shrugged.

Braithwaite said, "Vince said, in apprecia-tion, I better help him. Or word might get out that I'd done it, or had someone do it. The man's a goddamn manipulator. But I don't care. I don't want to be under his thumb anymore."

"I don't think you have to worry about that," Gordie said. "I think I can speak on Mr. Fleming's behalf that your services will no longer be required."

Braithwaite looked uncertain. "Seriously?"

"Yup," Gordie said.

"That's . . . that's terrific. It's almost too good to be true. I appreciate it. I really do. Is that what you wanted to tell me? Because if it is, great, but I'd like you to drop me off."

"Not yet," Bert said.

"What are we doing? Why are we driving

around?"

"We're just looking for a spot," Gordie said.

"A spot?"

Gordie said to Bert, "How long we going to keep wandering? Gas ain't cheap, you know." Gordie had been so engrossed in conversation with Nathaniel Braithwaite that he'd lost track of where they were. But he was guessing it was the road that led up to Derby. Two lanes, regular traffic, but more isolated than stopping on the Boston Post Road.

"I think this is good," Bert said. "I can just pull over to the side. It's not like anyone can see in."

The van's tires crunched on gravel as it veered from pavement to shoulder. Bert moved the column shifter up to park but left the engine running so the air-conditioning wouldn't shut off.

Gordie got up and slipped through the space between the two front seats. Braithwaite took a step back to make way for him.

"I don't want any trouble," he said. "If there's something you guys want, or Mr. Fleming wants, just tell me what it is."

"We want the truth," Gordie said. Now Bert was getting out from behind the steering wheel, moving into the cargo area, but

440

not before reaching under his seat for a small case made of rigid black plastic. On the side were the words Black & Decker.

Braithwaite wiped sweat from his brow. Even with the air going, it was hot in this metal cell that suddenly felt much smaller. Three grown men, jockeying for position.

"Sure, whatever you want to know," the dog walker said, glancing nervously at the case Bert was carrying.

"Where's the money?"

"I don't know, and that's the truth. I don't know what money you're talking about."

"The money you took from the Cummings house last night. Two hundred grand, give or take. Where is it? If you give it back right now, we'll only hurt you. But if you make us work for it, well, it's gonna be very bad."

"I didn't take any money. Are you saying there was money in the house? Was that why your boss wanted to get in? To hide money?"

"You ready?" Gordie asked Bert.

The other man nodded and set the case on the floor. He flipped back two clasps, opened it, and brought out an orange and black cordless drill.

"What the hell?" Braithwaite said.

Gordie suddenly moved on the dog walker, hooking his foot behind his leg and driving him back with two hands to the chest. Braithwaite landed hard, with a loud metallic thump. The van jostled. Gordie jumped on top of him, straddling him. He grabbed the man's wrists and pinned them to the floor alongside his head, sitting on him like a schoolyard bully.

"Get off me!" Braithwaite said.

Bert stepped around them and stood just beyond the man's head, looking down, holding the drill in his right hand. He gave the trigger a quick squeeze, the quarter-inch drill bit spinning furiously as the device emitted a high-pitched whirring sound.

"I think you might have a cavity," Bert said. "D'ya ever see *Marathon Man*? That was like getting a flu shot next to this. I'm gonna need you to open your mouth wide."

"No," he said quickly, then clenched his jaw.

Bert got down on his knees, hovered over the man's face. Teased the trigger of the drill.

Whizz. Whizz. Whizz.

Nathaniel continued to clench his jaw and press his lips together.

Gordie offered a suggestion. "If he won't open his mouth, just drill into his forehead."

Bert said, "You got one last chance to tell us where the money is." The drill bit was an inch from the man's lips.

Spinning.

"Don't know!" he said through clenched teeth.

Bert touched the tip of the drill to the man's upper lip for a millisecond. Tender flesh ripped and blood sprayed. Nathaniel screamed.

"Oh shit, you got some on me," Gordie said.

"Sorry," Bert said. "Maybe if I forget the teeth and go in through the ear. Might be less messy."

Nathaniel's eyes widened with even greater fear.

Bert was repositioning himself when there was the sound of a cell phone. The two thugs looked at each other, wondering for a moment whose phone it was.

"Not me," Gordie said.

"Shit," Bert said. He set the drill on the floor and reached into his pocket for his phone. Glanced at the screen and winced.

"Jabba?" Gordie asked.

Bert nodded and put the phone to his ear. "Yeah? I told you, I can't make the meeting. Just tell them to keep the old bat. We can't take her. Yeah, that's what I said. The old —"

Nathaniel saw his chance.

He'd only made it to a purple belt in karate, but he remembered at least one move. When someone is straddling you, holding your wrists down, gravity is on your opponent's side. You can't raise your arms.

But you can make them go sideways, and use your attacker's weight against him.

Nathaniel swept his pinned arms down across the van's floor to his side, quick as lightning. Gordie, his hands still locked on Nathaniel's wrists, found himself pitching forward. Nathaniel scurried out from beneath him, and as Gordie started to turn over, Nathaniel drove the palm of his hand into the man's nose with everything he had.

Gordie screamed, "Fuck!"

It all happened so quickly, Bert was caught unprepared. He still had the phone to his ear as it all went down.

Gordie put both hands to his face, over his nose, while Braithwaite scrambled, crablike, to the van's side door. He pulled on the handle, kicked the door open, and leapt from the vehicle.

The car was parked so far onto the shoulder that the ground sloped immediately away into tall grass. Braithwaite quickly found his footing, pivoted left, and ran toward the front of the van.

Bert caught a glimpse of the man streaking past the front window, running across the road.

"Fuck!" Gordie said again. But he'd taken his hands away from his face and was getting up, blocking Bert, who was about to give chase, from moving around him.

Gordie stumbled out into the grass. There was loose gravel underfoot, too, and he needed a second to get purchase. He charged around the front of the van, started running across the road.

That was when Bert heard a panicked screech, rubber sliding on dry pavement, and a very loud *FWUMP.*

Sounded like a side of beef dropping from a second-story window. That moment when it hit the sidewalk.

A man shouted, "Jesus!"

Rather than go out the side, Bert threw open the rear doors. A FedEx truck was stopped parallel to the van, engine rumbling. Bert ran between the vehicles, stopped when he got to the courier truck's front bumper.

Gordie lay on the pavement, his body a bloody pretzel. The FedEx driver, kneeling close to Gordie but too horrified to touch him, saw Bert and said, "He ran right out in front of me! I swear! I couldn't stop!"

Bert forced himself to look away, scanned

the surroundings for Nathaniel Braithwaite.

Not a sign of him.

He ran to the back of the FedEx truck, looked again. There were a thousand places where the dog walker could have disappeared. A wooded area. Half a dozen houses he could have sought cover behind.

Fuck it.

Bert slammed shut the rear doors of his van after first snatching his phone off the floor, opened the driver's door, and got in behind the wheel. The engine was still running.

Without bothering to close the side doors, he put the truck in drive and hit the gas, speeding past the FedEx guy, who'd backed away from Bert's dead coworker and had a cell phone to his ear.

"Hey!" he shouted as Bert raced past. "Hey!"

Bert kept his foot to the floor. He didn't know where he was going, but he knew for sure he wasn't headed back to the body shop.

And he wasn't headed to the nursing home.

And he wasn't going home.

He'd been thinking about this, planning for this, for a long time.

Bert was done.

FORTY-EIGHT

TERRY

Once Teresa had been dismissed, Cynthia and I continued to search the house. We finished with the boxes we'd dragged out from the furnace room and turned our attention to a crawl space under the stairs. There were another half a dozen boxes in there. I hauled them all out into the middle of the room and then we each grabbed one and went to town.

I'd briefly considered waiting until Vince showed up — assuming he kept his word and came over — and letting him lead us to it, but the thought that something in our home had been secreted there was so unnerving we both wanted it found, and out of there, as soon as possible. Especially if its presence made us some kind of target.

Grace came back down and asked what we were doing.

"We're looking for money," I said.

She blinked. "This is where you keep your money?"

"No. We think there may be some hidden in the house."

"What? Why?"

"All good questions."

"Can I help look?" she asked.

"Knock yourself out," Cynthia said.

"It's somewhere in the basement?"

"We don't know where it is. It just seemed a logical place to start," I said.

"If I find it, can I keep it?" our daughter asked.

Together: "No."

She didn't look happy about that, but was still intrigued. "Do you know how much it is?"

We told her we did not. She said she was going to look in the garage, and we gave her our blessing. Cynthia, who had just emptied a box of Grace's childhood drawings, stopped and blew some hair out of her eyes.

"What if it's not in any of these boxes?" she asked. "What if it's, I don't know, in the walls?"

I stopped. "It's possible. But no, I don't think so. If he hid money in our house, he'd want to be able to get to it quickly. He's not going to want to rip off drywall to get to it. And besides, he'd have had to get it *in* there.

448

I don't exactly remember returning home one day and finding one of the walls replastered."

"Then it must be tucked away somewhere. After you pulled all these boxes out, did you see if maybe it was jammed in between the studs or anything?"

That seemed like a good idea, since the walls were unfinished in there. I crawled over on my hands and knees and went back into the storage area under the stairs, feeling around between the studs. I didn't come up with anything.

"What about under the beds?" Cynthia asked.

"Too obvious. Too risky, too. We keep small suitcases under there. Something hidden there could be stumbled upon."

Upstairs, the doorbell rang.

We looked at each other nervously. We didn't want Grace answering. She'd be able to hear the bell from the garage. I charged up the steps two at a time, shouting, "I'll get it!"

Grace was coming through the doorway that joined the kitchen to the garage. "Who is it?" she asked.

"Just stay there."

I got to the door and took a quick peek through the small pane of glass that was at nose height.

Vince Fleming.

I turned the dead bolt, opened the door, and said nothing.

"I'm here," he said. With forced politeness, he added, "Can I come in?"

I let him in. Cynthia reached the top of the stairs and stopped when she saw who it was. "You son of a bitch," she said.

Vince said nothing. He looked like he was expecting this.

"You goddamn lousy son of a bitch," Cynthia said, putting a little more into it this time. "I shared a beer with you. You sat there and talked to me about your life like you were almost a human being. But that was an act. You're something vile. Something absolutely despicable."

Vince looked very tired. "Go ahead. Get it out of your system."

"You blackmailed Teresa. To get into our house whenever you want."

He shook his head. "Not blackmail. I offered to help her son."

Her cheeks flushed. "Why us?"

"Why not you?" he shot back. "You're perfect."

"I still don't quite get this," I said. "What it is you're doing. How you used us."

"I hide things for people," he said. "People

450

who can't afford to have these things found by the authorities. Money, drugs, guns, jewelry, anything. I hide it where no one would think to look. In the homes of people who are above suspicion. Good, upstanding folks whose places would never be searched by the police. You fit the profile."

"If I'm supposed to feel flattered," I said, "I don't."

"There are lots of people that fit that profile," Cynthia said. "So again, why *us*?"

Vince ran his tongue over his teeth. "I drive by here once in a while. I saw your cleaning lady arrive one day. I got this idea, a service I could offer. I decided to start with you. Seemed like the least you could do for me." He paused. "Considering everything."

"I don't believe this," Cynthia said.

"I started recruiting others. Other cleaning ladies, babysitters, nannies. People who are trusted by their employers."

"Let me guess," Cynthia said. "At least one dog walker."

Vince nodded.

"Nate told me, last night, he had something going on with you that he wanted out of. He wouldn't say what. You dragged him into this after you met him at my apartment."

Vince said nothing.

"You're some piece of work," Cynthia said.

"Someone took what you had stashed at the Cummings house," I said. "But it wasn't Stuart. He and Grace were there when someone else was ripping you off."

"Yeah," Vince conceded. "Which is why my guys have been checking out our other locations, to see whether we got hit in more than one place. That's what Bert was attempting to do here."

"Where is it?" I asked.

His eyes went north. "Attic," he said. "That's where we usually tuck stuff. No one ever goes up in the attic. We put it in between the joists, under the insulation. No one's going to find it."

"Unless they already know it's there," I said.

He looked at me with dead eyes. "Yeah." He rubbed his hands together.

"This money you're hiding," I said. "How much of it's yours?"

"None of it. I take my cut off the top. Like I said, I store it for others."

"So if it goes missing," I said, "you're in deep shit."

He smiled patronizingly at me. "Yeah, I am. But you don't have to worry about me

452

leaving anything with you anymore. I'm here to take it off your hands." A pause. "Assuming it hasn't been taken. There's not all that much here, at least not in cash."

"So we're just supposed to let you go up there?" Cynthia asked.

"I can wait here if you'd rather do it," he said. "Might take you a while."

We both hesitated, glanced at each other. "I'll get a ladder," I said.

I was turning to go get it when Vince's phone started to ring. He reached into his pants and pulled out his cell. He looked at it, said, "It's Jane."

"She know all about this?" I asked.

He shook his head as he put the phone to his ear.

"What is it, honey?" he said. But his expression changed from mildly curious to deeply concerned. "Who the fuck is this? This Bryce?"

He listened. His face darkened.

"Wait a minute, wait a minute. Who the hell is — ?"

He said nothing for several more seconds, then exploded.

"If you hurt her, I'll fucking kill you. I will rip out your fucking heart. I will —"

Someone at the other end was trying to tell him something, but Vince wasn't done.

453

"No, you shut up, you — you gotta be fucking kidding. There's no way I can pull that together, no way! You put her on the phone! I wanna talk to her! I wanna hear her voice."

He waited. I didn't know whether he was holding his breath, but I was, and I was pretty sure Cynthia was, too.

"Baby?" he said tentatively.

When Jane came on, she shouted loud enough that we could hear her, too.

She said, "Vince, don't —"

Nothing more.

"Put her back on!" he shouted. "If you — Okay, okay, just don't hurt her. Don't hurt her. Tell me what you want." A pause. I saw color draining from his cheeks. "That could take some time. It's not all in one place. It's complicated. I'm not trying to bullshit you. It's spread out for security —"

He stopped talking, took the phone away from his ear. He'd been hung up on.

Very softly, Cynthia said, "Vince. What's happened to Jane?"

But Vince was already entering a number into his phone, putting it to his ear. "Come on, pick up, pick up. Son of a — Gordie! Call me! Right fucking now!"

He ended the call, entered another number. Droplets of sweat had broken out on his forehead.

"Jesus, pick up . . . Bert! Is that you? Okay, okay, look, are you with Gordie? I tried to call and he — *what*? Slow down! *Slow down!* How did that happen? A FedEx truck? How the hell did he get hit — and what happened to Braithwaite? Jesus, he *walks dogs.* He's not fucking James Bond!"

He put a hand to his forehead, held it there. "Look, look — I don't care about any of that right now. Just — *shut up and listen to me* — don't worry about that now. We've got a situation . . . Yeah, something else . . . yeah, *more* important. Somebody's got Jane!"

More questions from Bert.

"That's what I said. They've got Jane and they say they're going to kill her if we don't — Don't tell me you don't care!"

Vince's eyes looked as though they'd pop out of his head. He'd taken his hand from his forehead and put it over his chest. "Are you listening to me? Listen! I'm at the Archer house. Whatever you're doing, come by here and pick me — What?"

His face was dark like the bottom of a well.

"No, you listen. You still work for me. You get your ass here right —"

And then he stopped. A second hang-up within as many minutes. Slowly, he slipped

455

the phone back into his jeans and looked at us, a man who'd lost all hope.

"They've got Jane," he said. "And I got nobody."

He reached out to the front hall table to steady himself, but his hand slipped on some mail lying there from the day before.

That was when his legs melted under him, and he went down.

FORTY-NINE

It was the blood on the train of Claudia Moretti's wedding dress that prompted the owner of the bridal shop to call the police.

Claudia had the first appointment of the day for another fitting for her gown, which she would be wearing in two weeks when she married Marco Pucic, an out-of-work electrician who Claudia's parents believed was nothing less than a total schmuck. She'd been zipped into the gown when she noticed she had something sticky on her hand, and, rather than run the risk of getting whatever it was on the dress, slipped through the shop's back door and into a short hallway, where there were two doors nearly side by side. The first was for the bathroom, the second for private investigator Heywood Duggan.

She went into the bathroom, washed her hands, and when she returned, store owner Sylvia Monroe noticed a dark red mark on the train. When she examined it, she discovered it was still wet. In the hallway, Sylvia spotted the small trickle of blood coming out from under the door of Heywood's office.

No way she was going in there. But she did call 911.

Rona Wedmore got a call not long after the uniformed officers arrived.

It was an execution.

One bullet to the head. Wedmore figured the killer must have used a gun with a silencer. Even though that still would have made a sound someone nearby might have heard, Joy Bennings, the lead crime scene investigator, figured Duggan had been dead an hour or two before anyone had turned up for work at the bridal shop.

"We'll work our usual miracles," Joy told Rona.

Rona said, "I want to know whether the gun that was used here is the same one that killed the Bradleys."

Joy said, "Those two retired teachers?"

"That's right."

"This is connected to that?"

"It might be," she said. "Same kind of execution."

"You okay?" Joy asked while Rona stood there and looked down at the body. "You're not your usual chipper self."

"Duggan's an ex–state trooper," Wedmore said.

"Shit," Joy said. "You knew him?"

"Yeah," she said. "I interviewed him last night. He's been sniffing around the Goemann murder, and Goemann used to live next door to the Bradleys."

"What a summer," Bennings said. "I was thinking of taking a week off, going to the Cape. But people are dropping like flies around here lately."

While the medical examiner dealt with the body, Wedmore searched through Duggan's desk, then sat down in the office chair and, with a gloved hand, nudged the computer mouse to bring the monitor to life. She handled it gingerly, knowing they'd be dusting it for prints, even though she had zero expectation of finding any other than the deceased's.

She opened the mail program and sighed.

"We're going to have to take this in," she said. "See what we can get off it. All the e-mails — sent, in-box, trash — have been deleted. Might still be something there."

Like something that would point Wedmore in the direction of Heywood's client. Find the client, find out what he was working on, find out who'd want him dead.

Yeah, simple as that.

Wedmore noticed there was no landline on the desk. Like an increasing number of people, Heywood must have worked solely with a cell phone, the number she'd used to call him last night after finding contact info on his Web site.

"You find a phone on him?" Wedmore asked Joy.

Joy shook her head.

Shit.

Wedmore would be able to track down his cell phone provider and get a list of calls from them, but it would have been nice if the killer, or killers, had left the phone behind so she could check it out.

She left Duggan's office and sought out Sylvia Monroe. Wedmore found the bridal shop owner in a closet-sized office off her showroom, which now had a CLOSED sign in the window. She was sitting behind a postage-stamp-sized desk that was obscured by receipts, fabric, and a bottle of bourbon and a shot glass.

"Ms. Monroe?"

She glanced up, grabbed the bottle, and shoved it back into a desk drawer. "Sorry," she said. "I'm a wreck."

"Of course. I wanted to ask you a few questions."

"Sure, yes, of course."

"What time did you open up this morning?"

"Just before ten."

"You notice anything unusual, anything out of the ordinary?"

"No, nothing. I usually come in through the front door, not the back, so I hadn't even been in that hallway."

"You didn't hear anything?"

"Like?"

"An argument? A shot? Footsteps in the hall?"

The woman shook her head hopelessly. "Nothing. It must have happened before I got here."

Wedmore figured that was the case.

Sylvia said, "We've had trouble here before, but never anything like this."

"What kind of trouble?"

"A few years ago we had a break-in. Someone made off with nearly a hundred thousand dollars' worth of wedding gowns. Who steals wedding gowns? Insurance only covered a fraction of it. I thought, when Mr. Duggan set up his office there, that maybe we'd be safer. It was like having a security guard here, you know? Because he used to be a cop. Did you know that?"

"I did," Rona Wedmore said.

"It never occurred to me that him being here was just going to attract trouble. Look at my hand. It's shaking."

"You never had any more break-ins?"

Sylvia shook her head. "Never. Spent a fortune on cameras for nothing."

"Excuse me?"

"The surveillance cameras we put up out back." Monroe looked at Wedmore as if she'd just remembered where she left her car keys. "Should I have mentioned those to you?"

FIFTY

TERRY

Vince went down to his knees, then threw out both his hands to brace himself. I thought he was going to pass out, but he spent a moment on the floor there, on hands and knees, panting and catching his breath.

"Call 911," Cynthia said to me.

"No!" Vince bellowed.

She struck off for the kitchen.

"Don't call!" he yelled, looking down.

She returned with a glass of water. "Drink this," she said, holding it in front of his face. He took one palm off the floor so he could do as he was told. Grace was perched halfway up the steps to the second floor, taking it all in, her eyes fixed on Vince.

He took a couple of sips and handed the glass back to Cynthia. I was next to her now, extending a hand.

"Here," I said. He grasped it, hard, and

with great effort got back up on two feet. "Over here," I said, moving him to the closest living room chair.

"No time," Vince said, his voice breaking.

"Just for a minute," Cynthia said. "Till you have your strength back."

"I have to . . . have to start making the rounds."

"Damn it, sit for a minute," Cynthia said. "Do you have chest pains?"

"No."

"You're sure?"

"Just . . . I'm just tired. A wave kind of came over me . . ."

"Drink some more of this."

"Something stronger . . ."

"Drink the water."

He took two more gulps, handed the glass back again.

"Fill us in," I said.

"Some guy. Using Jane's phone. He said they've got her. They want everything."

"Did you talk to her?"

"She got one — *two* words out. Mine, and then she said, 'Don't,' and then they wouldn't let her say anything else. But it was her." He made fists with both hands, opened them, closed them again. "I'll kill them," he said quietly. "All of them."

Cynthia glanced at me, then said to Vince,

"No one doubts you for a second about that, but right now you have to figure out how to get her back."

"You think I don't know that? But after I do, I swear to God . . ."

He looked at both of us, and for a moment I thought I saw a flicker of self-pity in them.

I asked, "What did you mean when you said they want everything?"

"Everything!" he said, as if it should be obvious. "Everything I've got! Everything I've put away for people. The money, anything else. They want it all." Vince shook his head. "If that's what it takes to get Jane, fine, they'll get it. But after that, I'm a dead man. And if I'm a dead man, I'm taking them with me."

I had an idea what he was getting at, but he must have seen confusion on our faces, so he spelled it out more clearly.

"I'm paying a ransom with other people's money and property. One day, they're gonna want it back, and they're not gonna be happy when I tell them I gave it all away. These are not forgiving people. I'm talking bikers. I'm talking bank robbers. I'm talking drug dealers. I'm a dead man walking, in more ways than one. So these fuckers who took Jane, I don't care how many I take down, or what happens to me after."

"It'll matter to Jane," Cynthia said.

Vince shrugged. Defiantly, he stood bolt upright out of the chair. But his top half swayed slightly and he had to put his arms out for balance.

"Shit," he said.

"You can't do this," Cynthia said. "You're not well. You've got to let somebody else handle this. You *have* to call the police, Vince."

"No!" he shouted. Weak as he was, he could still make his words echo off the walls. He pointed a meaty index finger at both of us. "No police."

"Vince, for God's sake," Cynthia said, keeping her voice calm. "They've got experience with this kind of thing."

"They got no experience with handling this kind of thing the way I intend to handle it," Vince said. "Christ, can you imagine if I called the cops? They'd love that. They'd put the cuffs on me and spend a week busting my balls before they got around to looking for Jane."

I thought he was probably right about that.

"No, no way. I'll handle this."

"Do you know who has her?" I asked.

His head went side to side slowly. "But I

466

got an idea. I think I recognize the voice. A woman. Someone who brought some cash for me to hide a few days ago. Now I think maybe she was sizing me up, seeing how the operation works. I was wondering that about those two guys who came to see me last night, too. Maybe they're in this together."

"What two guys?"

"Logan, and his asshole brother, Joseph. The donut eater."

I had no idea what he was talking about.

"There was something about them didn't smell right. But the woman, she must have an idea how much money and stuff there is. She said bring it all. Said if I didn't, she'd know. Son of a bitch. If she really knows, then I'm gonna be coming up short."

"The Cummings house," I said. "You got ripped off last night."

"Two hundred grand, and incidentals," Vince said, his jaw tightening. "I gotta go."

He took a couple of unsteady steps toward the door.

"What about your guys?" I asked. "You said you've got nobody."

Another shrug. "Eldon's dead. Gordie's dead. And Bert, he's bailed. Abandoned me. Disloyal fuck."

Cynthia gasped. "Two of your men are

dead? These people who have Jane, did they kill them?"

A shake of the head. "No. Eldon . . . had a problem. And Bert said Gordie was in an accident. Minutes ago. Hit by a truck."

"You mentioned Nathaniel," Cynthia said. "You said dog walker."

"They thought he might have ripped off the stash last night. Picked him up for a chat. Things didn't go right."

"Is Nate — what happened to Nate?" Cynthia asked.

"Got away."

Cynthia looked relieved. "What are you going to do?" she asked.

"Pull together what I can, in the time I've got. Bert, Gordie got to a few places where we tucked stuff away. But not all. They were running out of time — some people were home; they couldn't get in without causing a scene. Had to find out if we'd been hit anywhere else. They pulled together a few hundred thou, some other stuff. I can raise maybe another couple hundred, buy myself some time."

"How much time do you have?"

"She's calling me again after one. Gives me better part of four hours. Gotta get moving."

"Wait. Just hang on," Cynthia said. "Let

me get this straight. You have to go to how many homes? Where the money's hidden?"

He rolled his eyes up into his forehead, thinking. "Five — maybe six — oughta do it. If the money's there. If we didn't get ripped off like at the Cummings."

"And you've got keys and security codes?"

"At the office."

"And if the people are home? What then? You going to shoot them? But get them to hold the ladder first so you can get into their attic? You're already woozy. I don't see you crawling around cramped spaces. There's no way you can do this."

"This has nothing to do with you," he said and took another step toward the door.

But it did. What happened at the Cummings house had everything to do with us. Grace had been there. Someone had seen her, and might still consider her a threat. Until we knew who that was, we were still very much involved.

Cynthia pressed on. "You don't want to call the police, but you think you can barge into people's homes and they won't dial 911?"

He had the door open, then raised a hand high and placed it on the jamb, leaning into it.

"What the hell am I supposed to do?" he

asked, his back to us, his voice breaking. I could see his body heaving with each exhausted breath.

"Give us a minute," I said, then touched Cynthia's arm and led her into the kitchen, past Grace, still sitting on the stairs.

"What?" she whispered once we got there. I closed the door so Vince, as well as Grace, could not hear what I was going to say.

"I can't believe I'm thinking this way, but maybe we should help him," I said.

"The only way we can help him is to call the police."

"I don't know about that. You were saying, what happens if he goes to these houses and someone's home? What's he going to say? 'Hi, I hid money in your attic. You mind if I come in and get it?' For sure that'll get him arrested. But the alternative, going to the cops, that may not work, either. He needs to be able to get into those houses and get the money if he's got a shot at saving Jane."

Cynthia wasn't certain. "But if he explains things to the police, makes them understand, quickly — You remember that detective? The woman? Rona Wedmore?"

"I remember."

"If Vince talked to her, if we talked to her with him, maybe they wouldn't waste a lot of time worrying about Vince's business. They'd worry about Jane."

"It's not just about Jane," I said. "I mean, I don't want anything to happen to her, but there's more at stake than just her."

Cynthia looked at me blankly for a second, but then she got it. "Grace."

"Yeah. Once this whole can of worms gets opened, everything's going to come out. Including the business about our daughter breaking into that house. And there's the matter of who was there, who may be worried that Grace got a look at him."

She was shaking her head. "But nothing that bad even happened in the house. Grace has *heard* from Stuart. Those texts. He's okay. If we call the cops, Grace may not be in as much trouble as we first feared, and we'll be helping Jane at the same time."

I wasn't so sure.

I decided to try another tack with Cynthia.

"That man out there, I know what he is. He's a thug. I get that. But I still feel I owe him. For how he helped us before. If he hadn't come with me that night, I wouldn't have found you — you *and* Grace — in time. And like they say, no good deed goes unpunished. He nearly died."

Cynthia's eyes softened. "I don't feel any

different. I know the sacrifice he made. But what can we do? Jesus, Terry, what the hell can we do?"

"I have an idea how we can get into those houses so he can get the money. Any house where there are people."

"How?"

"Mold."

She blinked. "I'm sorry?"

"Mold," I repeated. "Your latest project. Mold infestation in houses. In damp attics. Health risks. Fucking spores floating around in the air getting into people's lungs."

"I'm not following."

"Get your purse," I said.

She didn't ask why. Instead, she went out into the hall and was back in ten seconds.

"They're talking out there," she said.

"What?"

"Vince and Grace. They were talking, and then stopped when I came in."

I couldn't care about that right now. "Get out your ID."

"What ID? My driver's license?"

"No. From the health department."

Something sparkled in her eyes. She knew what I was thinking. Cynthia dug into her bag, pulled out her official ID from the Milford Department of Public Health.

"That's what you're going to show when

they answer the door," I said.

She nodded. "I tell them we're checking homes in the area. That there's some kind of mold epidemic."

"Has there ever been a mold epidemic?" I asked.

"Not that I know of," she said. "But I've got pamphlets on household mold in the car. It outlines the risks. There's pictures in them that'll scare any home owner to death."

"We tell them we need to see the attic. That that's where it grows."

"We?"

"You tell them," I said. "But I'll be with you. With a ladder. We leave Vince in the car because he'll scare the hell out of people."

"It's beyond crazy," Cynthia said.

"I know."

I could tell she was considering it, though. She said, "If you thought you had mold in the attic that could make you sick, wouldn't you want to know? We get in, we get up in the attic — that can be your job — you get the money, and we get out."

"Yeah."

I thought I'd won her over to the idea, but then she shook her head. "No, it's too crazy, too risky. I want to help Vince — I

473

really do — and I want to help Jane, but the best way to do it is to call the police. And with Stuart alive —"

On the other side of the door, Grace let out a mournful wail.

We found her in tears, her back leaned up against the wall, standing across from Vince.

"He's dead," she told us. "Stuart's dead. They made it up. The texts, they were all bullshit. Vince told me."

Vince looked at us with heavy eyes. "I needed you to stop nosing around. But we're past that now. There's no sense lying about any of this anymore."

Through tears, Grace said, "He says I didn't shoot him."

Vince nodded wearily. "Last night, I was using the gun as leverage. But Eldon's gun, the one Stuart gave your kid, it hadn't been fired. Full clip."

Cynthia turned and said to me, "I'll get the pamphlets."

FIFTY-ONE

She had no idea where she was.

In a room, of course. In a house, somewhere. Felt cool, so she was guessing a basement. *Duh.* They did walk her *down* a flight of stairs once they got her here. They'd driven into a garage, and then she heard the noise of the door rolling down once they were inside.

They'd kept the cloth bag on her head since the moment they'd grabbed her, except for a few seconds after they'd thrown her into the car, when someone pulled it up just far enough that they could slap some tape over her mouth. Then they'd done a loop of tape around the bag at her neck so it wouldn't fall off, which scared the hell out of her at first. She thought they intended to strangle her. But they hadn't made that tape so tight that she couldn't breathe. They bound her wrists together behind her back, and ended up roping her ankles, too, when she started kicking wildly. They kept her down on the floor of the backseat, two of them, because she could feel the weight of two pairs of feet holding her down. One pair on her back, the other on her thighs.

Reggie, the so-called life coach, was driving. She wasn't saying much. It was the two men in back who were making sure Jane stayed down on the floor, who were doing most of the talking. And most of that was about how much money they were going to get.

"You got any idea how much it might be?" one asked.

"It's gonna be a lot," the other said. "Probably more than a mill. Reggie, you think it'll be more than a mill once he empties out all the houses?"

Reggie: "We'll see."

They did talk about some other matters. About the call they had to make to Vince, how this really was a better, quicker way to do it. All that other energy they'd wasted, hiding GPS tracking devices in the bags with the cash, trying to figure out which houses, when it made more sense to let Vince just bring everything to them.

She guessed it took ten minutes tops to reach their destination. So they were probably still in Milford, although they could be almost to New Haven, or Bridgeport, or even up to Shelton, if the traffic wasn't bad. But she didn't think they'd taken any highways, so Milford was most likely.

She wondered how long it would be before anyone at work noticed she wasn't there. It wasn't likely she could count on Hector, that little shit, to call the police. Her failure to return to the office would be his opportunity to speculate to the rest of the staff that she'd fucked off for a very early, and very long, lunch.

Would anyone even make the effort to notice that her purse was still there? That her Mini was in the parking lot?

Jane wondered whether she should have made more of an effort to get on Hector's good side.

Lying on the floor of the car, her bagged face pressed against the mat, Jane had wondered whether they were going to kill her. And even if they didn't, she was wondering what they might do with her in the meantime, because one of the guys in the backseat was giving her a very bad feeling.

He was exceedingly creepy.

"She's pretty, don't you think?" he asked. "Nice ass."

"Stay focused, Joseph," Reggie said. "Logan, control your brother."

"He's just admiring the scenery," said the other one, whose voice was deeper.

Joseph and Logan. Brothers.

"Whaddya think?" Joseph said quietly. "Be nice to have a bit of that."

"When we get the money," Logan said, "you can buy yourself the best piece of ass in the country. You don't have to settle for what's thrown in front of you."

"Yeah, but still. It's right there."

Jane felt a hand on her butt and tried to shift her position, to shake him off.

"Now, now," said Joseph. "I bet she'd be a wild one."

As much as Jane wanted to get a look at these fuckers, she wondered whether being blindfolded was a blessing. If they were going to kill her, they wouldn't want her to see their faces. But then again, she'd seen Reggie. And they were calling one another by their names. It didn't sound as though they were struggling to remember fake ones. Wouldn't it be kind of stupid to use their real names if they were going to let her go? Wouldn't they figure she'd tell Vince, maybe even the cops, their names once they'd let her go?

Which made Jane think, no matter how things went down, they weren't going to release her. They'd put a bag over her head to make her more docile. It had nothing to do with protecting their identities.

When they'd pulled into the garage, Logan had said, "We're gonna untie your legs so you can walk in. Don't start kicking or anything."

Jane moved her head up and down.

"Okay, then. Free up her legs," he said to his brother.

"Just let me get out my knife," Joseph said. He leaned over, put his mouth close to her ear. "It's a mighty sharp knife." Then she felt tugging at her ankles as he cut through the rope.

"Okay," Joseph said, and she felt his hand graze along her thigh. It was like having a tarantula crawl on you.

Logan got her up into a sitting position, helped her work her butt over the hump, and her legs started extending out the open back door.

"I'll lead you in," Logan said.

They walked slowly around the car, their footsteps echoing on cold concrete. There were two steps up into the house, maybe ten paces down a hall. Then they stopped.

"Stairs down," the man said.

She took them one at a time. They were just wide enough for two, which allowed the man to walk down with her, a hand at her elbow the whole way.

"Now turn left here. Okay, turn around — you can sit down. There's a soft chair here."

She sat. There was a cushion on the seat, but the back was wood. It felt like a kitchen chair.

"Okay, well, we'll be in touch," Logan said.

She sensed his retreat, then heard the sound of a door closing. She didn't know whether he'd left a light on. The bag on her head didn't allow any light through, although the weave was not so tight as to keep out air. Good thing, too, since she had only her nose to breathe through.

As she sat there in her own world of darkness, she struggled to free her wrists, but the rope was tight and cutting into her skin.

Jane could hear voices upstairs.

There had to be a kitchen or living room directly above her. The voices sounded almost tinny, as though they were reaching her through a heat vent.

"I think he'll deliver," said someone. A man, but it didn't sound like either of the two men who'd been in the car with her.

"I think Wyatt's right," Reggie said. "He's not gonna let the girl die."

Wyatt. The husband. The one who'd

480

bagged her head and pushed her into the car. He must have driven here separately. So there were at least four of them. Reggie, Wyatt, Logan, and Joseph.

For a while, she heard nothing other than footsteps occasionally going by overhead. Then, from another part of the house, someone talking angrily, but no one was responding. Jane figured he had to be on a phone.

The door opened.

"Hey." Reggie. "Your dad, or whatever the fuck he is, wants to hear your voice."

She unwrapped the tape around her neck so he could lift the bag up far enough to get at the tape on her mouth.

"Hang on," Reggie said into the phone. "Here she is."

Jane shouted, "Vince, don't —"

Reggie slapped the tape back into place, let the bag fall down. She left the room without taping the bag around Jane's neck, and closed the door.

She thought she'd heard Vince say something, even though the woman hadn't put the phone to her ear.

One word.

Baby?

Had he ever called her that before? Sweetheart, maybe. Honey. But never Baby.

Jane wanted to cry. She wanted to panic, too. But she kept herself from doing either.

She had to be tough.

She'd always been tough. She'd always known how to look after herself. She had to figure a way out of this.

They were going to kill her. She was sure of it. Didn't matter whether Vince delivered or not.

They'd probably kill him, too, unless he had some brilliant plan to outsmart them.

She heard the door open again. Someone was entering the room.

Jane made a noise from behind the tape. *"Mm, mm, mm?"* It was the best "Who is it?" she could manage.

Whoever was there said nothing. But she could hear breathing.

They'd sent someone down to kill her. They'd convinced Vince she was alive, and they didn't need her anymore. She bent forward and shook her head, trying to get the bag to fall off, but it stayed put.

"It's okay," a man said. "I just thought I'd come down and talk to you for a while. Keep you company. Help you pass the time."

Joseph.

FIFTY-TWO

TERRY

Vince took less convincing than I might have thought. Cynthia showed him her Milford Department of Public Health ID, with photo. "This'll persuade a home owner to let us into the attic without you having to threaten to blow their brains out."

"I guess that's better," he said. The man seemed to be in a fog. He had to be thinking about Jane. I knew I was.

I went to the garage and returned with a stepladder and four short bungee cords with hooks at each end. I tipped my head back, as though looking through the ceiling to our own attic, and said to him, "We'll start here?"

Vince hesitated. "No. I haven't got much time, and the other houses have more cash in them."

So I carried the ladder outside and strapped it to the roof rack of the Escape with the bungee cords. It made sense that we all go in one car, and that included Grace. We didn't have anyone to leave her with, and we certainly weren't going to leave her at home after the terrifying events of this morning.

Once we were all in the car — Cynthia offered Vince the front seat next to me, not so much out of courtesy, I figured, but because she didn't want him sitting in the back with Grace — we had to first go by Vince's body shop headquarters. He had to collect any keys he'd need, plus a small notebook with addresses and security codes, that would get us into any house where no one was home. Also, he had to pick up what Bert and Gordie had already retrieved from their various hiding places around Milford. He'd stuffed it all into a couple of reusable eco shopping bags from Walgreens.

"We'll — actually, Cynthia — will do the talking," I said to him, glancing in the mirror in time to see him scowl. "And if you can tell me where exactly the money is in each house, I can scramble up there and get it."

"You better not be thinking of ripping me off," he said.

I was about to go after him for that, but held back, figuring Cynthia would tear a strip off him.

But it was Grace who said, "Wow, what a totally asshole-ish thing to say."

Vince shifted in his seat to get a look at her.

"Yeah, that was me," she said. "Look at all the shit your problems have put me and my parents through since last night — and yeah, okay, I screwed up big-time, too — but this was your bright idea to hide money in people's homes and it's all gone to shit and now my mom and dad are trying to save your ass and Jane's, and you accuse them of trying to rip you off? Excuse me and all, but if that isn't being a dick, I don't know what is."

Vince turned his eyes on me and said, "How long's she been hanging out with Jane?"

"Long enough to learn how to talk to you, evidently," I said.

He turned his head, stared straight ahead through the windshield. Without looking at any of us, he said, "Just what I need. Two kids busting my balls."

At the first house on the list, we got off easy. The driveway ran all the way to a two-car garage that sat behind the house. We parked alongside it; then Cynthia and I walked around front to ring the bell. When no one came, we went back and told Vince, who got out, key in hand, and went around to the back door. The property was well shielded with trees and tall bushes along the property line, so we felt reasonably confident we could get in the house unseen.

Vince opened the place up and approached the beeping security pad. He entered a four-digit code and the beeping ceased.

"Teresa work here?" Cynthia asked, with just a hint of a sneer.

He shook his head. "We got it from the babysitter."

Cynthia opted to stay by the car with Grace and keep watch. She'd phone me in the event of trouble. I got the ladder off the roof and followed Vince up to the second floor, careful not to bang the legs of the ladder into the walls.

"Easy one," he said, pointing to the attic access, a panel in the ceiling in the upstairs hallway.

I opened up the ladder, pushed aside the panel when I'd reached the top step, and hauled myself up into the attic, where it was hot as hell. If it was eighty degrees outside, it had to be a hundred or more in here.

It was dark, too. Some ventilation slits built into the wall at one end cast a few pale

486

slivers of light, and the opening I'd come up through provided more, but it still wasn't easy to see.

"Coulda used a flashlight," I said. "Or a fucking miner's hat."

"Next time," Vince said, standing at the base of the ladder. "Not sure where exactly the stuff is. Gordie handled this place. We usually don't like to put it too close to the opening. Go toward a corner."

Getting around was no picnic. There was no floor. Just studs, with paper-backed insulation stuffed between them. There was just enough height for me to stand, and I angled my feet on the studs, straddling them so I wouldn't slip through and possibly put a hole in the ceiling underfoot. I took out my phone and once again used it for a flashlight.

I squatted down, reached between the studs, and lifted up chunks of insulation. When I didn't find anything, I moved over to the next set of joists.

It didn't take long to find something that caught my eye.

The light from the phone bounced off the shiny plastic of a dark green garbage bag. "I think I got it," I said. I tucked my phone back into my pocket, pulled the insulation out, shoved it aside, grabbed hold of the bag, and lifted.

It was heavy with cash.

"Jesus," I said under my breath. Like a tightrope walker moving from one wire to another, I stepped across the joists until I was over the opening.

"Look out below," I said, and dropped the bag down alongside the ladder into Vince's arms. "I gotta go back and replace the insulation." No sense leaving evidence that we were here. I continued my high-wire act, moving from joist to joist with only limited ambient light.

My foot slipped.

My right shoe rode over the edge of the stud, down through the insulation, then hit something moderately solid, but not solid enough. My whole body dropped and my arms went out, my hands scrambling to catch nearby studs.

There was a loud crunching sound.

"What the hell was that?" Vince shouted.

"My foot," I said. "I put a hole in the ceiling."

I managed to work my foot back up, ragged drywall edges cutting into my ankle as I freed it. When I peered down where my foot had been, all I saw was darkness.

But then, suddenly, there was light, and Vince's face looking up at me.

"It's a closet," he said. "You fuckin' incompetent."

"I'm fine, thanks for asking. So what the hell are we going to do?"

"Nothin'," he said. "Nothin' we can do. Let 'em think it was raccoons." Any raccoon that could have done this could star in its own horror movie.

I still threw the other insulation back into place, although I don't know what point there was in doing it, and maneuvered my way back to the opening. I dangled my legs down through the hole until I felt the ladder under my feet, took a couple of steps down, got the panel back in position. Vince was standing at the top of the stairs, bag in hand, looking at me impatiently as I folded the ladder.

"How many places did we hide money in, and we never went through the ceiling?" he said.

"No," I said. "You just *lost* the money."

As we emerged from the back door, Cynthia ran over from the car, saw the green bag hanging from Vince's hand.

"Mission accomplished?" she asked.

We both nodded but neither of us spoke. Now that we had what we'd come for, we wanted to get the hell out of there. Vince reset the alarm, locked up, and got into the car as I was securing the ladder with the bungee cords.

As I got behind the wheel, I said, "Next?"

"Viscount Drive," he said.

I backed out of the driveway and headed for the next house. From the backseat, Grace said, "Do you think, if you give them everything they want, all the money, they'll let Jane go?"

Cynthia whispered something to our daughter, probably along the lines of, "Let's not talk about that."

But Vince answered anyway. "Probably not."

"Why?" Grace asked.

"They'll kill her, and me, too, because I'm not the kind of person to let this go."

I felt a chill that had nothing to do with the AC. "Then is there a point to this?" I asked. "Emptying out these houses."

Vince kept staring straight ahead. "Oh yeah."

"What? What's the plan? If you figure they're going to take the money and kill you and Jane anyway, what's the plan?"

"I'm working on it," Vince said.

"Would you like to let us in on it?" I asked.

"Make a left up here," he said.

The house on Viscount was another two-story. A modest home, white siding, no garage.

"Cleaning lady? Nanny? Furnace repairman? Who you got on the inside here?" I asked.

"Does it matter?" Vince said.

We pulled into the driveway. There was an old faded red Pontiac Firebird parked there, had to be more than thirty years old. Cynthia was out of the Escape first. As she got to the door and was ringing the bell, I was three steps behind her.

Ten seconds later, the door opened. A man in his early seventies, I guessed. Neatly dressed, shirt buttoned at the collar. Thin and tall, with a few straggly gray hairs atop his head.

"Yes?" he said.

Cynthia apologized for disturbing him, flashed her creds, and went into her spiel.

"We've had a disturbing increase in reports of household mold," Cynthia said. "Perhaps you saw something about this in the paper or on the news?"

"Uh, the wife might have," he said, angling his head back into the house. "Gwen!"

Seconds later, a silver-haired woman of similar age appeared, crowding the doorway. "Yes?"

"These people here are from the health

department asking about mold."

"Oh my," she said. "We don't have any of that."

Cynthia nodded. "You're probably right. The trouble with mold, of course, is that often you're suffering the effects of it before you actually see it in your home. Mold grows most often in damp places, often behind walls or furniture, and more often than not in attics, maybe as a result of a leaky roof."

"Oh my," the woman said. "That sounds awful."

"Which is why," Cynthia said, motioning to me and the car with the ladder still attached to the roof, "we are making random attic inspections to check for any mold infestation."

"I don't know," the man said. "I really don't think that's necessary."

Cynthia said, "As you may know, mold presents a greater threat to infants and children, as well as individuals who may already have a compromised immune system. That would be people with, for example, HIV, or who have breathing difficulties associated with allergies or asthma, and of course the elderly are also more prone to infection as a result of mold spores. Can you tell me whether you've had any headaches or skin irritations, perhaps dizziness or itchy eyes, even a dry hacking cough?"

I could see worry working its way across their faces. Even I was feeling a little concerned. I'd had all those symptoms at one time or another in the last few months.

"Harold," the woman said, "if we've got mold growing in the attic, we need to know about it."

"They're just trying to sell us on some expensive repair job," he said.

"Not at all," Cynthia said, handing them an official pamphlet. "We're not in the business of doing that. If we do see mold, we have a list of bonded companies we can refer you to. Garber Contracting is one that comes to mind off the top of my head, but there are many more. We don't do the work ourselves."

I was starting to wonder whether it wouldn't be faster to do this Vince's way. Just shoot them.

"Well, okay, then," the man said, at which point I walked back to the car to take off the ladder.

Vince powered down the window and said, "Try not to go through the ceiling this time."

"Where should I look?" I asked.

"Along the east wall."

As I was coming back into the house, I heard the woman ask Cynthia, "Who's that in the car?"

"It's Take Your Daughter to Work Day," she said.

"But school's out."

"True," Cynthia said slowly. I could almost hear the wheels turning. "But it's a Chamber of Commerce thing, not school related. But I can't bring her into the house because health regulations stipulate we can't expose her to the kinds of contaminants that may exist in your home. And that gentleman in the car is a city health department supervisor."

"He just gets paid to sit on his ass?" the man asked.

Cynthia did a minor eye roll and said, "Your tax dollars at work. But really, if we find a problem, he's the one who puts the hazmat suit on and goes inside."

The man paled at the word "hazmat."

The wife led me to the second floor and into a bedroom that had been turned into a sewing and crafts room. She opened the closet door and pointed to the hatch in the ceiling. This was going to be a tight one.

I set up the ladder as Cynthia entered. The wife was standing nervously in the middle of the room, and the last thing we wanted was her hanging around when I dropped wads of cash down from the attic.

Cynthia, who had clearly thought this scam through, pulled two surgical masks from her pocket. She handed one to me and slipped the other one on over her face, looping the small straps over her ears.

"I wish I had a third one for you," she said to the woman, who then decided to wait downstairs.

I stuffed mine into my pocket as I moved the hatch aside. I hoisted myself up into the attic, yet another sweltering environment awash in the musty smells of stale air, wood, and what I thought might be mouse droppings. I directed the flashlight to the east wall.

There wasn't enough room to stand upright, so I moved bent at the waist. My eye caught something on one of the ceiling planks. Something dark and, well, yucky.

"Cyn, can you hear me?"

I heard the ladder rattling, turned, and saw her head poke up into the attic. "Yeah, I'm here," she said.

"I think they've got mold," I said.

She went back down the ladder.

When I got to the east wall, I started lifting up insulation. In a couple of minutes, I found what I was looking for. A clear plastic bag, about the size of a thick binder, sealed with duct tape and stuffed with neat stacks of bills held together with rubber bands.

I also found something else.

Several small freezer bags, tucked into a larger clear bag, filled with what appeared to be splinters of broken glass, or ice. Except it couldn't be ice, given how hot it was up here. There were hundreds of these crystal-like pieces, some very small, some as big as the tip of my finger.

"What in the hell is — ?"

Then it hit me. It was crystal meth.

When Vince said he was stashing stuff besides money, he wasn't kidding.

FIFTY-THREE

Rona Wedmore got on the phone to one of the department's tech guys, who went by the name Spock. She wasn't even sure what his real name was.

"I'm at a bridal shop downtown and I need you here ten minutes ago," she said into her cell.

"Did I propose and it slipped my mind?" he asked.

Spock showed up twenty minutes later. At five-five and two hundred fifty pounds, he bore little resemblance to the Vulcan, but he seemed to share his smarts. Once Rona let him loose on the store's surveillance system, which was set up in a storage room filled with hundreds of wedding gowns, he was all business. He'd brought along some equipment of his own, including a laptop, and was plugging things in and running wires here and there.

Instead of reviewing the surveillance data

from that morning on the cheap monitor set up in the storage room, Spock was able to see it on his own high-resolution screen.

"What time we looking at?" he asked Wedmore.

"Not sure. Before ten. Can you work backwards, or do you need me to give you an earlier time and you go ahead?"

Spock, eyes fixed on the screen, said, "I can do anything."

"Let's go back to eight and work forward."

Spock went back nearly four hours, then set the footage to play at fast-forward. The camera was positioned over the back door, angled in such a way as to catch the parking area and some of the street that ran behind the shop.

"There," Wedmore said. "A car just parked across the street."

"Yeah."

"What is that? A BMW?"

"I don't know anything about cars," Spock said. "I don't have a driver's license."

"What are you? Fifteen?"

Even on Spock's expensive laptop, the footage was grainy and indistinct. A man and woman got out of the car, started crossing the street, but bore right, and exited the frame. But a few seconds later, they entered the screen from the bottom right corner, so close to the wall that the camera picked up little more than the tops of their heads.

They spent a few seconds outside the door, then entered the building.

"She put in cameras," Wedmore said. "But she hadn't set the alarm. Start fast-forwarding again."

It wasn't much longer before another car showed up, but instead of parking across the street, this one pulled in right in front of the door. A beige four-door Nissan. Heywood Duggan got out.

Wedmore felt a tightening in her throat. She made a fist with her left hand, digging her nails into her palm.

"This the guy?" Spock asked.

"Yeah," she said quietly.

Another five minutes went by. The door opened again, and the man and woman exited. A shot of their backs as they walked past Duggan's car, crossed the street, and got back into the BMW. The car started, did a U-turn in the street, and disappeared in the direction it had come from.

"Go back — freeze that."

"Freeze what?"

"When the car's turning around, we've got a shot at the plate."

Spock froze the image. The car and the plate were equally blurry.

"Can't you blow that up?" Wedmore asked.

Spock said, "It's not going to get any better." And it didn't. He enlarged the image, but the numbers and letters on the license plate were too indistinct to make out.

"Shit," Wedmore said.

"I can tap into the traffic system. Check their cameras. Look for that car, in that area, around that time. I'll have a better chance pulling a plate number off their system."

"If you can do that, I'll buy you a full set of *Star Trek* action figures," Wedmore said.

"I hate *Star Trek,*" Spock said.

FIFTY-FOUR

TERRY

"Cyn!" I whispered. It was a pretty loud whisper. I wanted to be sure she heard me, but didn't want to get the attention of the elderly couple who lived in this house.

Her head popped up into the attic for the second time.

"I'll tell them about the mold," she said.

"I need to talk to Vince."

"You can't find the money?"

"I found money. But I found something else." I held up one of the bags of crystal meth.

"What *is* that?"

I tossed the bag in her direction. It landed a couple of feet short of the hatch, and she reached over, grabbed the bag, and examined it. She looked at me.

"You know what this is, don't you?"

"I've got a pretty good idea," I said. "It's one thing driving all over town with cash, but what if we get pulled over with that in the car?"

"Give me a minute."

Her head vanished. I tried to find a way to get comfortable while I waited for her return. I parked my butt crossways on one of the beams, rested my feet on one in front of me, placed my two hands on another behind me, and leaned back. I'd have much preferred a leather recliner.

Five minutes went by. I began to hear voices below me, then the rattling of the aluminum ladder.

A second later, Vince's head came into view. I held up the bag and said, "You think we should be wandering around with this?"

"You're wasting time," he said. "They said they wanted everything. So we're giving them everything. Maybe they know about this. Maybe this is part of what they want. I'm trying to save Jane and you're going to get picky about what we've got in the car?"

"I'll toss it over. You can drop it down to Cynthia," I said. When all the stored drugs and cash had been removed, I tamped the insulation back down.

By the time I got down to the front door with the ladder, Vince was back in the car and Cynthia was giving the home owners a short list of contractors they could call to take a look at their problem.

"Whaddya know," she said, getting into the backseat next to Grace. "We did a good deed."

Vince looked at his watch. It was already past noon. He'd be getting a call soon. He gave me directions to another house.

We got lucky there. Like the first place, no one was home. Vince and I went in while Cynthia and Grace kept watch out front. I had to lift up almost all the insulation to find the cash. Vince had thought it was on one side of the house, but it turned out to be on the opposite.

"Eldon," he muttered under his breath.

"What happened there?" I asked while I was bent over hunting for money and Vince was watching me from the access hatch. "Bert took off. Gordie got run down by a truck. You said Eldon's dead, too."

"Yeah," Vince said.

"How?"

"Don't ask," he said.

"Could it have been him?" I asked.

"Him what?"

"Who ripped you off? Was his son helping him? Him and Stuart? Something went wrong?"

Vince shook his head. "I don't think so."

"But it had to be someone who knew the

money was there. You never told Teresa why you wanted into our house. And you didn't tell the dog walker, either."

"No. Unless he figured it out."

"You saying it couldn't have been one of your own people?"

It was suddenly very quiet in the attic. It was several seconds before Vince spoke. "I suppose one could think that. But that's my problem. Not yours."

We finished up, did our best to make it look as though no one had ever been there, and left the house. I got the ladder strapped back onto the roof rack.

"Where to now?" I asked as I got back behind the wheel.

Vince looked again at his watch. "They're supposed to call in half an hour. We haven't got time to do any more." He talked in a monotone, as if on autopilot, his mind elsewhere.

"What are you thinking?" I asked.

"I don't know," he said slowly, which told me he did. "She said she wanted everything, like maybe it's not just about the money. It's the needle in the haystack."

Grace asked, "What?"

"Maybe it's that crystal meth. The people who left that with me have been perfecting their product for some time. Maybe someone wants that batch to figure out how they did it. Or maybe it's some documents, tucked in with some money from another house. Something they know is in one of my hiding places, but they don't want to ask for it outright so I could just go to the right house and get it. They don't want me to know what it is. Because if I knew it was that valuable, maybe I'd want to hang on to it myself."

"So we might not even have it yet," I said.

"Yeah." He thought some more. "That's kind of what I'm hoping."

I shot him a look. "What?"

"But if we do have it, I still have to tempt them with something more." He wasn't talking to us. He was talking to himself.

His interior monologue got cut short. His cell phone was ringing. He grabbed it from his jacket, looked at the screen, and said, "It's them."

FIFTY-FIVE

Jane, still bound and hooded and sitting in the chair, heard Joseph drag something across the floor from somewhere else in the room. She kept very still, listening, trying to figure out what he was doing.

The noise stopped abruptly, directly in front of her.

"Just want to make myself comfortable," Joseph said. A chair. He'd dragged over a chair, one with wooden legs, she bet. She heard the rustling of fabric, a slight shift in the air as the man sat down.

Suddenly, she felt something touch her knees, and she flinched.

"Hey, don't worry," he said. "That's just me. I pulled my chair up close so we could sit knee to knee."

She tried to force herself back farther into her chair, but there was no place to go. He opened his legs so he could trap hers between his two knees.

"That's nicer. I like that. You like that? You don't say much, do you? You know something? I like that in a girl."

He patted her knees with his palms, as if he was drumming.

"Badoop, badoop. Hey, I bet you're wondering whether your dad is going to get you out of this. I know, I got that wrong. Reggie says he's not your dad, that he's your stepdad. I had a stepdad for a while. Me and Logan, there was a couple years our mom lived with this asshole named Gert. He was from Bavaria or someplace. My mom liked him, till she got to know him and found out he got his kicks from bending her fingers back till they nearly snapped if she didn't get his dinner on the table on time. What he liked to do to me was — and I gotta admit, I was kind of a pain in the ass — was put me in the dryer. You know, this big white Kenmore. Well, it probably wasn't any bigger than a regular dryer, but when you're a little kid and you can't even see over the top of it, it's big. So when I was a pain in the ass, he'd open the door and shove me in, and then he'd prop a chair up against the door so I couldn't get out. I know what you're thinking. Did he turn it on? You know, and like spin me around and toast me to death? Naw. I mean, he might have wanted to, but I was too heavy, it would have busted the machine, and the last thing he'd have wanted to do is pay a repairman to fix it. So he'd just leave me in there, all bunched up. One time, he musta forgot he'd put me in there, or just didn't give a shit, because he went out for the afternoon to go drinking with his buddies. Your mom ever do anything like that to you? Did she have a nice body? Because you do."

A hand came off her knee and touched the side of her head. Caressing her through the hood.

"So, anyway, we saw your stepdad last night, and I couldn't believe it. He pissed his pants. I guess we scared him. He must scare easy, because we weren't being threatening or anything."

He took his hand from her head and rested it back on her knee. "Anyway, about when I was in the dryer."

Jane made a mewing noise of frustration.

"Don't interrupt. I used to go to this place, like, in my head, when Gert would do shit like that to me. Somewhere far away, so I wouldn't think about what I was going through. It was really helpful. Sometimes I'd imagine I was on a ship out in the ocean, or maybe on a rocket going to Mars — anything like that. I wondered, is that kind of what you're doing now? Imagining you're someplace else? Because if you're not, I think that's what you might want to start doing."

From upstairs: *"Joseph!"*

"Shh," he said to her. "That's my brother. He probably wants me to do something. Whatever it is, it can wait. I thought we'd have a little fun first. Even with a bag over your head, you're nice-looking. Some girls, you'd *want* to do them with a bag over their head. I have to stand up for a second."

He released his grip on her knees, stood back. Jane wondered whether he was leaving, but she didn't sense him moving away. She could hear his breathing. Then she could hear something else. A clinking, like the sound of a belt buckle. Then the unmistakable sound of a zipper.

Descending, in all likelihood.

"Go to your special place," he said, his voice sounding very close.

"Joseph!"

She could feel his breath on her face, even through the fabric of the hood. His face directly in front of hers.

Jane figured, if she was ever going to try something, it was now. It didn't take her more than half a second to figure out what it would be, and to execute.

She leaned back, to allow herself a few inches to build up some momentum, then shot her head forward.

Fast.

Whole thing couldn't have taken more than half a second.

She couldn't know exactly where he was — where, specifically, his *nose* was — but she had a pretty good feeling about it. She tipped her chin down, brought her forehead forward, and drove it as hard as she could to whatever part of him was there in front of her.

Contact. It lasted only an instant, but it was enough to feel bone meet flesh and cartilage. To feel Joseph's nose crushed into his face.

His scream was ear-piercing and immediate.

"Ahhhhh!"

Which was quickly followed by, "Oh my God, oh my God!"

Jane felt warm drops land on the thighs of her pants. Upstairs, the sound of people's feet pounding on the floor.

"Joseph! Where are you? Where — ? Jesus!"

"My nose!" he cried. "She smashed my nose!"

"Holy shit!" The voice of the woman. Reggie.

"Logan, it's broken!" Joseph said, weeping. "It's goddamn broken!"

"Okay, hold on, hold on." Sounding frantic.

"I'm gonna kill her!"

She felt hands, wet and slippery, grab her by the neck just below the hood, smear her skin. He wrapped his palms around her throat, started to squeeze.

"Stop it!" Logan. "Joseph, stop it!"

Someone dragged him away. "Jesus, he's bleeding like a faucet." Another man. Had to be the one called Wyatt.

"Get something for his nose," Logan said.

More screaming.

"I'm going to have to take him to the hospital," Logan said.

"Are you kidding?" Reggie said. "You can't go to —"

"Look at him! He's gonna choke on his own blood!"

"What the hell are you going to tell them at the hospital?" Wyatt said.

Joseph, his voice gargling: "That this bitch did it! This fucking bitch broke —"

"No!" Logan said. "You'll tell them you tripped and fell flat on your face — that's what you're going to tell them."

"I need a doctor," he said frantically. "I need a doctor bad."

"Fine, shit, okay," Reggie said. "Take him to the hospital. Just have a good story."

"I don't know how long we'll be," Logan said. "It could take a while. God, I don't even know if they can set that."

"How bad does it look?" Joseph asked.

"What the hell are you doing with your pants down?" Reggie asked. "Honest to God. We've got shit to do and you're down here fuckin' the help."

"What about the meet?" Wyatt talking.

Reggie said, "We can do that without them. You guys go to the hospital and we'll regroup back here after."

"We still want our share," Logan said.

"Don't worry about that. God, get him out of here — he's making a mess. Look at the goddamn carpet."

Jane heard Joseph's whimpers recede as his brother led him out of the room and upstairs. But she could sense someone still in the room.

Reggie said, "Did he touch you?"

Jane shook her head under the hood.

Reggie sighed. "It'll all be over soon enough," she said, and left the room.

FIFTY-SIX

TERRY

Vince Fleming put his cell phone to his ear and said, "Yeah." His jaw was set tight as he listened to the person on the other end.

About thirty seconds passed before Vince said, "I understand." He ended the call and put the phone away.

"Well?" I said.

"I give them the money in half an hour."

"Half an hour?" Cynthia said.

"We have to go back to your place," he said to me.

"Why?"

He cocked his head toward the backseat. "We have to get rid of them."

"We have names," Grace said.

Vince half turned in his seat so he could see her and Cynthia. "I need to borrow Terry for this. I need a driver. But you can't come along. They see a car full of people and they're going to get spooked. I don't think it's going to be dangerous — I'm just handing stuff over and then they're going to tell me where Jane is — but you can't come."

"How can you say it won't be dangerous?" Cynthia asked. "What if these people take the money and . . ." She struggled to get the words out. "What if they take the money and shoot you or something?"

"That won't happen," Vince said.

"You can't know that," I said.

"I do," he said.

"You know Cyn's right. There's every reason to believe they'll shoot you and take the money and you'll never see Jane."

"That's not how it's going to go down."

"So you do have some sort of brilliant plan?" Grace asked.

He didn't respond for a moment. "Yeah," he said. "And the sooner I get rid of you and your mother, the sooner I can get to it."

Sometimes Vince made it very hard to like him.

I took my foot off the brake and aimed the car for home. I could sense Cynthia wanted to talk to me, but couldn't say what was on her mind in front of Grace, or Vince. I knew she didn't want me heading off with Vince alone, but she also had to know it wasn't a good idea to make Grace a part of this continuing adventure, either. It actually made sense to drop the two of them off and for me to stick with Vince. I was still mulling over whether, and when, to put in a call to the police, and wondered whether Cynthia, once I'd dropped her off, would do it.

We were almost back to our place when Vince said, "We'll take my truck. They'll probably be looking for it, but you can drive."

Once I'd turned into the driveway and turned off the car, Vince said to Cynthia, "Don't hang around here."

"What?" she said. "Why not?"

"I can't say for sure someone won't come back here. It won't be anyone working for me — that much I know. Until this is over, you two take off. Go for a drive. Go to the mall. I don't know. Just don't be here. We'll call you when we're done."

I said, "That's a good idea."

We all got out of the car. Vince gathered together all the bags of loot he'd collected, including the ones he'd taken from his body shop, and carried them over to his truck. He set them down, got the keys from his pocket, and, once the doors were unlocked, tossed the keys my way.

I missed the catch and had to bend over

515

to grab them off the lawn. I thought I saw a small frown on his face, wondering, no doubt, whether any confidence he might have in me was misplaced.

I'd say yes.

He was walking with a decided limp and, while not collapsing, seemed even weaker than he had a couple of hours earlier. He went around to the passenger side of his pickup and got in, stuffing the bags behind the seat.

"Where are we supposed to go?" Grace asked.

"Go to your mom's apartment," I suggested.

"I need to talk to your father," Cynthia said, shooing Grace away. "I don't like this. It's one thing gathering up that money, but it's another delivering a ransom to kidnappers."

"It's not exactly how I'd expected my day to play out," I said. "You want, I'll pull the plug on this now. I'll call the cops. Vince'll be mad, but there won't be a damn thing he can do about it. And as far as Grace is concerned, we'll still get that lawyer and do whatever it is we have to do."

Cynthia hesitated.

"Right now, right this minute, it's about Jane," she said. "What if bringing in the police — what if that really does screw things up somehow? And ends up getting Jane killed?"

"Honestly, I don't know what to do. But my gut tells me this is Vince's call, how to play this. She's his stepdaughter. I'm not sure it's up to us. And if it isn't, I don't see how I can let him handle this alone. All his people are dead or have abandoned him. Right now, we're all he's got."

Cynthia laid a hand on my shoulder. "Just be careful, okay? Promise me that? Don't do anything stupid?"

"You're a bit late with that advice."

I wanted desperately to make some kind of joke, to not make this a scene where the soldier is heading off into battle. I gave her a quick kiss. Too long a one, I thought, would give the impression I wasn't coming back.

I was coming back.

Cynthia grabbed my hand and gave it a squeeze. I opened the door of the pickup, hauled myself in, and got settled behind the wheel.

"You remember what I told you seven years ago?" Vince asked.

"Huh?"

"When you and I set off in this very same truck, me helping you figure out what happened to your wife's family? The night I ended up getting a fucking bullet in my gut?"

"You said don't fiddle with the radio. Don't touch the stations, or you'd fucking kill me."

Vince nodded agreeably.

"Nothing's changed," he said.

FIFTY-SEVEN

TERRY

"They want to do the handoff in the cemetery," Vince said once we were on the road. "You know the one, on the way out to the mall?"

"Yeah," I said. "Isn't that a bit clichéd?"

Vince gave me a look. "Is that your concern? That they're not being original enough?"

"Look, I'm going to take one last shot at this. Call the cops."

"No."

I brought my voice down. I didn't want to be arguing with him. I just wanted to make my case. "You've already as much as admitted to me your future's kind of bleak at the moment. If these people who kidnapped Jane don't kill you, the people whose money you're using to save her will want to when they come to collect. So we're not talking about saving your ass here. We're only worried about Jane. The cops have a better shot at getting her back alive than you do."

"They'd fuck it up," he said.

"They've got helicopters and tracking devices. They know how to tap into everybody's surveillance cameras. They can have all kinds of cops in ordinary cars following these people. You're just one guy. With me, you're about one and a half guys. If you called them right now, they could get someone in place near the cemetery. They could watch what went down. They'd be like backup."

"We've got backup," Vince said.

I took my eyes off the road a second to look at him. "What?"

"Right here," he said, opening the glove compartment. I saw what looked like the butt of a gun in there. He wrapped his hand around it and took it out.

"You know what this is?" he asked.

"Oh, great. Yeah, that's a Mixmaster."

"Do you know what *kind* of gun it is, smart-ass?"

"No."

"It's a Glock 30."

"Well," I said. "So that's the plan. That's always been the plan. You're going to shoot everybody."

"No. At least, not at the beginning." He

leaned across the seat so the gun was no more than two feet from me. "You got any idea how to use one of these things?"

"Jesus, Vince."

"Do you?"

"You pull on that thing there." I pointed to the trigger.

He grasped the gun in his right hand, then with his left slid back the top. "That's how you tell if there's a round in the chamber. And this is how you remove the magazine, not that that matters."

"Why are you telling me this?"

"Just shut up and listen. There's no safety, you understand? Once you put your finger on the trigger, the safety is off, and once you squeeze, the goddamn thing goes off. If you can figure out how to use this one, you can figure out any one of them. It's not brain surgery."

"You're giving that to me?"

"No."

"If you've got a second one in there, I don't want it."

"I don't," Vince said. He held the gun on the top of his right leg.

"You're going to walk into this meeting with a gun."

"I am. I'll have it tucked into my belt where they can see it."

"They may not like that," I offered.

"I 'spect they won't."

"If there's more than one of them, they'll just take it off you."

"That's what I'd do if I was them," Vince said.

"You're not Bruce Willis in *Die Hard*. You haven't got another one taped to the back of your head."

"I know."

"And you haven't got a gun for me. I'm not going to be hiding behind some tombstone covering your ass."

"I know that," Vince said.

"So you're going to walk into this meeting knowing you haven't emptied out all your houses yet, not knowing whether you've got what they want or not, and you're going to let them take that gun off you?"

"I'm counting on it," he said.

I kept my foot on the gas. I was starting to think Vince was the one Cynthia should have told not to do anything stupid.

"Vince, I swear, if —"

"You trust me?" he asked.

I laughed. "Seriously? You co-opt our cleaning lady, hide money in our house, won't tell us what really happened to Stuart, and you've got the nerve to ask if I trust you?"

Vince went quiet briefly.

Then he said, "Like I told your kid, Stuart was killed in the house. By someone other than Gracee. I had my guys text her today with Stuart's phone, so you'd think he was still alive and back off. But you didn't."

"What did you do with him, Vince?"

Another pause, then, "After Grace phoned Jane, Jane phoned me, filled me in. Me and Gordie and Bert swooped in, found the kid. Took a bullet right about here." He touched his left cheek, close to his nose. "Died quick, I'd guess. Wrapped the kid up in plastic, put him in the trunk. Cleaned the place up best we could, intending to go back, do an even better job, fix the window, which is still wide-open. House probably full of goddamn squirrels and God knows what else by now. We checked the attic, to see if the money and whatever was still there, and it wasn't."

Again, I asked, "What did you do with him?"

Vince looked my way. "We fed him to the hogs."

That left me speechless.

Vince filled the void. "He'll never be found." There was sadness in his voice.

I managed to find some words. "And Eldon?"

"I killed him."

For a second time within ten seconds I had nothing to say.

"He took the news badly," Vince said. "I mean, who wouldn't? I understood that. I expected that. But he started accusing me of doing it. Said he was going to the cops. He was out of his head."

Long pause. Made me think I'd suggested for the last time going to the police.

"You said the future for me was bleak. You're right. These assholes who left their stash with me, if it ends up I can't get it all back, well, they'll get over it. I don't really give a shit about that. But Eldon" — he shook his head — "that was the end of the road for me, I think. I don't know if I knew it at the time, but I do now. I'm done. I'll get Jane back, and then, what happens happens."

I still had nothing to say.

"You laughed when I asked if you trusted me. So I'm laying it all out there. That's what's going on — that's what I did. You don't have to like it. But it's the truth. So when I tell you I'm going into this meet with a plan, I want you to trust me on that. So do you?"

My mouth was dry. "Yes," I said.

"I know what you think of me. I know you think you're better than me, and maybe you're right. You think I'm this unfeeling piece of shit, that I got no heart, and you might be right about that, too. You want the truth? I wish I was a better man." He paused. "Like you. But I'm not. This is what I am. I can't pretend to be anything else. But it doesn't mean I don't give a shit. I do. About Jane. Pull in here."

We were coming up on the cemetery entrance. I slowed, turned the wheel, drove slowly through the gates. Vince said, "They said look for a Beemer."

We moved at about five miles per hour along the narrow paved roadway that wound its way through the gravestones. I looked off to the right and saw a car, and a woman standing by the driver's door.

"Beemer," I said.

"She looks familiar," Vince said. "Her name — at least, the name she gave me — is Reggie."

I looked for the next lane to the right, made a careful turn so as not to drive over the grass. A hundred feet up, the lane was blocked by the BMW.

"When you're about five car lengths away, stop."

And that's what I did.

"Kill the engine," Vince said.

I did that, too.

Reggie was slim, brown hair, about five-five, dressed in a black pullover tee and a pair of jeans that looked like they cost more than everything I was wearing, including my phone. She'd moved since I'd first spotted her, her butt perched on the hood, arms folded across her breasts. I thought I could see the outline of a cell phone in her right front pocket.

"I don't see Jane in the car," I said. "Unless she's crouched in the back or in the trunk."

"They won't have brought her," Vince said. "They got to know they got the money first." He squinted. "This woman made a deposit with me a week ago." Quiet for a moment. "Why go to all that trouble, then kidnap Jane?"

"Fishing," I said.

"Huh?"

"They were dropping their line in, seeing where the fish were."

He thought about that. "If the bags were baited with GPS . . . They were trying to figure out where I hid the stuff, but there were too many locations. That might be it."

He slipped the Glock into the waistband

of his pants, off to the side by his hip, where it would be in plain view. He opened the passenger door slowly, put one foot down on the ground.

"You coming?" he asked.

I hesitated.

"I'll ask you again. You trust me?"

I nodded.

"Don't worry. You just roll with things. Follow your instinct. When an opportunity presents itself, go for it."

"What kind of — ?"

"Let's go."

He got the other leg on the ground, kept the door open, and stepped out beyond it.

"Hey," he said to the woman. "Nice to see you again, Reggie."

She nodded, then tilted her head toward me, still behind the wheel, both hands gripped to it. "Who's he?" she asked as I got out of the truck.

"He works for me," Vince said.

"He a cop?"

Vince actually laughed. "Yeah, he's with the FBI."

"You bring it all?" Reggie asked.

Vince reached into the truck and brought out the Walgreens bags by the handles, three in one hand, four in the other.

"Where's Jane?" he asked.

"She's fine."

"I didn't ask how she was. I asked where she was. You need to open your fucking ears."

She looked taken aback by that. She pushed herself off the car, but didn't move any closer.

"We'll release her when we've got what we want. Don't even think of pulling that gun."

"You never know what you're walking into, dealing with the criminal element," Vince said.

"You think I came here alone?"

"No."

"You're right. You're being watched right now. You touch that piece and you're dead and so's your kid."

I wanted to look around, see whether I could see who else was here, but resisted the temptation. I didn't think she was lying.

"I understand," Vince said.

She looked at me. "You carrying?"

"What?" I said.

"She wants to know if you have a gun," Vince said.

"No," I said.

Reggie kept her eyes on me for several seconds, then turned them back on Vince. "Bring it over."

"Why don't you come and get it?"

She stared at him. "Get your flunky to bring it to me."

Vince looked my way. "Do it," he said.

I came around the front of the truck, took the bags from him, walked them over to the woman, set them on the ground in front of her. Then I went back and took my post by the truck.

The woman glanced down into the bags, then back up at Vince.

"There's something you need to know," Vince said.

"What's that?"

"It's not all there."

Reggie looked at him with stunned silence for a moment. "What?"

"I wasn't able to collect everything. There wasn't enough time. There's one place remaining with a pretty fucking large sum. Maybe that's the one you're after. I don't know. I get the idea maybe you're not just looking for money. One of these bags, there's a lot of crystal in it. That what you wanted?"

Reggie got down on her knees and started rooting around in the bags, one after another. When she'd searched the last one, she looked up and said, "Shit."

"You don't see anything you like?" Vince

asked her, like she was looking at shoes.

"I see lots of money. That's good. But there's something in particular I'm looking for."

"What?"

She hesitated. "It's . . . a vase."

Vince was thinking. "Yeah. A kid named Goemann left it with me. Kind of powder blue, about this high?" He held his hands almost a foot apart. "Wedgwood or something, with little cherubs or some shit on the side."

"That's it."

"Along with a lot of cash."

"Yeah," she said.

"You're in luck. That's in the place I didn't have time to get to. But I can still get it. So how do you want to handle this?"

"If there's so much stashed there," Reggie asked, "why didn't you go there first?"

"The house wasn't empty. But it is now. Woman who lives there works an afternoon nursing shift at Milford Hospital. Lives alone, no kids. House is safe to enter now. Have to get up into the attic. Tell you what. You wait here. We'll be back in an hour or so."

She stood up. "I'm not letting you out of my sight. Not now."

"So where does that leave us?"

"We come with you," Reggie said.

"I don't know about that."

"No, that's what we'll do. We come with you to the nurse's house, get the last of it. Then we let Jane go."

Vince let out a long sigh, looked at the ground, kicked a small pebble. "I don't like it."

"That's the way it is."

After a moment's thought, Vince said, "Okay."

"And you lose the gun," she said.

"I don't know about that."

Reggie looked off to the right, beyond the truck. "Wyatt!"

Vince and I turned and saw a man step out from behind a broad-trunked oak. He had a gun in his hand that was pointed straight at Vince.

"I remember you, too," Vince said. "You made a deposit as well. Quite a few, between you two, and the others. Let me guess — GPS?"

"Put your gun on the ground," Wyatt told him.

Vince slowly took the gun out of his waistband, leaned over, and when the gun was a foot off the ground, he let it go. It dropped noiselessly into the soft grass. Wyatt motioned Vince to step away from the weapon, then leaned over and scooped it.

"You need to check him, too," Reggie told him, indicating me. Wyatt handed her Vince's Glock, which she trained on me while Wyatt patted me down.

"I told you I didn't have one," I said to Reggie after Wyatt backed away from me.

"Okay, then," Reggie said. "Looks like we're good to go. We'll take my car." She handed me the keys. "You drive."

Wyatt told Reggie to get up front with me while he got in the back with Vince. They'd each be able to keep a gun pointed at us, he said.

As we were taking the few steps to the car, Vince caught my eye and smiled.

FIFTY-EIGHT

TERRY

Once we were all in the car and Wyatt had put into the trunk all the bags of money and other assorted items that had been recovered from the homes Vince had used as safe-deposit boxes, Vince tapped me on the shoulder and said, "Get us out of here and go left on Cherry. When you get to Prospect, go left."

I did as I was told.

"So, I'm curious," Reggie said. "How do you do this? You hide the money in regular people's homes, right? But is it without their consent, or are they in on it?"

"They don't know," Vince said.

"Brilliant. But then how do you keep them from stumbling onto it? If you put it in the walls, between the studs, you'd have to cut into drywall, do all kinds of repair, paint, that kind of thing. I mean, if you were going to leave something there for ten years, that'd

533

be okay, but it's not like that, right?"

"Attic," Vince said. "Under the insulation, usually."

We no longer had a ladder with us. I hoped, whatever house we were going to, the attic was going to be easily accessible.

"Two men, brothers," Vince said. "Logan and Joseph. They're with you."

"Yeah," Reggie said. "We all left some money with you to see where it would end up. And you're right about the GPS. Every time we gave you money, we watched it go to a different place. But we had no idea how many spots there are. If it was just one, we could have handled this some other way. In the end, it made more sense to grab your kid and get you to bring it all to us."

Was Vince thinking what I was thinking? If they knew where some of the money had been stashed, maybe they'd been the ones who'd hit the Cummings house last night. They'd scored there, but it wasn't as big a score as they'd thought it would be.

"How'd you hear about me?" Vince asked.

"One of your other customers. Goemann. He was hiding some things that didn't belong to him. Took them from my uncle. Couple hundred thousand, and the vase. Said he entrusted them to you, couple of weeks ago, because he figured my uncle would come after him before he could sell them to another interested party. How would Goemann have heard about you?"

"He been staying with some girl whose biker boyfriend mentioned me to him. At least that's what he said."

"Hiding stuff for biker gangs, too?" Reggie asked.

"Go on with your story."

"So, Goemann fills us in on this unique banking service you offer. We asked him which house the stuff was hidden in, figuring maybe you told your depositors that, but he said he didn't know. Me and Wyatt pressed him on that, and he came up with this house where a couple of old retired teachers lived. Turns out Goemann just pulled the address out of his ass, because we searched that house from top to bottom. Attic, too."

The Bradleys. These two had murdered Richard and Esther Bradley. Reggie and Wyatt were more than a couple of crooks trying to rip off another crook. They were stone-cold killers.

Vince said, "Hang a right here."

I did. Now we were driving through the old downtown, along Broad Street. A minute later, we were on Golden Hill.

"Left up here," Vince said, "and then stay

on Bridgeport." To Reggie, he said, "Now I've got a question for you."

"Go ahead. We're all friends here."

"That was a lot of seed money you put in. Maybe not the biggest deposits I ever had, but cumulatively that was a chunk of change."

"Well, first of all, we're getting it all back, aren't we?" she said. "But even if we didn't, we did have some money to throw around. Ever heard of filing bogus returns to the IRS?"

"Let me guess," he said. "Rip off identities, file returns in their name that claim decent refunds, have them sent to a PO box."

"More or less. Wyatt here — he's my husband — is the brains behind that." I glanced in the mirror, saw the man smile.

Reggie continued. "We got refund checks coming in pretty steadily. Great line of work. Not like robbing a bank. You don't get hurt. Maybe some RSI, all that time you have to spend at the computer, but other than that, it's great. That's Wyatt's baby. I take on other jobs that are more physically demanding."

"Like killing people?"

"Whatever."

"So why this, then?" Vince said.

"Hmm?" Reggie said.

"Ripping off what's in my houses, all this bullshit, when all you want is what Eli left with me."

"Like I said, it's a favor for my uncle. Getting back what belongs to him. But you can see how this has turned into a golden opportunity. It's like fishing with nets. Maybe you're just out for salmon, but if you end up with a ton of lobster, you don't throw it back into the ocean."

"Left at the lights up here," Vince told me.

I put on the blinker and moved into the turning lane.

I slowed, tapped the brake, put my left blinker on. Once I was through the intersection and heading south, Vince gave me a couple more directions. Now we were heading down a street I knew very well.

"It's up here," Vince told me. "Turn into that house up there with the small SUV with the ladder on the roof."

I pulled into the driveway, killed the engine. I'd had a feeling this might be where we were headed. No wonder Vince had told Cynthia and Grace to get lost.

I was home.

FIFTY-NINE

TERRY

Vince had hidden Eli Goemann's stuff in our attic?

If so, it hadn't been there long. Reggie had made it clear that it had been left with Vince in only the last couple of weeks.

When the hell had he been in our house? Him, or one of his crew? And if there was nearly a quarter-million dollars hidden over our heads, why had Vince not wanted to bother getting it before we left to clear out other houses?

It wasn't as if I could ask him right now.

"Nice little house for a nurse," Reggie said as she took the keys from me and the four of us opened the doors of the BMW. I noticed she had Vince's gun in her hand, and once Wyatt was out I saw he had his tucked into his waistband.

Vince struggled some to get out of the car, and he wobbled some when he got on his

538

feet. He didn't look well.

"I need to find a can," he said. "I'm gonna overflow."

"Huh?" Reggie said.

"My goddamn bag," Vince said to her.

She blinked, taking a moment to figure out what he might be talking about. "Oh," she said. "Well, let's get inside."

Vince pointed to my Escape. "Grab the ladder off that car. We could use that."

Wyatt had a puzzled look on his face. "If the woman who lives here is at work, whose car is that?"

Shit.

Vince didn't wait a beat. "The hospital's only five minutes from here. She bikes it."

"How do you know?" he asked.

Vince shot him a look. "You think I'm gonna leave money in people's houses and not know their routines?"

I went over to the Escape. Normally, to get something off the roof racks, I'd open a door or two and stand on the sill to make it easier to undo the bungee cords. But I wasn't supposed to have a key to unlock it, so I had to stand on my toes to get the job done. I dragged the ladder down carefully.

I carried it to the front door, where everyone was waiting for me. "You've got the key, right?" Vince asked.

I reached into my pocket. "I do," I said, pulling out a ring that included the keys to the Escape sitting in the driveway. If Wyatt or Reggie thought it odd that I kept my car remote on the same ring as the key to just one of the many houses Vince had access to, they didn't mention it.

"And you know the code?" he asked.

"I've got it written down," I said, and made a show of looking in my wallet for a scrap of paper — in fact, a gas receipt — which I then shoved back into my pocket. "Yeah, I'm good."

I moved ahead of Vince and the others to get to the front door first. I fumbled some, getting the key in and turning the lock, and when the door opened and the security system began to beep, warning me that I had only a few seconds to disable it, I feigned a moment's confusion, wondering where the keypad was.

I entered the four-digit code to stop the beeping, then went back out to bring in the ladder. Everyone moved a few steps into the house, at which point Wyatt took the gun from his waistband and held on to it.

"Bathroom," Vince said.

I said, "It's —"

And stopped myself.

Then, barely missing a beat, I said, "I

think it's just up the hall there. I used it last time I was here."

Vince was really limping. He walked a few steps, found the ground-floor powder room, and stepped in. As he went to close the door, Wyatt held up a hand, blocking it.

"Not letting you out of my sight," he said.

"Great," Vince said. "You can see how I do it."

From my position down the hall, I couldn't see a thing, but I could imagine. I wondered how long Wyatt would really want to watch Vince empty a urine-filled plastic bag.

"Oh man," Wyatt said.

Not long, as it turned out. Wyatt stepped out into the hall, just outside the door to the kitchen.

The kitchen.

There were family pictures plastered all over the refrigerator, held in place with decorative magnets. If Reggie or Wyatt wandered in there, looked at the fridge, saw me in one of the snapshots, how was I going to explain that?

I backed into the kitchen, glanced at the fridge, gave the pictures as fast a glance as I could. Given that I was the one who had taken most of them, it was rare that any of them featured me. Plenty of Grace, and

Cynthia, and Cynthia and Grace together. Of the dozen or more pictures, I was pretty sure I was in only one of them. I was with about twenty of my students, a three-year-old shot taken just before we all got on the bus to go see a play on Broadway. A rare excursion for my creative writing students at the time. My head was so small in the pic that even if Wyatt or Reggie saw it, I wasn't sure they would recognize me.

"Let's go upstairs," Reggie said after we heard a toilet flush and Vince came out of the bathroom.

"D'you wash your hands?" Wyatt asked.

Vince limped toward the stairs and began to climb them, followed by Wyatt and Reggie, and then me. I needed some distance ahead of me because I was carrying the ladder.

I had to pretend I didn't instantly remember where the attic access was.

"In here, isn't it, Vince?" I asked, standing outside the door to the room Cynthia and I used as a study.

"Yeah," he said.

I entered the room, crossed it, and opened the closet. The panel to the attic was up there, and because the closet was deep, with the shelf and the rod for hangers recessed, it wasn't hard to reach. I opened up the lad-

542

der, made sure it was steady.

"Who's going up?" Reggie asked.

"You go ahead if you want," Vince said. "But it's not gonna be me. I can't handle all the bending over. My legs and knees are killing me. And it'll be hot as fucking hell up there."

"I'm not going up there, either," she said. "And I don't know where it's hidden." She looked at me. "I'm guessing you do."

"Yeah," I said. "I'll go."

"Me, too," said Wyatt. "I'll follow you up."

I looked at Vince, who offered me an almost imperceptible nod.

"I could use a flashlight," I said. "I've been using my phone all day, but it's not the handiest thing."

Everyone just shrugged. It wasn't as if anyone was going to run out to Home Depot and get me one, and I couldn't tell them I knew they could find one in a kitchen drawer next to the sink.

"Fine, I'll do without," I said. "Which corner'd we put it in again?" I asked Vince.

"Dig around. You'll find it." He probably didn't know. Gordie or Bert or Eldon had probably been up here, not him. "Try the farthest point from the opening, work your way back."

I started up the ladder and stopped when

I was close enough to move the panel out of the way, which created an almost two-foot-square opening. I shoved it off to the side, then poked my head through.

Another dark, hot environment. The opening was in the northeast corner of the house, so odds were the money was hidden in the southwest corner. I hauled myself up, then stood, awkwardly. There was enough room at the peak to stand totally upright. I moved over a few steps to make room for Wyatt, who still had the gun in his hand.

"Tell you what," I said, handing him my phone, on which I had just opened the flashlight app. "Can you hold this, shine it in my general direction?"

"Sure," he said, taking it with his left hand.

"Watch your step," I warned him. "There's no floor. Just the open studs. We used houses that hadn't floored over the attic so we could get at the insulation easier."

"Okay," he said.

I walked across the studs, putting my hands on the inside of the roof to brace and balance myself. I followed the ridgeline until I reached the far wall, then had to stoop over to go into the corner.

I got down on my knees, straddling myself between studs, and reached down under the insulation. I kept running my hand along, hoping I'd bump into something.

I didn't find anything between the first two sets of studs. I shifted myself over so I could check between the next set of studs.

Ran my hand along. And along, and —

I hit something. It felt like a cardboard box.

"Hang on," I said, and started lifting out the insulation.

It was, indeed, a box. Long, low, and narrow. Most of the light from my phone in Wyatt's hand was hitting my back, casting my discovery in shadow.

"You see okay?" Wyatt asked. "Or do you need me closer?"

"It's okay," I said. "Long as I know it's here, I can kind of feel my way around."

Which was what I did. I lifted the flaps on the box and reached inside, expecting to feel wads and wads of paper.

And I did, in fact, feel some of that. But it was all crumpled, not in stacks. It had been used as packaging. My hand wasn't finding anything that felt like cash, or a vase.

What I was touching was something very different.

This item was cold and hard and metallic. And there wasn't just one. There were several. I traced my fingers along them, translating those tactile sensations into a

mental image.
Guns.

SIXTY

Before he did anything else, Nathaniel Braithwaite felt he had to find the dogs. Once that was done, well, he was *gone*.

Once he'd escaped from Vince Fleming's two goons, he ran straight into the woods. Tripped twice. Took branches in the face. But he just kept going until he came out the other side, behind some small strip plaza. Out front, he found a woman sitting behind the wheel of a taxi drinking a coffee, and he got her to take him back to the neighborhood where he'd been walking Emily and King and where he would find his Cadillac.

"You walk into a propeller?" she asked, looking at his lip.

He'd heard the crash seconds after he'd bailed from the van, before they were able to perform any further Black & Decker dental surgery on him. Braithwaite glanced over his shoulder just for a second, long enough to see the mangled body of one of the men on the pavement in front of the FedEx truck.

He didn't know what to feel. It wasn't joy. Not at that moment. Just relief. The dead guy sure wasn't going to be coming after him, and the accident would keep the other man too busy to pursue him.

But that didn't mean he wouldn't be looking for him later.

Nathaniel got lucky soon after the cab dropped him off. King was scratching at the back door of his own house. Emily, rather than go back to her home, was still hanging out with King, stretched out on the grass, watching him try to carve his way back into his family's residence.

When the dogs saw Braithwaite come around the corner of the house, they both ran to him, their tails wagging so hard their bodies were gyrating.

"Okay, okay," he said. "Natey's back. It's okay."

He unlocked the door to King's house, put the dog inside, then locked up again. Then he walked Emily to her place, which was only four houses down the street, and did the same.

The dogs were safe.

The other dogs he should have gotten to

that day — well, they were just going to have to do their business on the floor. At least, when their owners got home that night, their pets would be there. They wouldn't be off roaming the neighborhood. So what if they messed a few carpets?

If he had a chance — and he wasn't sure that he would — Nathaniel would call these people and tell them he was quitting. Effective immediately. Yeah, they'd be upset. Some of them would start screaming at him over the phone. It was like your day care telling you they wouldn't take your kid anymore, starting tomorrow. Work out some other arrangement.

Some of his clients, Nathaniel knew, would phone in sick until they found someone else to take their dogs out for a poop and a run through the day.

It wasn't his problem.

Nathaniel had bigger problems.

He got behind the wheel of his car — God, how he loved this Caddy, the only reminder of his once successful life — and pointed it in the direction of home.

Which wasn't going to be home for much longer.

Not only might that other guy from the van be looking for him, but there was Vince to worry about, too. The man who'd dragged him into all this. Braithwaite never wanted anything to do with that man again.

Nathaniel drove past his place slowly, looking for Vince's truck, or the van that had been used to kidnap him. He didn't see them out front of his place, but they wouldn't be dumb enough to park there, would they? So he did a quick tour of the neighborhood. The street behind, the next one over. When he didn't see any vehicles that set off alarms for him, he drove back.

Then thought, *Shit.*

If one of them drove by anytime soon, they'd see *his* car and know he was home. Being kidnapped once in a day was enough. So he parked the Caddy one street over and hoofed it back. As he was mounting the steps to the porch, he encountered Barney, who had turned a couple of the chairs into a sawhorse, across which he'd placed a lengthy piece of sculpted wood. The handrail from along the stairs. He had some tools scattered about and a cell phone rested on one of the chair arms, but instead of working, he was leaning up against the wall, smoking a cigarette.

Orland was sitting in a porch chair, staring vacantly at the street.

"Nathaniel," Barney said.

"Hey," the man replied, not even glancing

at him as he reached for the door.

"You okay? What happened to your lip there?"

"I'm fine."

"Well, you sure don't look fine."

"Mind your own goddamn business," Braithwaite snapped.

Barney took a long drag on the cigarette and blew the smoke out through his nose. "Okay, then."

The sound of a car coming to a halt out front of the house prompted Braithwaite to spin around. He felt his heart in his throat, but breathed a sigh of relief when he saw it was the woman from across the hall. Cynthia Archer. And she had a teenage girl with her. Her daughter. He'd seen her here before.

But the last thing he wanted was to lose time chatting with them. He had much to do, and not much time to do it in.

He took the steps up to the second floor two at a time. He was unlocking his door when he heard Cynthia call up to him.

"Hey, Nate, hold up!"

He pretended not to hear, got the door open, entered his apartment, and closed the door behind him.

Pack.

Under his bed he kept three empty suitcases and a fourth, smaller one that was already full. He hauled them all out, dropped the three empty ones on the bed, and placed the fourth in a chair. The others he unzipped, opened. Then he went to his four-drawer dresser, grabbed clothes, and threw them randomly into the cases.

Someone was knocking on the door.

He ignored it, went to his closet, ripped shirts off hangers, balling them up and tossing them into the suitcases.

"Nate!"

Cynthia's voice coming through the door.

"I know you're in there. I want to talk to you."

He stopped, froze. If he didn't make a sound, would she go away?

Another knock. "I'm not leaving till you open this door," she said.

He dropped some shirts onto the bed, crossed through the living area to the door, and opened it. Cynthia stood there, daughter next to her.

"I'm kind of busy," he said. "Come by later."

Grace looked at his mangled lip. "Eww," she said.

Her mother said, "I know what's been going on."

"Going on with what?"

"With you. And Vince Fleming. And today. His men — they grabbed you, right? They did that to you."

That caught him by surprise. How the hell did she know that? "I told you, I'm busy. Leave me alone."

Grace peered around him, got a view into the bedroom. "You taking a vacation?" she asked.

"What?"

"Look, Mom," she said. "He's packing."

Cynthia forced her way into the apartment, headed straight for the bedroom. She stood at the door, took in the scene.

"This has nothing to do with you," Nathaniel said, sliding past Cynthia and flipping the lids of the suitcases closed. Now Grace was crowding into the room, too, standing by the chair where the fourth suitcase rested.

"It's got everything to do with us," Cynthia said. "We're all wrapped up in this together. You and me, we both got used, one way or another, by Vince. He used you to get into houses and hide drugs and money and other stuff there. And he used us by making our house one of his storage units."

"I never would have met that man if it wasn't for you," he said. "When he found out what I did, he . . . he coerced me."

"I know, and I'm sorry. But what's done is done. You made your choice to help him, and now you're paying for it."

"He's not an easy person to say no to. Had my ex-wife's boyfriend beat up. I felt if I said no, he'd find a way to tie me to that. I didn't know what to do."

He flipped the cases back open. He hadn't wanted to pack in front of them, but he was wasting time. He opened another drawer. Socks, underwear. He grabbed everything and tossed it into a case.

"Where you going?" Grace asked. Her hand was resting on the handle of the fourth case.

"Away," he said. "Those men nearly killed me. They were going to take out my teeth. God knows what they were going to do next." He looked hopefully at Cynthia. "If I gave you some names, would you call some people, tell them they have to get someone else to walk their dogs?"

Cynthia said to Grace, "Who are the people who own the house you were in last night?"

"Cummings."

Cynthia turned to Nathaniel. "You walk the Cummingses' dog."

"Not this week. They're away."

"But you know how to get in. You have a key, know the security code. Right?"

Rather than empty the bottom drawer, he turned his attention back to the closet, dropped to his knees, and grabbed shoes. "How the hell else am I going to take their dog out?"

"Was it you?" Grace asked.

"Was what me?" he said. He was on his feet now, dumping the shoes into his luggage. He zipped up another one of the bags.

"Was it you who was there last night?"

"Jesus, you sound like Vince's flunkies. You going to start taking my teeth out?"

"Did you shoot Stuart?" Grace persisted. "Did you, you asshole?"

"This is crazy," he said.

Grace glanced down at the case she'd been running her hand on without quite realizing it. "What's in here?" she asked.

"Get your fucking hands off that!" he shouted. "I'm outta here."

"What are you running from?" Cynthia asked.

"Seriously? Fucking nutjobs, that's what."

"Answer Grace's question. What's in that case?"

"Papers," he said. "All the papers from my failed business. Legal shit. Documents. Patent stuff. Zip drives."

"Open it."

Nathaniel laughed. "You're something else — you really are. No wonder your family needed a break from you."

He knelt down again in front of the dresser and pulled out the bottom drawer. As he grabbed a bulky sweater, there was a clunking sound. The sweater had been wrapped around something large and heavy.

"What the . . . ?" Nathaniel said.

As Cynthia and Grace watched, he reached in and delicately lifted out a powder blue vase, nearly a foot high, the cover held in place with duct tape.

SIXTY-ONE

Shortly after Reggie had saved Jane from Joseph, Wyatt made the call to Vince about the ransom delivery. Jane could barely hear him one floor above talking to Vince, but she heard enough to know that the handoff was supposed to be in half an hour. In a cemetery.

She wondered, would Wyatt go alone? If he wanted any kind of backup, he'd have to take Reggie with him. But then they'd be leaving her in the house by herself. Logan was with Joseph at the hospital, getting the perv's nose fixed.

So if Reggie and Wyatt both went to pick up the ransom money, she was going to have the house all to herself.

Which was exactly how things turned out.

Reggie came back downstairs to visit her.

"We're going to meet with your stepfather. In the meantime, we're going to have to leave you here all by your lonesome. And even though we've got you tied up pretty good, you're not tied *to* anything, and I'm going to have to do something about that. Don't want you wandering around the house or trying to get outside while we're gone, do we?"

At which point Jane felt more ropes being wrapped around her torso and ankles, securing her to the chair.

"There we go," Reggie said. "You sit tight till we get back."

Not long after that, she heard them leave the house.

It became very quiet.

She tested the bonds that held her to the chair, and they seemed to be doing the job, but that didn't mean she wasn't going to give it her best shot to get away.

It seemed like a no-brainer that she had to try. What were the odds, really, that once they had what they wanted, they'd let Vince and her live? If you crossed Vince and wanted to live another day, what choice would you have but to kill him?

So when Reggie and Wyatt and Joseph and Logan rendezvoused back here, they'd have to kill her.

Jane needed to get the hell out.

Now.

She twisted and turned, trying to build

558

some slack, even the tiniest bit of play, into the ropes. If she could get just one hand free, the rest would be easy. As long as she got the job done in time.

She thought about Vince, how he'd handle something like this. He was no fool. Okay, sometimes. Like maybe this whole business model of hiding money in people's houses hadn't turned out to be the most brilliant plan ever.

But one thing Vince did know was how people like him thought, what they were capable of. So he'd know Reggie and Co. would try to kill him, and her, once they had what they wanted.

So he'd plan for that.

He'd have Gordie and Bert in position. Hiding in the bushes, or behind a tombstone. Eldon, she figured, would be out of the picture. He'd be mourning somewhere, grieving. But Vince wouldn't go into a meet like this without having someone watching his back.

Maybe, just maybe, he'd pull something off.

Because he loves me.

She had no doubt of that. Vince thought the world of her. It wasn't as if he was going to tell her kidnappers to get stuffed. She couldn't imagine a scenario in which he'd refuse to pay, even if he might not be able to give the kidnappers everything they wanted.

Jane began to cry.

Suck it up. Suck it up and get yourself out of here.

She struggled for so long that she started losing track of time. But at one point, while she was stopping to catch her breath, it occurred to her that her hosts had been gone for quite some time.

Jane was pretty sure it had been well over an hour.

She figured, ten minutes for them to get to the cemetery, ten minutes tops for the handover of the ransom, another ten to get back. That was half an hour.

Build in another fifteen minutes for traffic. Even ten minutes for Vince to be late, which didn't seem likely.

They should have been back by now. Reggie and Wyatt. Or Vince.

Somebody.

But more than an hour — she was willing to bet it was getting closer to an hour and a half — and not a soul?

She wondered what to make of that. One way or another, someone should be coming back to this house.

To set her free, or to kill her.

They couldn't just leave her here. If someone didn't come eventually, and she couldn't get herself free, well, how long could a person survive this way? A couple of days? Half a week, maybe?

What could have happened? She thought up a number of scenarios. Maybe they'd taken shots at each other. Wyatt — now there was a perfect name for a guy who'd start an Old West–style shoot-out — pulled his gun, and Vince pulled his, and everyone started firing, and everyone got hit.

It could have happened that way.

Or maybe —

What was that?

She went still, stopped breathing. Listened.

Upstairs, the sound of a door opening, and then closing.

Someone was in the house.

Please be Vince.

Please be Vince.

Please be Vince.

SIXTY-TWO

Detective Rona Wedmore left Spock to work his magic, intending to go straight back to the station to follow up on other possible leads. She'd work the phones for a while. Talk to relatives, old coworkers, friends, of both Eli Goemann and Heywood Duggan. Anyone she could find. She'd check in with Joy, see what she'd learned.

But en route, Rona decided she needed a moment.

Alone.

She pulled into the parking lot of the Carvel on Bridgeport Avenue. Went inside and bought a chocolate milk shake. Wedmore could not remember the last time she'd treated herself to a milk shake.

Rather than drink it there, she drove back downtown, grabbed a parking spot on South Broad Street alongside the Milford Green, left the car, and found herself a park bench under the shade of a towering tree. She took a seat and sipped her milk shake.

What was it Heywood had said to her the night before? About his client?

Basically, he was trying to get back what you were to me. He was trying to get back the love of his life.

The son of a bitch. Why'd he have to say something like that? And if he'd felt that way, why'd he have to be such a bastard?

She'd loved him, too, back when they were seeing each other. God knows, she loved the sex. Between his shifts and hers, and the fact that he was living in Stamford and she in Milford, their times together were irregular and rushed. Sometimes they'd meet at motels in Fairfield or Norwalk, slip between the sheets, have a quick drink afterward, and off they'd go, their separate ways.

But then she found out she wasn't the only one. Snooped through his cell phone once when he slipped out of the motel to buy them some cold beer. Found e-mails.

What could she say? She was a cop. It was in her nature. He should have known better than to leave his phone there.

And then, holy smokes, the phone rang. Right in her hand. Rona had debated whether to answer. What if it was work related? What if it was something really important?

"Hello?" Rona said.

A woman: "Oh, uh, I think I must have dialed wrong."

"You looking for Heywood?" Rona asked.

"Um, no, I don't think so." She hung up.

The poor bastard didn't know what hit him when he came back with that beer. Things went south after that, despite his protests that the other girl meant nothing to him. Rona refused to see him anymore. Before long, she'd met Lamont, and the love they had for each other was the real thing, no doubt about it, even if he was never quite the lover Heywood had been. They had the church wedding, the big reception, honeymoon in Vegas, the whole deal.

Then Lamont went to Iraq and came back a shell of a man.

It was months before he even spoke. But he was doing well now. She knew he'd never forget the things he saw, but she believed he was going to be okay.

Wedmore had a long sip of her milk shake. Still icy cold. She had to be careful not to drink it too quickly. She'd get a brain freeze.

She felt herself wanting to cry.

Rona Wedmore was not going to cry sitting on a park bench in the middle of the

Milford Green.

But she wanted to. For Heywood. For Lamont.

For herself.

She watched three small children run past with balloons. A woman in her eighties walking her dog. A young couple on another bench having an argument. Too far away to hear the details.

Her cell phone buzzed.

Wedmore sighed inwardly. Took another sip of her milk shake, then rested the takeout cup on one of the park bench planks. She reached into her purse, found the phone, glanced at the screen, and saw that it was work calling. She put the phone to her ear.

"Wedmore."

"It's me."

Spock.

"Yeah," she said.

"I found the car — pretty sure it's the same one — on one of the traffic cameras. Got a clear look at the plate."

"Give it to me. I'll run it down."

"Way ahead of ya. Got a name and address here if you've got a pencil."

Wedmore got out her notebook.

SIXTY-THREE

TERRY

Vince called up to me from the study of my house, where an armed Reggie was babysitting him.

"You find it?" he asked. There was something in his voice. Was it . . . mischief?

"Yes," I said, my body blocking Wyatt's view of the guns that had been secreted under the attic insulation. There was a hint of light filtering its way around me from the opening in the ceiling and from my phone, set to the flashlight app, which Wyatt was holding up by the rafters.

"That's good," Vince asked.

Reggie called up, "Is there a vase?"

I was running my hands over the contents of the box, all the guns. I was guessing at least a couple dozen.

"I'm not sure yet," I said. "I'm still feeling around."

"How hard can it be to tell what you're

feeling?" she shouted.

Vince, of course, had to know what I was going to find up here. I remembered what he'd said to me.

If an opportunity presented itself, take it.

What was it he wanted me to do when I found these? Come out shooting? Kill Wyatt, then Reggie?

No, that made no sense. We had to find out where Jane was, and that wasn't going to be easy if Reggie and Wyatt were dead. As if shooting a couple of people was even within my capabilities.

As I'd told Vince, I didn't know a lot about firearms, but I was betting these weapons were Glocks, just like the gun in the glove box of Vince's truck.

There is no safety.

So if these guns were loaded, all one had to do was point and pull the trigger. Maybe some were loaded, and others not. Kind of like playing the Connecticut lottery.

I glanced back over my shoulder at Wyatt. Phone in one hand, gun in the other.

I said, "I need to pass you some of this stuff — you can pass it through the hole down to them."

He'd have to take a step closer and bend down to do that. Plus, he was going to have to put away either the phone or the gun, or both.

"Hang on a sec," he said.

He chose the phone. He slid it into the front pocket of his pants and started to crouch down.

"Christ's sake," I said. "I can't see a damn thing."

He stood up again. "Okay, fine." The phone came back out, the flashlight app reactivated. This time, Wyatt tucked his gun into the waistband of his pants. But as he started to kneel, he realized tucking it in front was pretty uncomfortable, so he shifted it around to the side.

He knelt down, fumbling with the phone, trying to shine the light where he thought I wanted it.

I swung around, squatting on my haunches, and touched the barrel of the gun to his temple.

I whispered, "Not. One. Word."

Wyatt took a breath.

"If you move an inch I'll pull the trigger," I said.

And thought, *Please don't move.*

"Vince," I called out softly.

"Yeah, Terry?"

"Could you tell Reggie that our situation has changed up here?"

"What are you talking about?" she said.

"I'm guessin'," Vince said, "the balance of power has shifted."

"What are you talking about?" Reggie said again.

"That be fair to say, Terry?" Vince said.

"Yeah, that's fair. I've got one of these Glocks pressed up against Wyatt's head here."

Wyatt twitched, like maybe he was thinking of going for his gun, but it would have been an awkward move for him to make, and not something he could do quickly, kneeling as he was.

Reggie said, "What? Wyatt?"

"It's true," he said. He'd set my phone, faceup, on the narrow side of a stud, the upward cast of light highlighting the droplets of sweat beading up on his forehead.

"How the hell'd that happen?" she asked. "Jesus! How'd he get your gun?"

"He didn't! It was already up here."

Vince said, "Hand your piece over, Reggie, or Wyatt's brains become part of the insulation."

"No! No way!" she shouted upward. "You take that gun off Wyatt, or I swear to God I'll shoot your boss!"

Sweat was trickling down my forehead, too. A drop went into my eye and stung like the dickens. I blinked several times.

I said, "How would you like to handle this, Vince?"

Vince, directing his voice my way, said calmly, "Shoot him."

"Wait!" Wyatt shouted. I couldn't have been more grateful.

"No!" Reggie screamed. "I swear, if you do, I'll shoot him one second later. You — you get your ass down here now, you fucker, and let my husband go, or I'll kill Vince. You think I won't? You want to try me?"

Vince said to her, "Go ahead. Shoot me. And then my friend will kill your husband. That's what you stand to lose. Your *husband*. But all my friend'll lose is an asshole boss he's never liked much anyway. But if you hand over your piece, I can talk my friend into not putting a hole in Wyatt's head."

"Reggie," Wyatt said, trying to keep calm, "I don't want to fucking die up here." And then he said an interesting thing. "Babe, come on, you can't run the tax thing without me. You need me for that."

Like, if Reggie was going to save him, it was going to be for more than love.

I know it's a cliché, but things really did seem to be moving in slow motion. Every second I held that gun to Wyatt's head felt like an hour. It wasn't as if the Glock weighed twenty pounds, but holding it with my arm extended, I was feeling the strain. And my legs, hunched down the way I was, were screaming with pain.

I was a teacher of high school English and creative writing. Holding a gun to the head of a kidnapper did not fall into my general realm of experience. Sure, things got pretty hairy seven years ago, but even then, I hadn't found myself in a position quite like this.

"So what's the fucking deal, then?" Reggie asked.

"I want Jane," Vince said.

"Okay, fine, you get the little bitch back. Wyatt comes down. You get Jane. We're square. Just give me the vase and the cash that's up there."

"There is no vase," I said. "And there is no cash."

"Look harder!" Reggie shrieked. "The vase, it doesn't mean anything to me or you. It's got no value. It's my uncle's."

"If you're looking for something Eli Goemann left with me," Vince said, "it's not up there. Never was. We stashed his stuff elsewhere. Everything there? It's from those bikers you asked about earlier. From New Haven."

"Then we go to where you hid Eli's stuff,"

she said. "You take us there. Then you get Jane. That's the deal. Take it or leave it."

"No." Vince's voice was very calm. "That's not how it's going to work. I get Jane, right now, and you two live."

Wondering whether there might be a way I could move things along, I pressed the Glock harder against Wyatt's temple, to the point he nearly lost his balance. I said to him, "She needs to decide just how much she loves, and needs, you."

"Give him the gun, for Christ's sake!"

From below, near total silence. I thought I heard a muttered "Fuck." The tension probably didn't last more than ten seconds, but it seemed to stretch out for much longer.

It was a relief when I heard Vince say, "I've got it."

"Okay," I said.

"The two of you can come back down now. Wyatt, you first."

"He's got a gun on him," I said.

"Wyatt, be a good boy and let Terry relieve you of that," Vince said.

"Use your *left* hand," I said. I'd seen a movie or two.

Wyatt forced his left shoulder up and took the gun from his waistband. Holding it between his thumb and index finger, he dangled it toward me and I took it with my left. Without looking, I dropped it behind me on some insulation.

"I take it," I said to Vince, "that I don't have to bring all these guns down."

"Just the one in your hand."

Wyatt turned himself around and lowered his legs through the hatch, found a perch on the ladder, and descended. I grabbed my phone on the way to the opening, and by the time I was down, gun still in hand, Vince was stationed in a corner of the room with the gun trained on the happy couple, now standing shoulder to shoulder.

"We tell where she is, right now, you let us go," Reggie said, still an edge in her voice, still thinking she had some leverage.

Vince looked at me and sighed. "Do I look like I have some sort of mental problem?"

"It's okay. We'll take you," Wyatt said. "We'll take you to the house. We'll take you to her."

"Who's with her?"

"Nobody," the woman said. "She's alone. Tied up, but just fine."

Vince's eyes went from her to him and back again. He said, more to himself than anyone else in the room, "We only need one person to take us there."

I thought, *Please don't kill someone in my house.*

"Come on," Reggie said, a hint of pleading in her voice. "We're cooperating, we are."

"We'll get her back to you," Wyatt said flatly. "We'll do what you want."

"We're going back out to your car," Vince said, "and you're driving." He was looking at Reggie. "I'll be in the back with your husband."

Which put me up front, riding shotgun, as it were. Unless Vince no longer required my services.

I decided to ask, "You still need me?"

The man looked wounded. "Are you kidding? You're my number two."

SIXTY-FOUR

TERRY

Vince said I'd lead the pack and he'd take up the rear. So I went down the stairs first, followed by Wyatt, then Reggie. Vince, hobbling some, came down last. He and I maintained a solid grip on our weapons.

Vince had taken Reggie's car keys from her and had the presence of mind to ask Wyatt for his set, too, no doubt figuring that both of them would have keys to the BMW. He was right.

Vince tossed Wyatt's keys into the shrubs under the front window and held on to Reggie's. When we all came out of the house, he hit the remote to unlock the BMW. "Go on and get in," he said to the couple. "We'll be right along."

Reggie got behind the wheel and Wyatt settled in behind her.

I said to Vince, "You think they're telling the truth? That Jane's still okay?"

Grim faced, he said, "Gotta hope."

"You could have told me about the guns being hidden up there instead of money."

"I knew you'd figure out what to do. If you'd known ahead of time, you'd have been too nervous."

Like I wasn't already?

"Vince," I said, reaching out tentatively and resting my hand on his arm. He glanced at it and I took it away. "I wasn't going to say this again, but damn it, you really could call the police now. You've got these two. You can hand them over."

"Let's go," he said.

"I don't know if I can do this," I said.

"You have to," Vince said, his voice sounding weak. "Because I can't do it alone. If it's just me, they'll get the drop on me. I'm feeling like shit. Coming down the stairs there, things were spinning some."

I locked up the house while he limped to the car and got in the back next to Wyatt. Following his lead, I kept the gun down and close to my thigh so as not to attract the attention of anyone passing by. As I was getting into the front passenger seat, Vince was handing Reggie her car keys.

Reggie took us north out of the neighborhood and got on 95 heading east, but very soon she took the Milford Parkway north to the Merritt, then went west. She got off at Main, went north, passing Sikorsky on the right, then hung a left on Warner Hill Road. We made a left onto Colbert, and soon she was rolling the BMW up the driveway of a nondescript white bungalow, tapping a button on a remote clipped to the visor. Ahead of us a garage door rolled up.

Nobody had said a word the entire trip.

"Take the keys," Vince ordered me.

Reggie removed them and handed them over. I tucked them into the pocket of my pants as I got out of the car.

"Close the garage," Vince said, and she hit the button to make the door rattle down behind us.

In the garage, there was another door that led into the house.

"This your house?" Vince asked.

Wyatt nodded. "We live here."

I tried the door, but it was locked. "Which one is it?" I asked Reggie, holding her keys in front of her.

She pointed. "That one."

I inserted it into the lock and turned. The door was unlocked, but before I could push it open, Vince said, "Wait."

"There's no one else here," Wyatt said. "There's no other car."

"Go in first," Vince told him, and Wyatt

577

did as he was told. I went after him, then Reggie, and as always Vince was last.

We'd come into a laundry room off the kitchen. Just ahead of us, a set of stairs led down.

Vince shouted, "Jane!"

"She can't talk," Wyatt said.

His face went dark. "Where is she?"

Reggie said, "Downstairs."

"Let's go."

We went, in our regular formation, to the basement. We were in a wood-paneled rec room with a Ping-Pong table, a couple of old couches, and a big-screen TV on the wall. There was also a long desk set up with three laptops on it, and stacks of what looked like tax forms. For their IRS tax refund scam, I guessed.

"In there," Wyatt said, pointing to a door on the far side of the room. "It's a bed-room."

"I'll watch them," I offered, training my Glock on the two while Vince crossed the room.

He put his hand on the doorknob, held it there for a second, as if afraid to see what was on the other side. But then he gripped it and swung it wide.

We all looked.

At the empty chair, with lengths of rope scattered around it on the floor.

SIXTY-FIVE

When Jane Scavullo heard the door open upstairs, sensed footsteps coming into the house, she wanted to be hopeful. Right away, she could tell by the sounds overhead that there was more than one person entering. Two, maybe more, pairs of footsteps. That in itself was neither good news nor bad. Yes, it could be Wyatt and Reggie returning. But it could also be Vince, with at least Bert and Gordie in tow.

But her gut told her it was not going to be Vince, or Bert, or Gordie.

Her instincts turned out to be partly right. It wasn't Vince and his crew. But it wasn't Wyatt and Reggie, either.

That was confirmed as soon as she heard someone speak.

"I'm gonna kill the little bitch."

The voice wasn't quite the same as she remembered it, but she knew who it was.

Joseph was back.

Not exactly who she was expecting. Jane figured Joseph and Logan were out of the picture indefinitely while Joseph got patched up at the hospital. This was not a welcome development, particularly considering that there was no indication Reggie and Wyatt were here. Sure, maybe they were going to kill her anyway, but Jane believed Reggie might be quicker about it.

She was not confident Joseph would be merciful.

She heard running down the stairs. Then, seconds later, she sensed the door opening. A quick rush of air.

Before a word was said, someone grabbed hold of the hood over her head and yanked it off. The lights in the room had been turned on, and it took Jane a few seconds of rapid blinking to become accustomed. She'd been in darkness for hours now.

God, what a sight he was.

There were splotches of dried blood on Joseph's shirt, his neck, his cheeks. If he'd made any attempt to clean himself, he hadn't done a very good job.

Then there was the nose itself.

Jane couldn't see much of it, hidden as it was under a wallet-sized wad of gauze and white medical tape, much of it smeared with blood. Jane wondered whether the emergency room doctor had been blind. This was the worst example of first aid she'd ever seen.

"I'm gonna enjoy this," Joseph said, standing a foot away, waving a finger in her face. He sounded as though he had the world's worst head cold.

Logan appeared at the door, stepped in, and placed his hands on his brother's shoulders, pulled him away.

"Just hold on, for Christ's sake," he said. "You're a goddamn fool, you know that? A goddamn fool."

"I'm gonna do her," he told him.

"Yeah, yeah, I get that. It's all you've said the last two hours. What the hell were you thinking, walking out of the ER? Another ten minutes and someone would've looked after you."

"I took care of it," Joseph said.

"Oh yeah, right." Logan looked at Jane. "You see what he did? Bought some bandages and shit and tried to patch himself up because he couldn't wait to get back here and take care of you. Damn, why'd you have to go and do that to him?"

"Get out of my way," Joseph said, although it sounded more like, *Geb ou da my may.*

He lunged at Jane, went to put his hands around her neck. He got his hands on her for half a second before his brother ripped him away.

"Listen to me!" Logan shook his head in exasperation. "I get why you want to do this. If it was me, I'd want to kill the bitch, too. But you can't! Okay? You just can't. We don't know if the time's right."

"Let go." *Leb doh.*

"Listen! They're not back yet. Until they're back, we don't know if everything's gone down okay."

"It's been too long."

"Not *that* long. Maybe they ran into a complication. Maybe Fleming was late, had trouble rounding up the money. But here's the thing. They might still need her. Like, maybe the guy says he's got the money but he gets a bug up his ass about being able to talk to her on the phone before he hands it over or says where it is. Something like that. So what happens if they phone wanting us to put her on and you've already gone and wrung her neck? You want to fuck that up? You want us to lose out on the money? We're this close, Joseph. We're this close."

"She broke my nose," he said.

"I know, I know — I understand. I'm sure, when the time comes, Reggie'll be okay with letting you do it. But you can't do it *now.*"

"Call them," Joseph said.

"What?"

"Call them and see if they've got the money. If they've got the money, I can do it now."

"I'm not going to call them," Logan said. "We wait to hear from them."

"What if something went wrong?" Joseph asked. "What if the cops got involved? What if they got picked up? Maybe the cops are on the way here. That's why we need to take charge. We need to do her now, because she needs to pay for what she did to me, and because we don't want her talking to nobody about what she knows."

Jane made desperate noises behind the tape. She wanted to make some kind of deal. Tell them something that might get them to change their minds.

"Shut the fuck up," Joseph snapped at her.

Logan was thinking. That last part Joseph said, about the possibility that something had gone wrong, was worrying him.

"Okay," he said. "Here's what we could do."

"What?"

"Well, we were never going to kill her here. We talked about taking her out in the woods, doing it there. We could start heading out that way. Get her out of here, put her in the back of the Lexus, make the drive. Sooner or later they'll call and say it's done, and we can finish her. And in the meantime, if they need her to say something on the phone, we've still got her."

Joseph's entire body seemed electrified, like someone who'd had far too much caffeine. He was so itching to do this.

"When you said 'we finish her,' you mean me, right? I get to do her. I'm the one who gets to do her."

Logan smiled, nodded slowly, tried to calm him down. "You're the man, Joseph. You're the man. Let's get her out of this chair."

Joseph managed a tortured smile under all the gauze and blood. "You're a good brother, Logan. You really are. I don't tell you enough."

Sixty-Six

TERRY

"You happy?" Reggie asked. "She got away. So we're good."

Vince stepped into the downstairs bedroom to examine the empty chair and the bits of rope while I stood, gun in hand, in the rec room, watching Reggie and Wyatt.

"There's blood," Vince said.

"That's from Joseph," Wyatt said. "He was gushing it. Your girl broke his fucking nose when she head-butted him."

Vince came out of the room, looked over at the table supporting the computers and tax files. A landline phone was sitting on it. Vince walked over, picked up the handset, put it to his ear, then hung it back up.

"Dial tone," he said.

"So?" Reggie said.

I knew what he was getting at. "Jane would have called," I said.

Vince glanced my way. "Yeah. If she'd got

loose, she'd have called my cell, let me know."

"Maybe not," Reggie argued. "More likely, she was scared, wanted to get out of here as fast as she could. She didn't want to take the time to do it."

Vince raised his arm, aimed the gun at Reggie's head. "Bullshit. You've got five seconds to find out where she's gone."

She didn't blink. "How the fuck am I supposed to know? When I left, she was here."

"Four seconds."

"You remind me of my father," she said coldly. "May he continue to burn in hell."

"Three seconds."

"For Christ's sake!" Wyatt shouted. "It has to be Logan and Joseph."

Reggie looked at him. "They went to the hospital."

Wyatt looked at Vince. "I'll call him. I'll find out. Just put the fucking gun down."

"Before you call," Vince said, "here's what you're going to say."

"Tell me," he said.

"Say there's been a hitch. Tell them I'm ready to hand over the money, but not until I see Jane. Not talk to her on the phone. *See* her."

"I don't even — I don't even know for sure they've got her," he protested.

587

"I'm going to shoot your wife in the head," Vince said.

I had no doubt. He'd been hanging on by his fingernails for too long. Part of me wondered whether Vince just wanted to kill somebody. Didn't matter who.

"Wait wait wait," Wyatt said. He reached for the landline phone, entered a number.

"It's ringing," he said. "It's still ringing. Just stop pointing that gun at my — Logan! Logan, is that you? Where — ? No, I don't have the money yet but we almost — Just shut up for a second! Where are you? We just got back to the house and the girl's gone . . . Why did you do that . . . ? He didn't go to the hospital? Is he a total idiot? Yeah, okay, we agree, he is . . . You have to bring her back . . . He can't do that! Are you hearing me? I know he's pissed, but you can't let him do that. We don't get the money until he sees the girl . . . Yeah, okay, we'll talk about that after."

Vince whispered to Reggie, "Get on the phone and tell them to get back. I get the feeling you're the one everyone takes orders from."

She glared at him, then took the receiver from her husband and said sharply, "Logan! You and your brother better be back here in five minutes with that girl or your share is fuck all! You got that? Nothing! You get nothing. Not fifty percent, not twenty-five, not ten. Nothing." She waited while this sunk in with Logan. Reggie put her other hand over the phone and said to Vince, "He's talking to his brother. He just has to —Yeah, I'm here."

Back on with Logan. "The plan? Get your ass back here with her. By then we'll have worked out how we're going to show her off. Maybe a video thing with my phone. Don't you worry about that." She listened for another second, then lowered her arm. The call was over.

"He'll do it," she said to the rest of us.

Vince asked, "Where are they now?"

"About ten miles north. They were heading up toward Naugatuck, the state forest."

"They were going to execute her in the woods," Vince said.

Reggie's eyes had gone dead. "Yeah." She swallowed. "But we stopped that. They did that without my say-so. That was *not* supposed to happen."

"Not this soon, you mean."

She had no comment. Maybe she knew lying was pointless now.

I'd been feeling uneasy since Grace's call to me the night before, and could barely get my head around all the things that had happened since. But right now, at this moment, even though Vince and I had the upper hand, I felt myself in a darker place than any I'd been in up to now.

I needed to know how this was going to end. Vince was a man with little left to lose. I was on board with getting Jane back here, but then what? Assuming Vince got her safely released, what was the next step? What was he going to do with Wyatt and Reggie? With this Logan and his brother, Joseph, who I'd yet to set eyes on?

The clock was ticking toward a bloodbath.

"Vince," I said.

"Hmm?"

"I need to talk to you."

"So talk."

My eyes went to the other two, then back to him. He got the message. He said to Reggie and Wyatt, "Lie down."

"What?"

"Both of you. Get down on the floor, facedown — not too close to each other — and spread your arms and legs out, like you're starfish."

After our two hostages did as they were told, he said to me, "What?"

I drew him back toward the door of the bedroom where Jane had been held, far enough away that if I whispered, they wouldn't hear me.

"How does this end?" I asked.

"We get Jane back."

"Yeah, of course. But after that. What happens then?"

His eyes bored into mine. "I guess we'll see."

"I can't be part of that," I said.

"I didn't say anything."

"You didn't have to. It won't be enough to get Jane back. You're going to want revenge."

"Justice," he corrected me.

"You can't kill four people."

"They were planning to kill me and Jane. And rip me off for everything I had. You think I should just send them to bed without a story?"

I gave my head a short, adamant shake. Even considering this pair had murdered the teachers, I wasn't about to take on the job of being their judge, jury, and executioner. Maybe, once this was over, there'd be a way to point the cops in their direction. An anonymous call, something.

"I can't be part of anything like that," I said. "If you want to hunt these people down later and put bullets in their heads, that's your business, but it's not happening while I'm here."

"I could just shoot you, too."

Maybe I was naive. Maybe I was a total fool. But I didn't believe he would do that to me.

"Right now, you need me. Unless you think you can handle these two, and the other two who are on their way, and can get out of here alive with Jane. But if you're just going to lay waste to the lot of them, I'm out. I'm walking. And I wish you the best."

He ground his teeth together. "I can't predict how things will go down."

"But you can tell me what your intentions are."

He shot me a look. "You really do talk like a fucking English teacher."

"I have to know, Vince."

"Jesus, what the hell am I supposed to do? Let them walk? What kind of message does that send?"

"What have you got left? Your guys, they're either dead or on the run. Your business is fucked. On top of that, you're sick. I can see it. Any fool can see it. What's the point in upping the body count at this point?"

I could tell from his expression he didn't like being spoken to this way, but I wasn't done. "What about Jane? You kill everyone involved in this, you'll never see her again.

You'll get caught. Connecticut may not have the death penalty anymore, but you'll die in jail. You'll spend the rest of your life there."

"Not all that much of it left."

"Still, how's that help Jane? And what'll it do to her, to know she's the reason you executed four people? How do you expect her to live with that? What if these assholes have got family, people loyal to them, and they go after Jane to settle the score when they can't get to you in prison?"

He shook his head slowly. "You're saying I should let them go."

"For now. You hang on to all the money and drugs and shit you got out of those attics, and you save Jane. Let them make a run for it."

Vince said nothing.

"I need to know," I said. "I need you to tell me this isn't going to turn into Falluja, or I'm heading up those stairs." I took a breath. "Five seconds."

"What?"

"Four."

"Since when do you have a big enough dick to tell me what — ?"

"Three."

"Fine!" he whispered. "I'll do it your way. At least I'll try. I can't make promises, but I'll try. A lot of it depends on them." He lowered his voice even further. "And the only reason I'm not shooting you is because of Jane. For some stupid reason she likes you."

I nodded. I hoped he wasn't lying, that he would do as I'd asked. But damned if he didn't look like a kid who'd just found out he wasn't getting a pony after all.

SIXTY-SEVEN

TERRY

Vince told me to keep an eye on Wyatt and Reggie, still spread out on the floor, while he went into the room where Jane had been held. I watched him gather together several lengths of rope. He came back into the rec room and told Reggie to cross her wrists behind her.

"No," she said.

"Look at me," Vince said. She twisted her head around, saw a gun pointed to her head.

Wyatt said to Vince, "Come on, man. We're cooperating. We've done everything you've asked."

"Yeah," Vince said, not sounding particularly grateful. "But things'll get more complicated when your friends show up. I need to make sure you don't get rambunctious."

"Just do it," Wyatt said to Reggie.

Vince tucked his gun into his belt and knelt down so he could tie her wrists, which she had now placed behind her back. He used only a short piece of rope, but he made it count. I wondered how many times he'd done this. With another short length, he secured her ankles together.

"Now you," he said to Wyatt.

I could see the fear in his eyes as he craned his neck around, looked up at us from the floor. He believed this was a step on the way to execution. I felt I had to say something.

"It's going to be okay," I told him. "Like you said, you've done everything we've asked."

Vince gave me a disapproving look as he bound Wyatt's wrists behind him, then his ankles. He stood, with some effort, took a second to catch his breath, and said to me, "That takes the pressure off."

"Tell them you're not going to kill them." Not whispering.

Vince said to the couple, "If I told you I'm not going to shoot you, would you believe me?"

Reggie said, "We'd want to."

He nodded. "But you wouldn't be convinced, would you?" She shook her head, as best she could with her face pressed to the carpet. "Well, then there's not much point telling you."

For the next few minutes the four of us just waited, saying nothing. It had been about fifteen minutes since Wyatt had called Logan and Joseph. If they were ten miles away, I figured we'd see them pretty soon. I didn't know how Vince wanted to pull this off, choreograph it.

As if reading my mind, he said to our prisoners, "When they come into the house, they'll probably call out. You tell them to come downstairs. Nothing else. You understand?"

"Yeah," Reggie said.

"Yeah," Wyatt said.

"They got a remote for the garage?" he asked.

"Yeah," she said.

"They in a Lexus SUV?"

"Yeah," she said.

Vince said to me, "Upstairs."

Up in the kitchen, he said, "I thought they might come through the front door, but now I'm thinking, since they've got a remote, it'll be the garage." It was large enough for two vehicles, so that made sense. "If they're bringing in Jane, they're not going to run the risk of anyone seeing her being brought into the house."

I felt as though I'd had thirty cups of coffee. I was shaking.

"You okay?" Vince asked.

"No," I admitted.

"This is almost over. They bring Jane, we take her back. Simple as that."

"No one has to die," I said.

"No one has to die," Vince said.

I wondered whether he would feel that way when he saw her, found out how they had treated her. If I were in his position, how much restraint would I be able to show? Wouldn't I want to kill these sons of bitches if they'd done something to Grace? Even if she hadn't been harmed physically, wouldn't they deserve to die for what they'd put her through?

I needed to keep a level head. Not just for myself, but to make sure Vince kept his.

Vince investigated the area by the door that led from the garage into the house. "I'll stand there," he said, pointing to where the wall was recessed back of where the door opened in. "They'll be all the way in the house before they realize I'm behind them. I tell them to drop their weapons, and then you come through that door there, gun pointing at their heads. We've got them covered from both sides. We get Jane. But we take them downstairs, tie them up, give us time to slip away. We'll take the woman's car, go back to the cemetery, get my truck."

Sure. What could go wrong?

"I guess," I said.

Vince frowned. "No guessing. You need your head in the game. You can do this?"

"I can do this," I said.

"Get in position. Tell me if you can see the driveway from there."

I went around the other side of the wall, just beyond the door to the basement stairs. I was in the dining room, a few feet away from a window covered in white sheers — sheer enough that I could see outside. I had a view of the street and the bottom two-thirds of the driveway.

"I've got a good view," I said.

"Soon as you see them turn in, tell me."

"Like I'd keep it to myself," I said.

And we waited.

"Anything?" he asked me after about five minutes. Like, maybe I'd seen the SUV pull into the driveway but it had slipped my mind to mention it.

I just said, "No."

Seconds later I said, "Hang on."

An SUV was turning into the driveway. One man behind the wheel, another in the passenger seat. It was hard to tell from here, but the front of his face appeared half covered in white.

"They're pulling in now. They're —"

We heard the garage door rattle as it began to roll up. A car coming into the building. Car doors opening and closing.

Murmurs. People talking.

I peeked around the corner, saw Vince in his hiding spot. He waved his hand, motioning for me to get back behind the wall.

"Gonna be fine," he mouthed.

SIXTY-EIGHT

Nathaniel Braithwaite stood holding the vase in both hands. It struck Cynthia that he was spellbound by it, which struck her as odd. It was, after all, just a vase.

He looked at Cynthia and Grace, his expression a blend of confusion and guilt, and said, "I don't know where this came from."

Mother and daughter exchanged a quick glance. "Okay," said Cynthia. "Neither do we."

"It wasn't here when I moved in. I've used all the drawers in this dresser."

He gave his head one last shake, then decided it wasn't worth worrying about one second longer. He set it on top of the dresser and turned his attention back to the suitcases. He'd stuffed as much as he could into all of them, threw down the lids that were still open, and zipped them up.

There was no way he could manage getting all the cases to his car in a single trip. But to start, he grabbed the smaller one Grace had been touching — making him very nervous in the process — plus one of the other bags that was full of clothes, and scurried down the stairs with them.

Cynthia and Grace followed him down to the first floor and out the front door, where Barney was still having a smoke, Orland still staring blankly.

"What's up with him?" he asked as Braithwaite walked briskly down to the street and around the corner.

"I think you're losing a tenant," Cynthia said.

Grace asked her mother, "What do you think was in that bag he didn't want me touching?"

Barney said, "You telling me he's moving out? The son of a bitch didn't give me any notice. He's gone, just like that?"

"I think he'll be back," Cynthia said. "He's got more bags."

As if on cue, Braithwaite came around the corner in the Caddy. He pulled into the drive, killed the engine, locked the car, and came back up the porch steps.

Barney blocked the door and poked a finger into Nathaniel's chest.

"What's going on here?"

"Something's come up. I'm moving out."

"Well, just hang on a second, mister. People give notice when they're moving out. I expect two months' warning, my friend."

"I'm not your friend, and get out of my way."

Nathaniel shoved him aside and stormed back into the house. Barney nearly lost his footing and the cigarette slipped from his fingers.

"You okay?" Cynthia asked.

Barney ground out the cigarette with his work boot. "Yeah, I'm fine. If he thinks he's leaving without paying next month's rent, he's got another think coming." He took a breath, puffed out his chest, and went into the house, stomping his way up the stairs.

Cynthia and Grace were right behind him.

When Barney got to the open door of Nathaniel's apartment, he positioned himself there and said, "You pay me next month's rent, now, in cash, and we're square."

Nathaniel called out from the bedroom, "You'll get it — don't worry."

Cynthia squeezed past Barney, stood just outside the bedroom, and said, "Nate, he'll find you. Vince'll find you. And if it's not him, it'll be the police."

"I don't give a shit about the police," he said. "The police don't grab you off the street and shove a goddamn power drill in your face."

Barney came in from the hall, stood in the center of the room. "I need to check the apartment, because if you've done any kind of damage, you won't be getting back your security deposit."

Nathaniel, carrying his last two bags, charged out of the bedroom. "I don't give a fuck. I just don't."

Barney said, "You just hang on a minute while I have a look around." He stood there casting his eye across the kitchen area, walked over to the fridge, and opened the door. "You gonna clean this out?"

"Jesus Christ," Nathaniel said, dropping the two bags so he could get to his wallet. He opened it up and started taking out some bills. "Here's two hundred. I'll mail you the rest."

As Barney walked over to take the money, he took a quick peek into the bedroom.

Stopped.

Then he took three tentative steps to the bedroom door, stared, his eyes focused for several seconds on the vase. Then he turned on Nathaniel.

"Are you the detective?" he asked. "Is Braithwaite even your real name? Is your name Duggan? Have you been living here

604

spying on me?"

Nathaniel said, "What?"

"You heard me," Barney said. "Are you the detective? Quayle told me a detective had it. That it was being checked for fingerprints. *My* fingerprints." His eyes narrowed as he looked at his former tenant.

"Didn't my niece go and see you? Reggie told me she was going to see you. Answer me!"

Nathaniel slowly shook his head. "Mr. Croft, I swear, I have no idea what the hell you're talking about."

"I'm with ya on that one," Cynthia said.

SIXTY-NINE

TERRY

I slipped behind the wall as the door began to open. Listened. Hoped they wouldn't hear my heart pounding in my chest.

Someone shouted: "Hey! Where are you?"

Reggie: "Basement!"

A different voice, somewhat muddy, as if the man had a cold: "What the fuck! What the hell is going on?"

Then a voice I knew. Low and controlled. *"Don't move."*

"What the — ?"

"I don't want to have to tell you again. Terry?"

I came around the corner, arms straight out, both hands wrapped around the Glock I'd found in my attic.

Just like in the movies.

Vince was where I'd last seen him, tucked into the corner, arms outstretched like mine, his gun an inch away from the ear of the second man who'd come into the house. Between him and the second man, whose face was plastered with bandages and speckled with blood, was Jane. Hands behind her back, a piece of tape over her mouth.

There was a gun tucked into the belt of the bandaged man, and I saw his hand moving slowly toward it.

My turn to be tough. "Don't," I said.

He looked at me with empty eyes, inched his hand away.

"Terry, get their guns."

I walked six paces, stood gingerly in front of the man, and reached ahead with my left hand, pried the weapon from his waist.

"Step over there," I said, knowing Vince was watching him.

The bandaged man looked at Vince, grinned, and said, "Pissed your pants lately?" Not the smartest thing to say, I thought, to a man who's pointing a gun at you.

I edged past Jane, gave her a smile. "Hey," I said. "One second."

Her eyes were dancing.

"Where's yours?" I asked the other man, not seeing a gun on him.

"Left it in the car," he said.

"Pat him down," Vince told me, and I did, patting him pretty much all over, including places where I didn't usually touch people. I was going to apologize, then thought better of it. I found no gun. I gave the one I'd taken off the other man to Vince.

"Help Jane," Vince said.

She turned around to show me her wrists, and I picked away at the knot for several seconds before realizing it would be faster to use a knife. I led her, gently, into the kitchen and opened a couple of drawers until I found one with a short, sharp blade. Carefully, I sawed through the rope until it slipped off her wrists, then dropped the knife onto the counter. Her hands went immediately to her mouth, where she delicately peeled off the tape. Once she had it free, she balled it up, worked to get it off her fingers, and threw it in the sink.

She turned to Vince and started to move that way, drawn to him, but his arms were still outstretched, the barrel of the gun still positioned behind the other man's ear.

"Oh God, Vince — I knew — I knew . . ." She began to weep. No, more than that. She began to convulse. Her shoulders hunched as she sobbed. "Oh God, oh my God . . ."

I could see in his eyes that he wanted to comfort her but right now couldn't move. "You," he said.

Still holding the Glock in my right hand, I

tried to take her in my own arms, put my left hand on her back as she pressed her face to my chest.

"It's okay," I said soothingly. "It's okay."

"Logan," Vince said to the one closest to him.

"Yeah."

"Still want to keep your mother happy? Keep your shithead brother and yourself alive?"

"Sure."

"Then this is what you're going to do. My friend's going to go down the stairs, and the two of you are going to go down after him."

"Where are the others?" he asked.

"They're fine. Let's go."

I went down the stairs quickly so I could turn around and train the gun on Logan and Joseph as they descended. I saw Jane throw her arms around Vince just before he came down the stairs. Heard them speak softly to each other, a couple of nods.

Vince said, "We'll be out of here in a minute. Why don't you wait up here."

I didn't take that as a good sign. That things Vince didn't want her to see were about to happen.

Vince came down the stairs, entered the room where Wyatt and Reggie remained trussed up on the floor and where our new visitors were standing, looking very uncertain. There were still a few short lengths of rope scattered about.

"Terry, do Bandage Man." Looking at Joseph.

I grabbed a length of rope, twirled my finger to get him to turn around. "Fuck you," he said.

Vince's arm went up.

Logan said to his brother, "Joseph, just do it. If they were going to kill us, they could have done it by now." He looked hopefully at Vince. "Right?"

Vince smiled. "That's right."

"Wanna blow me?" Joseph asked. I wasn't sure whether he was asking Vince or me. I had a feeling he wouldn't take direction well, that if I tucked my gun into my belt, he'd whip around and try to grab it. So I handed the weapon to Vince. He stood there looking like Gary Cooper, two weapons drawn, as I pulled Joseph's arms behind him and tied the rope around his wrists.

It wasn't my area of expertise, but I did the best I could.

"Ankles, too," Vince said.

By the time I was done, he was on the floor like Reggie and Wyatt. Then I took care of Logan.

"Vince?" Jane called down from the top of the stairs. "I wanna get out of here."

"Almost ready," he said, returning the Glock to me.

We were, as far as I could see, ready to go. We had Jane. The money was in the car. The kidnappers were immobilized.

But Vince stood over them, his shoes seemingly glued to the floor.

"Vince," I said.

He didn't look at me. Instead, his eyes were on the four of them, transfixed. The gun in his hand.

"Vince," I said again. "You and I, we had a deal."

Slowly, he looked at me. "They've got it coming. They don't deserve mercy. They deserve some sweet justice."

"Not your kind," I said. "Shit, maybe they do deserve it. But I told you, I can't be a part of something like this."

He closed his eyes for a moment. His body wavered. His eyes reopened and he looked the same way he had when he'd collapsed in our house. He lowered the gun to his side, put out his left arm, looking for something to brace himself on. He found the back of the couch, supported himself against it.

"Don't feel so good," he said.

"We need to go. You okay getting up the stairs?"

He took his hand off the couch, testing to see whether he could stand. "I think so." Vince lowered his head, addressed the congregation. "Smartest thing you could do is disappear. Later, I'm gonna be sorry I didn't do something about you. I'll come looking. I'm gonna make this right."

"Come on," I said.

"Old man doesn't have the balls," Joseph said.

"Jesus, shut up, you dumb asshole," Reggie said.

I let Vince go up the stairs ahead of me. I was half expecting him to collapse on the way up and felt I needed to be there to catch him. Jane, like an angel at the entrance to the pearly gates, awaited him at the top of the stairs.

Once we were all in the kitchen, I wanted to get the hell out of there, but Vince and Jane were huddled in an embrace, whispering things to each other. I felt they needed a moment of privacy, so I walked into the living room, gazed through the sheers at the street.

After the better part of five minutes, and a lot of discussion between the two of them, Vince called out to me. "Terry, we're off."

His voice was quieter than I'd ever heard it before.

We opened the door that led from the house to the garage. Vince was moving like a wounded soldier, his arm around Jane. She opened the back door on the driver's side, helped him into the seat. He dropped into it like a sack of cement.

"He needs rest," she said to me as I opened the driver's door. "Has he told you?" Her eyes glistened.

"Told me what?"

"He's sick."

That was pretty obvious. "How sick?"

She took a breath. "Cancer. Pretty far along, he says."

I nodded. "It's been a long day."

"Yeah. I guess we should go." She rested her hand on my arm. "Thanks, Teach."

I smiled weakly. "Sure."

Jane took her hand off my arm and started to walk around the front of the car, which took her to within half a dozen feet of the door into the house.

It burst open.

I should have taken a knot-tying course when I was a Boy Scout.

It was Joseph. He came flying out the door, a knife in his right hand. The one, I presumed, that I had left sitting out on the

613

kitchen counter after freeing Jane's wrists.

His eyes, wide and crazy, were fixed on her. She screamed when she saw him and raised her arms defensively. But they weren't going to do much to save her against an enraged man who was larger and stronger than she was.

He had the knife raised high, clutching it in his fist the way you'd hold an ice pick.

His teeth were bared like an animal's.

The Glock, as it turned out, was loaded.

I didn't think about any of it. My arm went up. It would be an overstatement to say I aimed. I just pointed and then I squeezed the trigger.

No safety.

The shot echoed inside the garage. A red blossom appeared on the side of Joseph's neck, knocking him off course and away from Jane. He dropped to the concrete, vanishing beyond the front of the Beemer.

"No," I said.

The garage was suddenly very still. Jane had backed up a few steps, pressed herself up against the fender of the SUV, both hands over her mouth.

I heard something behind me, whirled around.

Vince had gotten out of the car. He shuffled past me, knelt down by the car's front bumper, his head just above the hood.

He turned and looked at me. "Good shot," he said.

I had to ask. "Is he dead?"

"That's what 'good shot' means."

Slowly, using his hand on the hood to help him, he got back up on his feet. He stepped toward me and put out his hand. "Give it to me."

"What?"

"The gun."

Dazed, maybe even in shock, I handed it to him.

"What are you going to do?" I asked.

Vince was quiet a moment, then reached out and put a hand on my shoulder. "I tried to play it your way," he said, "but you've changed the game."

SEVENTY

TERRY

Trying to recall what happened over the next few minutes is, even now, not unlike trying to remember a dream. I try to see it clearly, but it's like viewing an image through wax paper. Everything is slightly out of focus, softened, fogged. I can't say I was clinically in a state of shock, but at the very least I was stunned. I could not believe what had just transpired.

I could not believe I'd killed a man.

It did not seem real.

Yet, at some intellectual level, I knew this was happening, that it *was* real. But I still felt disconnected from the events. I seemed able to listen and observe, but unable to act. I was paralyzed.

I remember Vince talking to me.

"You saved Jane's life. That's what you just did. You saved her. You did the right thing."

"I have to call the police," I whispered.

"No, you don't have to do that. You know why? Because as far as they're going to be concerned, you didn't do that. You see who's holding the gun now? That's me. It's going to be my fingerprints on this gun. Not yours."

"My fault," I said. "Didn't tie him up good. The knife —"

"Don't worry about any of that shit," Vince said. He still had his hand on my shoulder. "You really are my number two. You came through."

Someone else was touching me. Jane. She had a hand on my arm. "Yeah, Teach. He'd have killed me. He'd have done it."

"So . . . it was justifiable," I said. "So if I tell the police —"

"Thing is, pal," Vince said, "we're not quite done yet."

He said to Jane, "The two of you go. Now."

"No," Jane said. "Come with us."

"I don't want you here," he said. "I want you to get away as fast as you can. It'll be okay. I'll see you soon."

Vince moved his hand from my shoulder to hers. They stood inches apart. Jane was crying.

"No, you won't," she said. "I can tell."

"Don't worry. And you're going to be just fine. Do what I tell you."

She fell against him and he wrapped his free arm around her. "I love you," she said. "I'm sorry about all this."

"Shh," Vince said. "You get Terry out of here. Right away. There's still the other car here. I can get the keys off Logan. I'll be okay."

I wanted to wake up. *Please let me wake up.*

"I think you better drive," he told Jane. "Terry's kind of out of it."

"Why?" I asked Vince.

"Huh?"

"Why do you have to do it?"

He smiled sadly. "It has to end here. If I leave with you and Jane right now, it's not over. It's gonna spin out of control in a hundred directions." He paused. "Trust me."

Jane was tugging on my arm. "Come on. We have to go."

I got into the Beemer on the passenger side.

Maybe, once I got home, I could still call the police. Confess my crime. They'd understand, wouldn't they? That I had to do it? To save Jane's life? But what would the cops think — what would a jury think — when they considered everything that had come before? Vince and I effectively kidnapping Wyatt and Reggie ourselves? Making them bring us back to this house? Tying them up?

That wouldn't play well.

Jane got in the driver's seat next to me, then looked at Vince. "Keys?"

Vince said, "Terry?"

I glanced over. "What?"

"The keys?"

I had no idea what he was talking about.

"You've got them. In your pocket," he said.

I reached down into my pants pocket, found the set I had taken from Reggie when we'd arrived. Jane took them from me and started the car.

Vince extended a hand to a button mounted on the wall. "I've got the door," he said.

He pressed the button and behind us the garage door noisily rose. Jane looked down between the seats, got the automatic shift into reverse, then twisted around so she could see out the back window to back the car out of the garage and down the driveway.

I kept eyes forward.

Vince watched us for five seconds, then hit the button to send the garage door back down. Just before it closed, I saw Vince go through the door that took him back into the house.

SEVENTY-ONE

TERRY

"Where are we going?" I asked Jane.

"To the cemetery," she said. "Vince said that's where his truck is."

Of course. That made sense. I wasn't thinking clearly yet. I needed to try to focus, to bring myself out of the fog.

"Trouble is," she said, "I have no idea where we are. They brought me here with a bag over my head."

Even I had to think for a moment. "Okay, um, up here, turn by that bench. Once we get out of this neighborhood, you'll probably get your bearings."

After a couple of more turns, Jane knew where she was. "Okay, we're good now."

"Vince give you the keys to his truck?"

She nodded. "Don't let me forget to transfer over all the stuff in the trunk."

"Yeah," I said. "Looks like Vince won't have to worry when his depositors come

621

back to make withdrawals." I glanced over. "Do you even know about that? This thing Vince had going on for a while?"

"I heard them talking," Jane said. "The ones who grabbed me. Vince had all kinds of money hidden in people's houses."

"Yeah. Last night, when Grace and Stuart got into that house, they ran into someone who was ripping Vince off. Someone who found out money was hidden there. I'm thinking now it might have been your kidnappers. They figured out one house where the money was hidden, but it was too much to figure out all the locations, so they grabbed you. Told Vince to clear everything out or they'd — you know."

"Kill me."

"Yeah."

"Well, they nearly did," she said. "Vince told me, fast, about what was going on. He says we have to get a whole bunch of guns out of your house?"

Jesus. I'd forgotten.

"Yeah, that's a good idea."

"You know what he's doing, don't you?" she asked.

"I don't want to think about that."

"He's protecting us. Both of us."

"I could see him doing that for you," I said. "Not so much for me."

Jane glanced over. "He respects you."

"What?"

"He does. He thinks you're a good man. He always has. He's just not that good at showing it."

I wondered why I should care. Vince Fleming was a thug. A killer. Did I need the respect of a man like that? And yet, knowing this, I felt something that was hard to explain. Some small measure of pride.

Was it because I was a killer now, too? No, that was a totally different thing. What I did had nothing to do with the kinds of things Vince was capable of.

"Pull over," I said suddenly.

Jane looked over. "What is it?"

"Pull over!"

She whipped the car to the side of the road and I threw open the door. I stumbled out, doubled over, and was sick. I couldn't remember the last time I'd eaten anything, but whatever it was, it was gone now.

I rested there a moment, hands on my knees, while the Beemer idled. I stood, took a couple of deep breaths, and got back into the car.

Jane continued on.

At the cemetery, we took everything from the trunk and put it behind the seats in Vince's Ram pickup.

"We have to wipe it down," Jane said to me.

I wasn't sure at first what she was talking about. She'd grabbed two rags from the truck and handed me one. "The Beemer. Vince said to wipe it down. Fingerprints."

She had the door open and was going over the steering wheel, gearshift, dashboard — just about everything — with the cloth. I did the passenger side of the front, then the backseat. Jane did the trunk lid and the door handles.

"The hood," I said. "By the front. Vince put his hand on it to get back up."

When he was looking at the man I shot.

"Vince wasn't so worried about his own prints," Jane said. "Just us. But I'll do it anyway."

The last thing she did was wipe down the key fob itself, which she tossed into the car through an open window.

Then we were off in the truck, Jane behind the wheel again. "Let's clear your place out," she said.

I told her how to get there, and ten minutes later I was in the attic, lowering the box of Glocks and Wyatt's gun through the hole to her as she stood on the ladder. I tamped the insulation back down, crawled back down through the hole, and slid the cover back into place.

I put the box behind the pickup's seats with the other bags of loot.

"Tell me you're not going to drive around with all that."

"Not for long," Jane said.

She stood solemnly before me, smiled weakly, and gave me a hug. She whispered, "I'm so sorry."

"Sorry?" I said.

"That you and Grace — that you all got dragged into this. I'm sorry about that, but grateful, too. For helping Vince. For saving me. You know, those kinds of things."

She squeezed.

"And for always believing in me, Teach," Jane said, putting her lips to my cheek and giving me a light kiss.

I hugged her back.

"Are you going to be able to do this?" she asked.

"I'm gonna give it my best shot."

"All you have to do is play dumb."

I almost smiled. "I should be able to do that."

"It'll blow over. It will."

"Tell Vince I'll try," I said.

She gave me a pitying smile. "You don't get it. We're never going to see him again."

I watched her get into the pickup, back

out of the drive, and head up the street. When she'd turned the corner, I went back into the house, through the hall, and into the kitchen.

I went to the phone, picked up the receiver, and entered Cynthia's number.

She answered on the first ring.

"Terry?"

"Come home," I said.

"Well," Cynthia said. "We've kind of got a situation going on here."

SEVENTY-TWO

Cynthia put her phone away.

Nathaniel was still insisting that his real name was not Duggan, that he was not a private detective, and that he was not trying to find fingerprints on that blue vase that was sitting on top of his dresser.

"What about the two hundred thousand?" Barney asked. "You got that, too? Did Eli give that to you? The little bastard. I gave him some work fixing up some of my other apartments, took pity on the little shit when I found out he didn't have a place to stay. But the little bastard was watching me, figured out where I kept my money. Thirty years! Thirty years it took me to save that much." He gazed longingly at the vase. "But what mattered most was getting back Charlotte. I never should have told Eli about her."

Grace spoke, in little more than a whisper. "Is that . . . an urn?"

Barney looked at her, his eyes softening. "It's Charlotte. We were going to be married. I had an accident, I was laid up a long time, and my best friend — my best friend! — went after her while I was recovering. The fucker. Won her away from me, married her. She was the only one I ever loved."

"I don't understand," Cynthia said. "If she married this other man, how could you have ended up with her ashes?"

"Because I stole them," he said, and smiled proudly. "When Charlotte passed away two years ago, I went to the service, heard that she'd been cremated. A couple of days later I was driving past the funeral home, saw Quayle coming out the front door, a package in his arms. I knew what it had to be. He got in his car and I followed him. He stopped along the way, went into a bar to deal with his grief." Barney laughed. "I smashed the window of his car and took Charlotte back. If I couldn't keep him from having her when she was alive, I could have her as she enjoyed her eternal rest."

"This is fucked," Grace said.

Barney walked slowly, almost reverently, into the bedroom and took the vase gently in his hands, cradled it in the crook of his arm as though it were a newborn. He worked the duct tape off the cover, peered

628

briefly inside, appeared pleased by what he saw, and reapplied the tape.

"She hasn't been disturbed," he said.

Nathaniel, who'd been in such a rush to get out of there, appeared transfixed by these developments. He stood alongside Cynthia and Grace, watching the man reunite with the remains of the woman he loved.

Barney, clutching the urn, trained his eyes on Braithwaite.

"I want to know how you ended up with this."

"I've got no fucking idea how that got here."

"I do," Grace said, and looked at Braithwaite. "And just so you know, I never actually saw you, so you don't have to worry about trying to kill me or anything, but it really must have been you."

"Must have been me *what*?"

"Who was in the Cummings house. You got the money, and you grabbed that . . . that thing, too. And killed Stuart."

"No," he said.

"And that case you didn't want me touching — that's the money, right?"

Barney came out of the bedroom, still watching Nathaniel. "I want my money, too. If you don't return it, I know someone

629

who'll find a way to get it out of you."

With one free hand, he reached into his pocket for his cell. Hit a couple of buttons and put the phone to his ear. "Come on, pick up, pick up," he said under his breath. Then: "Reggie, I found it. It's here. In one of my buildings. I don't know how, but it's here. I've found her. Call me when you get this."

He put the phone away. "You'd be smarter to deal with me, instead of her."

"Whoever Reggie is can kiss my ass," Braithwaite said, picking up his two last bags. "I don't know what the fuck is playing out here or what it is you think I did, but I'm gone."

He turned and headed for the hallway.

"You come back here, you bastard!" Barney said, pushing past Cynthia and Grace, hugging the urn to his chest, his arms encircling it.

By the time Barney reached the top of the stairs, Braithwaite was already running out the front door, not bothering to close it. Seconds later, he could be heard getting into his Caddy, turning the ignition.

"Come back here! Come back!" Barney shouted.

He started down the stairs, but he couldn't race down them the way Nathaniel had.

Four steps down, he stumbled. He took one arm from around the urn and reached out instinctively for the handrail, but it was not there. His hand brushed across the bare wall, catching nothing, and he tumbled forward.

Cynthia watched from above as Barney pitched headlong down the stairs, then heard the sound of the urn shattering beneath him as he slid down several steps on his belly.

Seconds after that, weeping.

Cynthia turned around and put her arm around Grace. "I'm going to call your father back, tell him we're on our way."

SEVENTY-THREE

Vince did it quickly.

Went back downstairs. Three people, three shots.

Made them count.

Did them all with the same gun that had been used to shoot Joseph in the garage.

No one left to talk now.

He went back up to the kitchen, looked for where Reggie and Wyatt kept their liquor, and stumbled upon a bottle of Royal Lochnagar scotch.

"That'll do," he said to himself.

He didn't bother looking for a glass. He opened the bottle and drank straight from it.

There were things he could do, he thought, but none particularly appealed to him. That small matter of the missing money from the Cummings house didn't seem like such a big deal anymore.

He could go after Bert. Track him down.

Vince didn't figure he'd be that hard to find, but really, did it matter?

And then there was Braithwaite, the goddamn dog walker. He'd given Bert and Gordie the slip, got Gordie killed. Vince figured Braithwaite was on the run now, too. He might be trickier to find. Vince didn't know his habits, didn't know who his friends were. But with enough effort, he believed he could hunt Braithwaite down.

But the hell with it. What was the point?

He'd rather drink this scotch.

Finally, there was the matter of Eldon. His body, still up there in his apartment. There was no one left to help Vince deal with that matter. If it was to get done, he'd have to do it himself.

Didn't have the energy. He could feel the cancer eating away at him these last twenty-four hours.

Too bad about Eldon, and his boy.

"Damn," Vince said under his breath.

He wondered whether he should do it right here. Put the gun in his mouth, pull the trigger, be done with it.

Jane was free. And she was well-fixed, too. He'd made it clear what he wanted her to do. Get rid of the drugs, guns, anything like that. Stuff that could be traced, identified. Dump it in the Housatonic. But keep the cash. Keep it all. Get yourself a safe-deposit box, in an actual bank.

Maybe take off for a while. Go to Europe. Take that asshole musician with you. Live it up. Have the life you deserve. Let this be my gift to you, my way of saying sorry for everything. For not being there for your mom when she needed me. And for all the other shit.

When the folks who'd left money with him learned what had happened — and they would, Vince was sure of that — and realized the only person who knew where their loot could be found was dead, what the hell could they do? Invade every house in Milford?

They'd have to write it off. That's what they'd have to do.

He set the bottle down on the counter. He'd made a decision. He really didn't want to do it here. He'd take Logan's SUV, drive back down to his beach house, and do it there. Maybe take his shoes and socks off and walk a few feet out into the sound, feel the water lapping about his ankles.

Yeah, that'd be nice.

Vince had to go back downstairs to find the keys on Logan's body. Coming back up was a struggle. It took everything he had.

He left the house with only one gun —

the Glock Terry Archer had found in his attic — as he went back into the garage. He went over to the garage door button, pressed it to open.

The door slowly rose.

There was a car parked across the end of the driveway. A plain black Ford sedan. An unmarked police car, Vince figured.

And that woman standing in the middle of the drive, looking into the garage, was a cop, he bet.

A black woman, stocky, about five-three or so. She had a gun in her hand, too. Both her hands, actually. She had her arms straight out and that gun pointed straight at him.

"Police!" she said.

Vince just stood there. With the BMW out of the garage, she'd be able to see Joseph's body on the floor behind him.

"Drop your weapon!" she shouted.

He glanced down at the end of his arm, saw the gun, but did not let go. He looked back up and said, "I think I know you."

"Sir, put down your weapon."

"I remember you asking questions years ago, back when I got shot. Wedmore, right?"

"Yes, sir, I am Detective Rona Wedmore, and I am telling you, drop your weapon."

But Vince held on to it.

"There's quite a mess in here," he said. "This guy behind me, and three more in the basement. I did it. Plus a guy who worked for me. Eldon Koch. You'll find him sooner or later. And his boy —"

"Drop it!"

Would have been nicer standing on the beach when it happened. But this would do just fine.

Vince raised the gun, fast. Pointed it right at her.

Didn't even have his finger on the trigger. *Bam.*

SEVENTY-FOUR

TERRY

That night, Cynthia started sleeping at the house again. There was no way we were going to be apart as a family. Not after all we'd been through. But she didn't move all her things back for another couple of days. It wasn't that she was hesitant about the commitment. She just didn't get to it.

Grace wouldn't let her leave the house.

Our girl phoned in sick for the next two days. Same with Cynthia. They spent a lot of time in Grace's room, sitting on the bed. Just talking. I popped in once in a while, but they seemed to be having such a good time in there, just the two of them, that I gave them their space.

I figured they were talking about the ordeal of the last few days, hashing it out, working on the theory that the more we confront our demons, the better we can deal with them. But when I walked down the hall past Grace's room and caught snippets of conversations, they weren't about guns and attics and death. They were about boys and movies and school and Angelina Jolie.

But not always.

Sometimes, all I heard was crying. From both of them. More than once, I peeked in and found they'd fallen asleep together on Grace's bed, Grace's back tucked up against Cynthia, her mother's arm draped over her.

I had to tell Cynthia some of it.

It was all over the news. A massacre, they called it. Four dead in a Milford house. Detective Rona Wedmore — we knew that name well — while trying to track down a car believed to be linked to a homicide, had arrived at the house just as notorious thug Vincent Fleming was attempting to flee the scene. He had as much as confessed to all four murders before Wedmore shot him dead.

I told Cynthia most of what happened. The meeting in the cemetery. Coming back to this house, getting the drop on Wyatt and Reggie, taking them back to their place, rescuing Jane.

Like I said, I told her most of it.

Everyone was tied up in the basement, I told her. Vince made Jane and me leave, said he would catch up with us. We had no idea

Vince was going to hurt anyone, I said. I speculated that after we'd taken off, the one called Joseph got free and tried to kill Vince. Vince shot him, and then must have felt he had no choice but to kill the others.

I was shaking as I told Cynthia my theory.

"My God," she said. "Oh my God, that's — it's unimaginable." She was shaken by how close I had come to such horrific violence. "If there's any silver lining to any of this, at least you got out of there before it all started."

Yeah.

The police said Vince had also confessed to the killing of one of his employees, Eldon Koch, as well as his son, Stuart, although the boy's body had not been found.

Grace saw that part on the news.

"No way," she said. "Vince was in the house? He shot Stuart? It was that guy who lived across the hall from Mom."

She and Cynthia had filled me in on that part, but I still didn't know what to make of all of it.

I read and watched everything I could find on the case. Even though the police believed they knew who had done what, they weren't sure why. What they did learn was that Reggie and Wyatt had been running a sophisticated IRS tax fraud scam. They determined that a gun found at the scene was in all likelihood the same one used to kill a private detective named Heywood Duggan. And they also believed the husband-and-wife team was responsible for the murders of those two retired teachers and someone named Eli Goemann, although they were still investigating.

Which wasn't really news to me.

One of the stories featured an interview with Reggie's uncle, who turned out to be Cynthia's landlord, Barney Croft. Cynthia watched as he told a reporter that while he talked often on the phone to his niece — including a call he'd made to her the day she died that went unanswered — he had not seen her in many months and was unaware of her involvement in any sort of criminal activity.

"Lying bastard," she said.

Another local TV station managed to track down Jane as she was coming out of work at the advertising firm.

Adopting a similar strategy as Croft, she said, "Yes, Vince Fleming was married to my late mother, but I hadn't seen him in months and I don't know anything about any of this. But my heart goes out to the families of those who Vince is alleged to have harmed. It truly does. I don't know what else to say." She got into her Mini and sped off.

One of Vince's former employees, Bert Gooding, was still missing.

There was another, seemingly unrelated story on the news one night about some people named Cummings who had returned home from a trip to find their basement window kicked in but nothing missing from the house. This, in and of itself, would hardly have been newsworthy, but it led to another story about onetime software millionaire turned dog walker Nathaniel Braithwaite.

He hadn't shown up to walk people's pets. People were starting to worry about him.

Every day that went by without the police coming to our door, I wondered whether our involvement in all this was going to go unnoticed.

"It's going to be okay," Cynthia assured me. "Vince thought it through."

Three days went by. Then four. Then an entire week.

I was starting to think maybe Cynthia was right.

The evening of the eighth day, an unmarked cruiser pulled into our driveway. I saw it from the window. I'd been sitting by the window a lot lately. Waiting.

"Cyn," I said.

She and Grace came into the living room. Cynthia said, "Grace, go to your room and don't make a sound."

Grace took off. She knew what was at stake.

"It's Wedmore," I said. "This is it. They've figured it out. They're going to take me in."

Cynthia looked at me. "You? I thought the one we were worried about was Grace."

The doorbell rang.

Cynthia studied me. "There's more, isn't there? You haven't told me everything. I know there's more."

I didn't want to lie, so I said nothing.

The chimes rang a second time.

Cynthia managed to get herself moving and opened the front door. "Oh my gosh," she said. "Detective Wedmore. I can't believe it. It's been a long time."

"It has," she said.

I came up alongside Cynthia. "Hello. Nice to see you."

"You, too."

It had been years since Cynthia had seen Detective Wedmore, but she had come to visit me at school a year or so before, asking some questions about a case she'd been working at the time about a bogus psychic Cynthia and I had had the misfortune to

642

deal with back when we were having our troubles. Our other troubles.

Wedmore asked to come in and we directed her to the living room, where we all took a seat. Cynthia offered to make coffee, but the detective declined.

"What's going on?" I asked her. "I'm guessing this is about Vince Fleming."

Be direct, I thought. Don't act like you're trying to hide anything.

"What makes you ask that?"

"Well, we watch the news. We know what happened. And Cynthia and I, we knew him. He helped us, you know. Got shot in the process."

Cynthia nodded. "I know what kind of person he was — we're not naive. But even knowing that, what happened, it's all pretty hard to believe."

"It is," Wedmore said. "I wondered if either of you had been in contact with him at all lately?"

Cynthia and I glanced at each other. I said, "We visited him when he was in the hospital, but since then . . ."

"I sent him a card," Cynthia said. "A sympathy card after his wife died. I ran into him a few weeks ago and we chatted."

"That's all?" Wedmore asked. "Nothing else?"

We both shook our heads. "No," I said. "Why?"

"Because you're on a list," she said.

I felt as though my heart skipped a beat. Before I could respond, Cynthia said, "What list? Terry and I are on whose list? Where?"

"Not you and Terry exactly, but your house," she said.

"You mean, like, in an address book?" I asked.

"Not exactly. We're slowly taking a look at the various things Mr. Fleming was involved in, and one of them appears to have been an operation where he would hide things for other criminal operations — cash, drugs, what have you — in the homes of individuals who were not on any police department's radar. Decent, upstanding folks." She paused. "Like yourselves."

"You're saying he used our house?" I asked. "To hide stuff? You're kidding."

"No, I'm not," Wedmore said calmly. "Most likely, in your attic."

"That's impossible," Cynthia said. "We've got a security system."

"Well, seems he may have found ways around that. Do you have a dog?"

"A dog?" I said. "No, we don't have any pets."

"That's one way he got access. You heard of dog walkers? People who come into your house through the day to take your dog for a walk? They have keys, access codes."

Cynthia took this one. "For a while, I had a place across town, an apartment. Terry and I — I just needed some time to myself, and the man who lived across the hall from me, he did that."

I wondered what she was doing. But I was betting Wedmore already knew Cynthia had lived, for a short while, across from Nathaniel Braithwaite. She'd have been waiting to see whether Cynthia volunteered this.

"That's right. That'd be Mr. Braithwaite."

"Yes," Cynthia said. "Are you saying he was doing this for Vince? He couldn't have had our key or access code."

"One way to be sure would be to check your attic. Would you mind?"

We said we thought she was wasting her time, but I got a ladder and set it up under the access panel upstairs. She climbed up and spent about five minutes rooting around up there before concluding there was nothing to be found.

She was hot and sweaty by the time she came down, and this time she accepted the offer of a cool drink instead of coffee. Back in the living room, Cynthia handed her a bottle of water from the fridge.

"So I guess this means that whatever Vince was up to, it didn't involve us," Cynthia said.

Don't be too eager.

"Maybe not," Wedmore said slowly, uncapping the bottle and taking a drink.

"Does this have anything to do with all those people who got shot?" I asked.

"It might," Wedmore said. "The Stockwells — Reggie and Wyatt Stockwell — were acquiring large sums of cash through fake IRS returns. They might have needed someplace to hide it. Maybe Mr. Fleming was hiding it for them and decided to hang on to it, and they didn't like that. But that's just one theory."

Cynthia and I both looked at her expectantly, as if we couldn't wait for the next tidbit of inside information.

"What's interesting," Wedmore said, "is how your names have popped up a couple of times in connection with all this."

"I don't know what you mean," I said.

"Your house is on a list Mr. Fleming kept of places where he might have hidden proceeds of crime. Your wife happened to live, briefly, across the hall from this Mr. Braithwaite, who may have been helping Mr. Fleming. And you both have a history with Mr. Fleming."

"I don't know what to say," Cynthia said, shaking her head in wonder at these coincidences. She looked at me. "You have any ideas?"

I shook my head, too. "I don't. But I'm glad no one got into this house."

"Well," Wedmore said, standing, "thanks for your time. If you think of anything — anything at all — please call." She left a card for us on the coffee table.

We showed her to the door. We all said our good-byes and closed the door behind her as she left.

"Dear God," Cynthia said, falling back against the wall.

I had a hand on my forehead as I caught my breath. "I thought I was going to have a heart attack."

"When she asked about —"

The doorbell rang again. We looked at each other, terrified. We took five seconds to pull ourselves together, and Cynthia opened the door.

Wedmore said, "Sorry. I meant to ask. What happened to your front yard?"

I'd done my best to repair the lawn where Cynthia had torn it up with the car, but there were still two parallel streaks where the grass was having a hard time growing back.

Wedmore motioned for us to step outside, and reluctantly we did so. "See what I'm talking about?" she asked, pointing to where the grass had been dug up to within a couple of feet of the shrubs under the front window.

Something caught my eye. Something bright. In the soil, at the base of the shrubs.

"Yeah, let me tell you about that," Cynthia said slowly, clearly struggling to come up with something. While Wedmore focused on her, I stole a quick look down.

It was the extra set of Beemer keys.

The ones that had belonged to Wyatt. When Vince had taken Reggie's and Wyatt's car keys, he hadn't needed both sets, and tossed one toward the house. How would I explain it if Wedmore found those? Keys not only to their car, but their house, too.

Those keys connected me to a house where four people had been murdered. Where one of them had been murdered by me.

"No, let me tell you how it happened," I said, taking three steps toward the driveway, forcing Wedmore to pivot and turn her back to the shrubs.

I looked her in the eye. Not just to hold her attention, but to stop myself from looking at the keys, which, at least to me, stood out like a garden gnome in a spotlight. I had to get Wedmore out of here, grab those keys, and drop them down the nearest sewer grate.

"The truth is, I'm actually a little afraid to tell you," I said.

Wedmore's head tilted slightly. "Why would that be?"

"I — I don't want to get charged with anything."

"What are you saying, Mr. Archer? Were you — were you driving under the influence?"

"Cynthia sort of intimated there that she'd moved out for a while, and I went through some periods where I was feeling pretty down, and one night, I was out, and I guess I had a little too much to drink, and I — this is the part I'm kind of reluctant to tell you — got in my car and drove home and totally missed the driveway."

Wedmore sized me up. I couldn't tell whether she believed it. She said, "That was an incredibly foolish thing to do."

"I know."

"You could have got yourself killed. Or someone else."

Cynthia had taken a step back toward the door. She probably wanted to get back into the house, for all this to end, but standing there, if Wedmore turned toward her . . .

"I know, I know. I scared myself half to death when I realized what I'd done," I said.

"Mr. Archer," Detective Wedmore said, "you've got a nice life here. You've got a wife who looks to me like she loves you, whatever troubles you two went through. As I recall, you've got a lovely daughter, although she'll have grown up a lot since I saw her last. You've got a family. Don't throw it all away by doing something crazy like driving around drunk. Don't take stupid chances like that."

"You're right," I said. "I'll never do anything risky like that again."

"See that you don't," she said. "Well, I guess I'm done here." Wedmore smiled at me, then turned to face Cynthia. "You have a good — hello, what's this?"

She put a foot on the lawn, learned forward, and scooped up the keys. Dirt clung to the remote.

"You lose some keys?" she asked, turning and extending her arm.

"Oh, thank God," I said. "I've been going out of my mind looking for those."

Wedmore dropped them into my palm. I closed my hand over them tightly.

"You folks take care," she said, and headed back to her car.

EPILOGUE

TERRY

It was Grace who gave us the news.

This was nearly a month after Vince's death. In all that time I hadn't spoken to Jane once, not since she'd dropped me off at the house and got all the guns out of the attic.

But Grace, as it turned out, had been keeping in touch. The occasional text message, two or three phone calls.

"She keeps wanting to know if I'm okay," Grace said. "I mean, if there's anyone we should be asking to see if she's okay, it's Jane, right?"

On this particular Saturday morning, Grace came down to the kitchen and said, "Jane's going away."

"Away?" Cynthia said.

"To Europe. She's going to France and Spain and Italy and all those places. She's going with Bryce."

651

"I thought you'd said they broke up," Cynthia said. That was news to me, but Grace and her mom were always updating each other on people's relationships without bringing me into the loop, mainly because I wasn't the slightest bit interested.

"They got back together," Grace reported. "I thought she was going to totally dump him. She thought he'd been messing around on her, and maybe he even was, but they patched it up, I guess, and now they're going away. She's giving up her apartment and quitting her job and everything."

"How long is she planning to be over there?" I asked.

"She doesn't even know if she'll come back."

"That's so exciting," Cynthia said. "We should do something. Have a little going-away party — a bon voyage party — for them." She looked at me. "What do you think?" Her look of excitement faded. I knew she was worried that doing anything with Jane might resurrect anxieties I was only now starting to get a handle on.

"Sure," I said. "Why not?"

"You won't have to do a thing. Grace and I will look after it. We should get them some kind of going-away present. It's so hard to pick things for people."

"Maybe just one of those Visa gift cards," Grace said. "They could use it anywhere in Europe, couldn't they?"

Cynthia asked Grace to text Jane about coming over to the house the following afternoon. Grace's thumbs tapped away at lightning speed, and within a minute Jane had accepted the invitation. They went out that afternoon to buy the fixings for a small party.

How could I rain on that parade? Cynthia and Grace had never been closer than in the last few weeks.

Jane and Bryce were invited for three o'clock. Grace began watching for them around a quarter to. She was peeking out the living room window every three minutes.

Cynthia sidled up close to me and whispered in my ear, "I did something without telling you."

I felt a shiver. "What?"

"I bought something for Grace. I was in the mall and I just happened on it, and when I saw it, I knew it was just the right thing."

"What?"

She told me.

When it got to be five after three, Grace said, "Where are they?"

"They're only five minutes late," Cynthia

told her. "Which isn't late at all. No one likes to arrive right on the dot. They'll be here soon."

Grace had her phone in her hand at the ready, as though she expected Jane to give progress reports on their drive from one part of Milford to another.

"Relax," Cynthia said.

"I've just never known anyone before, like, someone who was a friend of mine, who was actually going to go to Europe and just *stay* there."

I was passing through the living room when I saw Jane's Mini pull into our driveway. In the passenger seat was, I assumed, Bryce. As he got out, I could see he was a nice-looking guy. About six feet tall, slim. Hair tousled in that very careful careless way. He held a bottle of wine by the neck. Jane got out, hung a long-strapped purse over her shoulder.

The two of them were almost to the front door when Jane stopped, looked down at the purse, opened it, and reached in for her phone. Someone had called her. She put the phone to her ear, and I saw her mouth, "Hello?"

And then, behind me, I heard Grace say, "Jane? Where are you? Are you coming? What? Oh my God."

Grace was striding through the house now, edging past me so that she could be the one to open the door for them.

"I'm almost there," she said. "This is so funny."

She opened the door and faced Jane, both of them still holding their phones to their ears. They laughed, put their phones away, and hugged.

"So, you're Bryce!" Grace said.

He smiled, extended a hand. "Hey," he said reservedly.

"Come in! Come in!" Grace stood back, giving them room to enter the house. She glanced over at me, waved her phone in the air, and said, "It did that funny thing again."

I didn't know what she was talking about. "What?"

"You know? That night, I told you . . ."

She stopped herself because she didn't know how much Bryce knew about the evening she and Stuart had broken into the Cummings house. I hoped not a damn thing. I'd kept my mouth shut and trusted Jane had done the same.

"Is something wrong with your phone?" I asked.

"Sometimes there's this funny echoing. It happened just then, and twice that other time . . . you know. Once talking to you and . . ."

Grace glanced at Jane, then back at me. Jane was looking at me now, too. Her eyes searching mine.

In an instant, it all made perfect sense.

Bryce said, offhandedly, "That just happens when the person you're talking to is close enough you could practically touch them."

Cynthia appeared from the kitchen. "Hey, everyone's here!"

Bryce extended a hand. "Mrs. Archer. Pleasure to meet you."

"Call me Cynthia. Come on in. Would you like a drink? A beer? A glass of wine?"

I forced a smile and said, "I just need to talk to Jane for half a second. Grace, give this young man something to eat."

Grace smiled, said, "Sure!"

I didn't think she'd quite figured it out yet.

As everyone else moved toward the kitchen, I took Jane gently by the arm and led her out the front door.

"What?" she said.

I stared at her. "The phone thing."

"What are you talking about?"

"Just tell me."

"Tell you what?" She'd been studying my expression seconds earlier, but now didn't want to look me in the eye.

"When Grace phoned you that night, when she asked for help, before she called me, she got that echo on the phone. Like what just happened now."

"Cell phones are always doing stupid stuff," my onetime student said. It was the way she said it, the way she turned her head away, that convinced me I was on to something.

"You were already there." It wasn't a question. "If Grace had known, she wouldn't even have needed her phone to talk to you."

Jane squeezed the top of her purse with her left hand, her fingers kneading the leather. Her right hand tightened, opened, tightened again.

"I don't know what —"

"Cut the shit, Jane."

She looked out toward the street. After several seconds, she sighed, then said, "I thought, at one point, that she'd actually seen me. When she phoned. I thought she'd spotted me and that was why she called. But she hadn't. Grace was calling for help, calling to ask me what she should do."

I said nothing. I waited for more.

"Vince had screwed me over," Jane whispered. "And he wasn't there for my mother. I was furious with him." She paused. "At the time."

"So you decided to rip him off."

"My mother's house was supposed to go to me, but he kept it. I didn't know he was going to try to make it right. But he told me, when you guys saved me from those creeps."

I was feeling light-headed. "You were always good at listening in on people, snooping around. Let me guess. You knew all about Vince's business. You knew where the keys were. You found a listing of the security codes. You got into the house the easy way. Not like Stuart, who had to break in."

Jane nodded. "But I didn't realize how big a score was in that house. I had no idea. I thought it'd just be a few thousand. That Vince might not even miss it for months and months."

"How much?"

"There was two hundred thousand," she said. "That, and a vase."

I was amazed and horrified at the same time. "What were you going to do? When Vince figured out it was gone? When someone came back to claim that money? It could have turned out that way."

Jane kept her voice low, her head down. "I didn't think that far ahead. I didn't know what to do. And then things started happening so fast."

We still hadn't talked about the bigger issue.

"Stuart," I said. Jane started to turn away, but I reached for her shoulder and made her face me. "Stuart. You killed Stuart."

"I didn't mean to. That was a total accident."

"And taking a gun with you? That was an accident, too?"

"I just . . . There were always guns around. Seemed dumb to go into a house without . . . you know, anything. I heard him and Grace in the house, but I had no idea who it was at first. I was in the kitchen, and this person came in, and I just kind of . . . I got scared. I panicked."

"Jesus," I said quietly.

"I realized real quick who it was, who I'd shot. I had to get out of there. Grace was freaking out, had her hands over her eyes, screaming, and I ran right past her. I hid outside for a while — a cop car was coming down the street — and then I heard Grace coming out of the house and my phone buzzed. I saw it was her and, like I said, I thought she'd seen me. But she hadn't."

"Then you called Vince. So he could clean up the mess everyone had made."

"I told him," she said. "The truth."

"But not then," I guessed.

"Like I said, right after you two saved me from those creeps. You were in the other room. I told him. I thought maybe he was going to need the money. I had it in a bag, under my desk at work. I thought he'd snap, you know? But I couldn't keep it to myself any longer. I figured I'd take whatever he dished out. But he went all funny. Instead of being angry, he was really sad. Said he'd been awful to me. Said he'd work it out."

Then I realized something else.

"You kept it all," I said.

"What?"

"Everything he got out of the houses, all the money. You kept it."

She nodded. "Not drugs or guns or anything. Just the money. Vince told me to."

We were quiet for a moment. There was still something that wasn't clear to me.

"The vase," I said.

"What about it?"

"It ended up in Braithwaite's apartment. How?"

Jane looked like she was holding back a smile. "I put it there."

"Why?"

Jane hesitated, then said, "When I left Vince that night, I heard him talking on the phone about Braithwaite, that he was the most logical suspect because he had a key, knew the code. Vince mentioned an address. The next morning, when Braithwaite went off to walk dogs, I got into his place and planted it. I figured Vince and his guys would search the place eventually and pin it on him, even though that never happened. I'd be off the hook."

"How'd you get into his place?" I asked.

She frowned. "Please. Look who I've spent the last few years living with. Think I couldn't get into an apartment? There's no security system in that old house."

I was seeing Jane in a way I never had before. "Being mad at Vince, stealing the money, I can sort of see that. And shooting Stuart, that was pretty bad, but you never meant for it to happen. But setting up Braithwaite? An innocent man? Knowing Vince and his crew would probably kill him when they found that vase? That wasn't an accident, Jane."

"You still don't get it, do you, Teach? I'm a survivor. You do what you have to do." She searched my face. "What's goin' on in there? What are you going to do?"

"I don't know," I said honestly. "But you killed someone, Jane. You murdered Stuart."

She tilted her head back, a newfound confidence in the set of her jaw. "Then maybe you should turn me in."

I said nothing.

"You've got blood on your hands, too, Teach. You killed a man. And don't think I'm not grateful. And you've let Vince take the blame for that. Sounds like he even took the blame for Stuart. It's been a month. I wonder how the cops would look at that now, if they found out you'd really killed Joseph."

I felt a pounding in my temples.

"I'm the only one who knows what you did and you're the only one who knows what I did," Jane said coldly. "Maybe Grace is figuring it out, but I bet a couple of words from you could change that. You could say your phone's been acting up, too. Tell her it's time to get her a new, fancier one. They're always upgrading them. She'd love that. I'd even pay for it, if you want."

I didn't know what to say.

Jane blotted a tear with her sleeve, and with that, seemed to adopt a new face. She said, "One thing I figured out back when I was in school, around the time you were my teacher, is the only one who's going to look out for you is you. And then when my mom hooked up with Vince, well, watching him, that point of view really got driven home. You can't wait around for others to make your life better. You see what you want and you take it."

She patted my shoulder. I didn't like the feel of it. "That doesn't mean I don't appreciate everything you've done. You've been awesome. Right now, you need to think about what's best for *you*. You think calling the cops and telling them about what I did is going to work to your advantage? You're a teacher. You can figure that one out."

The door opened. It was Cynthia.

"What on earth are you two gabbing about? There's food and drink in here. Jane, I want to hear about all the places you're going."

Jane smiled broadly and went back into the house. When Cynthia saw me standing there not moving, she stepped outside.

"You okay?"

"Yeah," I said.

"I can see it in your face. Something's wrong."

I shook my head.

Cynthia took my hands in hers. "I know we've been to hell and back. You're having nightmares every night. We're all going through a posttraumatic stress thing. But I feel there's still something you haven't told me, that maybe —"

Inside the house, Grace screamed, "What's this?"

We both ran inside. Grace was hauling a tall, narrow box out of the front hall closet, reading the description of its contents.

"Nuts," Cynthia said to me. "She found it. Grace, you weren't supposed to — Oh shit. We were going to give you that later, after Jane and Bryce left and —"

Grace looked at her mother with tears in her eyes. "I love it," she said. "It's a way, way better telescope than I had as a kid."

"At least five times you said, when we were talking up in your room this past month, how you wanted to get back into the whole stargazing thing, how much you missed it."

Grace leaned the box against the wall and wrapped her arms around Cynthia. I stood there, watching, wanting to be part of this moment but holding back.

Jane glanced at me, smiled, and said, "Isn't that great? I could just cry."

Maybe Grace would let me borrow her new telescope. Let me scan the heavens for incoming asteroids the way she used to when she was seven. Grace used to worry one would hit the earth and obliterate us all.

That struck me, right then, as the only thing that might give me peace.

ACKNOWLEDGMENTS

It just might be in order to thank readers. There are more of you with each book, and to all of you who've said to someone else, "You should read this guy," I want you to know I'm grateful.

Ditto, booksellers. Thank you, thank you, thank you.

And there are a few individuals I need to single out: Kristin Cochrane, Mark Streatfield, Duncan Shields, Helen Heller, Juliet Ewers, Danielle Perez, Bill Massey, Kara Welsh, Heather Connor, Susan Lamb, Nita Pronovost, David Young, Gaby Young, Valerie Gow, Brad Martin, Camilla Ferrier and everyone at the Marsh Agency, Ali Karim, Cathy Paine.

Also, thanks to Spencer Barclay, his Loading Doc Productions team, and everyone else who works on my book trailers: Alex Kingsmill, Paige Barclay, Eva Kolcze, Elia Morrison, Nick Whalen, Martin MacPherson, Katie Brandino, Jeremy Kane, Ian Carleton, Misha Snyder, Nick Storring, Gord Drennan.